THE DEVIL'S SLAVE

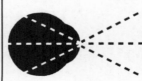

This Large Print Book carries the
Seal of Approval of N.A.V.H.

THE DEVIL'S SLAVE

TRACY BORMAN

THORNDIKE PRESS
A part of Gale, a Cengage Company

LIBRARY OF CONGRESS CIP DATA ON FILE.
CATALOGUING IN PUBLICATION FOR THIS BOOK
IS AVAILABLE FROM THE LIBRARY OF CONGRESS

ISBN-13: 978-1-4328-7098-0 (hardcover alk. paper)

Published in 2019 by arrangement with Grove/Atlantic, Inc.

Printed in Mexico
1 2 3 4 5 6 7 23 22 21 20 19

To Julian Alexander and Nick Sayers,
with heartfelt thanks

PART 1
1606

PROLOGUE
7 APRIL

The amber seemed to glow as Frances held it up to the candle that burned on her dresser. The beads were perfectly smooth and round, yet as the light shone through them, she could see the myriad dark flecks and shadows that made each one unique.

The rosary had been a gift from Queen Anne, who had slipped it quietly into her hands as Frances had taken her leave from court. 'Keep faith,' she had whispered, bending forward to kiss Frances on both cheeks. As she slowly threaded the beads through her fingers now, Frances wondered if Anne, too, would continue to abide by the faith that had bound her to the plotters — had made her countenance the murder of her husband and son. If so, then she would need to employ even greater discretion than usual. She knew that Cecil suspected the queen of involvement in the Powder Treason, as they were calling it, and would not rest until he had secured the proof.

Frances reached into the small linen purse that was concealed in the folds of her dress and drew out the letter. She had kept it with her ever since it had arrived three days earlier, not daring even to leave it in the locked casket where she kept her most precious herbs and tinctures. Slowly unfolding it, she read it again.

Lady Frances,

I know you were a good friend to my late brother Thomas. He spoke of you often, and in terms of great affection. His loss must be as great to you — greater, even — as it is to those of his family who still draw breath. To have lost two brothers as well as my husband John is almost more than I can bear, though I hear that they all died bravely. I thank God that I have my precious boy. I have named him Wintour, to preserve our family name. I wish that you had the same consolation.

Instinctively, Frances's hand moved to her belly, which she stroked distractedly as she resumed reading.

It is beholden upon those of us who remain to honour their memory by continuing to further the cause for which they died. Lady Vaux assures me that you can be trusted as a supporter of the true faith, and that you enjoy great favour with Her Royal Highness Princess Elizabeth. You must return to court as soon as possible. It is there that you can do most good for our cause. No matter how much you love Longford Castle — Tom told me it is dear to your heart — your love for him must surely be greater. I urge you, therefore, to make this sacrifice for his sake. I wish I could do the same, but I am now sole mistress of Norbrook and cannot leave my child at so tender an age. Though you will be returning to a place of danger, you will not be friendless. Lady Vaux tells me that there are many great persons there who conspire to return this kingdom to the Catholic fold. I beg you, make haste.

Your loving friend,
Dorothy Wintour

Frances's hands shook as she refolded the letter and slid it carefully back into the purse. She had never met Tom's sister, and he had rarely spoken of her — anxious, no doubt, to avoid implicating her in his plans. How had she known to write to her here? Lady Vaux must have enquired after her upon arriving at court — she was tenacious enough to do so. Or perhaps there were others there, besides the queen, who still watched her movements. The thought made her shudder.

I urge you to make this sacrifice for his sake.

The words sounded in her ears, but it was Tom who spoke them. She had heard them many times since the letter had arrived. She knew she should burn it, but somehow this single piece of paper seemed the only trace of him that was left to her. The thought of returning to court filled her with dread, and hers was not the only life to consider now. Surely Tom would not wish it, if he knew of the precious burden she carried. *No.* She would remain here at Longford, raise their child in the safety and comfort of her beloved home.

But how much longer would it be her home?

Frances pushed away the unwelcome thought. For as long as her parents lived, they would never allow Edward to turn his sister out of Longford, even though she threatened to bring shame upon the family. She knew that their father disapproved of his heir's haughty behaviour — even more

12

so of the Protestant doctrine he had spouted since his arrival at Longford. Frances suspected that her brother cared little for spiritual matters but had an eye to preferment at court. Please God, her parents would leave Richmond and return here themselves soon enough. Even as she mouthed the silent prayer, she knew it was unlikely to be answered. The king, capricious as ever, had made clear that he wished to retain her parents at Richmond, though he could have little need of them there. As Marchioness of Northampton and the old queen's closest favourite, her mother Helena deserved better — as did her father, Lord Thomas Gorges, who had the blood of the powerful Howard family coursing through his veins.

With a sigh, Frances stood, walked slowly over to the bed and pulled back the covers. Although her limbs sagged with fatigue, she had little desire to climb into it, knowing it would offer no repose. Instead, she would lie there for hours, as she had every night since Tom's death, waiting for the dawn.

CHAPTER 1
18 APRIL

Frances drew a sharp breath as she lowered her feet through the icy water until they brushed against the smooth pebbles of the riverbed. Her skin looked white, almost translucent, beneath the surface.

A tiny fluttering in her stomach made her sit up straight on the grass. She laid her hands gently over it and waited. There was the movement again, stronger this time. She smiled, then stroked the neat, warm swelling that lay beneath the stiff fabric of her dress. Ellen had been obliged to loosen her stays last week, and though her body was still slender, there was no longer any disguising her growing belly.

The surge of joy she had felt when the child moved dissipated as she recalled the angry words she had exchanged with her brother Edward the night before. He had returned to Longford the previous summer, having at last completed his studies in

Cambridge. She guessed that Theo, who was still there, had proved something of a distraction. With just a year separating her two brothers, they had always been close. She could remember many occasions when, as children, they had run off into the woods straight after breakfast, only returning as the light was fading. Her mother had chided them for missing their lessons, and for their dishevelled state, cuts and grazes on their skin, their fine linen shirts spattered with mud.

How different Edward was now. Frances had noticed the change as soon as she had arrived two weeks before. It wasn't so much physical — though he had certainly grown into a tall, muscular young man — but rather in his manner. There had been something distant in the way he had bent to kiss her, his eyes coolly appraising. As the second son, he had enjoyed a carefree youth, with no expectations of inheritance. But the death of their elder brother, Francis, had changed that. Edward, then aged seventeen, had shared his siblings' shock and grief, but Frances would always recall seeing excitement in his eyes, even as their father told them the news, his voice cracked with sorrow.

Edward had left for Cambridge soon

afterwards, and Frances had seen little of him, or her three other brothers, since. But now it was clear that he revelled in his status as heir to the Longford estate.

Her thoughts were disturbed by a movement at the edge of her vision — her old nurse, Ellen, walking slowly over the bridge. She stopped to rub her back, then plodded on, wincing at the pain in her hip. It had grown a good deal worse since Frances had last seen her almost two years before. Ellen had been standing on the threshold of the castle as Frances's carriage had made its steady progress along the drive a fortnight ago. Frances had felt the bones of Ellen's shoulders as her nurse had embraced her. She had tried to hide her dismay at the sight of Ellen's grey hair and pinched, sagging skin. In those two years, she had become an old woman.

It seemed to Frances as if a lifetime had passed since she had last sat here by the Avon, in the shade of her beloved home. She herself had changed, she knew. How naïve — arrogant, even — she had been when she had first arrived at Whitehall Palace a year after King James's accession. Despite her mother's warning, she had made little effort to conceal her skills at healing, as if the herbs could somehow protect her from the evil that pervaded the new king's court. She had soon learned, to her cost, that they were as nothing against his perverted obsessions or the twisted schemes of his closest adviser.

Cecil.

Frances felt the familiar loathing at the thought of the king's crook-backed minister. He had been a constant, menacing presence throughout her time at court. Even in the privacy of her lodgings, she had felt his eyes upon her. He had conspired in her arrest for witchcraft, had watched, impervious to her screams, as the torturer had searched her body intimately for the Devil's Mark. She remembered the elation she had felt upon hearing that Tom and his fellow plotters had succeeded: that Cecil had been blown to the heavens, along with the king and his entire parliament. But the news had proved false. Fawkes had been discovered with the gunpowder just hours before the lords assembled in the ancient hall above.

Frances shook her head as if to dispel the thoughts that she knew would follow. Of Tom, his body racked with pain, being pulled along to his death.

'Wintour looked as pale as a dead man when he mounted the scaffold,' she had heard someone say as, a few days later, she had hastened through the public rooms of the palace, desperate to avoid the subject that was on everyone's lips.

'Fear makes cowards of us all,' another had responded. Frances had rounded on them then, all of the grief she had tried to contain spilling out in her fury.

'Are you well, my lady?'

Ellen's brow was creased with concern. She was breathing heavily from the exertion of her walk. Frances gave a weak smile of reassurance. 'Do not trouble yourself, Ellen. I am quite well, thank you.'

Her gaze moved to the basket that the older woman had set down upon the grass. 'Were you able to find the willow bark, and the hyssop?' she asked.

Ellen nodded as she sank down next to her. 'Yes,' she replied, 'though I searched in the woods a long time. My eyes are not as sharp as they were, so I had to stoop down on my knees.' She kneaded them as she spoke.

Frances suppressed her impatience. 'I am sorry for it, Ellen, but with the herbs you have gathered I will make you a salve to ease your aching limbs.' She paused. 'I wish I could have gone myself.'

Ellen clicked her tongue in disapproval. 'And risk your secret being discovered?' she demanded, then gave a sigh and reached over to pat Frances's hand. 'You know you must have a care, now that your young knave is starting to show himself.' Her voice was softer now.

'It might be a girl,' Frances pointed out.

Ellen shook her head. 'Not when you carry the child like that, all at the front.'

They sat in companionable silence for a few moments. Frances watched as a hawk circled over the woods, dipping down now and again as it sought its prey. How she longed to be among the ancient oaks, to smell the sweet scent of the primroses, which she knew would be in bloom now. Though she cherished her home, it had felt more like a prison this past week. She chided herself for the thought. Her only solace during the long days and nights that followed Tom's death had been the prospect of returning to Longford. Now she was here, yet the restlessness and misery still hung over her.

'The pain of parting will lessen in time,' Ellen said, as if reading her thoughts. Frances opened her mouth to reply, but the older woman continued: 'I do not ask you to name him. I respect your parents' wishes, and would not vex you by pressing the matter — not for the world. Whatever the reason you have returned here unmarried, yet with child, I will not attempt to discover it. I want only to care for you, when the time comes —' She broke off, her eyes glistening with tears.

Frances swallowed her own. She had wept so much these past weeks that she wondered there could be any tears left. But soon she must go in for dinner, and she was determined to avoid her brother's scorn by concealing her grief.

'Thank you, Ellen,' she said quietly. 'You have always been like a mother to me, and I have missed you sorely since we were parted at Whitehall.'

'And I have fretted about you endlessly, my lady,' the old woman replied, her forehead furrowed with deep lines. 'The court is a good deal more dangerous since King James took our old queen's throne. There are many who would rejoice to see him murdered.'

'Hush, Ellen,' Frances remonstrated, her voice low. 'You know it is treason to speak of such things.'

Her old nurse gave an indignant sniff. 'I hated to think of you in that place, friendless and alone, while plots gathered about the king. When news reached us of the Powder Treason last November, I begged

21

your brother to bring you home. But he would have none of it.'

Frances gave a sardonic smile. 'I am sure he did not wish to upset the king by taking away his daughter's favourite attendant,' she said quietly. 'Besides, Ellen, I was neither alone nor friendless. The princess was a kind and loving mistress and, though still a child, an excellent companion. There were others, too.'

She fell silent, then took the old woman's hand and smoothed her thumb over the swollen joints. A little marjoram and a few sprigs of rosemary ground with the willow bark Ellen had gathered would make enough paste to ease the discomfort.

With a sigh, Frances lifted her feet out of the stream and dried them on the grass. 'I must make shift,' she said regretfully. 'The viscount is strict in his hours of dining.' She could not quite keep the scorn out of her voice as she spoke the title her brother insisted upon using. As the son of the Marchioness of Northampton and heir to Longford Castle, it was his right, she supposed, but to ensure that it was upheld here, in the quiet domesticity of their home, was absurd.

Edward was already seated at the head of

the table — her father's chair, she noted — when she entered the dining room. She gave a brief curtsy and waited.

'Sister,' he said, gesturing towards a place halfway along the table. Frances walked slowly to the chair and sat down.

A selection of dishes was laid out in front of them. Frances breathed in the aroma of capon with orange sauce, baked venison and fried whiting. Each was presented on the silver plates that their parents reserved for distinguished guests. Frances took a sip of the red wine that had been poured into her glass and recognised the fine Burgundy vintage her father usually reserved for their Christmas feast.

'The wine is not to your taste?' Edward asked, noting his sister's look of disapproval.

She forced a smile. 'On the contrary, brother. It is excellent — surely one of the best in our father's cellar.'

Frances saw annoyance in his face as she turned to the dishes in front of her and helped herself to some capon.

'It is not often that a prodigal daughter returns,' he replied smoothly. 'I wish only to extend my hospitality, to make you feel welcome.'

In my own home? Frances bit back the remark and took another sip of wine.

'I understand that you had Ellen foraging in the woods this afternoon, like some peasant girl,' her brother said. 'Really, Frances, you should have more consideration for her age and infirmity. She will not live to see many more summers, so please try not to ruin this one by troubling her with such needless tasks.'

Frances knew he was taunting her, but she was determined not to lose her temper. He would derive too much satisfaction from it. 'Hardly needless, brother,' she said pleasantly. 'Ellen suffers with the pain in her bones. The herbs I asked her to gather will ease it greatly. Besides, I would gladly have gone myself but —'

'And heap yet more shame upon your family?' Edward retorted.

Frances saw that his neck had flushed, as it had in his childhood whenever he was angered. She smiled. He might strut like a peacock now he fancied himself lord of the estate, but to her he would always be her foolish little brother.

'I wonder that you find it so amusing, sister,' he continued, his voice now dangerously low. 'You, who have destroyed our parents' standing with the king, threatened us with ruin — all to satisfy your selfish desires.'

24

Frances stared at him, colour rising to her cheeks.

'Now it seems that you would ruin Longford too. I begged our parents to send you well away from here, to a place where our family is unknown, so that you might birth your bastard in secret. They could have paid a local wet nurse to take it away so that you might return to your duties at court. God knows enough ladies did the same in the old queen's time.'

He took a gulp of wine and Frances noticed that his hand shook as he set down the glass.

'But they would not hear of it,' he continued, so loudly that Frances feared the servants would hear. 'They insisted upon abiding by their precious daughter's wish that she might bear her bastard here at Longford.' He drank more wine. 'This is our father's doing. You were always his favourite.'

Frances forced herself to take a deep breath. 'Longford is my home, Edward,' she said quietly.

His mouth curled into a slow smile. 'For now, sister,' he replied. 'For now.'

CHAPTER 2
21 APRIL

The smell of freshly baked bread wafted up the stairs, reaching as far as the library, where Frances was in her favourite window seat reading a collection of psalms translated by Sir Philip Sidney. She had loved his writings ever since Tom had bought her the cherished copy of *Arcadia* that now took pride of place among her father's volumes. Her stomach rumbled, even though she had breakfasted just an hour ago. The child must be growing fast, she thought.

She closed the book and swung her feet to the floor. Even this small movement obliged her to rest and catch her breath before standing. Glancing over her shoulder, she saw her brother riding along the drive, away from the house.

Good.

Her relief that she would be spared his company for the rest of the day was tempered by envy that he could ride about so freely while she was cooped up here, like one of the old queen's canaries. With a sigh, she set off for the kitchens.

Many times, as a child, she had stolen down there to watch the cooks at work, their nimble fingers plucking the tiny sprigs of thyme, marjoram or rosemary with which to flavour the meat or sauces. She had begged to be allowed to help, and eventually the housekeeper had agreed that she could gather the herbs from the woods that lay between Longford and the village. Soon, Frances had learned the many varieties by sight and smell, and would return with an overflowing, fragrant basket.

'They say she sickened last week, after returning from the market at Salisbury.'

Frances recognised the lilting voice of Mrs Lamport, the housekeeper. She paused at the foot of the stairs and listened.

'Is it the sweat?' Frances heard terror in Ellen's voice. 'Bridges said that two cases had been reported in the town just last week.'

'She has no fever, but there is a great swelling in her neck and she cannot swallow food or water these past two days. The Reverend Pritchard has already delivered the last rites.'

Frances felt a surge of anger. The poor

woman's condition could hardly have been improved by the rector's over-hasty ministrations. He would have done better to offer her words of comfort, to assure her that God would ease her suffering, as the Reverend Samuels would have done. The old priest had been as gentle in his manner as he was skilled in his healing. The villagers had been truly blessed during his tenure, even if it made the shock of his successor harder to bear. Although she longed to be able to walk to Britford, Frances was thankful that at least her enforced confinement meant she could not attend St Peter's. Pritchard's moralising sermons were as dreary as they were lengthy.

'Then there is no hope?' Ellen's voice brought her back to the present.

'Not unless something can be done.' Mrs Lamport lowered her voice, so that Frances was obliged to lean closer to the door: ' 'Tis a pity she cannot be treated by a wise woman, but the priest says such practices are the work of Satan.'

Frances's heart was hammering. Pritchard had as good as condemned the woman to death. His meddlesome actions would win favour with King James, who had made it his personal crusade to rid the world of witches, as he claimed all wise women and healers were.

Instinctively, Frances pressed her fingertips to the smooth ridge of skin at the base of her neck. The scar was barely visible now and the rest had healed. But she knew that the memories of her ordeal in the Tower would never fade. She flinched as she thought of the witch-pricker's knife jabbing at the freckles on her skin as he searched for one that would emit no pain.

James had looked on eagerly as his servant performed the grisly task. Frances felt the familiar surge of fury at him, mingled with frustration that she could not attend the sick woman in Britford. The Reverend Pritchard would delight in having her arrested and sent to the king. She would not escape his justice a second time.

But Frances knew she could not stand by and do nothing. With a sudden resolve, she hastened back up the stairs. By the time she reached her chamber, she was panting, but she did not allow herself to rest. She lifted the casket out of the dresser and fumbled for the key that hung from a ribbon about her neck. Not troubling to untie it, she leaned forward and jabbed at the lock with trembling fingers until the key slid into it.

The rosemary released its pungent aroma as she plucked the tiny dried leaves from the stem and ground it into a powder with the pestle. She added a few sprigs of rue and then, more sparingly, hartshorn, binding the mixture with a little oil. If she had judged Mrs Lamport's description of the symptoms correctly, then the woman was suffering from the same defluxion in the throat that had afflicted the late queen in her final days. Her tincture had eased Elizabeth's breathing and helped her to sleep. She hoped it would do the same this time.

Carefully, Frances poured the mixture into a small glass phial and stoppered it with a piece of thickly woven linen. Not pausing to pack away the contents of the casket, she called for Ellen. Soon she could hear the old woman's shuffling footsteps as she made her way up the stairs from the kitchens. Her face was red when she reached the top. Without explanation, Frances pressed the phial into her hands. 'You must take this to the sick woman,' she said.

Ellen looked at her in confusion. 'Mistress Gardner?' she asked. 'But —'

'I overheard you speaking with Mistress Lamport,' Frances explained quickly. 'If her symptoms are as grave as she said, then you must make haste.'

Ellen looked down at the dark green tincture, which glistened in the sunlight.

'My lady, you know such things are forbidden. If anyone were to see me —'

'Then you must not be seen,' Frances interrupted, pushing down her sense of foreboding. 'I wish I could attend the woman myself, but you know that I cannot venture from here. Yet neither can I leave her to suffer, when God has given me the skills to help her — cure her, even.'

Her nurse eyed her uncertainly before looking back at the phial.

'Please, Ellen,' Frances urged. 'I can trust no one else.'

The old woman fetched a deep sigh, then drew a kerchief from her pocket and wrapped it around the tincture. 'I pray that you will not ask this of me again, my lady,' she said.

Frances leaned forward and kissed her cheek. 'Thank you,' she whispered. They walked slowly down the stairs and outside, where Frances watched anxiously as Ellen hobbled towards the bridge, fighting a sudden impulse to run after her. It was madness to have put her at such risk. But she could not let the poor wretch in Britford choke out her breath without trying to help her. No, she had done the right thing, she told herself, pushing down the fear that gnawed at her breast.

Once the child was born and the swelling in her stomach had subsided, word could be put out that she had recovered from the sickness that had obliged her parents to release most of the servants, for fear of contagion. Only those whom they were sure could be trusted remained. Frances had been surprised by how few they were. But she trusted her father's opinion implicitly.

He had decided that, after several months had passed, his grandchild could be passed off as the orphaned offspring of some distant relative, whom he had agreed could be raised at Longford. In the meantime, Frances would make sure to be seen often in Britford and Salisbury, while her baby remained closeted in the nursery. She felt a rush of gratitude towards her father — her mother too — as she thought of what they hazarded for her sake. Most other daughters in her position would have been sent to a nunnery, their child taken from them as soon as it was born. If her father's plan worked, she could raise her baby, while escaping the censure of society.

Frances watched until Ellen was out of sight, murmuring a prayer that God would keep her safe. She was loath to go back indoors just yet. Edward did not like her to stray from the privy garden behind the house, which was enclosed by a thick yew hedge, and her refusal to obey had prompted several arguments. But he was not here and she must take advantage. Perhaps she might even wander as far as the wilderness that lay at the edge of the estate, close to the woods.

A chill breeze blew across from the river and Frances shivered. She experienced a pang of guilt that she had not thought to give Ellen a cloak for her journey in case the weather turned, as it did so often at this time of year, with little warning. She decided to fetch her own cloak and was starting towards the house when she heard the distant rumble of a horse's hoofs. Turning back, she squinted towards the road that led to Salisbury, and could just make out a cloud of dust in the distance. Even from here, she could tell that the rider was moving at speed. Surely Edward had not returned already? No, he did not ride with such skill. She felt a jolt of fear. There had been many such hasty messengers during the desperate weeks before Tom's plot had been discovered. They had rarely brought welcome tidings. She knew that she ought to return to the house, but felt unable to move.

Gradually, the outline of a rider emerged

from the plume of dust. There was something familiar about the slender frame that was slowly coming into view. At least it was not her uncle, she reflected wryly. His girth had expanded in recent years and he rarely travelled on horseback now.

At the long, final sweep of the path he disappeared from view for several moments. Frances held her breath as she waited for him to reappear. When at last he did, she exhaled.

Sir Thomas Tyringham.

She had not seen Tom's friend and patron for almost a year now. He had taken leave of court the previous summer, on the premise of urgent business at his Buckinghamshire estate. She had barely given him a thought since. God knew there had been enough else to occupy her mind.

Sir Thomas drew up his horse a few feet in front of her, then swiftly dismounted. He swept a deep bow. His long boots were spattered with mud, and his neatly cropped hair was dark with sweat at the temples. 'Lady Frances,' he said, with apparent good humour. But though his mouth lifted into a smile, his eyes were grave as he studied her.

'Sir Thomas,' she replied. 'I am surprised to see you.'

'Forgive me. I did not have time to send

word of my arrival.' He looked momentarily shamefaced. 'I trust you are well? I heard a report of some sickness.'

She watched his eyes flick over her body, and thought she saw them linger a moment too long on her belly. Folding her arms across it, she said brightly: 'I am afraid my brother is not at home, but do come inside for some refreshment. I will send for someone to tend your horse.'

Not pausing for an answer, she walked briskly towards the house. Her thoughts kept time with her steps as she crossed the hallway, calling for the stable boy and house-keeper.

Sir Thomas had been one of several suitors whom her uncle had tried to foist upon her. She had thought of their first meeting many times, at the dinner he had hosted in his apartments at Whitehall Palace. But the vividness of the memory was not because of Sir Thomas. It had been the first time she had spoken to Tom. She could remember almost every word of their conversation as he had escorted her to her chamber after-wards. Sir Thomas gave a small cough, bringing her back to the present.

Why was he here? Had her uncle encouraged him to renew his suit, now that Tom was dead? He would hardly have done so if he had known of her condition, she reflected bitterly.

As they entered the hall, Frances gestured for Sir Thomas to take a seat next to the fire. She sat opposite, in her father's chair. Mrs Lamport broke the brief, awkward silence that followed as she bustled in bearing a tray of wine and sweetmeats, set it down and left, closing the door behind her.

Frances poured wine for her guest, then sat back and waited. She had no patience for pleasantries.

Sir Thomas took a slow sip, then put the glass down. 'I am sorry for the loss you have suffered, my lady,' he said, eyeing her intently.

For a moment, Frances did not know what to say. It could hardly have escaped Sir Thomas's notice that she and his protégé had become close companions by the time he left court. But did he know that they had been much more than that? The earnestness of his tone — of his gaze now — suggested so. Not trusting herself to speak, she inclined her head and shifted her focus to the fire.

'Tom's death was a loss to me too,' he continued. 'I loved him as a brother and would have done anything for him — as he would for me, God rest his soul.'

He took another sip of wine, and Frances noticed that his hand trembled slightly.

'You know that I furthered his legal endeavours, putting him in the way of some influential clients?'

Frances nodded, still mute. *Where was this leading?*

'The queen was among them,' he continued. 'I initiated the introduction at Tom's request. He and his . . . friends were eager to make her acquaintance, as I think you know.'

Frances's pulse quickened.

'She proved a powerful supporter of their cause.' He leaned forward, his gaze intensifying. 'As did I, my lady. It was my connections — at court and abroad — that swelled their ranks, my gold that paid for the house in Westminster, the weapons with which they fought at Holbeach . . .' he took a breath '. . . and the gunpowder.'

Frances's heart was now thudding painfully as she stared at him. Was this a trap? Had Cecil sent him to secure a confession? No. The Earl of Salisbury had greater subtlety than that. Did Sir Thomas speak truth, then? She could not understand why else he would make such treacherous claims, and to a woman he hardly knew.

'You know, I think, that I secured the

king's consent to leave court for a time last summer, so that I might resolve an issue that had arisen at my estates.'

She nodded again, and he continued, 'I was not in Buckinghamshire all those months, but in Flanders. Tom and his companions had already gathered a considerable body there — armed men, ready to do battle. I was to lead them across the Channel, as soon as I received word that the plot had succeeded. But, of course, that word never came.'

By now his breathing was rapid and his eyes blazing as he stared at Frances, searching for reassurance — forgiveness, even.

'I know that I should not have encouraged their schemes,' he went on, his voice steadier. 'That it was madness to imagine they could destroy a king and his entire regime. I should have made them see reason — made Tom see reason — but I was too caught up in their fervour, in the blindness of my faith.'

He could no longer look at Frances, but her eyes never left him. As she watched him now, his gaze fixed upon the fire and his lips pressed tightly together, she pictured him as a rebellious traitor. She had remembered him as a mild-mannered, affable man, whose breeding and discretion made him an ideal courtier. How well he had concealed his true beliefs, his true nature.

It was not the first time she had been fooled by a man of the court. Tom's revelations had been strikingly similar, yet they had shaken her to the core. There was a time when she had believed Tom's dishonesty had been more than just concealment: it had been a betrayal of everything they had had together — their intimacy, their trust, their love. She knew later that he had kept the truth from her simply to protect her.

'Why are you here?'

Sir Thomas looked up at her. Frances knew her abruptness surprised him but cared little for that. He sipped his wine, then set the glass on the table. 'I know what you and Tom were to each other,' he said quietly.

Frances held back the tears that threatened to betray her. His eyes softened as he looked at her. *I do not want your pity,* she thought.

'I know, too, that a part of him has stayed with you.' His voice was barely a whisper. 'The queen sent for me upon my return to court, I thought, to warn me that her husband knew me for a traitor, though I had remained in Flanders until I could be sure my name was not among those he still seeks.' Another pause. 'But it was of you that Her Majesty wished to speak.'

Frances's head jerked up.

'She told me you are with child,' Sir Thomas said bluntly.

Instinctively, Frances's hands flew to her belly. *How could Anne betray her secret so readily? Had she told others too?*

'You must not be angry, my lady,' Sir Thomas said soothingly. 'She wished only to help you.'

'By betraying me to a man I hardly know?' Frances retorted.

'Her Majesty is aware that, even here, you are in danger. Though I am sure your servants can be trusted, it would take only an idle slip to ruin your reputation, and that of your family.'

'Do you think I do not know that, Sir Thomas?' Frances demanded, her face now pale with fury. 'My parents have taken great care in this. None of us is as thoughtless as you suppose.'

'Please — let me continue. Though nobody but the queen and I knows that the child is Tom's, if your pregnancy were to be discovered beyond the confines of this estate, it would not take long for Cecil to hear of it. And he would use it as proof that you conspired with a notorious traitor to destroy the king and his entire parliament. You would be put to death — the child too.'

The truth of his words smote her. Though she had known the dangers of her situation, she had been so consumed by grief for Tom that they had lurked at the edge of her vision. In truth she would care little for what might happen to her, should her part in the plot be discovered. She had stood ready to deliver the Princess Elizabeth to the plotters once they had blown up the king and his Parliament, so that they might set her upon the throne and marry her to a Catholic prince. That was high treason. Yet, on some days, she felt she would welcome death as a release from her wretchedness at losing Tom. Her desire to protect the child always proved stronger, though. It was the only part of him that she had left.

'Then what do you propose, Sir Thomas?' she asked.

He leaned forward and took her hands in his. 'To marry you,' he said simply.

Frances recoiled. 'You think I am a chattel to be bought? That I could transfer my affections to you now that the man I loved more than my own soul — the man you claim was a dear friend — lies cold in his grave?'

She made to snatch away her hands, but

41

his grip was stronger.

'You are in great danger, Lady Frances.' His eyes bored into hers as he spoke. 'I promised Tom that if he were to perish, I would do everything in my power to protect you. When the queen told me of your condition, I knew what I must do — as, I think, did she. If you accept, I will raise the child as my own and tell my household we married last year, shortly after I took my leave of absence. They will not think to question it — I have been a virtual stranger to them these past few months.'

Frances struggled to order her thoughts. Though her anger had abated at the mention of the vow Tom had obliged his friend to make, the idea of marrying a virtual stranger was abhorrent, even if it brought her his protection. She had surely lived long enough on her own wits to safeguard herself and her child.

Sir Thomas continued, 'I expect nothing from you. I do not ask for your love,' Frances flinched at the word, 'or even your esteem. It would be a marriage in name only. But I make this offer on one condition: you must vow never to make contact with any of Tom's family or associates, or with any of those who seek to finish what he and Catesby started. You must utterly relinquish any allegiance to the Catholic cause.'

Frances shot him a scornful look. 'You would so easily abandon the cause for which you have fought all these years? For which Tom and his friends died?' She stopped abruptly, trying to control her rising fury. 'Well, if *your* principles are so malleable, then mine are not. I will abide by the true faith and support those who seek to destroy this heretic king.'

Sir Thomas stared back at her, his chest rising and falling. 'We would live as the king's faithful subjects,' he said, his voice low. 'Though we may believe differently in our hearts, the days of plotting are over. There are many others of our faith who have chosen to conceal their true beliefs and conform to the king's so that they may live in peace. Only those too blind to see still cling to the hope that the Catholics will prevail. You must open your eyes, Frances, as I have done. If you do otherwise, you will destroy yourself and your child.'

He stood, and the sound of the heavy oak chair scraping on the flagstones echoed around the hall. 'I do not expect an answer now,' he said. 'I have lodgings in Salisbury and will return the day after tomorrow. If you accept my offer, we will leave for Buckinghamshire the same day.'

Frances sat quite still, long after the echo of the front door slamming had faded into silence.

'Sister, calm yourself,' Edward said irritably.

Frances turned from the window. 'I wish you would let me go and look for her. It is almost dark now, so nobody would see me. I know those woods better than anyone. She might have fallen and be lying hurt. She did not even have a cloak with her. She will surely freeze.'

'She will have stayed gossiping with one of the women in the village and lost track of time. I wonder you should trouble yourself so much about her.'

'Ellen raised us!' Frances cried, rounding on him. 'She loved us as her own and always will. It would grieve her sorely to hear you speak of her as if she meant no more to you than a passing acquaintance.'

Edward had the grace to look ashamed, but he soon recovered himself. 'I hear that just such an acquaintance paid you a visit today, Frances,' he said, smiling at her obvious discomfiture. 'When were you planning to tell me? You cannot have thought to keep your admirer a secret in such a backwater as this. There is little enough else to talk about.'

Frances would not let her brother goad her into losing her temper, as she had seen him do to their elder sister Elizabeth many times as children.

'Sir Thomas Tyringham is an acquaintance from court,' she replied calmly. 'I was introduced to him by our uncle upon first arriving at Whitehall, but have hardly seen him since. He did not stay for long.' She lifted her chin as she returned Edward's gaze.

'Is it not strange that a gentleman whom you know so little should travel all this way for such a brief and inconsequential meeting? His estates are in Buckinghamshire, I understand, so Longford is hardly on his way to anywhere.'

Frances knew that Edward would have made enquiries about her visitor. 'Perhaps he had business in Salisbury. I hardly know or care, brother,' she said airily, but the flush that was creeping up her neck betrayed her. She noticed her brother's smile broaden.

He rose to his feet and came to where she was standing. 'Is it him?'

Frances jumped back as if he had struck her. Her face was deeply flushed now, and her hands shook with fury. 'Who?' she demanded, though she understood her brother's question well enough.

'Your feckless suitor, the one who has shamed you — shamed our family. Father told me he was dead, but that's a little too convenient, don't you think?'

'He *is* dead!' Frances cried, brushing away the tears that filled her eyes. She hated to show such weakness in front of her brother. She made as if to leave, but he gripped her arm, his fingers digging deep into her flesh.

'Forgive me if I no longer take your word as the truth, sister,' he sneered. 'Tell me, has Sir Thomas been pricked by his conscience, or did Father bribe him to make you an offer?'

Frances glared at him. 'Sir Thomas is not the father of my child,' she said. 'Father spoke the truth — that man is dead. You will never know his name.' Her brother's eyes flashed. 'But Sir Thomas did ask me to marry him. He knows of my situation and is willing to claim the child as his own. He does this to honour his late friend.'

Edward released his grip, his eyes narrowing. 'If this is true, then it is a good deal more than you deserve,' he said, with the

petulance she remembered from their childhood. 'I presume you accepted.'

'No.'

She was gratified to see his eyes widen in
shock.

'Why ever not?' he demanded, incredulous. 'Do you expect to receive a host of
other suitors, to have the same luxury of
choice as your former charge?'

'Princess Elizabeth is not yet of an age to
marry, brother,' Frances replied smoothly.

'Do not toy with me, Frances,' he spat.
'You were always obstinate, but even you
must see that Sir Thomas's offer is better
than any other you may receive — better,
certainly, than you deserve. How could you
refuse him?'

'I did not refuse him, Edward,' she said.

'But you said —'

'I said only that I did not accept. Sir
Thomas has given me two days to consider.
It seems he has the qualities of a true gentleman, unlike those who merely pretend to be
so.'

She swept from the room, slamming the
door behind her.

Frances rose early the following morning.
She had slept only fitfully, troubled by fears
for Ellen. An image of the old woman lying

injured and unable to move in the woods flitted before her. She cursed her brother for refusing to let her look for her — and for making no move to do so himself. Well, she would no longer be gainsaid. She glanced at the clock in the parlour. Half past six. Edward would not be up for another two hours at least. With sudden resolve, she dressed and walked purposefully from the room.

The stable boy was already at work forking out the soiled straw. He jumped in surprise when he saw her, and bowed his head respectfully.

'I am sorry I startled you, Robert,' Frances said kindly. 'Ellen has not yet returned from the village, so I would be obliged if you would ride there to enquire after her.'

The boy flicked a nervous glance towards the house and seemed to hesitate. 'The master —'

'Do not concern yourself. You will be back before my brother has risen. Take Hartshorn,' she said, patting her horse's neck. 'He is the surest-footed through the woods.'

Robert hastened to fetch the tack. Frances helped him saddle the horse, then watched as the boy nimbly mounted. 'Please — take care to look about you,' she urged. 'Ellen may have fallen and be lying hurt. Take this blanket with you so that you might keep her warm if you need to go for help.'

The boy reached for it, then tapped his heels into Hartshorn's flanks and rode briskly away. Frances watched until he was out of sight, drawing her cloak against the chill morning air. With luck, he would return within the hour, Ellen in the saddle behind him. Her old nurse would be glad not to suffer the long walk home, Frances reflected, forcing herself to believe Edward's theory that the old woman had lost track of time and decided to stay with a friend in the village.

She glanced back at the house but had no desire to go inside just yet. Turning, she strolled in the direction of the wilderness. The hem of her dress soon grew damp where it brushed against the dewy grass, and the cool moisture seeped through the soft leather of her shoes. It was no matter. They would dry in front of the fire while she ate her breakfast.

Her agitation began to subside. She felt a little better for having done something to find Ellen, and the tranquillity of the garden worked as a balm upon her soul. But soon the memory of Sir Thomas's visit intruded upon her thoughts. How would she answer when he returned tomorrow? She had no desire to marry any man, let alone one she hardly knew. It felt like a betrayal of Tom, even though his friend had pledged to protect her. Sir Thomas must be a man of great honour to sacrifice his own happiness for the sake of such a promise. Would he really expect nothing from her? She could hardly believe it, though he had seemed in earnest. There would be no heirs of his own body if he stayed true to his word. He would surely then resent Tom's child as a daily reminder of what he had sacrificed.

She had reached the edge of the wilderness now. The grass underfoot was longer, the path less defined. She breathed in deeply, catching the scent of the woods that lay tantalisingly close. She took another step. Edward was probably still sleeping. He would never know if she defied his orders. With a few more paces, she could be among the ancient oaks, gathering the sweet violets and soft yellow primroses that would be opening their delicate petals to the early-morning sunshine.

Just then, she caught the distant chimes of St Peter's. *Six, seven, eight.* How could it be so late already? She had lost track of time as she had wandered, consumed by her thoughts. Reluctantly, she went slowly back towards the house.

She was surprised to see Edward already sitting at the breakfast table when she entered the parlour. 'Good morning, sister,' he said coldly. 'I trust you have not been wandering far — though the state of your dress suggests otherwise.'

'I went only to the edge of the wilderness,' Frances replied. 'I rose early and sent Robert to look for Ellen.' She had judged he would find out soon enough anyway.

'You had no right to do so,' he said irritably. 'I alone direct the servants in this house.'

Frances opened her mouth to object, but the sound of a horse's hoofs fast approaching reverberated around the room. She rushed to the window, but her brother was there before her.

'Robert has returned. No,' he said, pushing her back. 'You will stay here while I go and talk to him. You have meddled enough already.'

Soon Frances heard his footsteps crunching on the stones of the path as he strode to meet the stable boy. She felt the panic rise in her chest as she waited, straining for any echo of their conversation. But she could hear only the chattering of the birds as they flitted between the branches of the trees that bordered the estate.

She started at the slam of the front door. A moment later, her brother appeared, flushed and agitated. He closed the door behind him and guided Frances roughly to the far side of the room.

'Did he find Ellen?' she asked urgently. 'Is she safe?'

'She is in safe-keeping, that is certain.' Edward snorted.

Her relief drained away as she looked at her brother, a muscle in his jaw pulsing.

'The Reverend Pritchard has detained her on suspicion of witchcraft.'

'No!'

The tincture. The priest had condemned such practices from the moment he had arrived in the parish, eager to win favour with his sovereign. Frances herself had come under his suspicious gaze on more than one occasion. Only her father's intervention had saved her from any reprisals when she had last lived here. But her beloved Ellen had not been so fortunate. Frances chastised herself for placing her in such danger.

Edward was regarding her closely now. 'She was tending some sick woman in the village. A potion was found on her person, though she tried to conceal it when the priest came to minister to the woman.' His

53

eyes bored into Frances's and she forced herself not to look away. 'I wonder that Ellen would have taken such a risk,' he added.

'He has no right to detain her against her will,' Frances murmured, her teeth clenched.

'He has every right!' Edward shouted, then glanced quickly back towards the door. 'He has every right,' he repeated, more quietly this time. 'The king has pronounced that witchcraft in all its forms is heresy, punishable by death, and has charged every priest in the kingdom to be vigilant. If they discover anyone practising such foul arts, they have full powers to arrest them and have them brought before the assizes.'

'But Ellen is innocent,' Frances urged. 'It was I who made the potion. She was simply administering it on my behalf. You know full well that I would have tended the woman myself, had it been possible.'

Edward looked at her with a mixture of horror and disgust. 'I suspected as much,' he said, 'though I hoped I was wrong. It seems you will stop at nothing to bring this family to ruin and disgrace, sister. Is it not enough that you will taint the house with your bastard? Now you would have us all branded for witchcraft.'

He had brought his face so close to hers

that she felt his spittle on her cheek as he spoke. 'You will tarry here no longer,' he continued. 'You will accept Sir Thomas's proposal and go with him tomorrow.'

'You cannot force me to leave Longford.' Frances tried to keep her voice steady, though she felt sick with fear.

'Even Father would not stop me if he knew what you had done,' her brother retorted.

'He would not wish me to leave Ellen to her fate,' she countered, 'particularly as it is clear you will not lift a finger to help her.'

'If you intervene in this matter, it will be the surest means of condemning the woman to death,' Edward declared. 'Do you think I know nothing of your own arrest for witchcraft? Such news travels fast, even outside London. If Pritchard thinks to risk visiting you here at Longford and discovers the real source of your affliction, he will mark you as Ellen's accomplice and have you both hanged.'

Frances's heart was pounding as she tried to come to terms with the full horror of the situation. Though her brother's words were born of malice, she knew he spoke the truth. The only way she could help Ellen was to make sure that the priest did not hear of her involvement.

'That is, of course, unless the old woman has already betrayed you,' Edward continued.

'Ellen has sworn to tell no one I am here,' Frances said. 'I would trust her with my life.'

'You may have to. Who knows what a woman will say under threat of torture?'

'I know it well enough, brother,' Frances hissed. 'I have felt the torturer's blade pierce my skin until the blood poured from my body. Yet still I would not confess to a crime of which I was innocent. I pray that God will give Ellen the same strength.'

Edward stared at his sister as if she was suddenly a stranger to him. 'Once Ellen has been taken from the Reverend Pritchard's custody, it will not be long before he comes to make enquiries here,' he said slowly. 'You must be gone by the time he arrives.'

Frances fell silent, considering. When at last she spoke, it was with greater resolve. 'I will do as you wish, brother, but only upon this condition. You must go to Salisbury assizes to plead for Ellen yourself. As the head of the household, it is your duty to defend your staff. Father will think you unsuited to your position if he hears that you have neglected your responsibilities.'

Edward looked at her with resentment. He had always hated to be bested. 'Very well,' he said at last. 'I will perform my duty on Ellen's behalf. But you will not set foot in this house again. After tomorrow, Longford will be as dead to you as the man who sired your bastard.'

■ ■ ■ ■

Part 2
1610

■ ■ ■ ■

■ ■ ■ ■

Part 2
1610

■ ■ ■ ■

CHAPTER 4
26 JANUARY

Frances shivered and drew her cloak more tightly around her. A bitter east wind howled through the ramparts of the castle as she cowered against the thick stone wall of the postern gate. To her left, the motte dropped steeply away, and below she could see the dark waters of the swollen river glisten as they caught the moonlight.

She stole another glance over her shoulder. Nobody was there, yet she had the creeping sensation of being watched. She crouched closer to the wall, as if it could shield her from view. He had followed her to Thomas's estate, she knew. She had spied him on the road from Oxford, the deep blue velvet of his cloak marking him out as Cecil's man. Though she had not seen him for several weeks after her arrival at Tyringham Hall, she sensed that he was close by. Then, one bright autumn day when she had been walking in the woods that lay to the north of the

Hall, her infant son cradled at her breast, she had caught the flash of gold as he slid silently behind one of the large chestnut trees that were scattered across the estate.

For a moment, she thought of running. It was madness to have come here. Even if Cecil's man had not followed her, Thomas might discover the reason for her journey. She had seen the doubt in his eyes when she had told him of the relative who lay sick at Northampton, but he had not questioned her as to why she felt the need to visit someone of whom she had never previously spoken. He had, though, sent one of his servants to help her pack seeking assurance, no doubt, that there were no herbs or tinctures among the few clothes and other belongings she chose to take with her. His interference had annoyed her, though he had done little else to deserve her censure.

As a husband, Thomas had been attentive, ensuring that she had everything for her ease and entertainment. His library, which was far more extensive than her father's at Longford, had been at her disposal from the moment she had arrived at Tyringham Hall. It had been one of her greatest diversions, second only to her precious son for the comfort it had brought her. She had spent countless hours among the works of Homer and Ovid, their ancient prose delighting her with its humour and warmth, or browsing the impressive array of books on plants and their medicinal properties. She suspected that some of these had been newly acquired — their pages were by no means as worn as her own copies of Gerard and his fellow botanists. Whenever George was sleeping or with his nursemaid, she would come to the library, its now familiar shelves and volumes distracting her from thoughts of the past, of Tom.

The reminder of Thomas's kindness induced fresh guilt. Frances had striven hard to abide by the terms he had laid down for their marriage. Though in private she still cherished her rosary and prayer book, she was as outwardly conformist as her husband, accompanying him to church, whenever he was in residence, to hear and utter the words of worship prescribed by the king. She had been careful to show no interest when her husband's acquaintances had gossiped about the latest Catholic plot to oust James from his throne. Even during Thomas's long absences, when he accompanied the king on the hunt as master of the buckhounds — a privileged position, given that James was said to be fonder of his dogs than of his favourites — she had had no contact with Tom's family or associates.

Until now. Dorothy's letter had arrived two days ago. Frances had not heard from Tom's sister since her brief time at Longford almost four years earlier, though she had often wondered if Dorothy had sent other letters. Edward would have had no scruple in opening them. She only hoped that he would have had the good sense to destroy them. This letter had been brief, giving the time and place that she wished to meet, and urging Frances not to forsake her. As her fingers closed over the folded paper now, she wondered again if it was a trap. She had destroyed Dorothy's first letter before leaving Longford, but had read it so many times that she had recognised the woman's hand on this one as soon as her husband's attendant had brought it to her. Her first thought had been to consign it to the flames, but the urgency of Dorothy's words, the untidiness of her script, had prevented it.

Without pausing to think, she had rushed to Thomas's study and sought his permission to go. She had hated lying to him, but there had been nothing else for it. It would be the only time, she promised herself.

A sudden noise behind Frances made her turn. The ramparts were still deserted. After a few moments, she heard it again — like a sharp whisper. Peering into the gloom, she could just make out the edges of the chimney breast that jutted from the wall. As she stared, its base seemed to dissolve and billow in the wind. She took a step backwards, but lost her footing and felt herself begin to fall. Suddenly, an icy hand grasped her wrist and pulled her back onto the narrow path. Panting with fear, Frances stared at the woman before her, but her face was shrouded in the folds of her hood.

'I was afraid you would not come.' Her voice, though soft, had the same lilt as Tom's.

'Dorothy.' For a moment, Frances was unable to say anything more. She allowed herself to be led along the path towards a small recess in the wall that offered shelter from the howling wind. Dorothy lowered her hood, and Frances caught her breath. The resemblance was astonishing. It was as if Tom's large brown eyes were steadily appraising her.

'You did not answer my last letter.'

It was a statement rather than an accusation, but Frances felt ashamed. Dorothy must have thought her fickle to have turned her back on the cause for which Tom had died.

65

'I heard that you had left Longford soon afterwards, to be married.'

There was an edge to her voice now, and Frances's guilt and shame deepened as she realised how she must appear in the eyes of Tom's sister. As faithless to his memory as she had been to her fellow Catholics. 'Yes,' she answered. 'Sir Thomas Tyringham was a true friend to Tom. It was for his sake that he married me.'

'And for the sake of your son.'

Frances started at her words. *She could not know.* As she struggled to control her rising panic, she forced herself to hold the other woman's gaze. '*Our* son,' she replied carefully.

Dorothy continued to stare at her, then shook her head. 'Do not try to deceive me, Frances. I know that the boy is my nephew. That it was why you left court so suddenly.'

Frances felt hot, despite the bitter wind.

'Sir Thomas is a man of honour and sacrificed a great deal for the cause,' she continued, when Frances did not answer. 'It must have cost him dear to pass off the boy as his own, though I hear he dotes upon him now.'

Had Dorothy set spies to watch her too? The thought alarmed her.

'You are mistaken,' Frances replied. 'Grief

for your brother has given you false hope that a part of him lives on. I wish it were so. I loved him truly and would gladly have forfeited my life for his.'

She looked down at her hands as she struggled to maintain her composure. Dorothy reached forward and took them in her own. 'I understand your fears, Frances,' she said softly. 'These are dangerous times for those of us who share the true faith. I know that you wish to protect your son, as I do mine. But you cannot condemn him — and yourself — to a life of falsehood, of heresy. To do so would be to damn him in the next life, as well as this one. You cannot think that is what Tom would have wished for his son.'

'Tom would have wished for him to stay alive!' Frances cried, the tears now streaming down her cheeks. 'What would you have me do? Parade him as the son of a condemned traitor? Forfeit his safety, his happiness, his life? And all for what? A cause that died with Tom and the rest.'

Dorothy fell silent, but her grip on Frances's hands tightened. 'It did not die, Frances,' she said. 'It is stronger now than ever. The death of Tom and his companions has intensified people's hatred of this heretic king and drawn thousands more to our

67

cause. I do not speak out of blind faith,' she continued, as if reading Frances's thoughts. 'We have learned from the lessons of the past. Cecil's spies are now outnumbered by those of our cause. How do you suppose I was able to find out about my nephew? The time is almost ripe to act. We have powerful supporters at court, and the King of Spain stands in readiness with a huge army.'

Frances's mind was reeling. Amid the shock and fear that Dorothy's words had engendered, she felt a surge of hope, such as she had not experienced since Tom's death. It was as if she had been living in a trance, devoid of any real feeling, save the fierce love and protectiveness she harboured for her son. Time and again, she had told herself that this was the only way: Tom would not have wanted her to hazard her life and that of their young son by furthering the cause for which he had died. And she had almost believed it. But now it was as if Dorothy had opened a door into her old life, the one she had shared with Tom. She felt the familiar rush of anticipation at the thought of wreaking vengeance upon the king and his advisers. Though her fear had not left her, she felt alive for the first time in years.

Frances was only vaguely aware of Dorothy, who was watching her, as if following the thoughts that were racing through her mind.

'What would you have me do?' she asked at length.

Dorothy's lips lifted into a smile. 'The princess is still at the heart of our plans. Though she pretends to the same heresy as her father and brother, she will be crowned a Catholic queen. When the time comes.'

Frances thought of her former charge. Elizabeth would be thirteen now, she realised — old enough to be married. She tried to imagine the young woman she had become. When she had last seen her four years earlier, she had already had the elegance and charm of a lady twice her age — and the intelligence to match. But in other respects she had been very much a child. Frances recalled the petulant outburst that had marred their farewell, the princess berating her favourite attendant for deserting her, and swiftly withdrawing her hand as Frances had tried to kiss it. She had often thought of writing, but fear that she would implicate the girl in some way, should Frances's part in the Powder Treason be uncovered, had always prevented her.

'But our plans will be in ruins if she marries according to her brother's wishes,' Dor-

69

othy continued, interrupting her thoughts. 'Already he has paraded several heretic princes before her. None has been to the king's liking, thank God, but there is always a danger that the next one will be.'

Frances looked at her in confusion. 'But she is surely bound to marry according to her father's faith? The king will hardly countenance a Catholic husband.'

'The king hankers after earthly rather than heavenly treasures,' Dorothy replied, with a sneer. 'The King of Spain has a nephew of about the same age as the princess. If Elizabeth proves amenable, her father will overlook his religion in the interest of securing a powerful ally — and several coffers of Spanish gold. He does not know that Philip intends to use this match as a means of restoring England to the papal fold — and as a premise for invasion.'

'What has this to do with me?' Frances asked, pushing down the excitement that flared in her breast. 'I have been a stranger to the princess since leaving court. You cannot hope that I still have any influence over her.'

'You were as dear to her as a sister, and will be again,' Dorothy told her. 'No other attendant has come close to replacing you in her affections, and the queen is only seldom at court, preferring the solitude of Greenwich. The princess longs for a confidante once more.'

'I no longer have a position at court,' Frances countered, 'and my uncle is hardly likely to petition for one on my behalf. He and I have been estranged these four years.'

'You have no need of his assistance. The queen can arrange everything. Though she has taken care to distance herself from the Catholics at court, there can be no doubt that she remains true to the faith. And she always held you in the highest esteem. If she were to offer you a place in her daughter's household, you could hardly refuse — neither could your husband.'

'And, once there, I will regain the princess's trust and persuade her towards a Catholic marriage?' Frances said doubtfully.

Dorothy nodded encouragingly, her eyes bright with fervour.

'What of my son?' Frances asked, after a long pause. 'I could not bear to leave him behind, but neither would I place him in danger by bringing him to court.'

'My nephew cannot remain hidden from the world for ever,' Dorothy said firmly. 'Besides, there is as much danger in Buckinghamshire as at Whitehall.'

Frances thought of the man who had followed her to Tyringham Hall and lurked there still, watching and waiting. She shuddered. Quite apart from the dangers that surrounded her at Sir Thomas's estates, she had never felt welcome there. The household staff had always viewed her with suspicion, their conversations often ceasing abruptly when she entered a room. She knew they had not believed their master when he had told them he and Frances had been married several months before their arrival. Even though he had taken care to be seen visiting her bedchamber regularly, it was as if they knew that their master and his wife did nothing more than converse or play cards.

'You will arrange it all?' she asked.

Her companion nodded. 'I will write at once to Lady Vaux. She has a great patron at court who can petition the queen on your behalf. Sir Thomas already has lodgings there, so it will not appear strange that his wife and son should wish to join him. George has reached an age when it is expected that he will be sent to court to further his education.'

Frances was terrified at the thought of her young son in that vipers' nest. She wanted to keep him cocooned at Tyringham Hall, well away from the evil and corruption of the court. But Dorothy had spoken the truth. Perhaps the best protection she could offer George was to return and fight for his father's cause. Only when this heretic king was dead could England's Catholics and all others who had suffered at his hands truly live in peace.

Her mind was drawn back to her old nurse. She had tried hard to shut out the painful memory, afraid that the grief would overwhelm her. But an image of Ellen as she had last seen her flitted before her now: her back had been hunched and her limp pronounced as she set out on the agonisingly slow walk to Britford, Frances's tincture clasped tightly in her hand.

Many times, Frances had imagined the Reverend Pritchard's satisfaction as he had given Ellen into the sheriff's custody. After a miserable few weeks in Salisbury gaol, she had been acquitted by the assizes, thanks in no small part to the intercession of Frances's father. Though the king had forbidden him to attend, he had worked tirelessly to secure Ellen's release, fulfilling the role that his son Edward should have taken. He had expended a great deal on lawyers and other agents whom he could trust to act on his behalf. Thomas had lent his assistance too, dispatching his own lawyer to advise upon the matter. It had proved decisive. But the ordeal had taken its toll upon the old woman's health and she had died a few weeks later. Thomas had brought Frances the letter as she had sat cradling her newborn son in the warmth of the July sunshine.

The memory sparked a fresh wave of remorse, closely followed by an intense fury against the king, who had decried all forms of healing as witchcraft, punishable by death. He had as good as tightened a noose around Ellen's neck, choking the breath from her frail old body.

A sudden gust of wind brought in its wake the distant chimes of a church bell. It was late. Frances knew she must return to her lodgings before they were locked for the night. 'For love of Tom and his son, I will do as you ask,' she said. 'But my husband must never hear of it. If my part in this is discovered, he must remain entirely without blame. I will not reward his kindness by hazarding his life, as well as my own.'

Dorothy bent to kiss her hands, but Frances wrenched them away and strode purposefully down the hill. She did not pause to look back.

Chapter 5
27 January

A high-pitched squeal pierced the stillness as Frances dismounted and led her horse towards the stables. Rounding the corner, she smiled as she saw her young son sitting astride a pony, his small hands gripping the reins as if his life depended upon it.

'Remember to keep your back straight,' Thomas called, as he led the pony around the yard. He smiled indulgently as the boy lifted his chin and assumed a superior expression, every inch the young gentleman. But as his mount broke into a canter, George forgot any pretence at decorum and whooped with delight.

Neither he nor Thomas was aware of Frances as she watched from the shadows of the archway. Many times she had observed them thus, hidden from view as they walked together in the park, or practised archery and swordplay. Thomas had even had a hawking glove made for the boy so that he could hold one of the great falcons from the aviary and launch it into flight.

From the moment of her son's birth, Thomas had loved him like his own. Frances could not have wished for a better father for George, who adored him in turn and always missed him sorely whenever his court duties took him away from Buckinghamshire. Though she loved to see the bond between them growing stronger, it pained her too. It should have been Tom who had experienced the joy at seeing his son take his first tottering steps, who had helped shape the boy into the man he would become.

How like him George was, she reflected again as she watched him now, his dark brown eyes sparkling, cheeks flushed with excitement. Anyone who had known Tom would see the resemblance at once. She had often felt thankful that none of the household at Tyringham Hall had travelled further south than Bletchley. Certainly they had not been to court, Thomas preferring to keep a separate staff there. But if she did as Dorothy had asked, many people who had known Tom would see his son — Princess Elizabeth included. She experienced fresh anxiety at the thought. How could she expose George to such danger? And her husband? Looking at them now, she was consumed by remorse. Her son was happy here with his adored papa, free from the dangers and conspiracies of the court.

But for how long?

The same thought had plagued her many times since their arrival. Cecil had sent his spy not only to report on her movements but to convey a clear message that she had not been forgotten. She knew from bitter experience that he was a patient man. Was it really better to stay here, living this half-life and waiting for him to pounce, than to grasp the chance to help destroy him and his heretical master?

Her horse gave a whinny of impatience. She had almost forgotten him behind her as she gazed at her son and husband, lost in thought. They turned towards her now.

'Mama!' George exclaimed, letting go of the reins in his excitement.

With a deft move, Thomas stepped forward and caught him before he slipped from the saddle. As soon as he had been set safely upon the ground, he ran towards Frances and she swept him into her arms, planted several kisses on his warm cheek, then swung him around as he giggled with glee.

'How I have missed you,' she said, as she stroked his hair.

'Papa says I can soon ride in the park!'

George exclaimed. 'I have been practising all day.'

'You are a fine horseman,' Thomas said, with a smile, 'though you must be patient. Duke will not take kindly to being made to gallop before he is ready.'

At the mention of his beloved pony, George squirmed to be free of his mother's embrace and ran over to pet the animal.

'We did not expect you back so soon, Frances,' her husband said, stepping forward to embrace her. 'I trust all was well with your cousin.'

'I arrived to find her quite recovered,' she replied, keeping her gaze fixed upon George, who was now feeding Duke some hay. 'Thank you for giving me leave to go.'

'Think nothing of it. It would be a coldhearted husband who kept his wife from visiting a sick relative.'

Frances could feel his eyes upon her, but she continued to look towards her son. 'You have always been kind to us, Thomas,' she said.

'Your cousin must have been glad to have you as a guest.'

Frances hesitated. 'I did not wish to impose, so I found lodgings nearby.' She took care to keep her voice light.

'I am sure they would have been only too

happy to accommodate you. They asked you to come, after all,' Thomas persisted.

'Be careful, George!' Frances called, as she saw her son climb the mounting block. Unheeding, he leaped down from it and landed safely on the cobbles, then raced around to do the same again.

'I am sorry if my absence caused you any inconvenience,' she said tersely, turning to face him at last. 'It is the first time I have been away from this place since you brought us here.'

'You make it sound like a prison, Frances.'

Though he spoke gently, she caught the hurt in his voice and was instantly abashed. 'Forgive me — I am tired from the journey and slept little last night. I will rest now, before dinner, if you will excuse me?'

He looked at her closely, his eyes filled with doubt — and, she thought, some sadness. 'Of course,' he replied. 'George and I will continue our lesson a little longer. With luck, it will tire him out before bedtime,' he added, with a rueful smile.

Frances nodded her thanks. Then, casting a final glance at her son, she walked briskly towards the house.

As she opened the door into the dining room, Frances breathed in the aroma of roasted meats and spices. A rich array of dishes was spread on the table before her — venison studded with cloves, sweet chicken pâté and baked trout. Though she had little appetite, she knew that her husband had arranged this to welcome her home so she must not appear ungrateful.

He rose as she entered and smiled pleasantly, all trace of the earlier tension gone. 'Good evening, Frances. I hope you are rested?'

'Yes, thank you,' she replied, taking a seat close to him. 'And, as you predicted, George needed little persuasion to take to his bed.'

Thomas smiled. 'He is a credit to you, Frances.'

'And to you,' she replied warmly.

'His father would have been very proud of him,' he said quietly.

Frances was unable to reply. She took a long sip of wine as silence descended. The only sound was the ticking of the clock above the fireplace. It seemed to grow louder as the moments passed.

The opening of the door that led to the entrance hall made them both start. A second later, the steward appeared, flanked by two serving boys bearing more dishes. He bowed deeply to Thomas, then motioned for the boys to set down the steaming plates in the centre of the table.

'Thank you, Taylor,' Thomas said.

The serving boys retreated, but their superior remained standing by the fireplace. Frances looked at her husband, waiting for him to dismiss the man, but he made no move to do so. 'That will be all,' she said.

Taylor bestowed on her a look of disapproval and sniffed. She should not have infringed upon her husband's authority, but she could not bear to have the man present while they ate. Usually, he stayed only for the formal dinners when they entertained guests. At least then there was other company to distract her from his cold stares and curt remarks. Ever since her arrival at Tyringham Hall, he had made clear that she was not welcome.

The man turned his gaze to his master. 'Sir Thomas?'

'You may leave us.'

Taylor bowed stiffly and walked from the room, closing the door a little too firmly behind him. Frances waited until his footsteps had faded into silence, then addressed her husband. 'He still despises me.'

Thomas sighed. 'Taylor has served my family since I was a boy. He is loyal and able in his duties, though perhaps a little too officious at times. I am sorry that he is not more courteous towards you, but his discretion can be relied upon — as can that of the other servants.'

Frances fell silent. In her situation, discretion was of far greater value than friendliness, yet still she longed for the closeness she had enjoyed with Ellen. With her husband away so often, and precious few acquaintances of her own close by, she lacked company. It was a far cry from her years at court, when she had been hard-pressed to win a moment to herself.

The court.

For all its dangers, it offered her a purpose. God willing, she would serve it well this time. Tom had died for his faith; she would no longer keep her own secreted, like a long-faded jewel. She hoped that the queen's summons would be swift to arrive.

'Well, now,' Thomas said, interrupting her reverie. 'It seems we are to be parted again. The king has declared his intention to return to the hunt. I will leave for Whitehall tomorrow so that I can make ready.'

Frances thought quickly. Dorothy had told her to wait for word from the queen, but this was surely too good an opportunity to miss. 'Might I accompany you this time?' she asked, as casually as she could.

Thomas looked at her in surprise. 'I did

not think you would ever wish to return to that place.'

Frances was aware of the flush that was creeping up her neck, threatening to betray her, but she persisted. 'For myself, I would gladly stay away. But George should soon be introduced at court. No matter how much I might loathe the place, I wouldn't want to hinder his prospects — and neither would you.'

Her husband's expression darkened as he stared at her. She had aroused his suspicions, but she forced herself to hold his gaze.

'George is flourishing here and hardly lacks diversion,' Thomas said. 'Many a young gentleman has made his way in the world without recourse to the dangers and temptations of the court. By the time he comes of age, he will be as accomplished as any courtier and will know enough about this estate to take over its management. It is my intention to bequeath it to him.'

'I know it, and owe you a greater debt than I will ever be able to repay — for this and many other things besides,' Frances replied softly, reaching out to touch his hand. 'But you must recognise the truth of what I say. You are beyond compare as a father to George, and I would not wish to see him grow to resent you for denying him the opportunities that the court can offer. Besides,' she added, 'there must be gossip about why you keep me here, when most other gentlemen bring their wives to court. Surely the king himself has remarked upon it.'

The look on Thomas's face told her that her words had hit their mark. He opened his mouth to reply, then sighed as if resigned. 'Where would you live? My lodgings at court are by no means as spacious as we are used to here. There is only one bedchamber. It would be harder to maintain the pretence that we live as husband and wife.' He looked down at her hand, which still rested upon his, and shifted uncomfortably.

Sensing her advantage, Frances forged ahead. 'That is of little matter. There will be room enough for the three of us.' She did not add that, if George was obliged to share a bedchamber with them, there would be even less opportunity for intimacy than there was now, with their separate sleeping quarters.

Thomas rubbed his brow, as if trying to smooth out the creases. 'You know the risks that this would carry, Frances. The last time you were at court, Cecil almost had you arrested for involvement in the Powder Treason. He suspects you still.'

Frances held his gaze. 'But if what you have told me is true, he has been eclipsed by other favourites, and the king is too pre-occupied with hunting and hounds to trouble himself with affairs of state.'

'Has your sudden desire for court anything to do with your visit to Northampton?'

The abruptness of his question startled Frances, and it took her a few moments to recover her composure. 'I do not understand your meaning, Thomas,' she replied.

His gaze sharpened. 'I will take you at your word, Frances,' he said, his voice low. 'But you must promise me that you will not become embroiled in the plots that still swirl about the Crown. Tom would not have wished you to place yourself and your son in such danger. It will spell death for all of us if you disobey me.'

Frances nodded, mute. She took a sip from her glass and her hand shook as she set it down. With an effort, she swallowed the wine, which burned her throat.

'Then it is settled,' her husband said, after a long pause. 'I will send my steward ahead to make arrangements. We will leave as soon as it is light.'

CHAPTER 6
29 JANUARY

The sun was already sinking behind the towers of the palace when their carriage turned onto the Strand. Frances's heart lurched as she recognised the turrets of the Holbein Gate silhouetted against the deep crimson sky. She did not allow herself to glance right, towards Westminster Hall. It had been almost four years since she had visited the site of Tom's death, but the pain of the memory was still raw.

The cry of a trader made her look across to the houses that lined the south side of the street. Suddenly there it was: a tall, timber-framed lodging that seemed to lean precariously against the one next to it. Frances raised her eyes towards the tiny garret at the top of the house. The casement window was closed against the chill winter air. It was from there that she had seen Tom for the last time, his emaciated body jolting painfully over the cobbles as he and the other condemned plotters were dragged to the horrors of a traitor's death.

'Mama?'

George's voice brought her back to the present. She turned to her son, who had woken and was eyeing her uncertainly.

'Why are you crying?'

Quickly, Frances brushed away the tears she had been unaware were running down her cheeks. Thomas reached forward and stroked her hand, but she pulled it away, then inwardly chastised herself as she saw the hurt in his eyes. 'Forgive me, it is nothing. I was remembering old friends,' she said, giving her son's hand a squeeze. She was aware that her husband was still watching her closely.

'When will we be at the palace?' George asked. 'We have been travelling for weeks!'

Frances smiled indulgently. It had been just two days since they had left Buckinghamshire, but the journey had seemed arduous to her, too. Thomas had insisted they rest at St Albans for a night, rather than attempt to cover the fifty or so miles in a single day. He had been right, of course — the horses were tired after trudging along the seemingly endless tracks that lay between the Tyringham estate and the old abbey of Woburn — but Frances had been impatient to reach their destination. Now, though, she was filled with foreboding and almost wished she had stayed in the relative safety of her husband's estate.

'We are only moments away now, George,' Thomas said. 'Look! That tall gatehouse ahead is the entrance to the palace. King Henry built it to impress all those who visited.'

The boy's eyes opened wide as they followed the direction in which his papa was pointing. 'Even Hartshorn could pass under that,' he said in wonder.

Frances and her husband laughed, dispelling some of the tension that had crept in almost imperceptibly the closer they had come to London.

'Your mother's horse and many more besides,' Thomas replied. 'It was even high enough for the old queen's giant sergeant porter to pass through without bumping his head.'

George loved to hear stories of Thomas Keyes, who had guarded the riverside gate of palace. At almost seven feet tall, he had towered over the rest of the court. But Frances's mother, who had served in Queen Elizabeth's court for more than thirty years after her arrival from Sweden as a girl, had remembered him as the gentlest of souls.

Pity for him that his choice of wife had been so unfortunate. The diminutive Lady Mary Grey, one of the sisters of the ill-fated Jane, had had royal blood. Her failure to seek Elizabeth's permission for the marriage had led to her and her new husband being thrown into prison, never to see each other again. Frances shuddered at the unwelcome reminder of the dangers of court.

The carriage rumbled over the cobbles that led under the gateway and into the main courtyard of the palace. Although there were numerous other courtyards in the maze of buildings beyond, this was by far the largest and could easily accommodate a dozen carriages or more.

After a moment, a groom opened the door. George jumped to his feet and made to descend the steps the man had set in place, but Frances caught his arm just in time and pulled him back onto his seat. He scowled up at her.

'We are here as guests of your papa, George. He must go first.'

Thomas winked at the boy as he climbed down onto the cobbles, then turned and offered his hand to Frances. She hesitated, suddenly overcome with the enormity of what she had done. She could feel George wriggling next to her, desperate to explore the royal palace that was to be his home for — how long? A month? A year? Longer, perhaps. With a deep breath, she gathered up her skirts and alighted from the carriage.

Frances stood for a moment, gazing around the courtyard. In contrast to most others, it was far longer than it was wide and stretched the full length of the privy garden that lay on the other side of the courtiers' lodgings. Ahead was another gatehouse, smaller than the Holbein Gate but even more lavish in decoration, with domes atop its four towers and three storeys of luxurious accommodation within.

All of a sudden, there was a flurry of activity around one of the three arched passageways beneath the gatehouse. Frances watched, shielding her eyes from the dying rays of the sun, as the yeomen of the guard raised their halberds and a small figure emerged from the shadows of the central arch. As she strained to see the man who had caused a hush to descend across the courtyard, and the numerous servants and courtiers within to bow low as he passed, her heart contracted. Though she longed to run back through the Holbein Gate and far away from the palace, she stood stock still, unable to wrest her gaze from the figure as he walked haltingly but with purpose towards them.

'My lord.'

Frances was vaguely aware of her husband bowing low next to her. Only after a pause did she think to make a similar obeisance. She lowered her eyes to the ground and waited.

'Lady Frances.'

He spoke with the same mildly amused tone that she remembered, though his voice was frailer than it had been and she caught the faint wheeze as he drew in a breath.

'We had not expected to see you so soon.'

She raised her eyes to his and was shocked by how much he had changed. The years had not been kind to him. His hunch seemed even more pronounced, and he was leaning heavily on his staff. The skin on his face was pallid and pinched, and his neatly cropped hair was more white than brown. 'My husband kindly agreed that I might accompany him to court this time, Lord Salisbury.' Though she was careful to keep her tone light, she tasted bile as she spoke.

'Then we are fortunate indeed. The court has been a good deal less interesting since your departure and that of your . . . associates,' he said, with a smile. 'I have been hard-pressed to discover any news of you. Sir Thomas has kept you hidden away, like a prized jewel.'

Fury rose in her chest as she thought of the man whom Cecil had appointed to watch her ever since her arrival at Tyringham Hall. Thanks to him, his master was better informed about her movements than her own maid.

'My wife has had other demands upon her time,' Thomas cut in, before she could answer. He placed his hand on George's shoulder and gently steered him from behind his mother's skirts, where he had been hiding since Cecil's arrival. How much more afraid George would have been if he had known what Cecil was capable of, Frances mused.

She watched as Cecil looked down at her son. Though he affected a humorous expression, she noticed his eyes narrow as he studied the boy. Instinctively, she moved to stand behind George. It took all of her resolve not to wrap him in her arms as if to shield him from the man who had as good as murdered his father.

'You must be Master George,' Cecil said. The boy's eyes darted up to him, but he quickly looked down at his feet, which he scuffed back and forth across the cobbles until Thomas placed a restraining hand on his shoulder.

'Your son is a fine lad, Sir Thomas. I wonder that he is so tall. I must have mistaken his age. How old are you, boy?'

'He is but three years old,' Frances said quickly.

'I will be four in July,' George added, straightening his back and lifting his heels off the floor.

'Indeed?'

Frances could sense Cecil making a swift calculation. She glanced at her husband and noticed a tremor in his jaw.

'Then you were even more discreet than I gave you credit for, Sir Thomas. Though I had heard it said you had married Lady Frances months before she left court, I scarcely believed it. I had always thought that traitor Thomas Wintour had stolen your wife's heart.'

His smile never faltered as he looked from Thomas to Frances, whose hands were clenched at her sides.

'I am surprised that the king's chief minister would concern himself with such matters, my lord,' she said. Her eyes blazed as she stared back at him.

'It is a failing in me, I admit, Lady Frances. When he served the late queen, my father took an interest in all manner of things. He once told me it is often those which seem of little consequence that hold the greatest import. I have perhaps carried his lesson too far, but I am too old to change my habits now.'

There was an awkward silence. George had forgotten his shyness and was beginning to fidget. He yawned.

'You must forgive us, my lord,' Thomas said, seizing the opportunity. 'Our son is tired from the long journey. I will take him and my wife to our chambers now.'

Cecil spread his hands. 'Of course. How thoughtless of me to detain you for so long. I will have my page escort you there at once.'

'There is no need,' Frances said, as Cecil turned to one of his attendants. 'My husband knows the way well enough.' She did not add that she herself had visited the apartment once before. It seemed a lifetime ago now, though, and she had long since forgotten the way.

Cecil waved away her protest. 'It would be a pleasure, Lady Frances,' he said smoothly. 'Besides, I would not wish you to go astray, as you did upon first arriving at Whitehall all those years ago. Why, I believe you ended up in the apartments of one of the queen's own attendants.'

Frances opened her mouth to reply, but he gave a stiff bow, wincing, and gestured

94

for them to follow his page. As they made their way across the seemingly endless courtyard, she could feel Cecil's eyes upon her.

'Who is Wintour?' George asked, when they had almost reached the gatehouse.

Frances exchanged a look with her husband, who answered before she could. 'He was an old friend of your mother's and mine, George,' he said briskly. 'Now, which of these archways do you think we should choose? Careful now — select the wrong one and we could end up lost in the palace for ever.'

Instantly diverted, the boy pointed to the one on the left. Cecil's page, who was several paces ahead, had disappeared through the central one. Even though she knew they all led to the same courtyard beyond, Frances found herself hoping they could escape him. The encounter with his master had unnerved her. Though her husband had told her that Cecil no longer wielded the same power as he had when she was last at court, he was still a deadly adversary. He had known she had been up to her neck in the Powder Treason, but had lacked the proof to condemn her. And now he had a new focus for his schemes.

She looked down at her son, who was

scurrying ahead, eager to lead the way, though he had never before set foot in the palace. Her chest tightened with panic and she was consumed by remorse for bringing him into such danger. Tom would hardly have willed it. She shook the thought from her mind. It was too late now. She must fulfil the task for which she had taken such a risk. If she succeeded, George's future would be better assured than if they had stayed in Buckinghamshire.

After crossing another courtyard, Cecil's page disappeared through a large doorway on the right. This led into a passageway that ran the length of a small knot garden. Frances slowed her pace and took George's hand so that he might not stumble in the gloom. Her husband stayed close behind as they followed the young man up four flights of stairs to a series of apartments on the top floor. He came to a halt outside a large oak door.

With a jolt, Frances recognised the archway above, into which was carved the emblem of the House of Tudor. The first Stuart king to reside in the palace had not troubled to erase the many traces of his predecessors. She wondered briefly that Cecil's page had found Thomas's lodging in such a vast, sprawling palace without any false turns. Had Cecil been watching her husband too? It would hardly surprise her.

Thomas nodded his thanks to the young man, who waited until they had entered the apartment before going on his way. Frances stood on the threshold, struggling to control her emotions as memories of her last visit, six years before, filled her mind.

It had been the first time she and Tom had conversed together, after their fleeting introduction on the stage of the masque. Her uncle had arranged the invitation to dine with Thomas, whom he judged to be an ideal suitor for his niece. She smiled as she recalled his irritation at discovering their host had invited another guest: his friend Tom Wintour, a rising star at Gray's Inn. Tom had baited the earl over dinner, which had greatly enhanced Frances's enjoyment of the evening — that, and the conversation she and Tom had had when he had escorted her afterwards to her apartments. She had never met anyone like him and had been able to think of little else in the days and weeks that followed. By contrast, Thomas had faded rapidly from her memory. She would not have believed that it would be him, not his friend, whom she would marry.

'They usually light the fires before my return,' her husband said, with a hint of annoyance, as he walked over to a large dresser and rummaged in a drawer. The encounter with Cecil had unsettled him too, Frances realised. He brushed past her with a handful of tapers and returned a few moments later with them lit.

'My neighbour was obliging,' he said, as he handed one to Frances. 'I will start the fire if you light the sconces.'

She did as he bade her, and before long the room was suffused with a mellow light. Frances inhaled the warm scent of beeswax. Not all courtiers were afforded such luxury. Her husband must have succeeded in winning favour with the lord chamberlain, as well as the king.

The apartment was as tastefully furnished as she had remembered. Above the large stone fireplace in which her husband was crouched, attempting to coax the meagre flames into life, was a beautifully carved overmantel, with the same intertwined Tudor roses that could be found throughout the palace. The handsome oak dining table was still positioned on the opposite side of the room, close to the three large bay windows that overlooked the river and the mansions that clung to its southern bank. George had already scrambled onto one of the velvet cushions that lined the central window seat and was peering out, his nose pressed against the glass.

At the far end of the chamber, Frances saw that the full-length portrait of King James had been replaced by a fine tapestry, similar to those that hung on the other walls. She wondered if it had been reclaimed by the lord chamberlain for a public part of the palace, or if Thomas had arranged for its removal. She found herself hoping it was the latter.

'The bedchamber is over there, on the left,' her husband called over his shoulder as he continued to stoke the fire, which was now roaring in the grate. Though he tried to appear nonchalant, Frances knew he was as apprehensive as she.

'Thank you,' she replied. 'I will find our nightclothes from among the coffers and prepare George's bed.'

'But, Mama, it is still early,' her son protested. 'And I am not yet tired,' he added, stifling a yawn.

Frances smiled at him affectionately. 'That may be so, George, but we all need rest after our journey. Besides,' she added slyly, 'I am sure you would not wish to sleep too late tomorrow morning and miss any adventures that the court might offer.'

Her son gave a heavy sigh, then resumed

his careful study of the world beyond the windowpane. 'I have never seen so many houses,' he said, in wonder.

Frances turned and walked into the bed-chamber. Though she was familiar with the rest of the apartment, she had never stepped over this threshold. She held the taper in front of her. This room, too, was well appointed, though it was much darker than the rest of the apartment because there was only one small window, on the opposite wall to the fireplace. A large tester bed with crimson drapes dominated the room. Though she knew her husband to be a man of his word, Frances shivered as she looked at it. She had grown used to the convenience of their separate chambers at Tyringham Hall, and although she had brushed away Thomas's concerns about their sleeping arrangements at court, now that she was faced with the enforced intimacy they entailed, she felt uncomfortable.

She tore away her gaze and surveyed the rest of the room. She soon noticed that a small truckle bed had been positioned at one side of the large tester, furthest from the window. It was already made up with a rich coverlet and three pillows, so she had little to do except prepare their night attire. With customary efficiency, the lord chamberlain had ordered that their coffers be brought up as soon as their carriage had drawn to a halt, and she soon found the one that contained the shifts and other linens.

As she unfolded her husband's nightshirt on the chest next to her own and George's, Frances wondered how many other wives had first laid hands upon such garments after almost four years of marriage. An image of Tom came before her, so sudden that it took her breath away. She closed her eyes so that she might keep it there a moment longer, as she remembered his fingertips trailing down the length of her spine, his warm mouth pressed to her neck.

'I hope it is to your liking, Frances.'

The words, softly spoken, made her jump so that she almost dropped the taper. Her eyes snapped open and her fingers trembled as she watched the flame gutter, then burn as brightly as before. 'Yes — thank you. Though it has reminded me of how tired I am. I will retire as soon as George is settled.'

She did not look at her husband as she spoke, but she knew he was watching her carefully.

'Of course,' he replied. 'I have ordered some supper to be brought to our chambers — I did not think that you would wish to dine with the court this evening. We can retire as soon as we have eaten. I hope the food is swift to arrive — George is complaining that he is half starved,' he added. She heard the smile in his voice.

Less than half an hour later, there was a knock on the door and a page entered, bearing a tray of cold meats, bread and ale. Frances and her husband ate sparingly, in contrast to George, who devoured the food as if he had not eaten for a week. As soon as he had finished, Frances saw that his eyelids were heavy so she led him gently into the bedchamber, closing the door behind them so that she might change into her own shift after helping her son into his. Once they were dressed, they knelt beside his bed and offered up their nightly prayers. Frances made them shorter than usual lest George fall asleep before they were over. He climbed into his bed without protest, and when Frances bent to kiss his forehead, his eyes were already closed. With a smile, she began to walk towards her own bed.

'What is a traitor?'

She stopped at the small, sleepy voice and turned back to see her son peering up at her expectantly.

'That man said Wintour was one,' he added, when his mother did not answer.

Frances knelt by his bed. 'A traitor is

someone who betrays the king or tries to harm him in some way,' she said. 'But Thomas Wintour was no traitor,' she added, clasping his small hands in her own. 'He was a man of great courage, who fought hard for what he believed in. He —'

She stopped as she saw that her son's eyes had closed and his little chest was rising and falling in the slow rhythm of sleep. It was as well. She had already said too much. Slowly, she rose to her feet and walked over to the bed. Drawing back the covers, she slipped quietly between them, then blew out the candle on the small table next to her. She lay there for what seemed like an eternity. Though her bones ached with tiredness, sleep evaded her as she waited, listening for movement from the chamber beyond.

At length, there was a soft tapping on the door. Frances held her breath but did not answer. After a few moments, she heard the latch being carefully lifted and Thomas padded into the room. His footsteps stopped at the end of the bed and he stood there for so long that she wondered if he had stolen silently away. Then at last she heard him walk over to the chest and there was a soft rustling as he changed into his nightshirt.

Frances continued to feign sleep as her

husband climbed into their bed. She strained her ears to listen for his breathing becoming slower, deeper. But there was no sound as they lay there side by side, as still and silent as the carved stone figures of a tomb.

CHAPTER 7
31 JANUARY

Frances glanced around the deserted courtyard. The torches that had blazed in the sconces the night before had long since burned out. She would have welcomed a little of their warmth now, as she drew up her hood against the early-morning chill. A cold, damp mist hung low about the cobblestones, almost obscuring them from view. Ellen used to tell her that such mists were the shadows of unquiet souls, wandering the earth in search of vengeance or forgiveness. Frances could almost believe such tales now as she waited in the stillness, as if suspended between this world and the next.

It was four years to the day since Tom had died. She had lain in bed last night, pretending to sleep as she listened for the distant chimes. Time had not lessened her grief, only numbed it. But it often broke out without warning, prompted by some small recollection, and would sear through her.

Was Tom seeking vengeance, she wondered. Certainly he had never repented of his crimes and had died with the words of the Roman Catholic creed on his lips, begging all those of the faith to pray for him. The king's pamphleteers had seized upon this as a sign of his unrelenting wickedness, for which they declared he would suffer the eternal torments of Hell. Frances thrust the image from her mind. God would surely have claimed him for his own. It was Cecil and his heretic king who were damned, not those who had tried to blow them to the skies.

The mist grew thicker as she stood there, lost in thought, and the few tendrils of hair that were not hidden beneath her cloak felt damp against her face. She must make haste. The court would soon be stirring, and if her husband awoke to find her gone he would fear that she had betrayed him.

Keeping close to the easternmost wall, she made her way silently along the courtyard and through an archway that led into the privy garden. She could just make out the silhouettes of the brightly painted beasts that clung to a series of wooden poles speared into the ground. The mist had risen so high now that the panthers, leopards and griffins appeared to be floating among the clouds. Stepping carefully, Frances found one of the paths that led around the knot gardens, turning left at the corner of the first hedge. If she had judged correctly, she would soon pass by the magnificent sundial that King Henry had boasted could show the time in thirty different ways. There was little hope of it doing so now, she thought.

At length, she reached the long stone gallery that stretched across the southern side of the garden and ducked under the second of its ornate arches. Her old apartment lay directly above her. She glanced up, as if expecting to see the neatly appointed room that looked out over the Thames. She wondered who lived there now. Her place in the princess's household would have been quickly filled. Though there were more positions for ladies at a court that boasted a queen consort and her daughter, the competition for them was hardly less fierce than it had been in the days of the old queen.

Reaching out, she felt the smooth, damp oak of the door that led into the small herb garden beyond. As her fingers closed over the iron handle, she hesitated. This garden had been her solace during her time in the princess's service. She had spent many hours there, gathering herbs for her tinctures and salves, until Cecil had marked her for a witch and she had been obliged to employ greater discretion.

Slowly, she turned the handle. The sound of the latch scraping against the stone was deadened by the mist that had seeped into the passageway. Pausing on the threshold, she inhaled deeply to catch the familiar scent of myrtle or the sharp tang of rosemary. But there was only the same smell of damp stone that permeated the gallery behind her.

Frances took a step forward. In the small courtyard she could see the outline of the low box hedge that enclosed the garden. Crouching, she ran her fingers along the top and gave a low cry as one snagged on a sharp thorn.

As the mist was dispersed in the gathering light, she watched, with mounting dismay, as the features of her once-cherished garden gradually came into focus. The myrtle had been allowed to grow unchecked and was tangled with brambles. The neatly divided squares of turf it had once enclosed were now indistinguishable from each other, and the herbs she had tended so carefully were choked with weeds. The once bright green sprigs of thyme had withered into brown stalks, and as she reached out to touch the velvety leaves of sage that hung limply from the plant, they crumbled into dust.

Frances rose slowly to her feet. She felt exhausted as she gazed out across the long-neglected garden and wondered vaguely if anyone had set foot in it since she had last been there. Then, among the tangled weeds, she noticed a dark green sprig, its tiny leaves seeming to reach up towards the frail sunlight. Rosemary. She had come here to gather it, not for an ointment or potion — she knew better than to prepare such remedies so soon after arriving back at court — but for remembrance. She cast an anxious look at the sky, which was now the deep yellow of tansy. There was no longer time to walk to Westminster Palace as she had planned and lay a sprig of rosemary upon the place where Tom had died. But she would gather the herb nevertheless and keep it in the locket around her neck, close to her heart.

As she bent to pluck the delicate stem, a movement above caught her eye. She froze, heart thumping, and her eyes darted up to the windows that overlooked the garden. In the smallest, set in the southernmost wall, she thought she saw the pale skin of a woman's face, but it retreated from view. Quickly, she pulled at the rosemary with more force than she had intended and the entire plant broke free, fragments of dry soil scattering from its delicate roots. She had destroyed the only herb to survive in the wrecked garden. Tears rose, and she angrily brushed them away. Absurd that she should weep for such a thing when the tears she had thought would flow freely for Tom today were still choked in her throat.

There were sounds of the court gradually coming to life now as she stood motionless in the garden, the rosemary in her hand. Reaching into her pocket, she drew out a linen kerchief and wrapped it around the plant, then hastened from the courtyard. As she closed the door behind her, she felt those eyes watching her still from the window of her old chamber.

'We had almost given you up for lost, Frances,' her husband gently chided as she hurried into their apartment. She had run all the way back from the garden, and her cheeks were flushed as she bowed her head in greeting.

'Forgive me — I could not sleep so I decided to walk around the palace to remind myself of it and became rather lost.'

Thomas tore off another piece of bread and continued his breakfast. George, who was sitting next to him, was gobbling a thick slice of ham and hardly seemed to notice his mother's arrival. Frances took a seat next to him. Suddenly hungry, she helped herself to the generous selection of dishes that were spread in front of them.

'You are to be presented to His Majesty today,' Thomas said, without looking up from his plate.

Frances's heart skipped a beat. She had not expected it to be so soon — and on this day, of all days. Would James realise the significance? She had no doubt that Cecil would — indeed, he had probably planned it so he might watch her for any reaction.

'And I too, Papa?' George cut in eagerly.

'Of course. The king would not overlook so important a subject,' he replied, with a wink.

The boy's eyes shone with excitement. 'Will he wear a crown?' he demanded eagerly. 'And carry a sword, like King Arthur?'

Thomas grinned and ruffled his hair. 'I am sure he will dress in his finest clothes to meet you, George.'

Frances was hardly aware of her son's chatter as he fired off another volley of questions and began practising how he would bow before his sovereign. How far from the boy's chivalric image of a king James was.

111

George could not be other than disappointed when he met him. She should prepare him, but was too preoccupied by what lay ahead. The encounter with Cecil had been unsettling enough, but the idea of making her obeisance before a king she despised — and whom she had resolved to help destroy — was almost too much for her. With luck, he would pay her little heed — she was, after all, of the wrong sex to hold his interest for long.

'At what hour are we required to attend?' she asked, interrupting her son's animated babble.

Thomas gave her a long look. 'At eleven o'clock, just after he has breakfasted. He has a mind to go hunting in Greenwich today, to break in the horses before our excursion to Oatlands.'

'Then you must excuse me,' Frances said. 'I will prepare our attire.'

She did not look at her husband as she bobbed a swift curtsy and hastened into the bedchamber, closing the door firmly behind her.

Their brisk footsteps echoed along the corridor as they made their way towards the presence chamber. Frances clasped George's hand tightly in her own as he scurried alongside her. His chatter ceased as he looked about him at the tapestries and painted ceilings that grew ever more lavish as they drew closer to the king's private apartments.

Two yeomen of the guard were standing at the entrance, halberds crossed.

'This is Lady Frances, my wife, and our son George,' Thomas announced. 'We have an audience with His Majesty.'

Frances recognised the guard on the left, who was peering at her with interest. She prayed that he would hold his tongue. She had no desire to answer the many questions that George would ask if the man made any indiscreet remarks about her previous sojourn at court. Thankfully, he merely smirked, then nodded to his companion and they raised their weapons as the doors to the chamber were opened.

Heavy drapes were pulled across the windows and the room was dimly lit by the half-dozen candles that flickered in the sconces. It was stiflingly hot, thanks to the fire that roared in the grate. Frances regretted her choice of dress: its heavy brocaded silk was lined with sable at the neck and sleeves.

The chamber was dominated by the ornate throne that stood on a raised dais. The intricate gilded carvings on the arms and legs glimmered in the candlelight, and a sumptuous crimson canopy edged with gold thread hung above. On either side of the throne stood a gentleman dressed in the deep-scarlet velvet of the king's livery. George was staring nervously at them, all trace of his former ebullience gone.

After a few moments, footsteps could be heard, followed by a sharp rap of a staff on the wooden floorboards, which made Frances and her son jump. The doors to the left of the throne were flung open, and a cavalcade of young attendants — all male — walked briskly into the room, fanning out on either side of the throne. Frances cast a discreet glance at them but recognised only one or two. She had heard it said that James liked to keep a fresh supply of handsome young men in his chambers, lest he grow bored. It was just another way in which he differed from his predecessor, who had surrounded herself with the same faithful attendants for most of her reign.

Looking towards the throne, Frances noticed that a space had been left next to it. She did not wonder long who might fill it, for a second later a slender young man stepped nimbly into the room. The first thing Frances noticed was his bright red hair, which was combed back from his high forehead and curled at the stiffly starched collar of his shirt. He had a flamboyant moustache and a neat beard that narrowed to a long point. His dark eyes were coolly appraising as he stared back at her.

The shrill sound of a trumpet rang out, heralding the king's arrival. Frances and her husband sank to their knees and she tugged on her son's doublet, prompting him to do the same. It took all of her resolve to keep her gaze fixed upon the floor when she heard James huffing and cursing as he made his way onto the dais, then sinking onto the throne with a heavy sigh. A long silence followed. Frances felt a bead of sweat trickle between her shoulder blades.

'Sir Thomas,' the king drawled. 'Ye're welcome. Are my buckhounds made ready?'

His accent was even thicker than Frances remembered. She had heard that since the Powder Treason he had insisted upon being attended in his private domain only by Scotsmen. His face was ruddier than before, his hair more streaked with grey. Glancing down, she noticed that his white satin doublet was pulled tight over his stomach and the buttons looked set to give way at any moment.

'They are, Your Majesty,' her husband re-plied.

James grunted. 'And you have brought your wife with ye — your son too. Stand up, boy!'

George started at the king's command and looked across at his mother in alarm. Gently, she cupped his elbow and raised him to standing. His legs quivered as he stared at the floor.

'Come closer, so I can see you,' the king demanded.

George took a few faltering steps towards the foot of the dais. With an effort, James hauled himself up from his throne and leaned forward so that his face was almost level with the boy's. Frances might have been watching her son in a lion's den, about to be devoured by the prowling beast. She had to fight every instinct to run forward and sweep him into her arms.

'You're a fine lad, sure enough,' James said, as he pinched the boy's chin between his finger and thumb. George flinched as spittle fell upon his cheek. 'You'll make an even finer attendant one day,' he added, turning to share a knowing look with the red-haired man, who placed a delicate white hand to his thin lips.

The king gestured for George to return to

his place.

'And you, Lady Frances,' he said, as his gaze slowly travelled the length of her body. 'I did not think to see you here again. Your *husband*' — he emphasised the word — 'has always told me you were content to remain in Buckinghamshire.'

'Indeed I was, and would be still, Your Majesty,' Frances replied, holding his gaze. 'But our son is of an age to be introduced at court, and I would not wish to hinder his prospects, no matter how settled we were at my husband's estate.'

James eyed her closely. 'My little Beagle informs me that you kept better company there than you did when you were last at court.'

Frances had thought that Cecil's spy had been keeping his master informed, not the king. The chief minister must have delighted in letting James know that he had appointed someone to watch her. It was proof of his diligence, after all, and had no doubt been richly rewarded.

'I only hope that you will continue to do so now that you are here, particularly as I am about to deprive you of your husband's company for several weeks,' he continued.

'I am sure that I will not lack for diversion, Your Majesty.'

James sniffed loudly. 'Indeed ye will not. I know ye're a great reader, Lady Frances — ye certainly taught my daughter well enough — and I can give ye matter enough to hold your attention.'

Frances was at a loss. The king was not renowned for his literary tastes, and barely had patience for even the shortest plays during the entertainments at court.

'I'm sure your husband, faithful subject that he is, has told you of the oath of allegiance that all those who have come to my court since the Powder Treason have been required to swear.'

Frances felt suddenly cold, despite the rising heat. Thomas had been obliged to take the oath when it had first been issued, shortly after they were married. In so doing, he had sworn his fealty to the king and denounced the Roman Catholic religion as heresy, punishable by death.

'I will have no more of the damnable popish practices that almost led to my destruction!' James shouted, slamming his fist on the arm of his throne with such force that the entire dais shuddered.

Frances heard her son gasp and she put her arm around him as he cowered against her.

'The worst of those traitors went to their

deaths on this very day, four years ago. I will never forget it — nor will their heretic associates. So perish all enemies of the king!'

An ominous silence followed. Thomas gave a small cough, prompting. Frances steadied her breathing before she spoke. 'Of course, Your Majesty,' she said at last. 'I shall be glad to declare my faithfulness.'

James grunted. 'Even that troublesome woman has taken it,' he muttered. 'Arbella Stuart is a curse upon our name. I know she still hankers after my throne, for all her professed loyalty.'

Frances remembered the last time she had seen the haughty woman, at the christening of the king's short-lived daughter, Mary, almost five years before. She wondered that she had not yet been married off to some low-ranking nobleman who could keep her out of trouble.

She was still forming a reply when James stood abruptly. 'Well, now,' he said, turning to his favourite again. 'Before I leave for the hunt, let us have some other sport, Rabbie.'

Frances watched as the king gently stroked the young man's chin and playfully tugged on his beard. He stepped down from the dais and walked out of the room without a backward glance, closely followed by the red-haired attendant. After a pause, one of the servants walked slowly to the doors through which the pair had left and drew them softly shut. Frances could hear muffled laughter and cries from the bedchamber beyond as she led her son out into the public rooms of the court.

CHAPTER 8
12 FEBRUARY

'Be careful, George,' Frances called, as her son reached over the side of the boat to dip his fingers into the icy waters of the Thames. He sat back on the wooden plank that served as a seat and gazed in wonder at the huge expanse of water that stretched out on all sides. Though she had taken him sailing on the Great Ouse many times, he had never seen a river such as this, crowded with barges carrying courtiers, officials and goods back and forth between the palaces, small wherries bobbing in their wake.

They were nearing London Bridge now, with numerous buildings balanced precariously on top. George stared up, openmouthed, as they passed under one of the archways that was surmounted by what looked like a fortress, seven storeys high and with a turret at each corner that rose to a sharp point. Frances smiled to see her son crouch, as if expecting the building to crash down upon them. Indeed, it seemed a wonder that the bridge had not yet collapsed under all the weight it carried.

She shielded her eyes against the sun as they rounded another bend in the river. The day had dawned bright and clear, the first such since their arrival at court. Seeing the city through her son's eyes made her almost glad to be there, for all her anxiety about the task that lay ahead.

'Look, Mama!' George cried.

Frances turned in the direction that he was pointing. Her breath caught in her throat.

The Tower.

It was the first time she had set eyes upon it since the night she had visited Tom. She shivered at the memory of his cold, damp cell, the smell of decay clinging to its walls. She had thought to stop his breath with her tincture, to spare him the horrors of a traitor's death. But he had refused, knowing that it would be discovered and she would be condemned as a witch.

'Mama?'

'That is the Tower, George. It was built by the first King William more than five hundred years ago.'

'Where are the windows? It must be very dark in there.'

Frances nodded. 'It was built for defence more than comfort. King William knew that his people wanted him to go back to Normandy and never return. See that great house there, on the other bank?' she said, drawing her son's gaze away. 'That was built from the stones of Bermondsey Abbey, which was pulled down in King Henry's time.'

To her relief, George was easily distracted and soon they were beyond sight of the Tower. It would not be long before they reached Greenwich. The queen's letter had arrived the previous day. It had said little, beyond inviting Frances to attend her. She wondered if Anne herself had thought to write, or if she had been persuaded to it by one of Lady Vaux's associates. Frances had heard nothing from the latter since arriving at court, though she had expected it daily.

The red-brick turrets of the gatehouse came into view as the river twisted eastwards again. Frances was obliged to hold onto the back of her son's coat as he leaped from his seat. The oarsman grumbled as he tried to steady the boat, which swayed wildly from side to side. When he was able to row again, he did so with renewed vigour, eager no doubt to return to Whitehall, where there was a good deal more business to be had.

At length, they drew level with the landing stage and Frances stepped out, then turned to help her son from the boat. She pressed some coins into the oarsman's hand and watched as he manoeuvred the boat back towards the city. George tugged on her hand.

'Can we meet the queen now?'

Frances smiled and nodded, and they walked towards the two yeomen who were guarding the entrance to the first courtyard. A groom soon arrived to escort them through the deserted public rooms to Anne's apartments.

'Why doesn't the queen live with the king, Mama?' George asked, as they walked.

Frances saw the groom flinch at her son's words, and lowered her voice to answer. 'Her Majesty prefers the peace of Greenwich to the noise of Whitehall. Besides, the royal family is not like others. Even the children are sent to live in a palace of their own, away from their parents.'

George was clearly shocked. 'Shall I be sent away?' he asked, eyes wide.

Frances grinned. 'Of course not. I would not allow it — and neither would your papa. But we must soon find a tutor for you here, or you will quite forget your letters.'

George scowled. Though he had only

lately begun his studies, Frances judged that he was not a natural scholar. He preferred to be outdoors, running about the gardens or lunging at imaginary foes with the wooden sword her husband had given him for his last birthday.

The corridors grew gradually darker as they neared the queen's privy lodgings. Frances breathed in the scent of lavender, which was strewn over the rush matting. The walls on either side were lined with thick tapestries, keeping out the draughts that whipped around the larger public rooms.

When they reached the door to the ante-chamber, a page bade them wait while he announced their arrival. Frances smoothed her skirts and brushed the dust from George's sleeve. She had been surprised that the invitation had extended to her son, but was glad of it. She had no desire to leave him at Whitehall, now that Thomas was away at Oatlands.

The page reappeared and motioned for them to enter. George tugged back on his mother's hand, but she gave him a reassuring smile and led him gently forward. The queen raised her head from her needlework. She was sitting at the window, silhouetted by the bright sunlight. 'You are most welcome, Lady Frances,' she said, in her clipped tones. 'I have but few visitors here at Greenwich. Come — let me see you.'

Frances took a few steps forward. As she drew level with the queen, Anne's features were no longer obscured by the sun. Frances drew in a breath when she saw the change that had been wrought in her. Her high cheekbones seemed to have melted into the folds of her face, and her skin was now sallow rather than pale. Looking down, Frances noticed that the queen's stays had been loosened, though not for the usual reason. She had heard it whispered that there would be no more children, though she was only midway through her thirties.

'I am not as you remember me,' Anne said softly.

Frances flushed. 'Forgive me, Your Majesty. I am a little overcome. It has been so long since I was last in your presence.'

The queen gave a wry smile. 'You were ever of a gentle nature. But there is no need to hide your dismay. I hear it often enough from the king's lips. Little wonder he chooses to leave me for the hunt so often. I am sorry that, in so doing, he deprives you of your husband for many weeks together.'

'Sir Thomas is happy to do his duty, Your Grace,' Frances replied.

There was a brief silence, during which Anne eyed her. 'I trust he does his duty by you too?'

Frances forced herself not to look away. 'I am blessed to have such an attentive husband, Your Grace.'

There was a scuffing noise as George shifted impatiently behind his mother's skirts. Anne smiled. 'How rude of me! I should have introduced myself to your young master. Please, come forward.'

George bit his lip and stared down at his feet as if they demanded all of his attention. Gently, Frances coaxed him forward and laid her hands on his shoulders. He gave a stiff little bow, as she had taught him. Anne's smile never faltered as she gave him a long, appraising stare. 'How like your father you are,' she said, casting a glance at Frances.

'Papa?' George beamed with pleasure. 'Thank you, Your Majesty,' he added quickly, when Frances squeezed his shoulder.

'He must be very proud of you,' Anne replied. 'It is plain to see that your mother is. But we mothers are always proud of our sons. My own are a little older than you. I hope you will meet them soon — Henry, in particular. He will make a fine king one day.'

George looked thoughtful. 'Does he ride as well as me?'

The queen let out a bark of laughter. 'Of that I am not sure, though he is an excellent horseman. Perhaps you should challenge him to a race. The parkland around here extends for miles. You would tire out many horses, I am sure.'

The boy's eyes widened with excitement. 'I should like that very much, Your Grace.'

'Well, now,' Anne said. 'You must be hungry after your long journey. Lady Drummond.'

A young woman stepped out of the shadows. Frances had not noticed her before. She was of small stature, with jet-black hair that made her skin appear all the paler. Her slate-grey eyes regarded Frances briefly before she turned to her mistress.

'Will you take Master Tyringham to the privy kitchen and see what delicacies my cooks have prepared? I am sure there will be something to tempt him.'

The woman inclined her head and held out her hand to George, who took it without protest. Frances felt a pang as she watched him being led away.

'Do not worry, my dear. Jane will keep your precious jewel safe,' the queen assured Frances. 'I would trust her with my life.

Now, come and sit by me so that we may converse more freely.'

Once she was seated, Anne clasped her hand. 'I am glad to see you, Frances, truly I am. I have thought of you often since you left court. I know how you must have suffered. Do you miss him still?'

'With all my heart,' Frances whispered, looking down at the queen's hand. The large emerald ring glinted in the sunlight. 'But George is a great comfort to me, and Sir Thomas is a good husband — better than I deserve. I understand it is you I must thank for that.'

Anne gave her hand a squeeze. 'I know you wished to hide at Longford, but the world would soon have found you. It is better so.' She sank back into her chair and gave a heavy sigh. 'I have had my sorrows too, since we last met.'

'I heard of your loss and am sorry for it, Your Grace,' Frances replied. 'Mary was a sweet child.'

'Sophia too,' Anne added. 'She looked so much like Henry — and cried lustily like him too. Yet she drew breath for just a few hours —' She broke off and stared out of the window, her shoulders heaving with silent grief.

Frances wished she could offer some

comfort, but how could words ease the pain of losing two children in as many years? She could not imagine summoning the will to live if George was taken from her.

'Do you have need of my skills, Your Grace?' she asked gently, when Anne had regained her composure. 'I heard that you have been in poor health since — since your last lying-in.'

The queen sighed again and placed a hand on her stomach. 'My physicians have taken so much blood from me that I wonder there is any left. They say it is the only way to stop the menses that have flowed since Sophia's birth.'

Frances held back a scornful remark. 'I would be glad to assist you in any way I can.'

'Thank you, Frances. I am sure your remedies would do me more good than their leeches and purges,' the queen said. 'But we must have a care — you know that such practices are frowned upon, perhaps more than ever. Only last week there was talk of another witch trial at Southwark. Besides, that is not why I summoned you here.'

Frances felt her heart quicken.

'I wish you to join my daughter's household again,' Anne continued. 'Elizabeth is a young woman now and her father would have her married. He will use her to forge a powerful alliance — that is what daughters are good for, after all,' she added bitterly.

'Does the princess wish to be married?'

'It hardly matters — to her father, at least,' the queen replied. 'But she is even more susceptible to flatterers than she was when you knew her.'

The two women exchanged a knowing look. Frances had seen how easily the princess had been beguiled by Robert Catesby and his fellow plotters. Clearly she had learned little from the experience.

'She is also headstrong — even more so than when you served her,' Anne added, catching the look on Frances's face. 'She means to have a husband of the new faith, not our own, and will not be gainsaid — at least, not by me. Her brother Henry encourages her in this. She needs someone of greater wisdom to counsel her against making a choice that is as hasty as it is ill-considered.'

She hesitated.

'A friend has suggested that you can perform this service better than anyone else. The princess loved and trusted you above all others.'

So Lady Vaux had got word to the queen, as Dorothy had promised.

Frances was plagued by doubt. Four years was a long time to have been absent from the princess — almost half the girl's lifetime. She must have changed a great deal since they had last met, and may still resent Frances's hasty departure. Could she win back her trust, her affection? She felt far from certain.

'I ask only that you try, Frances. You know how much rests upon it. There is no other way to bring this kingdom back to the true faith.' A shadow seemed to flit across Anne's face. 'Many vest their hopes in the Lady Arbella. But though she professes herself a Catholic, she would as soon turn to heresy if she thought it would bring her to the throne. No, we must make my daughter realise the advantages of a Catholic match.' Her eyes blazed with intensity.

Slowly Frances inclined her head. 'You may trust me, Your Grace. I will do whatever I can to avenge Tom and rid this kingdom of heretics, no matter the cost.'

The queen smiled and extended her hand so that Frances could kiss it. 'I will have your letter of appointment drafted before you depart for Whitehall,' she promised. 'Now, you must go and find that son of yours before Jane Drummond stuffs him full of sweetmeats.'

Frances bowed her head and hastened from the room. Though she knew it was a deadly sin, she thrilled to the notion that the queen still hankered for her husband's deposition — his murder, even. If she could help to bring the Spanish marriage to pass, she might yet see her once-beloved mistress crowned in her father's stead. Mingled with the fear that had made her doubt the scheme in which she was now enmeshed, she felt a heady rush of anticipation.

CHAPTER 9
16 FEBRUARY

Hundreds of candles blazed in their golden sconces, illuminating the brightly coloured bejewelled swags that were strung across the pillars of the banqueting hall. Frances breathed in the enticing aroma of spiced wine and sweetmeats as she stood on the threshold. Though the king was away on the hunt, the reception was still crowded with courtiers, and as she slowly made her way to the seats in front of the dais, she was constantly jostled and pushed. By the time she reached the back row of chairs, she was hot and out of breath, and gulped down the cup of wine she had taken from a harassed servant on the way.

The excited chatter and squeals of laughter had risen to such a crescendo that the royal musicians, who were performing on the dais, could hardly be heard. She looked around at the ladies in gowns of peacock blue silk, scarlet satin and a riot of other dazzling colours, which caught the light as they swayed and curtsied, lowering their eyes coquettishly as the male courtiers swarmed around them. Frances recognised a handful. She would have felt just as much of an outsider at the court of Henri of France, she reflected.

Eager though she was to play her part, she wished herself back at Longford, strolling in the cool shade of the woods with George at her side. She did not belong there either, though — not any more. Edward had made sure of that. Neither did the rural beauty of her husband's estate hold any appeal. It seemed she was destined to spend her life like the restless spirits of whom Ellen had spoken, never finding that for which they searched.

A blast of trumpets jolted her from her melancholy thoughts. Immediately, the cacophony died down as the assembled throng looked expectantly towards the large doors to the right of the dais. A moment later, they were flung open by the yeomen of the guard and an elegant young woman stepped lightly through, head held high. There were gasps around the room as she walked slowly into the hall, the thousand or more gems on her exquisite gold and ivory gown catching the light from the sconces above. Her hair, which was swept into an elaborate coif in imitation of her mother's, had turned a deeper red than it had been when Frances had last seen her, and her face had lost its youthful plumpness.

Frances realised that all of the other ladies in the hall had dropped into a deep curtsy. As she hastily did the same, she thought that she caught the princess looking in her direction but forced herself to stare at the floor. The delicate tap of heels could be heard as the princess and her ladies took their places at the far side of the platform. There was a brief silence. Frances's back and legs ached as she continued to hold the curtsy. Clearly, she was out of practice, she mused — either that or her limbs were no longer as supple as once they had been.

The musicians struck up the overture and there was a rustle of skirts as the ladies sat down while the men moved to the back of the hall. Frances watched as a troupe of female players walked onto the dais, in sumptuous gowns of white silk and with gold coronets on their heads. There were eleven in all, and most were somewhat older than was usual for a masque. Frances knew Anne Clifford, who had been a favourite of Queen Elizabeth as a child, and Lady

136

Stanley, who had served her as a maid of honour.

On the right of the dais a beautiful young woman was carefully surveying the room, as if searching for someone. There was something familiar about her soft round face and small rosebud mouth, but it took Frances a moment to recognise her as Frances Howard, Countess of Essex. Her marriage to the third earl had taken place just a few weeks before Tom's execution. Lady Howard had been a girl of fourteen then, her husband a year younger. They had made a handsome couple, but there had soon been rumours of discord. Nevertheless the countess still drew as much attention from the men at court as she had before her marriage.

Another loud fanfare rang out and the eleven ladies curtsied as a figure walked haltingly onto the dais. She was older than the rest and portly. Although dressed in the same white silk gown as her fellow queens, her crown was much more lavish and seemed to glitter with real diamonds and rubies. As she neared the front of the platform, Frances drew in a breath.

Anne.

The queen had always loathed the ostentatious masques that so delighted her husband. Glancing down at the paper she had been given upon arriving at the hall, Frances saw that tonight's play was *The Masque of Queens,* written in Anne's honour by the celebrated Master Jonson. She looked back at her royal mistress, whose face was suffused with pleasure as she gazed imperiously across the audience.

After a few moments, Anne walked slowly to a throne that had been placed at the back of the dais, and the other ladies fanned out on either side of her. There was a thunderous drum roll and the entire platform was plunged into darkness. Frances could see shadowy figures running onto it, and as the sconces were relit, she stared in disbelief. They were dressed in ragged black shifts and were stooped over the wooden staves they carried. Their hair had been whitened with powder, and deep lines painted onto their faces.

Witches.

Frances had heard that other playwrights had taken up Master Shakespeare's theme to gain favour with the king, but she had not expected to witness one such example this evening. It was as if she had been transported back to that terrible evening, more than five years before, when Cecil had made her sit through a performance of *Macbeth* before declaring her a witch in front of

138

the assembled gathering. She watched the grotesque enactment with mounting horror. Surely the Lord Privy Seal had not arranged this too, knowing she would be there. In panic, her eyes darted around the room, searching for his familiar, hunched frame. But he was not among the dignitaries seated closest to the dais, and he would hardly be able to endure standing throughout the performance with the gentlemen at the back of the hall.

Aware that she was attracting curious stares from the ladies sitting next to her, Frances diverted her gaze back to the platform, where the princess seemed enthralled by the story playing out in front of her. Now and again, she would grasp the hand of the fair-haired attendant on her right, as if for protection against the hideous figures that kept leering in her direction. Elizabeth had always been fond of such entertainments, Frances remembered.

Applause sounded in Frances's ears as the players curtsied. She forced a smile as she stood to join in, anxious not to betray her private horror. After a final bow, the ladies filed off the dais. Only Anne remained, seated on her mock throne and smiling benignly at her court.

Frances was caught up in a press of

bodies, eager to pay homage to the queen, who had now taken her place next to her daughter. She tried to turn and make her way out of the hall, but it was impossible and before long she found herself within a few feet of the royal party.

'Lady Frances,' Anne called, above the cacophony, signalling for her to approach.

The people in front of her turned to stare, then moved aside so that she could pass. Frances stepped onto the platform. She walked slowly over to the queen and offered a deep curtsy. 'Your Majesty.'

'How did you enjoy the performance?' Anne asked. 'I'll wager you did not expect to see me among the players.'

'Your Grace played your part to perfection,' Frances replied.

'You must lack such entertainments in Buckinghamshire.'

The words rang out in a clear, shrill voice. Frances looked up and saw that the princess was regarding her closely, a smirk playing about her lips. The young lady whose hand she had grasped during the performance raised her own to her mouth, as if suppressing a giggle.

'Indeed, Your Highness. We enjoy no such spectacles, but take pleasure in simpler pursuits.'

Elizabeth's smile faded and she raised her chin a little higher. 'My mother tells me you are to attend me once more.'

Frances inclined her head. 'If Your Grace pleases.'

'It matters little whether it pleases me or not,' the young woman replied curtly. 'I will do as the queen bids me.'

'We are most grateful that you are willing to return to the princess's household, Lady Frances.' Anne directed a reproving look at her daughter, 'especially when you have ever preferred the peace of the country to the clamour of court. But your services will carry their own reward.'

Frances knew that she did not mean the riches that were to be won from attendance in the royal household. The queen was right: a far greater prize was to be had if she succeeded in her task.

'Well, it is of no consequence,' Elizabeth said, 'for I am soon to be married, so I will not require your service for long, Lady Frances. I will take only my closest attendants with me when I leave for my husband's kingdom.'

The young woman to the princess's right gave a self-satisfied smile and raised hostile eyes to Frances.

'You intend to marry a foreign prince,

then, Your Grace?' Frances was careful to keep her tone light, respectful.

Elizabeth stared coldly at her. 'I shall marry a prince of the true faith, one who can help my father to rid this kingdom of papists once and for all.'

Frances saw defiance in her eyes, and felt as if she was looking at a stranger. The princess had been utterly beguiled by Tom and his associates and had sought out their company whenever there had been an opportunity. Frances wondered how much of her new-found hatred of Catholics was inspired by loyalty towards her father, and how much by her humiliation at learning they had deceived her. It must have stung her vanity to find that they had courted her only to further their plot.

'I am sure many men will be eager to win such a prize, Your Grace,' Frances replied, with what she hoped sounded like sincerity.

She was gratified to see her former mistress's eyes light up at the compliment, before she remembered herself and reassumed her previously chilly demeanour. It gave Frances hope that, for all the princess's hostility, she might still win back at least a measure of the favour she had once enjoyed.

As if sensing she was at a disadvantage, the fair-haired attendant leaned over and whispered something in her young mistress's ear. Elizabeth nodded.

'Forgive me, Lady Frances,' she said in an imperious tone as she stood to leave. 'Blanche has just reminded me that I have been invited to sup with Baron Windsor this evening.'

'It is very late, Elizabeth,' her mother said, with a frown.

Frances caught annoyance on the princess's face. 'I am no longer a girl, Mama,' she replied scornfully. 'Lady Frances's attendance must have reminded you of the days when I was obliged to go to bed after the evening's entertainments. If you had not spent so much time at Greenwich, you would have known that I retire much later now.'

Shocked that Elizabeth should address her mother so, Frances shot an anxious look in the queen's direction. But Anne was smiling benignly at her daughter. 'Of course, my jewel. I have neglected you for too long. You must forgive me.' She held out her hand.

After a pause, Elizabeth bent to kiss her mother's ring, though Frances noticed that her lips did not touch it. With a nod in Frances's direction, the princess swept past her, the fair-haired young woman following in her wake, eyes downcast and a small

143

smile on her lips.

There was an awkward silence. Frances looked at the queen, fearing to see the hurt and humiliation that Elizabeth's words must have wrought in her. But Anne's smile had not faded — if anything, it had grown brighter still. She turned to dismiss the ladies who attended her. They seemed relieved to go, Frances thought. As soon as they were out of sight, the queen beckoned her closer.

'As you have seen, Lady Frances, I did not exaggerate when I told you that my daughter has grown haughtier since you last attended her. You must wonder why I did not upbraid her, as she deserved.'

Frances was unsure how to respond.

'Do not think that I have become an indulgent mother,' she continued. 'I know Elizabeth's faults well enough. But if I seek to correct them at every turn, she will grow ever more wilful and defy me even over trifles. I must appear unconcerned and let her think she has her way, as she chooses the path that I would have her take. It is you who must steer her towards it.'

Frances nodded, understanding and admiration dawning in equal measure. 'Of course, Your Grace. I will take care to let the princess believe she rules me, so that

144

she might prove readier to do our bidding.'

Anne smiled and rose slowly to her feet. Frances rushed to assist, but she brushed her hand lightly away. 'You will begin your service in my daughter's household next week. I have arranged for your son to join Charles in his lessons. Though my youngest boy is superior in years, he is hardly so in learning. George will soon catch him up.'

Frances swept a deep curtsy. 'Thank you, Your Grace. That is a great honour — to me and my son. I have no doubt that he will delight in the prince's company. He has spent precious little time with other children, and has stopped asking when he might have a brother or sister.'

The queen inclined her head. 'Then it is settled. God go with you — and your endeavours, Lady Frances,' she said, then moved slowly from the hall, which was now almost deserted.

Frances tried to concentrate on the intricate pattern that her stitches were slowly bringing to life, but her fingers did not seem to belong to her today and the thread kept snagging on the stiff linen. Her son had been fretful when she had left him that morning, clinging to her skirts as he used to on the rare occasions that she had been obliged to leave him for a few hours when they had lived at Tyringham Hall.

Although George had gone eagerly to the prince's household on the first day, filled with excitement at the prospect of meeting the king's son, he had been unusually sullen that evening. Frances had eventually coaxed the reason from him. Charles had not been a kind companion, it seemed, but had seized the opportunity to flaunt the superiority of his years and status over the latest boy to share his lessons. The other young men of his household had been quick to join in the

146

teasing, glad that that their royal master had a new focus for his jests. Their tutor had shown little interest when Frances had questioned him: his sole concern was to ensure that he remained in the good graces of the prince and his father. She would speak to the queen when she next had the opportunity, she resolved, as she jabbed her finger for the third time in as many minutes.

'Perhaps you would like me to help you, Lady Frances.' The silken voice broke the silence of the princess's antechamber. 'Our mistress praised your skill with the needle, but it seems she was excessively kind, as she is in so many things.'

'Thank you, Lady Blanche, I can manage.' Frances did not look up from the fabric as she spoke. 'My eyes are a little tired today.' With a sigh, she set the embroidery on her lap and gazed down into the herb garden below. Even on a beautifully clear day such as this, it appeared as dull and neglected as when she had crept unseen to visit it a little over two weeks before. If anything, it looked worse, the bright sunlight illuminating the withered plants and weeds that were enclosed by the overgrown hedges.

'You show a particular fascination for the Witch's Garden,' Blanche observed slyly. 'I wonder that nobody has pulled up all those dying plants by now and laid out a new lawn in their place. Perhaps the gardeners are afraid they will unleash some dreadful curse if they touch it.'

Frances stared at her companion. 'The Witch's Garden?'

Blanche bent her head to her needlework again. 'Why, yes. Has it not always been called so, Lady Frances?' she asked guilelessly. 'Certainly that is how the princess referred to it upon my first entering her service two years ago. I had thought it an old name, but perhaps it dates to more recent times.'

She raised her grey eyes to meet Frances's, her face a mask of innocence. Frances fought back the urge to slap it. Though she had been in Blanche's company for only three days, she already harboured an intense dislike for her simpering flattery of the princess, and her barbed asides to anyone she judged to be a rival — Frances in particular. She forced her attention back to her own embroidery.

'I knew it only as a simple herb garden,' she replied, as nonchalantly as she could. 'But, then, many things have changed since I was last here. I must learn to keep pace with them. Life passes more slowly in Buckinghamshire.'

Blanche gave a snort of derision. 'I wonder it passes at all! You must be so relieved that your husband finally chose to bring you to court.'

'Sir Thomas is a kind and attentive husband. He would have brought me here long before now, if he had fancied I had any inclination to leave the tranquillity of our estate.'

'I am surprised you did not. You were all but raised at court, I hear, and your mother was a great favourite of the old queen. Yet you gave it up so abruptly, the princess said, without a thought for those you left behind.'

Frances knew that Blanche was goading her, but refused to show her rising irritation. 'I was needed at my father's estate, so had little choice in the matter. But I did think of the princess often — and some other cherished acquaintances to whom I bade farewell,' she added, almost to herself.

'Then why did you not visit, or even write?'

The princess's voice made both women turn in surprise. Frances wondered how long Elizabeth had been standing in the doorway that led into her bedchamber. She and Blanche bobbed a hurried curtsy.

'Well?' The princess raised an eyebrow.

Her mistress's eyes were glinting with

anger, her lips pressed tightly together. Frances saw she had underestimated the hurt that her sudden departure had caused. 'Forgive me, Your Highness,' she said. 'I thought you would forget me all the sooner if I did not pester you with letters and visits, that you would soon find another to take my place.'

She glanced at Blanche, who was clearly enjoying her discomfiture.

'Perhaps your own affections are so lightly bestowed, Lady Frances, but mine are more enduring,' Elizabeth said.

Her eyes seemed to shine with something other than anger now, and Frances felt remorse that she had caused the girl such pain. Her desertion, so soon after the executions of Elizabeth's treacherous companions, must have dealt the princess a devastating blow. 'I am truly sorry to have grieved you, Your Grace. I hope I may make amends, now that I am in your service once more,' Frances replied.

'Oh, it matters little to me any more,' the princess responded. 'You were right — there were others to take your place.' She walked over to Blanche and took her hand. 'And my brother is even dearer to me now than he was when you last saw him. He has been my teacher, as well as my companion, and has brought me to the joy and comfort of the true faith. My only regret about taking a husband is that it will mean leaving him behind. But, as Henry has told me, through this sacrifice I will bring our father's subjects to salvation.'

'Indeed you will, Your Grace. And I shall rejoice therein,' Blanche declared.

'Well, now, we must make haste. My brother cannot abide lateness.'

Blanche went to fetch her mistress's cloak. Clearly she knew about whatever excursion the princess planned. Frances stood, uncertain whether or not she was to accompany them.

'Come, Frances! Did you not hear me?'

She decided not to ask where they were going, but busied herself with smoothing down her mistress's cloak before putting on her own.

The sun shone brightly and there was not a breath of wind as they waited at the landing stage, but the air was colder by the river and Frances could see her young mistress shivering beneath the folds of her gown and cloak. The bells of a church on the opposite shore began to toll the hour. Ten o'clock.

The three women turned at the sound of brisk footsteps and Frances recognised the prince approaching, flanked by two companions. Henry had grown a good deal taller than when she had last seen him, though he was just as thin. His hair was darker, which made his complexion seem paler than before, and he had the same air of fragility that she remembered.

'Good day to you, sister,' he said, as Elizabeth dipped a curtsy. His eyes soon moved to her companion. 'Lady Blanche,' he said, in a softer tone. Frances saw that the young woman's face was flushed with pleasure.

'And you, Lady Frances *Tyringham,* as I believe we must call you now. I had heard you were back at court.' He eyed her coldly.

His opinion of her had clearly not improved since their first meeting all those years ago, Frances reflected. She had been careful never to cross him, but suspected that her closeness to the princess had been the source of his antipathy. He had always guarded his sister's affections jealously. Well, that jealousy was needless now.

'Your Highness.'

As Frances rose from her obeisance she looked at the young gentlemen on either side of him. They were both a little older than the prince, but the one on the left was a good deal shorter. Even though she had not met them before, there was something familiar about both.

'May I introduce Sir John Harington?' the prince announced.

Frances started at the name.

'Of Coombe Abbey,' Henry added, with a small smile.

The young man bowed elegantly, then regarded her coolly with his pale blue eyes. He bore little resemblance to his father, except in his small stature. A delicate jewel hung from one ear, and he wore the same elaborate style of ruff as the prince.

'Delighted to make your acquaintance, Lady Frances. I believe you know my father?' His voice was as delicate as his appearance.

Frances inclined her head, taking care to keep her expression neutral as she thought of the turbulent time that she and the princess had spent as guests of old Sir John. Although Elizabeth had been sent to Coombe ostensibly for her education, it lay close to the plotters' estates, and Frances had promised Tom that she would keep her mistress safe there until such time as she could be crowned queen. But that time had never come. When Tom had finally arrived at the abbey, it had been with the news that Fawkes had been discovered with the gunpowder just hours before Parliament would

153

assemble.

'Sir John was a generous host to the princess and myself,' she said now, aware that his son was watching her closely. 'I trust he is well?'

'I thank you, yes. Though his generosity cost him dear. The estate is now ruined and he is yet to receive any recompense.'

He cast a sorrowful gaze at the prince, who bristled at his words. 'I have petitioned my father daily, but still he does not honour the debt.' Henry's voice rose with the petulance that Frances remembered. 'It is dishonourable to treat a loyal subject thus.'

Frances was surprised that he should criticise the king so openly, though she knew there had been little love lost between them.

The taller gentleman gave a small cough. He seemed uncomfortable with the turn of conversation. He must be twenty years old, Frances judged, and in both appearance and manner was the opposite of the prince's other friend. His large brown eyes and grave expression suggested wisdom and maturity, and though his dress was as fine as his companion's, his clothes were of a more sombre hue.

Henry scowled at him briefly, then resumed his pompous air. 'And this is Viscount Cranborne.' A pause. 'William Cecil.'

As Frances stared at the young man, it was as if his father's eyes were gazing back at her. How could she not have recognised him at once? His height had deceived her — he must be almost two feet taller than the elder Cecil. His hair was much darker too. But he had the same narrow face, the same neatly clipped moustache and beard. He seemed to be appraising her just as carefully. *Did he know?*

She was so lost in thought that she almost forgot to curtsy, and was grateful when Prince Henry declared that they must be on their way. He stepped into the magnificent gilded barge, ignoring the page, who stood dutifully by, waiting to assist, and held out his hand for the princess. Their attendants followed, Frances last of all.

Only as the oarsmen began to row the barge away from the landing stage did Frances remember that she had no idea where they were going. She was still reeling from the shock of meeting the prince's companions, who seemed to her as shadows of the future.

They were heading eastwards, and though the river was as crowded as usual, their progress was rapid, thanks to the barge, which was superior in size and manpower to the other vessels that bobbed in its wake.

Frances was hardly aware of the lively chatter between the prince and princess, which their other attendants occasionally joined in — Sir John more than most. She kept her eyes fixed upon the horizon as she struggled to calm her racing thoughts. When the domes of the Tower came into view, she instinctively turned away, but was aghast when Prince Henry called, 'We are almost there — see how bright the walls of the keep are today. They must have been newly whitewashed.'

The oarsmen seemed to pick up their pace, and Frances watched with mounting horror as they drew closer to the high stone walls of the fortress. She could see the characteristic scarlet uniforms of the yeomen who were standing by the steps of St Thomas's Tower, waiting to greet them. As they passed under the water gate, she shuddered. She clutched the side of the barge, assailed by a recollection of the last time she had been brought there, on Cecil's orders, as a suspected witch. Terror gripped her now as it had when the king's yeomen had dragged her from the barge, their rough fingers bruising her flesh. She clamped her eyes shut but now the blade was before her, glinting in the light of the fire as her blood dripped from it.

'Are you well, my lady?'

The quiet voice was close to her ear. She opened her eyes to see William Cecil looking at her with concern.

'Yes — thank you.'

She cast a glance at the princess, hoping she hadn't noticed her distress. But Elizabeth was laughing at some remark of Sir John's. Frances's misery increased as they mounted the steps, which were as slippery as ice.

Once inside the Tower, the prince led the way, surrounded on all sides by yeomen, and walked briskly in the direction of the western entrance. As they drew near the huge, squat tower in front of the drawbridge, a loud roar rang out along the passageway. The princess grasped Frances's arm in fright, but quickly released it when her brother laughed at her. Despite her own fear, Frances could not help but feel gratified that it was to her, not Blanche, that Elizabeth had turned for reassurance.

'King James heralds our arrival!' Henry called over his shoulder. Sir John let out a peal of laughter, but William Cecil continued to stare straight ahead, grave-faced.

As they passed under the gatehouse, they were plunged into darkness — or so it seemed after the dazzling sunlight that their eyes had grown accustomed to. Frances stumbled on one of the cobbles and almost fell, but a strong hand pulled her backwards and she regained her balance. 'Thank you, Lord Cranborne.'

He did not reply, but stayed close to her side as they made their way into a semi-circular courtyard. Five large archways were cut into the thick stone, each one closed off by a portcullis. The yeomen led them over to the one in the centre, and Prince Henry pressed his face against the heavy iron bars. The rest of the party gathered around him, trying to make out any shapes in the darkness.

All of a sudden, an enormous beast leaped from the shadows, its huge paws clawing at the bars and its razor-sharp teeth glinting white as they caught the sun. The prince gave a terrified yelp and jumped backwards. His sister screamed, and a commotion ensued as the yeomen rushed to their assistance. A deafening roar rang out across the courtyard, bringing everything to a standstill. Frances watched as the lion flung its weight against the bars again, causing them to rattle loudly in their stone casing. She feared that it would give way at any moment and made to grab the princess's arm so that she could lead her to safety.

'All is well, Your Highness,' a calm voice called.

They turned to see a man of middling years strolling towards them. A leather apron was strung about his waist and he carried a large stick in his right hand. He gave a stiff bow as he drew level with the prince. 'Jim is a bit fretful just now, Your Grace. He wants his breakfast, that's all. I like to keep him hungry before a fight.'

Henry straightened and gave an unconvincing bark of laughter. 'Do not concern yourself, Master Keeper. I merely wanted to surprise my companions. I knew we were in no danger.'

He almost shouted the words, but Frances caught the tremor in his voice and his forehead glistened with sweat.

'Now, if you will kindly show us to the gallery, we will not keep the king from his breakfast any longer.'

The keeper bowed again, then led them back into the gatehouse and up a flight of spiral stairs to a small chamber on the first floor. A row of seats had been arranged in front of the window overlooking the courtyard. Frances sat down with the others. The prince leaned forward eagerly in his seat. His sister did the same, though Frances noticed the fear in her eyes.

A loud creaking sound echoed around the courtyard and everyone watched as the central portcullis was slowly raised. A moment later, the lion leaped forward and began to pace the length of the courtyard, its head bowed as if ready to pounce. It stopped at the distant sound of barking. They all listened as it grew steadily louder, almost drowning the noise of another portcullis being raised. Frances watched in horror as five mastiffs tore out from underneath it. In an instant, they had surrounded the lion and stood growling, teeth bared and drooling. For a second, the lion stood stock still, panting in anticipation. Then it gave a loud roar and lunged at one of the dogs, its teeth sinking deep into its neck. The hound yelped, and the other four leaped upon the lion, tearing at its mane, its flank, its legs, their teeth sharp as blades. Soon, the cobbles beneath them were dripping with blood and flesh.

Unable to bear the sight of the massacre that was unfolding beneath them, Frances diverted her gaze to the prince: his eyes were alight with excitement as he cheered and shouted encouragement. On his right Elizabeth's face was ghostly pale as she watched the grisly spectacle, her chest rising and falling quickly — too quickly,

Frances knew.

A high-pitched howl reverberated across the courtyard, followed by the sickening sound of tearing flesh. Without thinking, Frances turned back to the window and saw the severed leg of a mastiff hurled from the lion's mouth. The beast had the dying hound pinned beneath its paws and as it lowered its head to deliver the killer blow, the other dogs skulked away, whining, their fur matted with blood. They clustered around the archway through which they had been released, but Frances knew with a sickening certainty that the portcullis would not be raised again.

A movement to her left caught her eye, and she turned just in time to see the princess fall to the floor. Blanche screamed in horror and the prince looked in dismay at his sister, who was lying motionless before him. Frances pushed past them and knelt by her mistress. Gently cradling her head in her hands, she leaned forward and pressed her head to the girl's chest. At first, she felt nothing, and her heart contracted with fear. After an agonising few moments, during which she was conscious that all eyes were upon her, she thought she detected a faint fluttering beneath the princess's ribcage. Slowly, she lifted her up to sitting.

Her head lolled forward, prompting another squeal from Blanche, but Frances could see a faint rosy hue begin to creep across her neck and face.

Reaching into her pocket, Frances pulled out the phial of rosemary oil she always carried with her to ward off the stench of the river and raised it to Elizabeth's face. After a pause, the girl wrinkled her nose and slowly opened her eyes. She blinked a few times and looked about her in confusion.

'Fran?' she said, in a small, querulous voice, reaching out to squeeze her attendant's hand.

'Do not worry, Your Grace. You fainted, but are quite well now,' Frances murmured. Relief that the princess was recovered mingled with a rush of joy that the girl's former affection towards her had returned. Even if it proved fleeting, it gave Frances cause to hope.

'Thank you, Lady Frances. I will attend to my sister now,' the prince interrupted, in his shrill voice. He bent and pulled Elizabeth to her feet. She wobbled and Frances put out a hand to steady her, but Henry pushed it away impatiently. As soon as the princess appeared more stable, he led her slowly out of the room, his arm clasped firmly around her waist. When they reached the doorway, Elizabeth turned and looked back at Frances. She stared for a moment, as if remembering another time. Then, slowly, her lips lifted into the faintest of smiles.

CHAPTER 11
22 FEBRUARY

'Your Highnesses must forgive me. I had not expected you to pay me this honour.'

They all turned to see a small, wiry man standing in the doorway. His features were obscured by the light that streamed from the window next to him, but Frances noticed that his legs were slightly bowed. As he stepped forward, she saw that he had a thin face and a long white beard. His doublet was trimmed with fur and on his head he wore a small velvet cap.

'Sir William,' Prince Henry addressed the old man as he stooped to bow. 'My sister fell faint at the lion-baiting and I wanted to ensure that she was fully recovered before returning to Whitehall.'

The old man looked across at the princess and made another obeisance. 'Your Grace does not share your father's taste for the sport, then,' he said, with a small smile.

Frances sensed Elizabeth bristle. 'I was a

164

little tired, that is all. I am quite well now,' she said briskly. 'We really need not have troubled you, Sir William.'

'Oh, it is no trouble, Your Grace. Most of my guests are a good deal less welcome.'

His eyes darted up to Frances. 'I do not believe I have had the pleasure, Lady . . . ?'

'Frances Tyringham.' She hoped he would soon move on to her companions.

But his small black eyes continued to appraise her. 'Sir William Wade, my lady,' he said. 'His Majesty's lieutenant of the Tower.'

Frances knew the name immediately and her blood ran cold. It had been he who had interrogated Tom and the other plotters. She had heard it said that he had personally superintended the torture of Fawkes, looking on as his limbs were wrenched from their sockets. Evidently the king had rewarded him for his trouble by making him lieutenant. Not trusting herself to speak, she lowered her gaze to the floor.

'Tyringham?' His voice again. 'I trust your husband is keeping the king's buckhounds in good order.'

'You have an excellent memory, for one of your years,' the princess said.

'Your Grace is most kind,' Sir William replied, ignoring the insult. 'I never forget a name — or a face, for that matter. That is

165

how I was able to bring the Powder Treason to light.'

So it was he who had uncovered the plot. Frances's thoughts ran back to those desperate days at Coombe Abbey. When Sir John Harington had told her and the princess that a great treason had been discovered, she had assumed Cecil had informed on them. Certainly, he had known of it for some time, thanks to the spy he had placed in their midst. But perhaps Sir William had found out by other means.

'And our father was most grateful, Sir William,' Henry put in, with a hint of impatience. 'Now, as my sister seems to have recovered, we will not keep you any longer.'

'Permit me to show you something before you depart, Your Grace,' the old man said. 'As you may know, I have been making improvements to these lodgings since I took residence. The room in which we are standing used to be twice as tall, but I have added an extra chamber above, which I use for — well, you will see, if you accompany me now.'

He gestured towards the door. The prince sighed, then walked briskly out of the room. The rest of the company filed out behind him, Frances last of all, and mounted the handsome oak staircase that led to the upper chamber. She could hear the lieutenant turn the key in the lock, then the door creak on its hinges as it was slowly opened.

The room was in darkness and Frances stood blinking on the threshold. She could just make out Sir William's stooped frame as he walked slowly to the furthest window. A shard of light illuminated the wall next to her as he pulled open one of the shutters. She drew a sharp breath. The plasterwork had been entirely covered with a huge painting depicting what Frances first thought was a scene from Hell. But as she peered at the figures writhing in torment, she realised that this was a depiction of earthly torture. Fighting the instinct to look away, her eyes alighted upon the figure of a man, his hand pinned to a table by his captor while another gripped one of his fingernails with a pair of iron pincers. Blood was spurting from two of his other fingers — the nails had already been wrenched off. Frances swallowed the sickness that was rising in her throat as she gazed at another scene, of a prisoner lying on the rack, his face contorted in agony as the ropes were tightened on his wrists and ankles. She reached out to grip the back of one of the chairs that were positioned around the long table in the centre of the room.

Sir William crossed to the other window and opened the shutters, casting light across the opposite wall. A large sculpted plaque dominated it. Intricately carved from marble, it resembled an elaborate funerary monument and was covered with inscriptions. As she looked more closely, Frances could see that most were in Latin, but in the lower left corner one was in Hebrew.

' "He discovereth deep things out of darkness, and bringeth out to light the shadow of death," ' Sir William quoted, following her gaze.

Frances stared. She had read that same passage in her prayer book as she had waited to see Tom taken to his death. As she looked above the inscription, her stomach lurched.

Thomas Wintour.

His name was at the top of the list of those described as 'conspirators of everlasting infamy'. It was almost as if he was in the room with her. With mounting horror, her eyes scanned the rest of the monument.

The atrocious conspiracy to blow up with gunpowder Our Most Merciful King . . . prompted by the mad lust of quenching the true and Christian faith . . .

On the right were the names of all the 'most illustrious men' who had brought the 'wolves' to justice. Scanning the list, Frances saw that of her uncle, the Earl of Northampton. His coat of arms was above, along with those of the king's other privy councillors.

'It is a fine monument, Sir William,' the prince said, his voice flat with boredom.

'I am pleased you think so, Your Grace,' Sir William replied eagerly. 'I laid out a considerable sum on it. But the expense was justified, for its purpose is more than merely decorative. I wish it to serve as a warning to other traitorous wretches who are brought here for interrogation. Through this they learn that the king's justice can never be evaded, that God will wreak his vengeance upon any who oppose him.'

Anger flared as Frances stared at the old man, his mouth curled into a self-satisfied smile. 'Surely the paintings are enough,' she remarked, gesturing to the opposite wall. 'You could have preserved your wages for wood to burn in winter or food for your table.'

Sir William turned to look at her. 'Ah, but such things are soon consumed, Lady Frances, whereas this monument will endure long after our bones have been laid in the earth.'

169

'Well, I think it an ugly thing!' declared the princess, breaking the silence that followed. 'And that is hardly a true likeness of my father,' she added, pointing to the painted wooden bust next to it.

Frances was gratified to see Sir William's jaw twitch.

'Fortunately Your Grace will not have to look upon either again,' he said tightly, 'since this room is intended for prisoners rather than honoured guests.'

Elizabeth took her brother's arm, a signal that she wished to leave.

'Thank you, Sir William,' the prince said firmly. 'We cannot tarry any longer.'

The lieutenant inclined his head and led them slowly from the room. Frances kept her eyes fixed upon the princess's skirts as she followed. She certainly hoped never to see that place again.

As they reached the bottom of the stairs, Prince Henry turned and addressed their host. 'I have a mind to visit Sir Walter before we leave. I trust he is at leisure to receive us?'

Frances saw the old man's eyes widen briefly in panic before he recovered himself. 'I usually require the king's permission for such a visit, Your Grace —'

'I hardly think you would refuse me, his

eldest son and heir, Sir William,' the prince interrupted.

The lieutenant gave a stiff bow. 'Of course, Your Grace. I shall accompany you.'

'There is no need — we have troubled you long enough.' Henry's tone made clear he would brook no opposition. 'I will be sure to tell my father that the Tower is in excellent safe-keeping. Good day.'

He walked briskly away before Sir William could reply, the rest of the party following.

'Pompous old fool,' Frances heard Henry mutter under his breath as he strode purposefully in the direction of the Bloody Tower.

The apartments in which Sir Walter Raleigh was lodged were so well appointed that Frances wondered if they were a prison at all. At the foot of the steps that led up to them a small, fragrant garden was filled with brightly coloured flowers and plants of such variety that she did not recognise them all. Perhaps some had been brought back from his many voyages overseas, she mused. She longed to study them more closely, but knew better than to do so in such company.

The door to the lodgings was opened not by a guard but by a servant wearing Sir Walter's livery. He bowed low to the prince and his sister, then led them into a brightly lit chamber, the walls of which were adorned with tapestries and paintings. A beautifully carved oak writing desk was in the centre of the room, and either side of a large window recess were two matching oak dressers.

'This is an unexpected pleasure, Your Highnesses,' drawled a well-dressed man as he strolled from an adjoining room and made an elaborate bow, then bent to kiss the princess's hand. Frances noticed her cheeks turn pink.

As he faced the rest of the company, Frances saw that Sir Walter was handsome still, though his hair was flecked with white and his figure was more thickset than she remembered. His beard was trimmed to a point, and a large pearl dangled from his left ear. Though he looked at her with the same smiling eyes that had so beguiled the late queen, Frances doubted that he had any recollection of her. After all, she had been little more than a child when he had last seen her.

'How are you faring, Sir Walter?' asked the prince, frowning a concern that Frances had not seen in him before. 'I trust you have everything you need for your ease?'

Sir Walter inclined his head. 'Thanks to Your Grace, I live in greater comfort here than I would at court.'

'Yet still you are a prisoner,' Henry protested. 'Daily, I have petitioned the king for your release. Only my father would cage such a bird,' he muttered resentfully.

'I am sure the king will pardon me, in time. His predecessor did so for a far more heinous crime.' He grinned at the reference to his clandestine marriage to Bess Throckmorton, a lady of the late queen's bedchamber.

'But for now I must rest at Sir William's pleasure. I am glad to provide a daily reminder of his assiduity in bringing treacherous subjects to light,' he added cheerfully.

'We have just endured an audience with that self-righteous ass,' the prince remarked scornfully. 'He wanted to show us that hideous monument to the discovery of the Powder Treason.'

'I wonder that he has not yet commissioned one to mark the plot in which I was thought to be involved,' Sir Walter replied. 'It is nigh seven years ago now — ample time for the stonemasons to fashion something suitable.' He glanced across at the princess and her companions. 'But I must not talk of such things now. Tell me, how fares the king's oath? I trust all of his subjects have proven their loyalty by taking it — or else choosing to be silenced for ever?' Though his smile did not falter, his eyes darkened.

'Of course,' Henry replied nonchalantly. 'The papists are dwindling by the day. Blind though they are, even they recognise that only the true faith can prevail.'

'Indeed?' Sir Walter asked lightly. 'Though their numbers may be dwindling outside these walls, it is a different matter within. There is hardly room enough to accommodate them all. I wonder that I have not been asked to share my lodgings.'

The prince laughed.

'I assure you I am not in jest, Your Grace,' Raleigh said. 'Our ranks are swelled by fresh Catholics every day, and still there are those lingering here from the days of the Powder Treason.'

He shot a look at Frances. *Did he know she had been involved?* She shook the thought from her mind. The visit to Sir William's chambers had unnerved her. That was all.

'I must think you insincere, Sir Walter,' chided the princess, with an arch smile. 'You said we should speak of other matters, yet still you bring the conversation back to papists and plots.'

Raleigh put his hand to his heart and

bowed low. 'Forgive me, Your Grace. Being cooped up here has evidently dulled my senses. I would have you and your ladies visit me often, so I will divert you with livelier conversation. My wife tells me that Mr Jonson's new masque was lately performed at Whitehall.'

Elizabeth brightened at once and proceeded to describe every detail of the lavish spectacle. Sir Walter pulled up a chair next to her and appeared just as rapt as he had when the late queen had regaled him with tales of the court upon his return from his adventures. Frances judged from the princess's animated expression that he had not lost the ability to make a woman feel as if she was the sole object of his devotion.

As her mistress rattled on, Frances gazed distractedly out of the window. To the right rose the imposing edifice of the White Tower. The sun had sunk behind it now, casting a long shadow across the royal apartments below. Now abandoned as a residence for the king and more often used to house high-ranking prisoners, they were in a sorry state of repair.

'I fear the time has come for us to return to the palace, Sir Walter,' Prince Henry said regretfully, when his sister had at last finished her description of the masque.

The prisoner stood and held out his hand for the princess. She placed hers delicately upon it and blushed again as he bent to kiss it. 'I pray that you will soon honour me with another visit,' he murmured. 'The hours will pass very slowly until you do.'

'I will think on it, Sir Walter,' Elizabeth replied, with a coy smile.

'Perhaps I can entice you with the prospect of a little surprise,' Raleigh replied. 'I would detain your attendant here for a moment, so that she can assist me in bringing it to pass.' He gestured towards Frances, who was bewildered. The princess narrowed her eyes as she stared at him, as if considering whether he was in earnest. 'I beg you to indulge me, Your Grace,' Sir Walter added. 'I know that you will soon be spirited away by some foreign prince, so I am eager to ensure that you will return to see me as soon as possible.'

Frances saw that his flattery had hit its mark. 'Very well, Sir Walter,' Elizabeth replied, her eyes sparkling with pleasure. 'But you must not keep Frances long or we will miss the tide.'

Before Frances could protest, her mistress had swept from the room, closely followed by her brother and their attendants. Sir Walter crossed to where Frances was standing and waited until the footsteps had echoed into silence.

'How easily the young can be won with flattery,' he said, with a sardonic smile. 'The prince even more so than his sister.'

'You and he are not so friendly as it seems, then?'

Sir Walter's eyes glittered. 'If you were to ask him the same question, he would have you whipped. But for myself, I will tell you that the admiration is on his side only. I think him a preening fool — more so even than his father, who placed me here.' His expression darkened as he held her gaze. 'But we have little time, Lady Frances, so I will not waste it on trivialities,' he said, in a low voice, pulling her closer. 'I am told that you are a friend to our cause and have agreed to use your influence with the princess to further the Spanish match.'

Frances dared not speak, but inclined her head slightly.

'I will assist you in any way I can,' he continued earnestly. 'Her pretty young head is easily turned, and between us we might fill it with the right thoughts.'

'The princess knows her own mind well enough, Sir Walter,' Frances said, bristling. 'It will not be as simple as you imagine.'

'You may be right, Lady Frances, but we

must not fail in our endeavours. There are many in this place who stand ready to act, when the time is ripe.'

'I will do my utmost to bring the marriage to pass,' Frances whispered.

'First, you must dissuade her from a suitor whom I have heard is making his way to England. The King of Sweden is an even stauncher Protestant than the heretic who sits on our throne and has sent his son to court the princess.'

Sweden. Frances had been raised to love her mother's native land. Was she now to betray it?

'Prince Gustavus is close in age to Elizabeth, but has already proved his worth on the battlefield. You must make sure that she is not won over by such bravado. They say that in appearance he is ill-favoured.'

Frances nodded. 'That is to our advantage, at least. But it will be no easy task to dissuade the princess from the match, if her brother approves of it — as he surely must, given the Swedish prince's faith.'

Raleigh gave a wolfish grin. 'A woman can always be persuaded to follow her heart, Lady Frances.'

She stared back at him, unsmiling. Clearly he had chosen to forget that the old queen had steadfastly resisted his charms, sacrificing her personal happiness in the interests of her kingdom. But it would not serve to remind him of that now. 'For the love of our faith, I will do as you ask,' she said quietly.

Sir Walter smiled and clasped her hands in his. 'You are a true subject, Lady Frances — even if the king would brand you a whore of Satan.' He paused. 'But the princess's marriage is not the only one that concerns you. There are plans for a much greater one besides.'

Frances wrenched her hands away and stared at him, aghast. 'I pledged no more than this and would not place those I love in any greater danger than I have already.'

Sir Walter lowered his face so that it was almost touching hers. She could feel his breath hot against her mouth. 'You have no choice,' he whispered, eyes glinting. 'If you make a pact with Satan, then he marks you for ever as his own. You are the devil's slave, Lady Frances.'

CHAPTER 12
1 MARCH

Frances tried to focus upon the intricate plasterwork on the ceiling as she waited for the privy councillors to appear. The criss-cross pattern had seemed random at first, but as she looked more closely, she realised that it comprised a series of interconnecting stars — a reference to the purpose for which this room was used. She had never been to Star Chamber before, but she knew that it lay directly beneath Westminster Hall, which still held terrible memories of Tom's trial. Looking down at the flagstones now, she wondered if the gunpowder had been hidden underneath this very spot.

The door to the left of the ornate fireplace at the far end of the room opened. Frances rose to her feet and waited, head bowed, as the lords filed in and took their places along the low bench, which was covered with a cloth of azure blue embroidered with tiny gold stars.

'Lady Frances — please.'

She raised her head to see Cecil pointing towards a spot just in front of the assembled councillors. She walked slowly over and bobbed a curtsy. Her eyes flicked across the group. She recognised the aged Charles Howard, Earl of Nottingham and Lord High Admiral, who had served the old queen so loyally. On his left was the king's chamberlain, the Earl of Suffolk, and next to him the dashing Edward Somerset, Earl of Worcester and Master of the Horse.

A loud cough drew Frances's attention to the opposite side of the bench where, staring back at her with eyes as cold as ice, her uncle, the Earl of Northampton, sat. It had been almost four years since their last, bitter exchange. He had berated her for giving up the position in the princess's household that he had gone to so much trouble to arrange. How much greater his fury would have been if he had known the true reason for her departure from court. Looking at him now, she saw that his face was ruddier than before, his hair more white than brown, and there were several folds of flesh beneath his chin. Clearly, he had been enjoying the fruits of his various offices. As well as being a member of His Majesty's Privy Council, he was also keeper of the

Privy Seal and warden of the Cinque Ports. Frances wondered how much time he spent on the latter. Lucrative though it no doubt was, she could not imagine that the Kent coast held the same appeal as Whitehall.

'For the sake of those present, please state your name.'

She turned to Sir Thomas Fleming, the Lord Chief Justice, who was dressed in the scarlet robes of his office.

'Lady Frances Tyringham, my lord.'

'You are brought before us to swear the oath of allegiance to our dread sovereign lord, King James,' he continued, 'as all true and faithful subjects are required to do, in the sight of His Majesty's council and before God.'

Frances tried to swallow but her mouth felt suddenly dry. She stared straight ahead, her lips pressed tightly together as if they might prevent her from uttering the words that she knew would deny everything she held dear.

'Do you solemnly swear that the pope has no power to depose the king, or to authorise any foreign prince to invade him, or to give licence to any to bear arms or raise tumults . . .'

Frances clasped her hand more tightly over the small amber bead that she had

182

carefully prised from the rosary early that morning, before George was awake.

'Do you further swear from your heart that you abhor and detest as impious and heretical this damnable belief that princes which be excommunicated by the pope may be deposed or murdered by their subjects, and that the pope has no power to absolve you from this oath?'

His words echoed into silence. Frances continued to stare at the carved marble overmantel above the fireplace.

'Lady Frances?'

Cecil's voice this time. His eyes glinted as he looked back at her, clearly relishing her discomfort.

Who would have thought that we would meet in such a place?

The words he had spoken to her in the Tower came back to her suddenly. Though she willed herself not to think of what had followed, images of Cecil's grim smile as the witch-pricker did his work flitted before her. Even when her shift had been ripped from her body, his gaze had never faltered, or when the knife had begun to probe her flesh.

Frances felt herself begin to sway and forced her focus onto a small indentation on one of the flagstones below. When at last

183

her breathing grew steadier, she saw that several of the council members had begun to fidget in their seats. At the far end, her uncle was glaring at her, his face now puce with suppressed fury. She had no idea how long they had been waiting for her to respond.

She tried to swallow again. An image of Tom filled her mind now as she opened her mouth to speak. He was holding out his hand to her and smiling. She took another breath.

'I swear.'

The words came out as a whisper.

'Speak up, my lady!' bellowed the Lord Chief Justice.

Above all else, guard your heart, for everything you do flows from it.

The words of the proverb came to her suddenly, like a balm to her tormented soul. These men might direct her words, but her heart was her own to command.

'I swear,' she repeated, so loudly that the words echoed around the chamber. Her uncle's shoulders sagged with relief, and the smile faded from Cecil's lips.

Sir Thomas Fleming rose to his feet and rapped his staff upon the floor three times. 'Then I declare before His Majesty's Privy Council that you are a true and faithful

184

subject, and that you shall be bound by this oath until you depart this earthly life.'

Frances bowed her head, as if in humble submission. She kept her eyes lowered as she listened to the scraping of chairs, followed by the shuffling of footsteps as the lords left the chamber. When at last the door had closed behind them, she raised her eyes to the ceiling.

'God forgive me,' she whispered, then sank down onto the bench, suddenly exhausted. The distant chiming of a bell sounded across the empty chamber. Frances counted. Eleven o'clock. She must return to the princess.

Slowly, she raised herself. Her limbs felt heavy and there was a dull throb at her temples that would grow worse as the day went on. Only sleep would clear her head and restore her strength, but there was little prospect of that until after her mistress had retired. Turning, she walked towards the door through which she had entered and began to make her way through the long network of corridors and courtyards that led back to the privy apartments.

As she passed her own lodgings, she had to fight the urge to enter and take her rest. Instead, she walked on towards the stairs that led up to her mistress's chambers. Just as she drew level with the last door, it was flung open and a man rushed out, colliding with her. She almost fell, but he grabbed her waist and pulled her to her feet.

'Forgive me, I —' He faltered as they stared at each other.

'Thomas!'

Frances stared in disbelief at her husband. She had thought he was still at Oatlands and would be for many weeks yet.

'Frances,' he said, with a swift, awkward bow, not quite meeting her gaze.

As the shock subsided, she studied him more closely. His hair was somewhat dishevelled and his shirt was untied at the neck. The surprise of seeing her still showed on his face, along with . . . *guilt*?

Her thoughts were interrupted by a rustle from the doorway behind her. She turned towards it at once and saw the flash of a woman's sleeve and the glint of a sapphire ring before both disappeared from view. Frances looked back at her husband, her expression hardening. 'I did not expect you to return so soon. You did not write to tell me of your coming.' Her words were sharp.

He cast a glance over his shoulder, then looked her in the eye at last. 'Forgive me. There was little time. The rains came suddenly and with such force that His Majesty decided to abandon the hunt and return to London. It was all done with such haste.'

'And yet you found time to visit an . . . acquaintance, before seeking out your wife?'

Frances's gaze was unrelenting and she felt a stab of triumph when she saw her husband cower beneath it.

'Come, Frances,' he said, agitated. 'We cannot talk here.'

He took her arm and began to steer her towards their apartment, but she wrenched herself free and stood stock still, eyes blazing. 'I have no time for such matters,' she said. 'I must attend the princess.'

She turned to go, but he stepped forward and grasped her shoulders, forcing her to look at him. 'You must hear me, Frances. God knows we talk about such matters little enough, though we are man and wife. I have honoured my pledge to be a husband in name only, but I cannot live without affection.' His gaze intensified. 'Please.'

To her dismay, Frances felt tears prick her eyes. She did not understand why she felt so bereft, so alone. It was as if he was a stranger to her. Yet that was what they had always been in a way. What did it matter if he had taken a mistress? His marriage bed was cold, so it was natural that he should seek warmth in another. But still his betrayal stung, more than she could ever have expected.

A tear ran slowly down her cheek. He reached out and stroked it gently away with his thumb. His palm felt warm against her cheek as he held it there, his eyes full of sorrow as he looked down at her. 'Forgive me, Frances. I —'

She pulled away from him again and was gratified to see the hurt in his eyes. His arm fell limply to his side but he continued to gaze at her, his mouth working as if he was trying to find the words to explain. Impatiently, Frances smoothed her skirts. 'As I said, I must go. My mistress will be asking for me.'

She walked briskly to the end of the corridor and through the doorway that led to the staircase. Mounting them two at a time, she broke into a run when she reached the gallery at the top that led to the princess's apartments. Though she did not pause to look back, she knew that her husband would be standing there still, gazing in her wake.

CHAPTER 13
3 MARCH

'You are very quiet again today, Frances,' the princess said, with a mixture of concern and impatience. 'I have hardly heard you speak two words together since you returned from the Star Chamber.'

'Your Grace must forgive me,' Frances replied. 'My son has been a little fretful these past two nights, so I have slept badly.'

It was not a complete lie. George had been troubled with night terrors of late. Though the queen had written to her younger son's tutors, there had been little improvement in Charles's behaviour and George had often returned from the schoolroom with his eyes swollen from crying. Frances had planned to talk to Thomas about it, but they had barely spoken since their meeting in the corridor. He had taken to sleeping on the settle in the parlour. She supposed that its stiff oak boards must offer more comfort than the bed they had shared.

'When will you bring the boy to me?' Elizabeth asked. 'You know that I am desirous to meet him.'

'Yes, Lady Frances,' chimed in Blanche. 'You cannot hope to keep him locked in your apartments for ever.'

Frances pushed down her irritation. The woman seemed to have a gift for knowing when her rival was trying to hide something. Though Frances knew she must soon accede to her mistress's request, she feared that Elizabeth would see the resemblance straight away. Tom Wintour had been one of her closest companions, after all.

'I promise I will arrange it as soon as George has a little freedom from his studies, Your Grace,' she said evenly. 'He is obliged to apply himself for many hours a day until the tutors judge that he has come within sight of your brother's learning.'

The princess gave a derisive laugh. 'I am sure that he has long since surpassed Charles!' she exclaimed. 'My little brother is such a dolt. Thank God Henry is the heir and not he, or the kingdom would be ruined.'

'Is there any more news of Prince Gustavus?' Frances enquired, changing the subject.

Elizabeth brightened at once. 'Your uncle

has sent word that he arrived in Dover yesterday. He will rest there for two nights before riding to Greenwich.'

Frances gave a wry smile. Her uncle must have proved a good deal more eager to exercise his duties as warden of the Cinque Ports since hearing of the Swedish prince's impending arrival.

'My mother will receive him there,' the princess continued, 'and I am to join her — with my ladies, of course,' she added, with a smile.

'Which gown shall you wear?' Frances asked. 'I will make sure that it is brushed and aired.'

'Oh, that is already in hand,' Blanche cut in. 'The princess made her selection yesterday and I have sent it to the laundresses.'

'You are a model of efficiency, Lady Blanche,' Frances replied.

Her eyes lingered on the young woman for a moment and she found herself wondering whether she would dislike her so much if their positions in the princess's household had not pitted them against each other. She knew that some of her antipathy derived from jealousy at Blanche's favour with their mistress; she knew, too, that she had no right to resent her, when she herself had deserted Elizabeth so suddenly. But looking at Blanche now, a simpering smile playing about her lips, she could not imagine her ever being a friend.

Frances turned to address her mistress. 'Have you been in correspondence with the prince, Your Grace?'

The princess set down her embroidery and strolled over to the window. 'There is hardly need,' she said nonchalantly, looking out across the Thames, 'since we shall soon be acquainted in person.'

'Of course,' Frances replied. She paused. 'I wondered if you knew anything of his character or interests.'

'Our mistress knows that her suitor is a staunch defender of the true faith,' Blanche remarked, in an imperious tone. 'That exceeds all other qualities — as your brother the prince has observed on many occasions, Your Grace.'

Frances felt as if she was engaged in a war of words, and that Blanche had struck a heavy blow. They both knew how much their mistress revered her brother and that she set his word above all others.

'Indeed,' she countered. 'After all, of what consequence are such matters as intellect, taste and appearance when set against devoutness of belief?'

She was glad to see Elizabeth's brow

crease with doubt.

'He looked fine enough in the miniature I received,' she said, a little too firmly. 'And my father says that in martial prowess he is unsurpassed.'

Frances framed her expression into one of admiration and fell silent, as if considering her mistress's great fortune in attracting such a suitor. 'Your mother must be delighted too,' she observed.

The princess pursed her lips, then turned so that her face was obscured from view. 'The queen sets her native land ahead of her daughter's happiness, it seems,' she snapped. 'Gustavus's kingdom is at war with Denmark, so my mother is against the match — though such petty disputes are hardly of concern to our kingdom.'

Frances bowed her head so that Blanche could not see the triumph in her eyes. She had heard that Anne had quarrelled with the king over the matter. Though she had little influence with her husband, she had made sure to voice her protests within earshot of several courtiers, who now whispered that the queen was right to insist James should not sever the alliance he had forged upon their marriage.

The silence that followed was broken by a sharp rap on the door. Blanche was first to rise and crossed quickly to it. No doubt she hoped it was Prince Henry, whose visits to his sister's bedchamber had become even more frequent of late. Frances kept her eyes fixed on her embroidery, waiting for the usual giggling and simpering as Blanche greeted him. But she had fallen silent, and instead of the brisk tap of Henry's footsteps, Frances heard the rustle of skirts. She looked up and her breath caught in her throat.

'Mother!'

Helena flashed her daughter a heart-warming smile before sweeping an elegant curtsy in front of the princess, who was regarding her with interest. She was dressed in an exquisite gown of russet silk edged with pearls, her old mistress's favourite. Her hair was of a deeper red than it had been when Frances had last seen her, but there was still no trace of grey. Though she was a woman of sixty, she could still outshine most other ladies at court, Frances reflected proudly.

Her mother had sent no word of her visit, and Frances could hardly believe she was there. How often these past five years had she longed to visit her parents at Richmond? Although they had written numerous times, she had always resisted their invitations, knowing that if she accepted, she would not be able to bear returning to Tyringham Hall. Neither had she wished to bring any scandal upon them. Her brother Edward had ordered her never to take her bastard son to Richmond, lest it spark gossip among the servants about the speed of her marriage to Thomas. Whenever she had been tempted to let them visit her instead, Edward's words had sounded in her ears: *You have shamed them enough.*

'My lady marchioness,' Elizabeth said, as she turned from the window and walked slowly to where Helena was standing. She showed none of Frances's surprise. 'We are grateful for your coming with so little notice.'

Helena inclined her head. 'I am glad to assist Your Grace in any way I can.'

Frances looked from one to the other in bemusement.

'The king invited your mother to attend us,' the princess explained, noting her confusion. 'He thought Prince Gustavus might welcome the presence of his countrywoman, and that the marchioness could help us converse.'

Frances was as surprised as she was delighted that James should have made such a plan. When he had given her parents charge of Richmond Palace at the beginning of his reign, it had been as good as banishment. They were never invited to attend any of the formal gatherings of court, even though her mother's rank demanded it.

The princess gestured for Helena to sit, and she chose the chair next to her daughter. Frances breathed in the familiar scent of rose and camomile, and smiled for the first time in days. She longed to reach out and touch her mother's hand. Having her so close was both comfort and torture. How many times over the past five years had she ached for her embrace, imagining it would soothe away all the torment she had suffered since they were last together? She lowered her gaze as she struggled to maintain her composure.

'I wonder that we have not seen you at court before now, my lady,' Blanche remarked slyly. 'Richmond society must be very diverting.'

Frances jerked up her head and glared at her.

'My husband and I are contented there, Mistress . . .'

'*Lady* Blanche Pembroke,' she retorted icily. Frances smiled at her obvious indignation.

'Well, we are very glad that you are here now,' the princess stated. 'We will leave for Greenwich the day after tomorrow so that we are in good time for the prince's arrival.' She looked at mother and daughter for a moment, then added, 'Perhaps you would show the marchioness to her apartments, Frances. They are close to your own.'

Frances's heart leaped at the prospect of spending some time alone with her mother, however brief. She beamed at her mistress and stood to make a deep curtsy, then held out her hand and led Helena from the room.

'How I have longed to see you, Frances,' her mother whispered, as soon as they were out of earshot. She grasped her daughter's hand and pressed it to her lips. Frances saw that her eyes glistened with tears. She swallowed her own so that she might reply, but could not find the words. As they emerged into the hall, Helena held her head high, conscious of the curious stares of the ladies who stood in small clusters around the room.

At last they reached the apartment that Frances guessed had been assigned to her mother: it had lain empty for some time. She pushed open the door and was glad to see that it was more spacious than her own, and richly furnished. As soon as the door

197

had closed behind them, the two women embraced each other. Frances clung to her mother as if she would never let go and closed her eyes so she might savour every sensation, committing them to her memory for the turbulent times that must lie ahead.

'You have been always in our thoughts and prayers,' Helena said, when at last they parted. 'You and our grandson,' she added, her voice breaking.

'He has asked many times to meet you both,' Frances replied softly. 'I have told him so much about you. I wanted you and Father to be as real to him as I am. I rejoice that you will see him at last.' She glanced at the clock on the fireplace. 'He will soon have finished his lessons.'

'Your father made me promise to remember every detail of the precious boy and relay all to him when I return. He would have sent Master Critz to take his likeness if he could.' She smiled.

'How is he?' Her own smile faded as she saw her mother's expression change.

'He suffered greatly with the ague last month,' Helena said. 'The chill of winter brought it on. He would not heed my warning to stay indoors,' she added sharply, as if chiding him still.

Frances felt a wave of anguish at the

thought of her father lying sick at Richmond while she had been here, unknowing. She could have eased his suffering with a tincture of willow bark and elder — but even if she had known, a visit to him would have carried too great a risk. Cecil's spies would have followed her there, and their master would have been delighted to hear the witch was making her potions once more. Well, she would find a means to prepare a phial of the medicine for her mother to take back to Richmond, in case the sickness should return. 'He is recovered now?' she asked, fearing the answer.

'Enough for me to accept the king's summons,' Helena replied briskly. 'Now, tell me more about my grandson.'

Frances studied her mother closely before she replied. The joy she took in describing George's character and accomplishments was marred by worry that her mother was concealing the extent of her father's illness.

'Thomas is a good father?' Helena asked, when her daughter had finished speaking.

'Very. George adores him.'

'A good husband too?'

Frances's face clouded at the memory of what had happened two days earlier. She nodded, unable to meet her mother's gaze.

'He is an honourable man, Frances,'

Helena said earnestly. 'Few men would make such sacrifices.'

Frances bit her lip. She had no wish to speak of her husband's infidelity — if she could even describe it as such. 'He gives me little cause for complaint.'

'It is thanks to Thomas that I am here, Frances.'

She looked up, surprised.

'The king would hardly have thought to enlist my help otherwise,' Helena continued. 'Your father and I have long since been forgotten. Your husband did you a great kindness in reminding him.' She took her daughter's hand and gently stroked it. 'He must have known that you were in need of comfort.'

Frances tried to order her thoughts. Her anger at Thomas's transgression had blinded her to the many sacrifices he had made on her behalf. Shame at her ingratitude mingled with her ongoing bewilderment at the strength of her reaction when she had seen him that day. Now that she knew of this latest service, she could not but feel remorse that she had been so quick to judge him. 'Then I am deeply grateful to him, Mama,' she said at last.

CHAPTER 14
6 MARCH

Frances shielded her eyes against the sun as she watched the river snaking into the distance. Soon the prince's barge would come into view. It had been half an hour at least since the queen's steward had arrived to report that the procession had reached Woolwich.

Beside her, the princess was fidgeting nervously, her fingers working at the grey satin sash that was tied at her narrow waist. 'He should be here by now,' she muttered.

'I am sure the prince is just as eager to see you, Your Grace,' Helena said. 'It will not be long.'

Frances glanced at her mother and smiled. George was at her side, his hand clasped in hers. He had soon overcome his initial shyness in meeting his grandmother, and in the space of just three days the pair had become inseparable. She watched as Helena smoothed his hair, then bent to whisper in his ear. He looked up at her adoringly.

Frances's gaze moved to her husband, who was standing behind them. His expression was, as ever, inscrutable as he stared at the horizon. Relations between them had thawed a little since her mother's arrival. She had found it impossible to remain angry with him now that she knew he was responsible for bringing her there. Helena had enjoyed his company, and seeing them together, Frances had been struck by how similar in character he was to her father. Little wonder they got on so well. Thomas looked at her now and their eyes held, until Frances glanced away.

A sudden fanfare of trumpets signalled that the prince was in view. Elizabeth grasped Frances's hand and held it tightly as the gilded barge drew closer, the pennants at either end fluttering in the breeze. At last, it reached the landing stage in front of them and a stout young man climbed out. He was shorter than Frances had imagined, and though he was dressed as might be expected of a royal prince, with starched white lace collar and sleeves, and, across his doublet, a sash that matched the princess's, he appeared rather awkward and ill at ease. He marched up to the assembled company and gave a stiff bow to the princess. As he raised himself, Frances saw that his face was flushed and there were beads of sweat on his high forehead.

'It is a pleasure to meet Your Highness.'

His voice was flat, as if he had learned the phrase by rote, and his accent was strong. It was fortunate that her mother was there to aid their conversation, Frances thought.

The princess made the briefest curtsy. 'You are most welcome, Prince Gustavus,' she replied, studying him closely. Frances heard the disappointment in her voice and felt a rush of hope. Perhaps her task would not be so difficult after all.

The prince glanced at the assembled company, his eyes darting from one courtier to the next. His neatly clipped blond moustache twitched occasionally, whether from nervousness or disapproval Frances could not tell.

'I bid you come and take your ease,' Elizabeth said as she gestured towards the palace. 'My mother is waiting to receive you.'

He took the hand she proffered and they walked slowly towards the gatehouse. Frances watched them closely as she and the rest of the company followed in their wake. Although her mistress's hand was now resting lightly on the prince's arm, she stared straight ahead. Neither she nor her suitor spoke another word.

The great hall was crowded with courtiers waiting to greet the royal couple, and a hush descended as they entered. At the far end of the room, Queen Anne sat enthroned on a high dais. She made no move to stand as she saw her daughter and the prince, but remained motionless as a statue while they approached, her eyes never leaving them.

Frances scanned the crowds on either side of her as she followed her mistress through the centre of the hall. She recognised several members of the Privy Council, before whom she had been obliged to swear allegiance to the king a few days earlier. The chamber was thronged with ladies, too, all dressed in their finest silks, jewels twinkling. Lady Howard shone brightest, as usual, and Frances saw Prince Gustavus's head turn towards her as he passed.

As Frances neared the dais, another figure caught her eye. The young man was leaning against a marble pillar with an air of nonchalance, but his features were suffused with tension. He was tall and muscular, with long fair hair and light blue eyes, which now and again glanced over to the courtiers who stood on the opposite side of the stage. She followed his gaze to a proud-looking woman, who was staring back at him, her small blue eyes burning.

Arbella Stuart.

Frances recognised her at once. She had aged considerably since she had last seen her, though she must only be in her mid-thirties, Frances calculated. Old enough to have been married long before now, if she had been content to take a husband without royal blood.

Frances glanced back at the elegant gentleman who held Arbella's interest. The look that passed between them unnerved her.

'Welcome to court, Prince Gustavus.' The queen, still seated, addressed him. All eyes were upon him as he knelt to kiss her hand. An awkward silence followed. The princess, who was standing behind him, eyes downcast, made no move to help. At last, her mother gave a signal to the musicians and they struck up a lively tune. The courtiers quickly formed themselves into a line and began to dance, their chatter soon rising above the sound of the flutes and violins. Thomas took Frances's hand and guided her over to join them before she could protest.

'He is not to her liking, I think,' he said in her ear, as they drew close and parted again.

Frances nodded. 'Though she will wish to

please her brother in this, as in all things.'

They followed the steps of the dance, their hands meeting from time to time as they weaved in and out of the long line of court-iers.

'Thank you,' she said, when next they came together.

Thomas looked at her questioningly.

'For bringing my mother here,' she explained. 'I am very grateful.'

He inclined his head and his shoulders sagged as if in relief. 'It was the least I could do after —' He stopped abruptly.

Frances forced herself to concentrate on her steps. Following the others, Thomas put his hands about her waist and lifted her into the air, but did not release her afterwards and instead guided her away from the throng. She could feel the warmth of his hand on the small of her back as he led her to a quiet corner, far from the dais.

'I beg your forgiveness, Frances,' he said. 'I cannot but be ashamed of what I have done, but I want you to understand the reason.'

'You owe me no explanation,' she replied coldly. 'Ours is a marriage in name only — as you promised it would be. How you choose to spend your hours of leisure is of no concern to me.'

His face showed he was stung. 'It is more than that, for me at least, though I know it will never be so for you. Your love for Tom is as strong now as when he lived — stronger, even, I think. Of course I knew you still loved him when we married, but I dared to hope that you might look upon me with affection, in time.'

Frances searched his eyes for any hint of deception, but they blazed with sincerity. Her love for Tom had blinded her to the true feelings of her own husband. She continued to stare at him, unable to form any words with which to respond.

At that moment, a loud fanfare rang out and Frances turned to see Prince Henry and his entourage enter the crowded hall. He stood for a moment, as if to ensure that all eyes were upon him, then made his stately progress towards the dais. Frances glanced at her mistress, who seemed delighted yet apprehensive to see her brother. She rose to greet him, but he brushed past her and swept an elaborate bow before Gustavus.

'Your Highness is most welcome,' he pronounced, so that all of the assembled company could hear. He took his sister's hand and joined it with that of her suitor. Elizabeth recoiled before she forced a graceful smile.

'Through this union, our kingdom will be saved from papists and heretics, and the devil will have no more to do with my father's people.'

An uncertain cheer rose from the crowd. Henry gestured for Gustavus to join him at the front of the dais. The Swedish prince walked stiffly to him and stood surveying the room, his expression grave. Behind him, Frances could see the princess, her smile fixed.

Suddenly, the queen stood. 'Please, stay and enjoy the entertainments.' Her voice echoed around the hall. 'My daughter and I will retire now.'

Elizabeth shot her mother a grateful look and followed in her wake, head bowed. Frances pushed through the crowds so that she might accompany them. This was too good an opportunity to lose. As she reached the door that led to the privy apartments, she looked back across the hall. The courtiers were talking in animated whispers, no doubt speculating upon the queen's sudden departure. But Thomas was still standing where she had left him, staring after her. For a moment, their eyes met, then Frances turned and half ran from the hall.

'Forgive me, Your Highnesses,' she said, as

she arrived, breathless, in Anne's presence chamber a few moments later. 'I feared the princess was unwell so was anxious to attend her.'

She glanced across at the young woman, who was sitting at the window, gazing out across the park.

'I am quite well,' Elizabeth remarked sullenly, without turning.

'But we are pleased you are here,' the queen said quickly, gesturing for Frances to sit.

'Tell me, what did you think of our Swedish prince?' she asked, after a pause.

Frances looked up at her, but Anne's expression was as inscrutable as ever. 'He seems the perfect model of an upright and pious young man,' she replied carefully. 'Even if he has not yet displayed any of the accomplishments that are prized so highly by the courtiers here, I am sure that he possesses many others.'

Out of the corner of her eye, she saw Elizabeth flinch but she remained silent.

'Indeed,' Anne agreed, taking up the theme. 'Besides, my daughter is well enough versed in dancing, conversation and other such trivial pastimes to make up for any deficiencies on the part of her husband.'

'They are hardly trivial, Mother,' the

princess snapped, turning to face them at last. 'Henry encompasses them all, yet is just as serious and devout as Prince Gustavus.'

Frances thought she saw a flicker of a smile on the queen's lips, but it was quickly suppressed.

'That is quite true,' Anne said. 'But we must not be too quick to judge poor Gustavus. Some men's qualities are slower to emerge than others. That is all.'

The princess scowled and turned back to the window.

'It is a pity that his kingdom is presently at war with your brother's, Your Grace.'

Frances had not noticed Lady Drummond enter the room. Her steps were as soft as her voice.

'Would that it were otherwise,' Anne sighed.

'Then this betrothal must be abandoned at once,' the princess urged, choosing to overlook her earlier disregard for the matter. Her eyes filled with indignation — and, Frances thought, hope. 'If my father knew of this . . .'

'He does know,' her mother snapped. 'But the king sets matters of faith above those of family loyalty — as is entirely proper. God must come before all.'

Frances held back a retort. It was well known that the king's conscience was little troubled when trying to secure the most advantageous alliance overseas. 'But surely there are other suitors, Your Grace,' she said. 'After all, your daughter is widely admired — both for her beauty and her accomplishments, and for the powerful alliance she would bring. Half of the princes in Christendom must be clamouring to marry her.'

A glance at the princess told her that her words had hit their mark.

'Of course there are other suitors.' Elizabeth raised herself to her full height. 'I will speak to my father. He is due to attend this evening's feast, is he not?'

'It will do no good, Elizabeth,' Anne replied softly. 'I raised the same objections when the match was first spoken of. You know how unyielding he is when his mind is set upon its course.'

'Then I shall ask Henry to plead my case. Though he favours the marriage, he would hardly do so if he knew how strongly opposed I am to it now.'

Frances exchanged a knowing look with the queen. 'I fear he will not be so easily dissuaded, Your Grace, given how greatly it will strengthen our war against heresy.'

211

'So I am to be traded like a chattel, with no thought to my own wishes or desires?'

'Such is the lot of princesses, my dear,' her mother said sadly. 'I know it all too well.'

Frances saw Elizabeth's face redden as it had when she had flown into one of her childhood rages.

'It is not to be borne!' she cried, then swept from the room and slammed the door loudly behind her.

The queen took up her embroidery. 'I had not expected the seed to take root so quickly,' she murmured, with a smile.

Lady Drummond moved to stand behind her mistress. As she rested her hand lightly on the back of the chair, a flash of blue caught Frances's eye. She looked at the woman's delicate white fingers and her heart lurched.

The sapphire ring.

Though she had seen it for just a second that day, she recognised it at once. So this was her husband's mistress? She stared up at Lady Drummond as if seeing her for the first time. The woman's eyes were lowered and her rosebud mouth was set in a demure smile. Frances judged that she was a few years younger than herself, and her small stature lent her an air of delicacy.

Suddenly her eyes flicked upwards and

Frances saw them glint with understanding. She held the other woman's gaze coldly, expecting to see contrition. But Jane Drummond's expression never faltered.

CHAPTER 15
28 MARCH

Frances closed the door softly behind her, but an echo still sounded across the empty pews. A solitary candle burned on the altar, illuminating the simple wooden crucifix above. As her eyes grew accustomed to the gloom, she could see that the church boasted few adornments. No hangings covered the cold stone walls, and only a row of empty plinths hinted at the former richness of the decoration. Even the Reverend Pritchard could find nothing at fault here, she reflected.

She walked slowly towards the altar, pulling her cloak more tightly around her shoulders against the chill. Looking up at the crucifix, she made the sign of the cross, then sank to her knees on one of the cushions beneath. 'Hail, Holy Queen, Mother of Mercy,' she whispered, her breath misting in the cold, damp air.

The tolling of the bells made her start.

She paused, counting. Midnight.

A moment later, she heard the soft click of the latch but forced herself to keep her gaze fixed upon the floor. She listened to the slow rustle of skirts as the woman drew closer, then knelt next to her.

'You have done well, Lady Frances,' she whispered, as she bowed her head. 'I hear that the Swedish prince is not to Elizabeth's liking.'

'That is not entirely my doing. My mistress was greatly grieved when she discovered that his kingdom was at war with her mother's, and the prince himself has done little to improve her opinion.' Frances thought of the previous night's assembly, the latest in a succession of entertainments staged in the prince's honour since his arrival three weeks before. But though each had been more extravagant than the last, the atmosphere had been progressively more strained. The courtiers who had attended could not have failed to notice the sour looks that had passed between the princess and her elder brother, or the cold formality with which she had greeted her suitor. The king had not troubled himself to attend any of the gatherings, which had given the princess cause to hope that he might abandon the negotiations.

'So it will come to nothing?'

Frances shook her head. 'The outcome is far from assured. Prince Henry still favours the match, and the king has expressed no opinion about his daughter's obvious aversion towards it.'

'Then you must keep up your persuasions.'

Frances fell silent. She had not seen Lady Vaux since their meeting at Coombe Abbey more than four years before, though in the past few weeks her numerous letters had made the woman seem a constant presence. Frances knew that she was one of the fiercest supporters of the Catholic cause and had almost paid for it with her life, yet she felt the same dislike she had formed upon first meeting her. She had always thought that Lady Vaux was motivated more by personal gain than by God's truth.

'Have you spoken to the princess about the King of Spain's nephew?' Lady Vaux asked.

'Not yet,' Frances replied. 'It would be precipitous, since the Swedish match has not yet been abandoned.'

'All the more reason to present her with an alternative.'

Frances bridled. 'I am better placed to judge the right time to act, Lady Vaux,' she said. Then, lowering her voice: 'If I lose my mistress's trust now, we are undone.' She felt remorse for seeking to manipulate the young woman for whom she cherished such affection. She was little better than the king or his ministers, who treated the princess as a pawn in the game of diplomacy.

'That may be so.' Lady Vaux interrupted her thoughts. 'But we do not have the luxury of time. The King of Spain grows impatient and our supporters here are beginning to lose faith.'

'What has Sir Walter Raleigh to do with this?' Frances asked abruptly.

She was gratified when Lady Vaux stared at her in surprise.

'He told me that the princess's marriage is part of a wider plot,' Frances continued. 'If I am to advance it, I must not be kept in ignorance.'

Lady Vaux hesitated but Frances kept her gaze steady.

'That does not concern you, Lady Frances,' she said at last. 'Neither will you know more until you have proven your loyalty by bringing the Spanish match to pass.'

Frances tried to calm her rising fury. Was she a mere puppet in the schemes of others, just like her mistress? Though she would gladly lay down her life for the Catholic cause Tom had so passionately espoused, she could feel nothing but distaste and mistrust for Lady Vaux and her associates. 'I took too great a risk by meeting you here,' Frances said, after a long pause. 'I will not do so again. Neither should you persist in writing to me. The princess will begin to suspect my reason for visiting the kitchens so often — Lady Blanche has already remarked upon it — and you cannot hope to find another place to leave your letters.' Lady Vaux opened her mouth to reply, but Frances continued, 'I know the part well enough that I am to play. Unless the situation changes, you must keep your silence.'

'Very well,' Lady Vaux replied tightly. 'But do not think to conceal anything from me. I have many eyes and ears at court.' She stood abruptly and gave a curt nod to the altar before striding back down the aisle. A moment later, the slam of the heavy oak door echoed around the church.

Greenwich Palace was still in darkness as Frances went through the park-side gate and locked it behind her, then crossed the small courtyard beyond. Her racing thoughts made her oblivious to the bitter chill of the night air. What was Raleigh's part in all of this? There had been something in Lady Vaux's expression when Frances had mentioned him that she could not quite fathom.

She was still turning over the possibilities as she fumbled for the key to her apartment. Her husband had been sleeping soundly when she left; she prayed he still was. *Perhaps he had sought diversion in Jane Drummond's chamber.* She tried to push away the thought. She had not troubled to tell him that she knew who his mistress was. It hardly mattered. If he had visited the young woman since his infidelity had been discovered, then he had been discreet.

Frances pressed her ear to the door but could hear nothing. Slowly, she lifted the latch.

'Frances.' Thomas's voice startled her as she entered the room. He rose from the seat by the fire and crossed quickly to where she was standing, the door still open behind her.

'Forgive me, I could not sleep.' Her words died as she saw the look on her husband's face. He reached out and clasped her hands tightly.

'What is it?' she said, panic rising. 'George?'

'He is fast asleep,' he replied quickly. 'It is your father.'

Frances felt the colour drain from her face.

'A servant arrived from Richmond an hour ago. Lord Thomas is gravely ill. You must make haste.'

Frances stared at him, as if uncomprehending, then wrenched her hands free. 'I must go to my mother. She can travel with me,' she said, as she turned back towards the door.

'She has been told, Frances, and is already on her way to Richmond,' her husband said, guiding her gently back into the room. 'She came here to see you and was sick with worry when we found you had gone, but I urged her to set out at once and promised you would follow as soon as you returned.'

Frances felt a wave of remorse. Was God punishing her for betraying her husband? She had taken a risk by agreeing to meet Lady Vaux, but had hoped Thomas would remain in ignorance. Would it be too late by the time she reached Richmond? She shook away the thought as she hastened to her room and, with trembling fingers, unlocked the chest that contained her herbs and tinctures. The glass phials clinked together as she stuffed them into a leather pouch. George gave a small moan from his pallet bed and she padded over to kiss his forehead, then hurried from the room.

'I have ordered a barge to be made ready for you,' her husband said, as he draped her cloak over her shoulders. 'With luck, you will be there before daybreak.'

Frances nodded but could not speak. As she turned to go, Thomas pulled her to him. She tensed, but the warmth of his embrace soothed her troubled soul and she surrendered to it, pressing her face against his chest. She could feel his heartbeat, fast and strong, and then his warm lips against her hair. Eventually she pushed herself free.

'Frances!' he called after her, but she was already out of sight.

CHAPTER 16
28 MARCH

The turrets of the palace were silhouetted against the dark grey sky as the barge at last approached the landing stage. It had been an agonisingly slow journey, the tide against them all the way. With every twist of the river, Frances had craned her neck, hoping to see the fields surrounding the city give way to the gently sweeping hillsides of Richmond. *Please God may I be in time,* she had prayed over and over.

Before the oarsman had even tethered the boat, Frances had leaped onto the wooden platform and begun to run towards the house, her heart in her mouth. It was still in darkness, save for a solitary light that blazed from an upper room in the east wing of the palace. Her father's bedchamber.

Frances hammered on the door and waited, panting. A few moments later, it was opened by the elderly steward. His features were grave, and she swept past him, not daring to ask if she was too late. She ran up the stairs, two at a time, and hurried along the dark corridor that led to her father's room. A soft light seeped under the door, but all was quiet within. Frances knocked, then pushed it open.

As she stepped over the threshold, she breathed in the stale aroma of sweat. The room was only dimly lit, and the curtains had been pulled around her father's bed. As she walked around it, she saw her mother sitting on the mattress, her head bent over her husband's hand. She turned at the sound of Frances's footsteps and leaped up to embrace her. Her cheek was wet against her daughter's neck and Frances began to weep. She could not bear to look past her to the bed and see her father's lifeless body.

'This is a fine greeting, after so many years.'

His voice was so faint that Frances wondered if she had imagined it. Gently, she released herself from her mother and stepped slowly forward. Her breath caught in her throat as she saw her father smiling up at her, his hand outstretched. With a cry, she flung herself down on the bed and pressed her lips to his fingers, smothering them with kisses. They felt cold and waxy, and though she continued to clasp them, she could not warm them. When at last she raised her eyes to his, her heart contracted. His face had the grey pallor she recognised all too well. Though she tried to reason that it was just the effects of the fever and that his strength might yet return, she knew that her herbs could offer no resistance to the inexorable march of death. The most that she could hope was to ease his suffering.

'Father,' she croaked, as she leaned forward to kiss his forehead.

With an effort, he raised himself on his pillows. Frances tried to hide her dismay at the sight of his wasted chest, the ribs showing through his nightshirt.

'My love,' he said, reaching out to touch her cheek. His hand soon fell away and he was panting as he tried to recover from the exertion. Frances's throat tightened as she tried to hold back her tears.

'How I have missed you.'

'And I you, Father,' she whispered, squeezing his hand. 'I have wished myself here so often, these past four years. It seems a lifetime ago that I was last in your presence.'

'Well, it *is* a lifetime.' He smiled. 'How fares my grandson? Your mother says he is a fine young man already.'

Frances returned his smile. 'He is very like you,' she said, taking out the miniature that

Thomas had commissioned shortly before they left Tyringham Hall. She handed it to her father.

'Ah, what a handsome fellow,' he said, stroking the picture with his thumb. 'A credit to his father.'

He raised his eyes to meet his daughter's. She swallowed, unable to reply.

'I should so like to have met him,' he added.

'I shall arrange it,' Frances said, as she got to her feet and began to unpack the herbs and tinctures onto the small table next to the bed, 'as soon as spring is here and the days are longer. I can be excused from my duties for one day, and George would so enjoy the boat ride. Or we could ride here, if the roads are good. He is an accomplished little horseman, thanks to my husband . . .' She sank down onto the chair, her chest heaving with silent grief. 'Forgive me,' she whispered.

'There is nothing to forgive,' her father said. 'Your herbs have worked many wonders in the past, but you know as well as I that I am beyond their help now. Do not weep, my love. I am at peace, and would that you were too.'

Her tears flowed as she bent to embrace him, her head resting lightly on his chest as

225

he stroked her hair, just as he had when she had curled up next to him as a child.

'Our faith will sustain us both,' he murmured. 'You must never forsake it, Frances, even though the path you have chosen is fraught with danger. It is better to hazard your mortal self than your immortal soul, though I pray God will keep you safe after I am gone.'

Frances turned her face to his. 'I promise, Father,' she said earnestly, then sank back down onto his chest.

After a while, her father's breathing became shallower. Frances glanced at him anxiously, but saw that he was sleeping. Slowly, she raised herself from the bed.

'You should rest now.'

Frances turned to her mother, who was sitting by the fire. She seemed to have aged overnight. Her pale skin sagged, and her eyes were filled with such sadness that Frances could hardly bear to hold her gaze. Her own grief at losing Tom after their brief time together had been so overwhelming that she had often thought it would stop her breath. How much greater would her mother's be for the husband she had loved deeply for more than thirty years?

She walked over and bent to kiss her. 'And you too, Mother,' she said gently.

Helena smiled but said nothing, and Frances knew that she would not leave her husband's bedside. She walked slowly from the room, casting a final glance towards the bed as she did so.

The thundering of horses' hoofs woke Frances. A moment later the front door slammed and she heard rapid footsteps mounting the stairs. She threw back the covers and hastily wrapped a shawl over her nightgown, then ran out of the room. It was pitch black and the clock in the hall chimed ten as she raced along the corridor towards her father's chamber, castigating herself for sleeping so long. As she neared the bed-chamber, she could hear muffled voices, one of which — a man's — was raised in anger. Not pausing to knock, she burst into the room.

Edward was standing next to the bed, one of Frances's tinctures clasped in his hand. He turned as she entered, his face puce with fury.

'Do you mean to damn us all to Hell, sister?' he demanded, his hand shaking as he thrust the phial towards her. 'Is it not enough that our father is dying but you must condemn his soul with your potions and witchcraft?'

'Edward, please!' Helena implored, clutching his arm. He shook it roughly away and continued to glare at his sister.

'Come, Frances,' he went on. 'You are not usually slow to express your opinions. What is the meaning of this?'

As she glanced from her mother's anguished face to her father, who lay senseless on the bed, a knot of rage uncurled in Frances's stomach. When at last she spoke, her voice was ominously low. 'You do more harm than I ever could. I mean only to help our father, but you — you cannot see beyond your selfish fury. Are you blind to how you grieve our mother? You would do better to return to Longford. I wonder that you came here at all, unless it was to serve your own ends.'

Edward's face turned a deeper shade of red. His mouth worked as if he was trying to form a response and his eyes blazed with hatred. 'And why are *you* here, sister?' he asked at last. 'I am surprised you troubled to make the journey from Greenwich. There is nothing for you here. I am our father's heir.'

So that was why he had come so quickly, Frances thought, no doubt breaking the wind of several horses in the attempt to reach his father before he breathed his last, not to say goodbye but to claim his inheritance. Would that she *was* a witch! She would curse him to Hell.

'Edward.'

They turned to their father, his eyes filled with such sorrow that Frances felt wretched with shame. She brushed past Edward and went to kneel by her father's side. 'Forgive me,' she whispered, kissing his wasted hand.

His fingers twitched, then were still.

'Please, leave us,' he said, looking from Frances to her mother. 'I would speak with my son alone.'

Frances studied her father's face. A thin sheen of sweat had formed on his forehead, and the skin beneath was a pallid yellow. His lips were dry and cracked, and his breath came in gasps. She reached for the glass of water on the table, but Edward swiped away her hand. 'You heard our father — leave us,' he hissed.

Helena placed a hand on her daughter's shoulder as she stood to leave. Reluctantly, Frances followed her, seeing triumph in Edward's eyes as she passed him.

As soon as they were out of the room, her mother clasped her hand and kissed it. 'You must not mind Edward,' she said, as they walked towards the gallery. 'He was always a headstrong boy, but he has a good heart.'

Frances squeezed her mother's hand in return but said nothing. She did not wish to vex her at such a time, and there was little she could say to change her opinion. The bonds of maternal love would not easily be loosened — she knew that.

'Will you stay here after . . .' Frances gazed out over the neatly manicured gardens, which were lit by braziers.

Helena shook her head. 'I cannot.'

Frances heard her mother's sharp intake of breath as she tried to halt her sobs.

'There are too many memories. It is seven years since my beloved mistress departed this world here, her favourite palace. And now your father . . .' She trailed off, her shoulders quivering with silent sorrow.

A fine drizzle had begun to fall, causing the braziers to spit and gutter. Frances took her mother's hand. 'You could come and live at court. The queen esteems you highly and would find you a place in her household. And I would love to have you near — George too.'

Helena smiled. 'I am too old for court life and cannot serve another mistress, even one I respect as much as our queen. I wish only to live in quiet retirement. Your father has bequeathed me a manor some forty miles from Longford. It will suit me very well.'

Frances felt a rush of resentment. Though her mother would never admit it, she knew Helena feared Edward would not make her welcome at Longford. His sights were set upon the future, not the past. Neither would he suffer any check to his authority, even from his mother.

She opened her mouth to speak, but at that moment Edward crashed through the door at the far end of the gallery and marched towards them, his hands clenched at his sides. He stopped when he reached them. 'I congratulate you, sister. You have achieved what you have been scheming for since we were children,' he snarled, trembling with rage. He pushed past her and strode out of the gallery, ignoring his mother's pleas, slamming the door so hard that several of the paintings shuddered on their chains.

'We must go to your father,' Helena said, before Frances could make any comment. Her face was ashen, but something in her eyes hinted that she knew the reason for Edward's fury.

Both women were breathless by the time they reached the bedchamber. Frances looked at her father anxiously. His breath was rasping in his throat, and his linen nightshirt was drenched with sweat.

'My daughter,' he whispered, and held out his hand.

Frances sat on the bed and stroked his cheek. Though it still glistened with sweat, it felt as cold as ice. As she gazed at him she saw his eyes mist.

'You were always my precious jewel,' he said tenderly. 'I wish I could have kept you safe.' A solitary tear trickled down his cheek.

Frances gave a sob as she pressed her fingers gently to his lips. 'You have, Father. You have given me so much, and I will always think myself the most blessed of daughters.'

'I would give you something more —' He fell into a paroxysm of coughing that left him fighting for breath.

Quickly, Frances reached for the tincture she had prepared upon first hearing of her father's illness several weeks before. She tilted a few drops into her palm and carefully smoothed them onto his chest. His nostrils wrinkled at the sharp aroma of hartshorn, but soon his breathing became steadier and his eyes fluttered open again.

'Though we have suffered for our faith — you more than any of us — you must always cherish it in your heart, Frances,' he said, when he had recovered. 'It will comfort and sustain you for the rest of your days, as it has for me. This heretic king —' He broke off, panting.

Frances was aware of holding her breath as she waited for him to continue.

'The kingdom will never flourish while he is on the throne. God speed the work of those who would wrest him from it,' he rasped, eyes blazing.

Did he know of her endeavours, of the wider plot that Raleigh had spoken of? She wanted to ask him, but the words stopped in her throat.

'I have bequeathed Longford to your son,' he said, after a long pause.

Frances was dumbfounded. There had never been any doubt that the estate was Edward's by right, as the eldest surviving son.

'George?' she whispered, when she found her voice.

Her father blinked slowly, as if in assent.

'Longford must remain in Catholic hands,' he replied. 'Your brother has sworn to uphold the religion of King James. He will not waver in this, I know — though I have not spoken of it to him, and neither must you. He cannot be trusted, Frances — even by his closest kin.'

Her father struggled for breath. Frances's mind was racing. Though her heart soared at the thought that her son would one day inherit the place she loved more dearly than any other, she knew it must be bought at a terrible price. 'But George has been raised a Protestant, Father,' she murmured. 'In my heart I will stay true to the Catholic faith for the rest of my days, but I cannot hazard his life by making him share it.'

'You will hazard his soul if you do not.'

At her mother's voice Frances turned. Helena's eyes showed the same fervour as her husband's. He had always implied that his wife knew nothing of his faith — and certainly not of the plots in which he and their daughter had become entangled. Now Frances saw she knew everything.

'You cannot keep your faith hidden from everyone, Frances. Our grandson must learn of the comforts it offers, when he is old enough to understand,' Helena continued. 'In the meantime, you are right to ensure that he conforms to that of the king — although you must take care to protect him from its worst excesses. His mind and heart must remain open to the true religion, when the time comes.'

Frances grasped the wisdom of her mother's words. It had always troubled her to see her precious boy being raised a heretic, to watch as he solemnly repeated the words of the Protestant prayer book. She had comforted herself with the knowledge that he could hardly understand their meaning. But that would not be true for much longer. George was a bright boy and quick to learn. She must keep him from those who would turn his mind from the true path — his own stepfather included — even if it meant breaking the promise she had made at her marriage.

Her father fell into another fit of coughing. She rushed back to his side and gently lifted his head to ease his breathing. Her mother knelt down next to them. When at last the fit had passed, he was so weak that his eyes kept closing.

'Edward will hold Longford in trust, until my grandson comes of age.'

His voice was so faint that Frances had to lean forward to catch his next words.

'It is written in my will and in the deeds of the castle, so it may not be altered — though Edward will try, you may be sure. Do not let him prevail, Frances,' he begged, clutching her hand. 'Do not . . .' He sank back on the pillows and closed his eyes. His breath now came in short, choking gasps. Slowly, his grasp weakened and his fingers grew still. The clock on the fireplace began chiming the hour, its high-pitched tone ringing out across the chamber.

Midnight.

As the last chime echoed into silence, Frances listened for her father's breath. But the only sound was her mother's muffled sobbing. Raising her eyes to her father's face, she saw that he had gone.

CHAPTER 17
18 APRIL

The carriage rumbled over the cobbles, jolting Frances and her son from side to side. She looked down at George, who was still sleeping peacefully, his head resting on her lap. His hair had grown darker this past year so that it now closely resembled that of his father. So much sorrow. Sometimes she did not know how she would bear it.

Her mother had been so brave when they had laid her husband to rest. She had borne herself with the same quiet dignity that had set her apart from the other ladies in the old queen's household. Frances had been glad that her father had chosen the cathedral at Salisbury as his final resting place, rather than the family vault at Britford. It would have been unthinkable for the Reverend Pritchard to officiate at the funeral — though, of course, he had expected it. Frances smiled at the thought that even in death her father had bested him.

All of the local nobility had attended the ceremony, along with scores of tenants, estate staff and the household at Longford. Her father had been greatly beloved of them all, as Edward had clearly grown tired of hearing by the end of the banquet that followed. He had maintained a frosty silence during the proceedings and had refused even to look at Frances. Once or twice, though, she had caught him staring at his nephew with an expression of such implacable hatred that her blood had run cold.

'You would do well to dry your tears, niece. The king will have no patience for weeping women.'

Frances turned cold eyes to her uncle. His legs were sprawled out and his belly protruded from the russet silk doublet that strained at the buttons so that he seemed to fill the entire space opposite her.

'I am sure you are right, Uncle,' she agreed. 'He has little enough patience for his own wife.'

The earl grunted. 'That damned woman. I paid dearly for the keepership of Greenwich Park, yet still she contests it. She should not trouble herself with matters that are beyond her comprehension.'

Frances suppressed a smile. Anne understood the issue well enough. She just wanted to vex the earl, knowing how he had tormented his niece in the past. As queen, her influence was limited, but she was determined to exercise what little power she had for the good of those who proved loyal.

'Tyringham is a dull fellow.'

She turned back to her uncle.

'He barely spoke two words together in Salisbury,' he continued. 'He seemed affable enough when I first introduced you. Perhaps marriage does not agree with him, eh?' He shot his niece a sly look.

Thomas had been even more attentive since her father's death and she had drawn comfort from his constant presence. She wished he was here now, but he had been unable to hold off the king's increasingly insistent requests to attend him and had set out for court early the previous morning.

'It was hardly the occasion for lively conversation, Uncle. My husband is as contented in our marriage as I am.'

'And yet you have given him no more children.' He glanced down at George, who was still asleep. 'Does he seek his pleasure elsewhere?'

Frances flushed with anger. 'That can hardly be your concern,' she snapped, then chided herself as she saw her uncle's grin widen. 'Besides, you should not judge all men by your own standards.'

The earl's smile faded as he looked down at George again. 'I wonder that your father should have bequeathed his estate to your boy, when he had sons of his own,' he said. 'Edward is a fine young man and has greater spirit than his father. He would have transformed Longford from a backwater into one of the greatest estates in the county.'

'Or run it into the ground,' Frances countered. 'He has already depleted the revenues with his extravagance. I just hope he will not ruin it entirely before George reaches his majority.'

'That is the least of your worries, niece. If George proves as troublesome as his mother, he will lose Longford altogether. A traitor's property is forfeit to the Crown, is it not?'

'Then it is well that my son has been raised a dutiful subject, Uncle.'

The earl's brow creased into a deep frown. 'I hope you speak the truth, niece — for your son's sake, as well as Longford's.'

He turned away as if suddenly bored.

Frances closed her eyes, feigning sleep to avoid any further conversation. God willing, they would soon reach Whitehall.

'I am sorry about your father, Frances.' Elizabeth's concern was clearly genuine.

'Thank you, Your Grace,' Frances replied, with a deep curtsy. Behind her mistress, Blanche shifted uncomfortably.

'But I cannot deny that I am glad to have you back,' the princess added, with a shy smile. 'I have missed you.'

Frances felt joy at her words, the first she had experienced since that night at Richmond. 'I am eager to hear what has passed during my absence. You must have had many diversions, with Prince Gustavus still residing here.' She caught a fleeting look of unease on the princess's face.

'I have had a great deal to occupy my thoughts,' the young woman replied quietly. 'But the prince is away from court at present. My brother has taken him hunting.'

Frances watched her for a few moments, considering. 'Perhaps Your Grace would also like to take the air,' she said. 'It is a fine day — the warmest one yet this spring. We could ride out to the old deer park.'

Elizabeth brightened at once. 'What an excellent idea!' she cried, leaping to her feet. 'Blanche, tell the grooms to prepare the horses. Frances and I will be at the stables as soon as we have changed our attire.'

Blanche hesitated. 'Am I to accompany you too, Your Grace?' she asked, darting a

241

look at Frances.

'There is no need,' the princess said, distracted. She was already riffling through her wardrobe. 'Besides, you are not as accomplished a rider as Frances so would only slow us down.'

Blanche pursed her lips and left the room.

As soon as she had helped her mistress into her riding boots, Frances hastened to her own apartment to make ready. Though she had suggested the ride as a means of gaining some time alone with the princess, her heart soared at the prospect of galloping through the park, breathing in the fresh, sweet air of spring.

A few minutes later she was at the stables, where the princess was already climbing into the saddle. She soon mounted the horse that had been prepared for her and they trotted off through the courtyard, which echoed with the sound of hoofs clipping on the cobbles.

There were many cries of 'God save Your Grace!' as they rode through the crowded streets. Elizabeth acknowledged every one, gracefully inclining her head and smiling. She would have made a fine queen, Frances reflected. God willing, she might still.

As soon as they had passed through the gates of Hyde Park, the princess dug her heels into the horse's flanks and galloped away, Frances following. The sweet tang of blackthorn filled her nostrils as she raced across the park, her hair whipping about her face. She closed her eyes, her senses alive with the freedom of being out in the open air, far from the stifling confines of Whitehall.

Focusing again on the horizon, she could see that the princess was pulling up her horse. Slowing her own to a canter, she drew level with her.

'Oh, Frances!' Elizabeth exclaimed, her eyes sparkling. 'I feel happier than I have in weeks.'

'As do I, Your Grace.' Frances beamed. 'Now that the weather has turned, we must ride out as often as we can.'

The princess nodded enthusiastically and reached over to clasp her hand. 'You always knew what would do me good, Frances,' she said. 'I have never had a friend such as you. I am sorry that I treated you harshly when you first returned to court.'

Frances smiled. 'It was I who was at fault, for leaving you so suddenly. I had little choice, but it grieved me sorely to think that you might suppose I did not care.'

Elizabeth looked towards the woodland that lay on the eastern edge of the park. 'I cannot think of that time without sorrow. I was a fool to be so easily deceived by those traitors.'

Frances chose her words carefully. 'You were not deceived. Catesby and his associates loved you truly and wanted only to serve you.'

'By murdering my father and brothers!' the princess cried.

Her horse shook his mane and whinnied, and she pulled sharply on the reins. 'How can you speak of them so favourably?'

Frances knew she must have a care. 'Forgive me, Your Grace. I did not mean that their crimes were not abhorrent, only that their intentions towards you were honourable — though horribly misguided.'

'Perhaps,' Elizabeth said uncertainly. 'But Henry says they will be burning in Hell, in the very fires they would have whipped up to destroy him and our father.' She bit her lip. 'Though I know he is right to rejoice in this, it grieves me sorely to think of it, Frances.'

Frances felt a surge of hope. She had supposed her mistress to be entirely in thrall to her beloved brother, but her true feelings clearly ran contrary to her outward obedience. 'And I too,' she said earnestly, 'though I cannot think that God would punish those whose faith was so strong.'

The princess gave her a long appraising look. 'You loved him, didn't you?'

For a moment, Frances considered feigning ignorance, but she knew it would be in vain. Though the princess had been little more than a child at the time, she was old enough to understand such things now. Besides, Frances had no wish to destroy the trust that had begun to flower between them again. Slowly, she inclined her head.

Elizabeth gave a sad smile. 'He loved you too — that was obvious to anyone with eyes.' Then: 'But you knew nothing of their schemes, did you?'

'Of course not, Your Grace,' Frances lied, looking down at the reins that were now slack in her hands. She patted her horse's neck.

'Though I know what you must have suffered by his treachery, I cannot but envy you,' the princess said.

Frances's head jerked up.

'You know what it is to love, and to be truly loved in return,' her mistress continued. 'I fear that I am not destined to enjoy the same good fortune.'

Elizabeth pressed her lips tightly together as if to stop herself saying more. Her eyes were filled with such sorrow that Frances was overcome with pity — remorse, too. She had been so intent upon using the princess's marriage to further the Catholic cause that she had given little thought to her personal happiness. In this, she was little better than the girl's father or brother, who looked upon her as a chattel to be bestowed as it suited them.

'You must not marry against your own inclinations, Your Grace,' Frances said softly. 'Though I know you wish to please the prince your brother, he would not wish to condemn you to a life of misery. Besides, many other suitors clamour for your hand, some of whom promise even greater riches than the Swedish prince.' She prayed her voice held more conviction than she felt.

'But Henry is resolved upon this match and will not be swayed from it. He thinks Gustavus possesses all the qualities that should be looked for in a suitor.'

'And what do *you* think of him, ma'am?' Frances ventured.

'I think him a bore and a brute!' she exclaimed, with sudden passion. 'I know I shall never love him.' She buried her head in her hands.

Frances drew her horse closer so that she could reach out and clasp the girl's hand in her own. 'Then you cannot marry him,' she said firmly. 'You must speak to the king your father. If he will not be persuaded by reasons of the heart, then employ those of the mind.'

Elizabeth raised her tear-stained face.

'Already there are murmurs against the match among your father's council,' Frances continued. 'They say it would bring dishonour upon this kingdom to ally with a country that is at war with his brother-in-law, the King of Denmark. If you join your voice to theirs, he will listen.'

Frances could see the princess's thoughts racing as she gazed back at her. Sensing her advantage, she pressed on: 'The queen will be our ally in this. As soon as you have planted the seed in your father's mind, she can speak to Prince Henry and insist that her honour will be compromised if he persists with the match. By these means — if we are patient — you will be spared a husband who can never make you happy.'

The princess's mouth lifted into a tentative smile. 'Thank you, Frances,' she whispered. 'I pray God it will turn out as you say.'

CHAPTER 18
3 MAY

Frances watched as Prince Henry downed the contents of his glass. His usually pale complexion was flushed, his hair dishevelled. Leaning across to Sir John, he laughed uproariously and slammed his palm down so hard on the table that it shook. The king shot a furious look at his son, but Henry seemed not to notice.

'The prince is in high spirits tonight.'

Though her husband's tone was light, Frances caught the concern in his eyes. She made no comment, helping herself to more of the capon. The feast was plentiful this evening. It had been intended to serve Gustavus and his entourage, as well as James's court, but they had left early that morning. The marriage negotiations had broken off the previous evening, the king declaring that for as long as Sweden remained at war with his wife's native land he could not consider an alliance. Henry had stood at his right side, sullen and resentful. To the left, his sister had kept her gaze fixed upon the floor. Frances had seen her shoulders sink with relief when Gustavus had bowed abruptly to her father and stridden out of the room, without bidding his intended bride farewell.

'How is your mistress?' Thomas asked.

Frances finished her mouthful. 'Her Grace is saddened, of course,' she said, not quite meeting her husband's eye. 'She has wept a great deal since last night and was too grieved to attend this evening's entertainments.'

That at least was true, though the source of Elizabeth's grief was not as most of those present supposed.

'I had not thought her so enamoured of the prince,' Thomas observed, 'but the secrets of women's hearts have always confounded the inferior sex. Perhaps Her Grace is grieving for a different reason.'

Frances forced herself to hold his gaze. They had not spoken of the matter after retiring to their chamber last night, though the rest of the court could talk of nothing else. She had allowed herself to hope that Thomas was content not to question the king's reason for rejecting the proposed match. She had been careful to avoid raising her husband's suspicions since her meeting with Anne Vaux, but she knew he still wondered at the cause of her absence in the middle of the night.

'The princess has a tender heart and is saddened that her brother's hopes are dashed — though she was hardly the cause,' she added quickly.

Thomas reached out and clasped his wife's hand. 'Are you sure that is all, Frances?'

His words were drowned in a sudden cacophony on the king's table. The prince had stood so abruptly that his chair had toppled off the dais, clattering onto the flagstones below. He was glaring at his father with undisguised fury. 'You treat me like a child!' he cried, fists clenched at his sides.

The king let out a bark of laughter. 'That's because you act like one,' he replied scornfully.

Beside him, Cecil smirked, his dark eyes flitting around the room. The company had descended into a deathly silence and everyone's gaze was fixed upon the dais. Frances was thankful that her mistress was not there. The poor girl's nerves were already in shreds after a bitter encounter with her brother, when he had upbraided her for defying him.

James continued to stare at his son, apparently oblivious to his gaping courtiers. A slow smile crept across his lips. 'I had a mind to make you Prince of Wales at last, but I see that you are still not ready for such an honour.'

Henry's face whitened. The whole court knew how impatient he was for the title that had been his right since his father had taken the English throne. He had made little secret of it, railing against his lack of authority to anyone who would listen.

William Cecil reached out a hand as if to restrain his master, but the prince batted it angrily away. He opened his mouth as if to speak, but then turned and strode from the platform instead, swiping at the table as he passed. The hall echoed with the sound of shattering glass.

James raised his cup in a mocking gesture to the prince's retreating form, then drained its contents. A trail of the ruby liquid slid from one side of his mouth, glistening in the light of the sconces. 'God save the prince!' he slurred.

The courtiers looked at each other in bemusement. A few echoed the king's words, but the rest remained silent. Several minutes passed before a low hum of chatter rose once more.

Frances and her husband resumed their meal. She ate slowly, picking at the array of dishes in front of them, glad of the distraction they provided.

'Forgive me, Lady Frances.'

She started at the soft voice behind her. She had not noticed Jane Drummond approaching — the woman seemed to glide noiselessly around the court. Frances glanced at her husband and caught his mortification before he lowered his gaze.

'The princess is asking for you,' the young woman said, her eyes fixed upon Frances.

Frances dabbed at her mouth with a linen napkin then rose to her feet, aware that her husband was watching her closely. 'Thank you,' she said coldly. 'I will attend her at once.'

Jane Drummond walked briskly away. Frances made to follow her but the young woman was soon out of sight.

'I will escort you there,' Thomas said, rising quickly to his feet.

'There is no need,' Frances replied curtly. 'I will not be long. The hour is late and my mistress will soon retire. Please,' she urged, when he hesitated, 'stay and finish your meal.'

She swept away before he could protest,

quickening her pace as she weaved through the long tables of diners, who were now engaged in such animated talk that they did not look up as she passed.

When she reached the courtyard that lay behind the great hall, she took a deep, cleansing breath of the cool evening air. The moon cast its silvery shadow across the cloisters that ran along each side of the quadrangle, illuminating the ornately carved stonework above the archways. Crossing to the opposite corner, her soft leather soles making no sound on the cobbles, worn smooth by the footsteps of many thousands of courtiers, she wondered briefly if she should collect some tinctures from her apartment first, in case the princess was ill. But she dismissed the thought. Even though she had regained her mistress's trust, it would offer little protection if she was found to have reverted to her old ways. Blanche would be only too happy to twist her rival's healing into an accusation of sorcery and report it to Cecil — of that, she was certain.

Passing under the archway on the far side of the courtyard, Frances found herself plunged into darkness. The page had not yet lit the sconces — supposing, no doubt, that the feast would continue long into the night. As her eyes adjusted to the gloom, she reached out to touch the inner wall of the cloister to use it as her guide, but an icy hand gripped her wrist. She made to cry out but another hand was clamped over her mouth and she was pushed roughly back against the wall, the cold bricks pressing against her neck.

'Do not speak or I will stop your breath,' the man whispered, his breath hot against her face, his hand gripping her throat. He was much taller than Frances, and though she strained her eyes to make out his features, they were entirely in shadow. She could feel her pulse throbbing against his fingers, which were soft. Gentleman's hands.

After a long moment, he relaxed his grip but kept his fingers close to her throat while his other hand still clasped her wrist. Frances tried to quell her fear, though her legs felt as if they would collapse.

'You have performed a great service by getting rid of the Swedish fool,' he continued. 'The princess would have married him to please her brother, had it not been for your persuasions.'

Frances opened her mouth to protest but he pressed his fingers to it. 'Now you must perform an even greater one.'

Whose schemes had she become involved

with now? Was this the plot Raleigh had hinted at?

'England will soon be saved from heresy by another marriage,' he continued.

Even though he spoke quietly, his voice was laced with excitement and Frances thought she caught the flash of a smile.

The King of Spain's nephew must have embarked for England. She had not wanted to speak to the princess of another marriage so soon, but she must find a way, before the prince reached these shores. Her mind raced on, despite the terror that consumed her.

'The negotiations for the princess's hand are as nothing to this — though they provide a useful distraction,' he said, 'and while the eyes of the court are focused upon the husband that milksop the prince will choose, a far greater alliance will have been forged.'

Frances stared at the dark outline of his face as she struggled to understand his words. *Another alliance? Surely Catholic hopes rested upon the princess alone.*

'Our plans are now almost in place. We await only the court's return to Greenwich, where my mistress resides.'

'The queen?' Frances whispered.

He pressed his fingers to her lips again. She inhaled the sharp tang of tobacco. 'No

— though my mistress will be called by that name soon enough.'

A shaft of moonlight pierced the gloom, illuminating his handsome features. Frances gasped as she recognised the serious young man she had seen at the Swedish prince's reception two months earlier. His sensuous mouth curled into a slow smile and his eyes glittered as he gazed down at her.

'William Seymour,' he said, and made an exaggerated bow.

Seymour. The name had been synonymous with royalty from the time that the virtuous Lady Jane had become King Henry's third wife. Though her triumph had been brief, her family had hankered after the Crown ever since. This latest scion was as blinded by the same ambition as his grandfather, who had married Lady Katherine Grey in secret. Frances's mother had told her of the scandal. Far from winning him the Crown, it had landed him in the Tower at the old queen's orders. Clearly William had learned nothing from his grandfather's example.

'Who is your mistress?' Frances asked, though she already knew the name before he spoke it.

His smile broadened. 'Arbella Stuart.'

Frances tried to order her thoughts. 'And what has this to do with me?'

'You will be our witness,' he said simply.

Frances stared up at him, incredulous. Why had they chosen her from all the courtiers who thronged the chambers of the royal palaces? She had not spoken a word to either of them until tonight.

'We are assured that you can be trusted,' he continued, as if reading her thoughts. 'God knows there are few others here who can boast the same qualification.'

Assured by whom? Frances thought at once of Lady Vaux. But then she remembered the look in the woman's eyes when she had mentioned the wider plot to which Raleigh had referred. Frances wondered whether her net was cast as wide as she liked to claim.

'I cannot imagine who told you that, Lord Seymour, but I assure you I am the king's faithful subject.'

His eyes lit with amusement. 'I have been at the card tables all evening and have no patience for more games, my lady,' he said, any trace of humour gone. 'You know as well as I that you are up to your neck in treason.' He took a step closer and trailed his fingers across the smooth skin of her throat. 'One word from me in the king's ear and he would gladly see it snapped,' he murmured, clicking his fingers so suddenly that she jumped back.

'I have committed no crime against His Majesty since coming to court,' Frances muttered, as soon as her breathing had slowed.

'Not on this visit, perhaps.'

Seymour's eyes never left hers as his words echoed into silence. He could not know about her involvement in the Powder Treason, about Tom. And yet something in his steady gaze told her he knew everything.

'It is treason for those of the royal blood to marry without their sovereign's consent,' Frances said. 'Why do you suppose I would hazard my life for your sakes?'

His smile did not falter. 'Ah, but there are other lives at risk aside from yours, are there not, Lady Frances? Your son is a fine boy. What a pity it would be if he were to wither suddenly on the vine.'

Frances's breath caught and she gripped the wall behind her. 'My son has no more to do with this than I shall!' she cried.

Seymour lunged forward and clamped his hand over her mouth again, pressing her so hard against the wall that she feared her skull might break. She struggled for breath as he held her there, his grip tightening.

Leaning towards her so that his lips almost touched her ear, he murmured, 'I shall send word when the time is ripe. You will not fail us.' He released his grip.

Frances stumbled forward and felt a sharp pain as her knees hit the cobbles. Panting, she watched his slender frame disappear into the gloom.

CHAPTER 19
22 MAY

George darted between the rose bushes, their heavy blooms obscuring him from view, as Jack, another member of the young prince's household, raced after him. Frances was glad that her boy had made a friend at last. These past few weeks, he had been happier than she had seen him since their arrival at court, and she could almost believe that they were settling into a steady and harmonious routine.

'You are pensive again today, Frances.'

Her husband's voice intruded upon her thoughts. She cast him a glance and saw that he was watching her with the familiar look of concern that she had intercepted many times lately. Though she had tried not to show the turmoil she had felt since that encounter with Seymour, Thomas always seemed to sense when she was hiding something.

'I worry for George,' she said, deciding to

stay as close to the truth as possible.

They turned in the direction of the child, whose high-pitched shrieks echoed around the garden as Jack wrestled him to the grass.

'But he is clearly thriving now and no longer pines for Tyringham Hall as he once did,' her husband reasoned. 'Children are much more accepting of changed circumstances than adults.'

George and his friend were now charging along the pathways between the plant beds.

'Perhaps,' she said. 'You must forgive an anxious mother. We naturally fear the worst.'

'And what of you, Frances?' he asked. 'You seem troubled. I know it has been a difficult few weeks, since your father . . .' He trailed off, as if regretting saying that much.

Frances felt an unexpected surge of affection. God knew there were few enough men at court who shared her husband's gentle nature. His mention of her father also caused her a pang of guilt: she had hardly thought of him over the past few days. 'I am well enough,' she replied, forcing a smile. 'Or as well as I can be, so far from the country. Masques and assemblies are a poor substitute for the fields and woodlands of Buckinghamshire.'

Respect for her husband compelled her to

name his home, rather than the one she really craved. *Longford.* Her heart contracted as she thought of her brother Edward there, striving to ruin the estate before her son could inherit.

'Perhaps I could persuade the king to release you from duty for a few weeks, so that you might take some rest. He is already planning another hunt so I will have ample opportunity.'

The prospect of escaping from court, its troubles and dangers, was appealing, and for a moment Frances was tempted. But even before she began to imagine being in the tranquillity of the Tyringham estate, she knew it was impossible. Cecil's spies had followed her there before and would do so again. As would Seymour. His eyes flashed before her again, and she felt the terror she had experienced that night. No, she must remain here and do his bidding, for George's sake. Besides, she had work of her own to accomplish with the princess's marriage. Not for the first time, she was trapped in an endless maze, with no prospect of escape.

'You are kinder than I deserve, but my duty lies here with the princess,' she replied. 'I cannot abandon her so soon after Prince Gustavus's departure. She is still racked with guilt and grief.'

'Better that than suffer a marriage without affection,' her husband said, almost to himself.

They walked on, and soon Frances's eyes were drawn to a flurry of activity ahead, where a dozen or more gardeners were hurriedly digging. As she and her husband drew level with them, Frances noticed a row of small shrubs lined up against the wall.

'You are admiring my new arrivals, Lady Frances?'

She and her husband turned sharply at the king's voice and swept a deep obeisance. Neither had heard him approach, as he was only sparsely attended. As she raised her eyes, Frances saw a groom standing two paces behind his sovereign. To James's right was the smiling Robert Carr, who gave the slightest of nods towards them.

'Your Majesty, forgive us.' Thomas spoke before his wife could reply. 'We did not mean to trespass upon your privacy.'

James waved away his apology. 'Dinnae trouble yeself, Tyringham. Rabbie and I wanted to see how my gardeners are progressing.' He looked across at the men, who had all ceased digging and were standing, heads bowed. 'Well, get on wi' it!' he cried irritably. 'The berries will wither on their branches if ye dinnae make haste.'

At once, the gardeners returned to their labours, digging even more frantically than before.

'Your hounds are made ready for the hunt, Your Grace,' Thomas said, deflecting his master's attention.

James grunted. 'They'll need to wait a while yet,' he muttered. 'Cecil has urged me to delay our journey until after the prince has been ennobled.'

So Henry was to have his wish after all and be made Prince of Wales, Frances thought. The king seemed to alter his course as often as his favourites.

'A most wise decision, Your Grace.' Carr simpered. 'This country sets great store by its titles and ceremonies. Your subjects here will surely be content for a while if you indulge them — though they little deserve it,' he added, with a sneer.

The king reached over and stroked the man's cheek. With a deft move, Carr turned and kissed his palm. Frances hoped the shock had not shown on her face. The old queen had excited enough gossip by tickling the neck of her favourite, Robert Dudley, as he knelt to receive a knighthood. How much more scandalised would Elizabeth's courtiers have been by her successor?

'When will the ceremony be held, Your Grace?' Thomas asked, his face a perfect mask of composure.

'In two weeks — or more, if my little Beagle has his way. I'll wager he intends to use it as a means of keeping me at court.'

Frances wondered if Cecil had grown used to the nickname his royal master had assigned to him. She rather hoped he had not.

'Such occasions require a great deal of organisation,' Thomas said tactfully. 'No doubt it will be attended by all of Your Grace's nobles and bishops, as well as those who reside here at court.'

'To Hell with that!' James shouted. 'Half of them would have had me blown to the heavens — still would, if my council's reports are true.'

He fixed his glare on Frances. She blanched as she lowered her gaze to the ground. A quick glance to her left revealed that George and his companion were hiding behind a rose bush. They had scampered there as soon as the king had arrived. She prayed they would not stir.

'There will always be those foolish enough to conspire for the Crown, Your Grace,' Carr said soothingly.

Frances did not dare to look up and see whether he, too, was staring at her.

'But your faithful subjects are far greater in number and will rejoice to see your son created Prince of Wales,' the young man added.

The king grunted again. 'Ill-deserving wretch,' he muttered under his breath. 'I wouldn't wonder if he petitioned me to invite his friend Raleigh. God knows he visits him often enough.'

Frances was holding her breath. James must know that she and the princess had accompanied Henry on one of those visits. Sir William Wade would have been quick to convey the news, she was sure.

'Your Grace has had reason to be vexed by your children of late,' Carr remarked slyly.

'Aye!' his master exclaimed. 'Lizzie was always a dutiful daughter, but even she has become obstinate. Well, she will learn soon enough that a woman does not have the freedom to choose her own husband.'

Frances tried to focus upon the spidery green stem of a weed that had forced its way through the gravel of the path. She could feel James's eyes upon her. Did he know of her part in persuading his daughter to defy him?

'Tell me, Your Grace, what are the saplings that your gardeners are planting? I have

266

never seen their like in this country.'

She shot a look of gratitude at her husband.

'Ah, these are more than saplings, Tyringham,' the king said, brightening at once. 'They will rescue this kingdom's fortunes, eh, Rabbie?'

Carr was preening himself, like one of his master's peacocks. 'Indeed, your Grace,' he replied.

James waited, evidently enjoying the interest on the faces of Frances and her husband. 'For too many years, the French have enjoyed the monopoly of the silk trade,' he began. 'No doubt their new king looks forward to filling his treasury with the profits, just as Henri did. Well, he is a fool.' He reached forward and plucked one of the dark green leaves. 'The silkworm is a particular creature and will only feast upon one thing.' He paused so that his words might take full effect. '*Morus negra,*' he said proudly. 'Black mulberry.'

Carr clapped his hands together gleefully and gave a high-pitched laugh. 'And so by cultivating the tree here in England, His Grace will be able to produce that precious commodity on a far greater scale than King Louis.' He beamed. 'It is with justice that you are called the wisest king in

Christendom.'

Frances looked at both men, understanding dawning. 'What an ingenious plan, Your Grace,' she said, with exaggerated deference. 'No wonder you have brought over so many.'

'Ha!' the king exclaimed scornfully. 'There are a great many more than you see here. I have had a four-acre field by St James's Park cleared so that the rest can be planted. All ten thousand of them,' he added, with satisfaction.

Frances struggled to maintain her composure. 'Then I hope they prosper — and your plans too, Your Grace.'

But James wasn't listening. He had turned towards his favourite and was toying with one of the buttons on his doublet. 'I think we have earned a small celebration,' he whispered to Carr, who smiled coyly.

Without troubling to take their leave, the two men walked swiftly back towards the palace, the king's groom following in their wake.

As soon as they had disappeared from sight, Frances burst into a fit of laughter. Thomas turned to her in surprise. 'What on earth can have made you so merry?' he asked, smiling.

'It is a pity the king condemns as witches

268

those skilled in the art of healing,' she said, when at last she was able to speak. 'If he did not, perhaps he might have sought our advice before emptying his coffers to buy all these trees.'

'Surely the king is not in error. I know little of plants myself, but even I have heard that silkworms feed on mulberries.'

'Indeed they do,' Frances replied, looking out across the long line of saplings that the gardeners were now beginning to plant. She turned back to her husband, her eyes still glistening with mirth. '*White* mulberries.'

CHAPTER 20
4 JUNE

'Be still, George,' Frances whispered, as she placed a restraining hand on her son's shoulder.

The curls at the nape of his neck were damp with sweat and he pulled at the collar of his shirt as if trying to free himself from it. Frances could feel a trickle of sweat running down her back. She drew her shoulder blades together so that the tightly laced bodice lifted away from her skin.

The lofty hall at Westminster had provided welcome respite from the oppressive heat outside, but the press of bodies had soon caused the temperature to rise. It had occasioned some surprise when the king had announced that the ceremony would take place in the Court of Requests, rather than the far larger main hall of the palace. While Frances was thankful not to have had to return to the place of Tom's trial, she wished that a more spacious hall had been chosen.

But this was one restraint that James had insisted upon. He would rather have had no ceremony at all, but Cecil had persuaded him of the political advantages to be gained from putting on a show of Stuart splendour.

Frances could not help but be impressed by the magnificence of the occasion. She had never seen such lavish decorations, even at the old queen's court, which generally far outshone that of her successor. She had heard several guests remark that it was like a coronation, and she could believe that this was no exaggeration. The stone walls were hung with richly embroidered arras, the gold thread picked out by the candles that blazed in the sconces above. A carpet of deep purple had been laid along the entire length of the aisle, and at the end of each row of seats a plume of feathers floated atop a golden pole, representing the prince's new title. Contrary to what the king had said that day in the garden, all of the nobility had turned out to pay homage to their prince, and Frances was dazzled by cloth of gold, cobalt silks and ruby red satins.

A cheer rose from the crowds that had assembled outside the hall. Everyone turned expectantly towards the great oak doors, which were now flung open. Frances shielded her eyes against the bright sunlight that flooded the hall. Silhouetted against it, she could make out the stooped figure of the king, a large crown balanced precariously on his head. His legs appeared even more bowed than usual, as if he was struggling under the weight of his finery. Robert Carr walked half a pace behind him, stooping occasionally to fuss over his master's train.

The queen followed in their wake. Frances knew how much the long walk must pain her, but Anne betrayed no hint of it as she held herself erect, an elegant and dignified contrast to the king, who seemed to stamp as he walked, like an angry child. The princess was breathtakingly beautiful in the ivory satin gown that Frances had chosen for her that morning. She bore herself with the same dignity as her mother. Frances felt a surge of affection and pride as she watched her gracefully acknowledge the courtiers on either side of her as she passed. She had called for Frances earlier than usual, unable to sleep because of her terror at the prospect of being seen in public for the first time since Gustavus's departure.

'They will look upon me with loathing,' she had sobbed, 'just as Henry does now.'

Frances had known better than to reason with her, but had carefully prepared her gown and jewels, then dressed her slowly, hoping that the familiar ritual would eventually calm her. By the time that Elizabeth had been escorted from her rooms by one of her father's grooms, her hands had ceased to tremble and she had even ventured a smile as she bade Frances farewell.

The princess was holding the hand of her younger brother Charles, who looked a good deal less assured. Frances watched as his eyes darted nervously across the crowds. Though he could now easily walk unaided, his gait was still awkward and his thin legs, like his father's, were slightly bowed.

When the royal party had taken their seats on the dais that had been specially built for the ceremony, the courtiers looked back to the entrance. A few moments passed, yet still there was no sign of the prince. A low hum of animated whispers echoed around the hall as they began to speculate on the reasons for Henry's absence. Perhaps he had quarrelled with his father again and decided to snub the occasion. Or some accident had befallen him on his way to Westminster.

George looked up at his mother in alarm. Frances smiled down at him and gave his shoulder a reassuring squeeze. She suspected the prince was simply biding his time so that his arrival would achieve the greatest possible impact. Thomas was on the opposite side of the dais. She caught his eye and he smiled, as if to assure her that he was unconcerned.

At that moment, a fanfare of trumpets rang out across the hall, causing many of those present to start. Frances turned back towards the doors and saw Prince Henry standing on the threshold, surveying the throng as if they were his subjects, not his father's. He was dressed in cloth of silver that dripped with jewels, and from his shoulders was suspended a long train lined with ermine.

After a long pause, he made his stately progress along the aisle. Though he knew all eyes were upon him, he kept his own fixed straight ahead. George craned his neck to get a better view.

The prince was now mounting the steps of the dais.

'In the name of the Father, and of the Son, and of the Holy Ghost . . .' The sonorous voice of Archbishop Bancroft echoed around the hall and the courtiers took their seats. He was elderly now and his shoulders were even more hunched than they had been when Frances had last seen him. His beard was still the colour of dark mahogany, though, and there was no trace of grey.

There was a long pause before the ceremony of investiture began. Frances looked across the aisle to Thomas, whose gaze was now on the prince, kneeling before his father. She was about to turn back towards the dais when she saw, a few rows behind her husband, a solemn-faced young man staring directly at her.

Seymour.

Her blood ran cold. She had not seen him for several weeks, and Arbella had appeared only seldom at court since Gustavus's reception in Greenwich. Frances had begun to hope that Cecil or one of his informants had thwarted their plans and that she would therefore escape any involvement. Now she feared not.

Frances held Seymour's gaze. His expression did not alter as he stared at her. A small movement at the edge of her vision made her turn. Thomas was watching her too. Frances forced herself to focus upon the ceremony of investiture that was now well under way on the dais.

'I, Henry, do become your liege man of life and limb and of earthly worship, and faith and truth I bear unto you, to live and die against all manner of folk.'

Though he was in his seventeenth year, the prince still spoke with the same shrill voice that Frances remembered from her first meeting with him. She wondered if it would deepen in time. It was hard to imagine him commanding a parliament or an army if he still sounded like a child. She smiled at the thought that a king whom his subjects could not understand would be succeeded by one they could not respect. God willing, she would help to spare them that fate.

The king was now standing over his son and placing a ring on his outstretched finger. Frances saw Henry wince as his father forced the bejewelled band over his delicate flesh. He then handed his son a sword with a ruby at its halberd that glittered in the light from the high windows. Finally, and with great solemnity, the aged archbishop passed the coronet to his sovereign. James lifted it above his son's head, then held it suspended, as if taunting him. Henry kept perfectly still, but Frances noticed a red flush creep up the back of his neck. At last his father lowered the coronet onto his head and the prince stood to face the assembled throng. He reminded Frances of a child who had been allowed to try on his father's clothes.

Archbishop Bancroft rose unsteadily to his feet and read out the investiture oath — first in Latin, then in English. When his words had echoed into silence, the prince gave a stiff bow towards the throne, then walked slowly down the aisle. Two yeomen of the guard opened the heavy oak doors as he approached, flooding the crowded hall with bright sunlight. A loud cheer rose as Henry stood at the top of the steps. Frances could just make out his slender form as, slowly, he turned from side to side, raising his hand in salute.

The rest of the royal party began to leave the dais, followed by the lords of the council. Frances stared resolutely forward as her uncle passed. She knew he was looking in her direction but could not bear to see him, self-satisfied in his robes of office. Behind him walked the Earl of Worcester, with his neatly trimmed white beard and pale grey eyes, which flicked from side to side, as if searching for a hidden assassin. Frances wondered idly whether his wife was still a favourite with her uncle. No doubt he lusted after younger flesh, these days.

As she watched the other councillors progress towards the doors, she realised that Cecil had not been among them. Instinctively, she looked behind her, as if expecting to see him there, watching her. But the only faces she saw were those of the ladies of the household, who were studying the procession of other dignitaries following the lords.

Where was he?

Perhaps his absence had something to do with Arbella. Frances had not seen her among the crowds either. She looked across and realised that Seymour had gone. She must calm herself, order her thoughts according to logic not fear, as her father had taught her. Cecil had invested an enormous amount of time and energy in preparing for this day. Even if he had uncovered Seymour's scheme, he would not choose this moment to pounce.

'Mama!' George was tugging impatiently at her sleeve. 'We must hurry or we will miss the prince.'

She felt an unexpected jolt of unease at her son's eagerness, but smiled down at him. 'We will see him at Whitehall, for the investiture feast,' she said. 'And there will be many celebrations to follow. I wouldn't wonder if you had tired of the sight of him by the time they are over.'

'Never!' George protested. 'He is the best prince in the world and will be my king one day.'

Perhaps.

Her son had already darted along the row of seats. She was hard-pressed to keep up with him as he scurried down the now crowded aisle, weaving between the brightly coloured skirts and silken hose. By the time she reached the small chapel that lay to the east of the nave, just before the main doors, she had lost sight of him.

'George!' she called, but her voice could hardly be heard above the excited chatter as the courtiers made their way out of the hall.

All of a sudden, she was being jostled towards the chapel. 'Lady Frances, please — come this way.'

Frances knew the voice before she saw him at her side, steering her firmly towards the small doorway. She was about to turn and walk away when she saw her son crouched on the floor of the chapel. She ran towards him and heard the door close behind her.

'George!' She scooped him into her arms.

He wriggled to be free, and Frances saw that a cluster of tiny bones and a bright red ball lay at his feet. Jacks. Her son had loved the game ever since Thomas had presented him with his first set the previous New Year.

'Go ahead, young master — see how you fare.'

She could hear the smile in Seymour's

voice before she turned to him. He was leaning against the door, his arms crossed. Casting a quick glance at George, who was now engrossed in the game, she walked over to Seymour. 'How dare you take my son?' she hissed.

The young man shrugged, clearly amused. 'I did not take him. He gladly followed,' he replied, flashing a smile at the boy. 'You should be more careful with him, lest he fall into the wrong hands. The court is full of villains, Lady Frances. One of them wears a crown.'

Frances glared at him, fear and fury rising in her breast. 'You will not touch him again. He has nothing to do with your twisted schemes,' she spat.

Seymour's smile broadened. 'Ah, but he does, Lady Frances — as you well know.' He glanced again at George. 'But so long as you play your part, no harm shall come to him.'

She fought the urge to lash out at him. Her breathing was rapid and she could feel her face burning, but she kept her gaze fixed upon him.

'God is smiling on us this day,' he continued at length. 'We have seen the prince ennobled, and we will soon have cause for further celebration.' He lowered his voice.

'Everything is made ready. The nuptials will take place as soon as the court moves to Greenwich two weeks hence. Let us hope that the king's little Beagle has not recovered by then. He would not be a welcome guest.'

'What has happened to him?'

'He has taken to his bed, complaining of stomach pains. Perhaps the lamprey had not been well enough salted or the Burgundy wine was too strong for his palate.' He smirked.

Frances stared in horror. *Had Seymour had him poisoned?*

Before she could reply, he continued, 'You will receive word of the time and place. Do not think to betray us. You know what you would hazard.'

She turned to follow his gaze. George had stopped playing and was staring at them, an uncertain smile on his lips.

'It was a pleasure to make your acquaintance, Master Tyringham,' Seymour said, as he made an elaborate bow. 'I hope we will meet again.'

George scrambled to his feet but the man was already striding towards the door, which slammed behind him.

Chapter 21
22 June

Frances padded silently along the corridor, heart pounding. The candle she held was guttering as she quickened her pace so she shielded it with her other hand. Though she knew Greenwich Palace well, she had only a vague notion of where Arbella's apartment lay and could not hope to find it in the dark.

She had not slept that night, tormented by thoughts of what lay before her. George had been dreaming peacefully when she had stolen out of their room, entrusting his care to Mistress Knyvett, the woman her husband had appointed to attend them. Frances was glad that Thomas was away on the hunt. He had left two days after the prince's investiture, his royal master not troubling to stay for the stream of celebrations that had followed. But his departure had been a mixed blessing, leaving her feeling relieved . . . and bereft.

There was no time to dwell upon that

now. Ahead, she could see a soft light spilling out from underneath one of the doors that lined the passageway. She stopped and strained her ears for any noise within. But the only sound was of her rapid breathing.

She walked slowly forward, pausing again outside the door. She closed her eyes briefly and uttered a silent prayer, then softly tapped on it. She heard a chair scraping on the flagstones, followed by footsteps, which seemed to pause on the other side of the door. Frances held her breath.

'Who is it?'

Seymour's voice.

'Lady Frances.'

She heard the latch being lifted and Seymour opened the door a crack, peering through it to make sure she was alone, then pulling her quickly inside.

The chamber was dimly lit and only sparsely furnished — certainly less than Frances would have expected for one of Arbella's rank. A young man dressed in black sat by the fire, clutching the large wooden crucifix that hung about his neck. He stood as Frances entered. She saw her own fear reflected in his eyes, which kept darting behind her to the door, as if he was expecting Cecil's men to arrive at any moment.

'Is she here?' a woman's voice called from

an adjoining room.

Frances caught irritation on Seymour's face. He strode to the doorway that linked the two chambers and gestured impatiently for her to join them. A sharp yelp made Frances and the young priest start. It was followed by a scuffle, then Arbella emerged, a tiny white and brown lapdog in her arms. Her dress was jet-black, with a white lace collar and ruff that made her already pale complexion appear almost ghostly.

She stared at Frances, eyes narrowing. The deep lines around her mouth and across her brow made her appear older than her years, and as Seymour stood next to her Frances thought them more like mother and son than bride and groom.

'I wonder that my cousin allowed you back in his court, given your associations,' Arbella said abruptly. 'More fool him,' she added, with a sniff. She turned to Seymour. 'And you are sure she can be trusted?'

'Quite sure,' he replied earnestly. 'She knows what will follow if she betrays us.'

Frances thought of her son, so young and so vulnerable. She was his only protector now, but her actions had also placed him in great danger. If her part in this marriage should be discovered, she would forfeit her life — and Longford. James would hardly allow the son of a convicted traitor to hold onto such an inheritance. Aiding this union also threatened the plans she had so carefully advanced these past weeks for the princess's marriage. The thought was bitter and she tried to push it out of her mind, as she had many times since Seymour had first involved her in his plan. Pray God the King of Spain's nephew would arrive soon. His presence would give the Catholics hope and surely dash those of Seymour and his bride.

'We must begin,' the priest said hurriedly, glancing again towards the door. He drew a small missal from the pocket of his gown and held it with trembling fingers as he began to read the familiar words.

Frances hardly heard them as she stared at the grim-faced couple. She had never seen so little joy at a wedding, even the many that had been arranged between noble families to further the prospects, rather than the happiness, of bride and groom.

'. . . and therefore is not by any to be enterprised, nor taken in hand, unadvisedly, lightly, or wantonly, to satisfy men's carnal lusts and appetites, like brute beasts that have no understanding . . .'

She could not help smiling at these words. Surely they had never been so little required. She wondered if there would be any fruit from their union. Even if Seymour was prepared to set aside his obvious distaste to bed her, Arbella must be approaching the end of her childbearing years.

The couple began to repeat their vows as if by rote, like novices in a play. Arbella still clutched the little dog to her breast, and when Seymour tried to slide the ring onto her finger, the creature snapped at him and the gold band clattered to the floor. Cursing, Seymour stooped to pick it up. 'Put the wretched animal down!' he muttered.

For a moment Frances thought Arbella would refuse, but then she bent to kiss the dog's head and placed the wriggling creature gently on the rug by the fire.

Frances tried to imagine the couple sitting side by side on their thrones. The idea seemed ludicrous. For all his twisted, heretical beliefs, James's royal blood was pure, uncontested — even the old queen had acknowledged that. It might save his subjects' souls to be ruled by a Catholic queen, but with a claim as questionable as Arbella's, it would surely also plunge them into civil war.

The rest of the service was soon concluded, the priest uttering the words so quickly that they could hardly be distinguished from each other. 'O Lord, bless them both, and grant them to inherit thy everlasting kingdom; through Jesus Christ our Lord. Amen.'

'Amen,' Frances repeated softly, hoping they might inherit it before their schemes came to fruition.

Frances's eyelids were growing heavy as she tried to focus on the masque that was being played out before them. An elegant young lady dressed in silks of azure blue was emerging from the lake, which was fashioned from long strips of white gauze held at either end by the other players. They flapped and twisted it so that it rippled around her like water, the tiny glass beads that had been sewn onto it glittering as they caught the light. The effect was mesmerising.

Jonson had written the masque in anticipation of the prince's investiture — although Henry had ordered the first performance in January. He had been so delighted with it that there had been several more since then.

'You do not find the entertainment diverting, Lady Frances?'

Cecil was crouching next to her, his face close to her ear so that his words would not be overheard. She had not known he was there. The other lords were seated on the far side of the dais, and though a chair had been reserved for Cecil at the centre of the row, it had stood empty. She had assumed he still lay sick at Salisbury House.

'It is an excellent masque, my lord,' she replied, without turning her head.

A groom hurried over with a chair, which he placed behind Cecil. Frances heard him groan quietly as he raised himself onto it. Glancing at him now, she was shocked by how frail he was. His cheekbones showed sharp beneath his pallid skin, and there were dark shadows under his eyes. Frances could see that his chest was rising and falling in a rapid, jerking movement, and it was several moments before his breathing began to slow.

'I trust you are recovered?' she ventured.

Cecil waved away her concern. 'It was nothing, Lady Frances, just an imbalance of humours in my stomach.'

She resisted the urge to press him further, but knew it must have been a good deal more than that for him to miss the prince's investiture and all that had followed.

The thundering of drums reverberated around the hall, heralding the arrival of a troupe of heavily armoured knights. Frances and Cecil watched as they proceeded to engage in mock combat, their swords swooping and clashing. Prince Henry was sitting forward on his throne, his face alight with excitement. His sister was equally enthralled — although afraid, too: she shrank back with each new thrust and parry. Frances's eyes strayed to the group of courtiers sitting just beyond them. She had surveyed the room upon entering in the princess's train, but had not seen Seymour or his new wife. Their absence was a source of anxiety, as well as relief.

'It is well that the king is not here,' Cecil remarked. 'He has not the same stomach for violent sports as his son.'

'And yet he loves to hunt,' Frances replied sardonically.

'You are quite right, as ever, Lady Frances. Have you received news from Oatlands?' he added. 'Your husband must have little enough leisure to write.'

She nodded. 'All is well.'

Cecil gave a heavy sigh. 'If only it was here too.'

'What do you mean?' Frances asked sharply.

He held her gaze, his brow furrowed. 'I have received news of an intended marriage,' he replied quietly.

Frances felt her scalp prickle. 'The princess's?' she asked guilelessly.

Cecil slowly shook his head. 'No, though I

289

am sure that will happen soon enough. This one concerns the Lady Arbella.'

Frances forced herself to focus on the figure of Merlin, who had just made his entrance on the stage, dressed in a dazzling gown of deep blue edged with gold. His long white beard almost trailed on the floor, and as she tried to steady her breathing, she watched it sway while he began his long, moralising speech.

'Oh?' she replied at last. 'I did not think the Lady was inclined to marry. She might have taken a husband long before now.'

'Ah, but the hearts of those with royal blood are not so easily bestowed, Lady Frances. The Duke of Parma would have married her to one of his sons, but the old queen opposed it — little wonder, too, given that even as he treated for the lady's hand, he was lying ready with a vast fleet to join the Armada.'

'And you think there is another Catholic prince now?' Frances asked carefully.

'No, no — or not a foreign one, at least,' Cecil replied. 'The King of Poland was the last of those. No, I am told that Lady Arbella plans to marry someone closer to James's throne. I only hope that I can discover who it is before she is foolish enough to act.'

Frances tried to swallow but her throat felt as if it was being squeezed. 'Do you have any notion of who it might be?' she whispered.

A pause.

'Certain names have been suggested, of course,' he said eventually. 'I hope that whoever it is does not greatly value their life. Marrying a person of royal blood without the sovereign's consent is treason — for all involved.'

Frances made herself turn to him before she spoke. 'Then God speed your endeavours, my lord.'

CHAPTER 22
9 JULY

Frances sat bolt upright in bed and listened. There it was again: a volley of thuds that echoed along the corridor outside her apartment. Beside her, George gave a small moan. It was pitch black, but as she scrambled out of bed she caught the flare of a torch outside her window.

Feeling her way to the door, she opened it as quietly as she could and came face to face with Mistress Knyvett. The light from the old woman's candle illuminated her panic-stricken eyes and deathly pallor, making her appear like some ghoul that was stalking the palace. Steering her back into the parlour and closing the door behind her, Frances strained to listen.

Another thunderous volley sounded in the distance.

'Open this door, in the name of the king!'

The voice was muffled. Too far away to be at her door, Frances realised with relief. She felt Mistress Knyvett tremble and gave her shoulder a reassuring squeeze, then padded quietly to the door and pressed her ear to it.

'What is the meaning of this?'

Another man's voice this time. Even at a distance, Frances could hear the terror in it. A moment later, there was scuffling and a door slammed. The man's protests could be heard above the swift clipping of heels on the flagstones. Frances listened as they faded into silence. Then, with sudden resolve, she reached for her cloak. 'Stay here with George, Mistress Knyvett,' she said, with greater determination than she felt. 'I must go to the princess.'

The old woman nodded, mute.

Frances slid back the bolt and lifted the latch. She took a breath before opening the door, her ears straining for any sound. All was silent. She let herself out quietly and stood blinking in the gloom. A dim light glowed from the stairs at the end of the cloister and she hastened towards it.

Quickening her pace, Frances was breathless by the time she reached the top of the stairs but broke into a run when she saw that several lights blazed outside the princess's apartments at the end of the corridor. Two guards were stationed outside and watched her closely as she entered.

The room was empty. She had not known what to expect, but it was not this. Looking around, she saw that the door to her mistress's bedchamber was ajar. She strode towards it and pushed it open, her heart in her mouth. The covers of Elizabeth's bed had been flung back, as had those of the pallet at its foot.

'The princess has been removed from here for her safety.'

Frances swung around to face the guard. 'To where?'

Without replying, he walked back to his post. After a few moments, Frances followed briskly in his wake. *Why wouldn't he tell her?* She was known to be one of Elizabeth's favourite attendants. Even if her life was in danger, surely Frances should be trusted to accompany her.

Unless she herself was under suspicion.

She broke into a run again, but as she fled down the stairs, she lost her footing and fell heavily down the last few, her face slapping against the cold stone floor. She lay there for a few seconds, then carefully raised herself. Her face felt bruised and pain shot through her left ankle as she put her weight on it. Reaching down, she could feel that it was already swelling.

Frances hesitated. She knew she should return to bed and get what little sleep she could before whatever awaited her in the morning. She should also rest her ankle so that the swelling receded. But the urge to find out what was going on proved stronger. She would go to the queen's privy chamber.

Hobbling painfully, Frances was obliged to keep stopping to rest her ankle. By the time she arrived, she was drenched with sweat and every bone in her body ached.

The guards eyed her closely before raising their halberds so that she could enter. Frances was relieved to hear voices within. The queen turned sharply as she crossed the threshold. 'Great God! What has happened to you?' she cried, gesturing urgently to one of her ladies to help Frances to one of the chairs close to where she was sitting.

'It is nothing, Your Majesty. I had a fall. I should have carried a lantern.'

As she spoke, the same lady brought her a damp linen cloth to wipe her face. Frances dreaded to think what she must look like. The hem of her nightgown was torn and covered with dust. Anne regarded her steadily.

'Where is the princess?' Frances asked, when she made no move to speak.

The queen hesitated. 'Cecil has arranged

for her to be taken to St James's, to be with her brother. He considers it safer there,' she added, with a touch of impatience.

'So she is in danger here?' Frances persisted.

Anne gave a heavy sigh. 'It is all nonsense, of course. He would have had me go there too, but I refused. There is little wonder that my husband jumps at shadows, with such a man as Cecil to advise him.'

Frances waited for her to continue.

'A secret marriage has been discovered,' she said at last. Frances's heart lurched. 'That foolish lady, Arbella Stuart, has wed another blood claimant — a Seymour, no less. It has been many years since one of their number has worn a crown,' she scoffed.

Behind the queen, Frances noticed Lady Drummond shift uncomfortably and heard the soft rustle of her skirts. Their eyes met for a moment.

'They were married here, according to Cecil,' Anne continued. 'To think that such a thing was happening under my very roof as I languished here, whiling away the hours with my ladies,' she added.

Frances chose her words carefully. 'They surely did not mean to seize the throne. Lady Arbella has few friends here at court, and fewer still beyond. She is well known to be a haughty, troublesome woman.'

She darted a glance at Jane Drummond and saw her expression harden.

Anne nodded. 'I agree with you, Frances, and if she had attempted it alone she would have presented no danger. She is a Stuart, after all. But the English are a sentimental race and still hark back to the glories of the Tudors. William Seymour is one of the last scions of that dynasty.'

Frances tried to slow her breathing as she held the queen's gaze. 'Have they been arrested?' she asked quietly.

'Yes — and various others besides,' Anne replied. 'Cecil is certain they had accomplices here in the palace.'

Frances hoped that the flush she could feel creeping up her neck would not show on her face. As she tried to compose herself, she heard Jane's skirts rustle again and looked towards her, glad of the distraction.

The young woman was staring steadily at her. Her eyes were grey and beautiful and her hair was as silky black as a raven's feathers. No wonder Thomas had been drawn to her. She thought of the awkward encounter between the three of them, the night when Seymour had first accosted her. Thomas had looked so stricken.

Her breath caught in her throat as another

thought occurred to her. It had been Jane Drummond who had summoned her to attend the princess that night. She had been so distracted by her husband's reaction to the young woman that she had not thought of it before. The realisation must have shown on her face because she saw Jane's eyes widen briefly, as if in panic. *So this was Seymour's associate.*

'One can never be too cautious in such matters.'

They all turned at the soft voice. The Lord Privy Seal was standing in the doorway of the queen's lodgings, his emaciated frame stooped over a black staff. He smiled pleasantly as he surveyed the room.

'My lord — what news?' Anne was the first to compose herself. She gestured for him to sit. He did so agonisingly slowly — whether through genuine frailty or a desire to increase the already palpable tension, Frances could not tell.

'Seymour is safely in his lodgings at the Tower, Your Majesty,' he said, after a long pause. 'I have entrusted the care of his new *wife*' — he emphasised the word — 'to Sir Thomas Parry at his house in Lambeth. He is eager to retain his place on the council so can be relied upon to watch her closely.'

'Good, good,' the queen said distractedly.

298

'But what of the others? The guards have woken half the palace tonight. I am sure they were not dragging people from their beds to enquire after their health.'

Cecil gave a little chuckle. 'Indeed not, Your Grace. We have apprehended several others who, we believe, were involved.' His eyes flicked across to Frances. 'There may be more arrests before the night is over.'

The queen gave him a long, appraising stare. 'You were always most thorough, my lord.' Her voice was as cold as ice. 'Now, if you will excuse me, I will return to my bed for what little is left of the night. Jane.'

She held out her hand. Lady Drummond hastened to take it, then gently helped her mistress to stand and guided her slowly to the door of the bedchamber.

Frances and Cecil rose, heads bowed. As soon as she heard the door click shut, Frances dropped a hasty curtsy and walked as quickly as she could from the room, gritting her teeth against the pain. She could feel Cecil's eyes upon her with every step she took.

CHAPTER 23
18 JULY

'You performed a great service that night, Frances.'

She did not turn to look at the woman but continued staring out of the window. Though it was early, the sun was already glittering off the river and the bank on the opposite side appeared hazy. It would be another sultry day. The walls of the palace seemed to soak up the heat, like those of the ovens in the kitchens below. It made the atmosphere at court even more oppressive.

'I had little choice in the matter,' she replied.

Jane Drummond came to stand next to her. Frances had to fight the urge to move away. 'I know what you must think of me, but everything I have done has been for the sake of the Catholic cause.'

Frances rounded on her. 'Even bedding my husband? Your dedication is commendable.'

She was gratified to see the other woman flush.

'Even that,' she replied quietly.

Frances's eyes blazed as she stared at her, waiting for her to continue.

'I needed to ensure your compliance. If it had been necessary to threaten you with exposing your husband as an . . . accomplice to our plans, I would have done so.'

Frances experienced such a surge of fury that she clasped her hands together to stop herself striking the woman. 'My husband has nothing to do with this. He is a loyal subject to the king.'

'That may be so, Frances, but his moment of weakness has placed him in danger.' She eyed Frances thoughtfully. 'Of course, I did not know that your marriage is a pretence, that you feel nothing for him. That is why we had to threaten your son instead.'

'That is not true!' Frances cried.

Her companion flicked an anxious glance towards the queen's bedroom door.

'I greatly esteem my husband,' she continued. 'Ours is a truer marriage than most others here at court.'

The young woman gave a small smile. 'Esteem?' she remarked quietly. 'That is admirable, Frances, but the success of my plan rested upon something stronger. You

301

would not have been willing to hazard the life of one you loved.'

Frances tried to steady her breathing. Tears filled her eyes but she blinked them angrily away. 'I wonder that you can play with people's lives with as little thought as you might give to a game of quadrille,' she said, as soon as she could trust herself to speak. 'You know nothing of my feelings for my husband, or of his for me. Things are not always as they appear to be.'

'Perhaps not,' Jane replied. 'It matters little now anyway. You performed your part without the need for any further incentive.'

Frances regarded her coldly. 'I risked a great deal — and to no effect.'

'On the contrary. Our plans have suffered a setback. That is all.'

'Arbella and Seymour are in the king's custody,' Frances replied scornfully. 'That is more than a mere setback. Surely you must abandon all hope of success now.'

At that moment, the door to the queen's chamber opened. Both women turned and fell into a deep curtsy as Anne walked slowly into the room. She looked from one to the other, an eyebrow raised, but said nothing.

'Forgive me, Your Majesty,' Frances said quickly. 'I must attend your daughter.'

■ ■ ■ ■

By the time Frances reached the Tower, the sun had sunk low on the horizon, casting streaks of deep pink and orange across the sky. The searing heat had begun to abate and she relished the cooling breeze that blew from the Thames.

It was foolhardy to come here, but she could no longer abide the endless waiting and watching at court. Cecil had as yet made no move against her, though she sensed he was merely biding his time. The conversation with Jane Drummond had gnawed at her constantly. She did not know what troubled her most: the unexpected feelings it had unleashed for her husband, or the hint that the Arbella plot was far from over. It was the latter that had driven her here, desperate for answers she hoped Raleigh would provide.

The yeomen showed little surprise when she told them whom she had come to visit. The former royal favourite was by far the most popular of the Tower's prisoners. As she mounted the steps to Raleigh's lodgings, she had a sudden urge to turn back. It was madness to consort with a suspected traitor when her own loyalties were in doubt. But her need to find out more about the plot into which she had been drawn drove her on.

'Lady Frances!' Raleigh rose to greet her like an old friend. He did not seem at all surprised by her coming. She gave a small curtsy and moved to sit in the chair he held out for her.

'What a pleasure it is to see you again,' he said, with genuine warmth. 'I had begun to think I had forfeited your good opinion when we last met. It was ever a fault of mine to speak too passionately to a lady — though the old queen did not object,' he added, with a grin. 'Please.'

He held out a glass of wine. Frances accepted it and took a long sip. It was delicious. Little wonder that Sir Walter seemed so accepting of his situation. She wondered how many other privileges he was afforded.

'What do you know of the plot to put Arbella Stuart on the throne?' she asked, deciding to set aside the usual pleasantries.

Raleigh's smile faltered for just a second. 'Why, you sound very like my host,' he replied smoothly. 'Sir William asked me that very question not two weeks ago.'

Frances remained silent, waiting.

'I hear many things in the Tower,' he continued. 'That the lady was secretly married to one of the Seymours, that they were discovered and are now in the king's custody . . .' A pause. 'That you yourself stood witness to the marriage.'

Frances's heart skipped a beat. She had been right to seek her answers here. 'Theirs was the marriage you hinted at when we last met,' she said quietly.

Raleigh studied her briefly, then slowly inclined his head. 'You have proved a true friend to our cause, Lady Frances.' He leaned forward and kissed her hand.

'I did not do so willingly, but to protect my son,' she retorted.

Raleigh was watching her intently now. 'And your husband?'

Frances felt herself redden. She pressed her lips together, determined not to show the same weakness that she had with Jane Drummond.

'You must forgive his transgression. The queen's favourite attendant can be most persuasive. And even a man as noble as Sir Thomas can suffer a momentary weakness.'

'Lady Drummond implied that the scheme is not yet over,' Frances cut in, eager to divert the conversation from the subject of her marriage.

Raleigh stood up and walked to the window, gazing towards the White Tower. 'Seymour is still awake, I see,' he murmured, almost to himself. 'His lodgings are even finer than these. But, then, he has royal blood.'

Frances rose and walked over to where he was standing. Following his gaze, she saw a light in a window of the royal apartments. 'Such blood has often proved more a curse than a blessing,' she observed.

'Indeed it has,' Raleigh replied. 'But we must not lose hope. God has seen fit to unite these two people and even His representative on earth cannot separate them for long.'

Frances turned to him. 'But Arbella is at Lambeth, in Sir Thomas Parry's keeping.'

Raleigh nodded slowly. 'For now, perhaps. But the Tower's walls are not so thick that they can keep out love's winged chariot.'

'Seymour plans to escape, then?' she demanded, her voice barely a whisper.

'He has no need,' her companion replied. 'We have friends enough here to help him visit his wife now and again, and Parry can be trusted to keep his counsel. He treats her more like a guest than a prisoner.'

Frances's mind was reeling. The tendrils of this plot stretched even further than she had thought.

'And who knows what might result from

such visits?' Raleigh continued. 'A would-be queen is one matter. But one who carries a son in her belly is another entirely. A prince born of two royal houses, and on English soil, would be a tantalising prospect.'

Frances felt as if the world had suddenly shifted, that nothing was as she had believed it to be. If what Raleigh said was true, then it was little wonder that Jane Drummond had seemed so assured. The discovery of Arbella and Seymour's marriage did not spell an end to their hopes, merely an impediment.

She thought of the proud, haughty woman, of her vain and feckless young husband. Were they really more appealing than the man who now sat on the throne? 'I will have no further part in this,' she said quietly.

'You must choose your own path.' Raleigh took her hands in his. 'Though there may be some who try to persuade you otherwise, in time.'

Frances gazed at the light that still burned in Seymour's window. Raleigh's hands felt warm, comforting. Such physical contact had been rare these past few years and, with a sudden pang, she realised how much she had missed it. She thought of her husband — how he had sometimes placed a tentative hand on hers, the look of hurt in his eyes when she had pulled swiftly away. A single tear rolled down her cheek.

Raleigh looked away discreetly, but squeezed her hands. 'I will always be a friend to you, Lady Frances,' he murmured.

Frances glanced at her husband, who smiled his reassurance. She was glad that he had returned from the hunt, though part of her wished he had remained longer in Hertfordshire. The controversy surrounding Lady Arbella's marriage had hardly abated, and she knew that Cecil's investigations continued. Living in constant dread of a summons was wearing her nerves to shreds.

'Am I to miss my lessons for the whole day?' George asked hopefully.

Frances smiled down at him. 'Just for an hour or so. The princess is paying you a great honour but she has many more people to meet so we must not steal too much of her time.'

The truth was, she would rather have avoided the meeting altogether, but Elizabeth's requests to have George presented to her had become increasingly insistent.

'Are we ready?' Thomas asked, straightening his back so that George would do the same.

Frances nodded, and he motioned for the yeomen to let them pass.

'At last!' the princess exclaimed as they entered. 'I feared that you had changed your mind, Fran.' She crossed to greet her and smiled her welcome to Thomas, who kissed her hand.

George shrank behind his mother's skirts, but Elizabeth spied him and sank to her knees so that she could peer round at him. The boy chuckled, delighted at the game. He soon emerged from his hiding place and, remembering what his mother had taught him, gave a stiff bow. 'It is an honour to meet you, Your Highness.'

'And to meet you, Master Tyringham.' Her smile faltered as she studied George's face. 'I heard he was very like his father,' she said thoughtfully, glancing up at Thomas.

'He has his mother's eyes, Your Grace,' Thomas said smoothly. 'And certainly her temperament. He is as stubborn as a mule.'

The princess laughed, her doubts apparently forgotten.

'I trust you were kept informed about the late controversy, being so far distant from court, Sir Thomas.'

Blanche had strolled from the princess's

bedchamber. Frances bit back a retort. The young woman had talked of little else these past few weeks. It was as if she could sense her rival's discomfiture every time the subject was raised.

'Of course, my lady,' Thomas replied evenly. 'The Lord Privy Seal was most assiduous with his dispatches.'

Frances gave a wry smile. She had little doubt of that.

'The king must have been most anxious to return,' Blanche persisted, 'especially after the Powder Treason.'

George stopped fiddling with his shirt cuffs and looked at her with interest.

'That was many years ago now, Blanche,' Frances said quickly.

'But everyone at court must still remember it as if it happened only yesterday,' the young woman said archly, with a glance at George. 'If those traitors had succeeded, the king would have been blown to the heavens.'

Frances saw her son's mouth fall open.

'Oh, do be quiet, Blanche,' Elizabeth said irritably. 'You will terrify the poor boy. Now, George, some sweetmeats?'

Frances felt a rush of gratitude to her mistress as she saw her son's face brighten, all talk of treason forgotten.

■ ■ ■ ■

'You are leaving again so soon?' Frances was dismayed.

'I am afraid so,' Thomas said, with a resigned shrug. 'Lady Blanche's remark was ill-judged. The king wishes to be far from court at this time. He lives in constant fear of an assassin.'

'That is nothing new, Thomas.'

Her husband gave a rueful smile, but it soon faded. 'I wish you could come with me. I fear for you here, Frances — George too. Every day that we were in Hertfordshire a new message arrived from Cecil, telling the king of someone else whom he suspected of aiding this late marriage.'

Frances looked at him sharply. 'And you think I might be one of them?'

Thomas seemed to hesitate, then crossed to her and took her hands. 'Of course not. I just hate to think of you alone in this vipers' nest. Cecil —' He pressed his lips together.

Frances's heart began to thud. 'Go on,' she whispered.

Her husband's eyes searched hers. Then he sighed and rubbed his hand across his brow. 'It is probably nothing, and I should not have mentioned it. God knows you have enough to occupy you at present, with the princess and George . . . The king shared all of Cecil's dispatches with those of us who attended him on the hunt. But there was one he did not read out. After looking through its contents, he summoned Carr to attend him in private and left the rest of us to wonder what it purported.'

Frances forced her breathing to slow. 'What has this to do with me?'

Thomas stroked the back of her hand with his thumb as he studied her face closely. 'I saw the king glance at me as he read the letter. From that day, he shared no more with us — or with me, at least. Though others of his companions seemed to know the latest news from court, I was kept in ignorance.'

Frances fell silent. Her husband was right to be concerned, but she could hardly say as much. 'This signifies little,' she said at last. 'The king favours you, but you have never been one of his intimates.'

She saw doubt in her husband's eyes.

'That is true. I must not let myself become as consumed by fear and suspicion as the king I serve.' He tightened his grip on her hands. 'But you would tell me if Cecil has any reason to suspect you, Frances?'

She felt the blood drain from her face but

resisted the urge to look away. 'Of course.'

She wanted to say more — that Cecil's suspicions were due to no more than his having been intent upon her destruction since she had evaded the charge of witchcraft six years earlier, that she had stayed true to the agreement they had struck upon their marriage. But the lies died on her lips.

Thomas studied her for a moment longer before releasing her hands. 'I must prepare for our departure,' he said, moving towards the bedchamber. 'I am glad now that I did not have time to fully unpack my coffer from the last journey.'

Frances remained standing by the fire, barely aware of the noise of drawers scraping and chest lids thudding in the adjoining chamber. *How much did Cecil know?*

'I think that is all,' Thomas said, as he came back into the parlour, dragging his coffer.

Frances inwardly shook herself. 'I wish you good hunting,' she said brightly. 'I hope it will restore the king's spirits.'

'As do I,' her husband replied, with feeling.

He set down the coffer and came to where she was standing. 'Take care, Frances,' he said quietly, then kissed her cheek.

She felt her body respond to the warmth

of his lips and closed her eyes so that she might summon up the familiar image of Tom, his mouth so close to hers that she could feel his breath. But it was her husband who appeared before her, his eyes alight with desire as her lips parted for his kiss.

Her eyes sprang open and a flush crept over her cheeks as she stepped quickly away from him. Thomas stared at her for a moment, then turned towards the door. As he lifted the latch, she saw his hand tremble and had a sudden impulse to run to him, encircle him in her arms and feel the warmth of his chest against her cheek. But she remained by the fire, as placid as one of the carved statues in the privy garden. Only when the door had closed behind him did she surrender herself to her grief.

Frances smiled and clapped as another arrow thudded into the target. Elizabeth grinned, then drew back her bow once more.

It was the first fine day in more than two weeks, so the princess had been determined to make the most of it. They had been riding that morning, much to Frances's joy. Feeling the wind whipping around her as they galloped through Hyde Park had given her a heady sense of release. She had spent the past fortnight indoors, feeling as if she were being slowly suffocated.

There had been three more arrests since Thomas's departure, including a lady of the queen's bedchamber. She had been released soon afterwards, but it had occasioned great alarm among Anne's household and had made Frances feel as if the net was closing. She found herself almost wishing that Cecil would make his move.

'Can I trouble you for a moment, Lady Frances?'

Jane Drummond's face was ghastly pale and her hair had come loose from its coif. Frances cast a glance at the princess, who had just loosed another arrow and laughed with delight as it hit the target. Beside her, Blanche was clapping enthusiastically, but Frances noticed the young woman stare briefly in her direction.

'What is it?' she muttered, her gaze fixed on the princess.

'Please — it will only take a moment.'

Frances caught the urgency in her voice. 'Very well,' she said curtly. She walked a few paces from the small gathering of spectators so that they would not be overheard.

'We need your assistance. Lady Arbella lies sick at Parry's house. If the source of her malady is discovered, the consequences will be grave.'

'And what is the source?' she asked, fearing she knew the answer already.

Jane hesitated. Then: 'She is with child.'

Frances felt a sudden chill. Many times these past weeks, she had thought of Raleigh's words during their last meeting, his plan to help Seymour visit his new wife. But she had reasoned that even if such visits

317

took place, the chances of their resulting in a pregnancy were surely remote. Certainly she had hoped so. More and more, she found the idea of this arrogant and head-strong woman on the throne utterly repellent. Queen Anne was right: Arbella served her own interests, not those of the faith. Frances regretted that she had been obliged to assist her.

'At least, she was,' Jane continued. 'But last night she began with such pains in her stomach that she could hardly rise from her bed.'

'Has she bled?' Frances asked.

Jane shook her head. 'But the pain frightens her and she is greatly agitated. While she continues like this, it cannot but do harm to the child. Please, Lady Frances. I know of none other who can help her.'

'I told Sir Walter I wanted no part of this,' Frances murmured.

'I know that,' Jane countered, 'and he told me not to involve you. But the fate of every Catholic in the kingdom rests upon the child she carries. As a prince of the houses of Stuart and Seymour, his claim would be uncontested. I cannot risk his life, or that of the lady.'

Frances thought quickly. It was common for a woman to suffer pains during the first few weeks, as the child took root in her womb. But they should not be as grievous as Jane had described. Perhaps Arbella was making too much of it — she was known to be of a nervous temperament. 'I can give you something to ease her pains.'

'It is not enough. You must attend her. That is our only hope. I have arranged everything. You will be conveyed there as soon as the princess has finished her game. It is but a short distance from here — you will be back before she needs you again.'

Her mistress was now engaged in an animated conversation with one of the onlookers. It was she whom Frances devoutly wished to see crowned queen of this kingdom, not the vain and foolish Arbella. Suffering the rule of a heretic king was preferable to that.

'Very well,' she muttered. 'I will do as you request. But I will have nothing further to do with you or your schemes. I do not wish to see you or have any correspondence with you hereafter. The service that I perform is as a healer, not an ally. I have no desire to see the lady or her child on the throne.'

Jane Drummond's expression hardened, but she gave a curt nod. 'Thank you, Lady Frances. Be at the water gate by dusk. A barge will be waiting for you there.' She turned on her heel and strode back across the park, her skirts billowing.

Sir Thomas Parry's house was one of a number of handsome mansions that lined the river close to Lambeth Palace, their lush green lawns sweeping down to the water's edge. As the barge drew level with the small wooden landing stage, Frances noticed the figure of a man at one of the downstairs windows. He disappeared from view as soon as she disembarked. She did not know if it was the same man who opened the door to her a few moments later. He was stooped with age and leaned heavily on a staff as he peered out at her.

'Sir Thomas Parry,' he said, giving a slight bow. 'You are come to help my guest?' The lines at the corners of his eyes deepened as he smiled. He shuffled back a few paces so that she might pass.

'Thank you, Sir Thomas,' she said, grateful that he had not asked her name. Frances suspected he wanted as little to do with this as she did.

She climbed the stairs and followed the corridor along to the end, as Parry had directed, and knocked quietly on the door of the furthest chamber. It was opened a moment later by a charwoman. She peered at Frances cautiously before motioning for her to enter. Frances watched until her stooped frame was out of sight along the corridor, then went quickly into the chamber.

A low keening emanated from the bed, around which heavy drapes were drawn. Frances walked to the head and set her salves and tinctures on the table. She took a breath, then pulled back the curtain. Arbella twisted in the direction of the dim light that glowed from the sconces. Her face had a yellowish hue and her shift was damp with sweat. 'You are come at last,' she hissed, teeth gritted.

Frances did not reply but turned back to the table and began decanting a tincture of willow bark and feverfew into a glass. She mixed it with a little water, then held it to Arbella's lips.

Arbella sniffed it. 'What is it?' she demanded.

'Something to lessen the pains,' Frances replied.

'Do not scowl at me so,' Arbella snapped. 'There are many who would gladly poison me. Perhaps they have already, intent upon murdering me and my child.'

She clutched her belly again and brought her knees up to her chest. Frances watched her panting against the pain, like an animal caught in a snare. At length it subsided and she offered her the tincture again. She drank it, shuddering at the taste.

'When my prince is born, England shall be saved from its heretic king,' Arbella said, once she was calmer. She gazed down at her belly and gently stroked it.

Frances said nothing. The woman was even more blinded by her arrogance and ambition than she had thought. How could she, a prisoner of the king, still cherish hopes of seizing the throne? As for her child, Frances doubted it would ever draw breath. These were not the pains of early pregnancy.

'I see you doubt me,' Arbella sneered, 'but you do not know the friends I have.'

Jane Drummond was a valuable ally, certainly, but Frances doubted that Arbella had many other supporters at court, despite what Raleigh had hinted. Lady Vaux had also claimed to have a wide network of allies, but Frances had seen little proof of that either. Not for the first time, she wondered if any of the Catholics in this kingdom were willing to stir themselves for rebellion. They had not done so for the Powder Treason, which must surely have inspired them with greater hope than the machinations of this haughty, volatile woman. Frances believed that most would rather live peaceably, keeping their faith in their hearts, as Thomas had urged her to do.

Arbella gave another cry, jolting Frances from her thoughts. She stepped quickly forward and took the glass from her fingers, then soaked a cloth in the ewer and pressed it to the woman's forehead. Arbella swiped her hand away and flung back the heavy covers of the bed. 'You must try to be still — for the sake of the child,' Frances urged.

Arbella quietened and lay panting for several minutes. As gently as she could, Frances eased her onto her back and placed more pillows under her neck for support. She then moved to examine her.

Arbella flinched as Frances lifted her shift and held herself taut, legs clamped together as if to stem the steady stream of blood that now seeped between them.

'I am sorry,' Frances said quietly.

Arbella's scream was so piercing that Frances feared it would rouse Sir Thomas and his servants. As it echoed into silence, she listened for the creak of floorboards in the corridor beyond. But the only sound was of pitiful sobs as Arbella watched her child bleed away.

Frances sensed that she would lash out if she tried to comfort her, so instead she busied herself with fetching fresh linens from the chest and placing a wad underneath Arbella's shift. She doused others with water and patiently cleaned the blood as it oozed steadily from her womb. It would continue for several hours yet, but already it was starting to diminish. From the remaining linens, she fashioned a pad such as a woman might wear for her monthly courses and tore off a long piece so that she could tie it into place around Arbella's hips.

When she had finished, the lady's sobs had subsided and she had fallen into an exhausted sleep. The herbs would be taking effect now, Frances judged. They would help her sleep until dawn.

Knowing she could do no more, and anxious to return to court before the princess noted her absence, Frances gathered the phials and pouches of herbs, and padded quietly towards the door.

'You must tell him.'

She turned back to the bed. Arbella's eyes were still closed and, for a moment, Frances wondered if she had spoken in a dream.

'Tell him this is an impediment only, that I will carry another child — and soon.'

'Seymour?'

'No, no — not him.'

Her voice was agitated now, but as Frances

waited for her to continue there was a sharp creak from the corridor.

'I must go,' she said, without pausing to hear who Arbella's message was for.

The old serving woman was standing outside when she opened the door. Frances gave a curt nod, then brushed past her. As she hastened along the corridor, she heard Arbella cry out again.

'Tell him!'

Sir Thomas was nowhere to be seen when Frances reached the entrance hall. She did not trouble to make her farewells, but left the house and ran down the path to the river. The boat was still tethered to the post and Frances could just make out the figure of a man waiting on the landing stage. She whispered a prayer of thanks that the boatman had proved patient, but it died on her lips as he turned to face her.

William Cecil.

'My father has summoned you to attend him,' he said, his mouth set in a grim line. 'You will come with me at once.'

CHAPTER 26
2 SEPTEMBER

Neither spoke as the barge glided along the dark waters of the Thames. As the initial shock of her arrest began to subside, Frances felt almost calm. Whatever Cecil had in store for her, at least the tortuous weeks of waiting for him to pounce were at an end.

Soon Whitehall Palace came into view. Frances could see the lights blaze through the windows of the great hall. Her mistress would soon be dressing for the masque. Blanche would be delighted when her rival failed to attend and would be quick to take advantage. How trivial such matters seemed now, Frances reflected.

It was moments before the vessel bumped against the landing stage of the palace. William stepped quickly out and grabbed Frances by the wrist as he helped her alight. He did not relinquish his hold as he strode towards the gate. The guards quickly raised their halberds and Frances could feel their eyes following her as she allowed herself to be dragged towards the inner lodgings.

The shouts of revellers rang out across the courtyard as they walked briskly through it. They must be nearing Cecil's apartment. Though she had never set foot inside it, Frances knew it lay close to the king's. The richness of the tapestries along the panelling of the corridor confirmed it.

William stopped abruptly outside a large doorway halfway along the passage. Glancing up, Frances recognised Cecil's coat of arms, surmounted by a coronet. She held her breath as she waited for William to open the door, imagining his father on the other side, a satisfied smile on his face. But the young man seemed to hesitate.

'Forgive me, Lady Frances,' he whispered. 'I did not know what else to do.' His expression had softened and Frances noticed how pale he was, how dark the shadows under his eyes. He no longer looked like her captor.

'There is little time,' he urged. 'My father is gravely ill. He refuses to see a physician for fear that his rivals will learn of it and use his weakness to their advantage. Lady Frances, you must help him. There is no one else here with your skills.'

Frances tried to come to terms with the

news that he had brought her to Whitehall to help his father, not to be interrogated. The idea that she should use her skills to treat the man who had conspired endlessly to have her condemned for witchcraft, who had watched, implacable, as the torturer's blade had pierced her skin, seemed preposterous. It would be as good as signing her own death warrant, given that his son now had evidence she had been in conference with Arbella. She wondered vaguely how he had known to find her there.

'If the earl will not accept the help of a physician, then he will hardly countenance that of a wise woman,' she said.

William winced at the bitterness in her voice. 'I know what he has done to you — that you have every reason to refuse me. But I cannot abide to watch him writhe in pain, knowing there is someone who might bring him relief.'

Frances tried to push down the pity she felt, to remind herself that this was the son of her enemy. 'What is it that pains him?'

'His stomach. The convulsions are so strong that they make him retch.'

Frances saw from the young man's face that he was in earnest: this was not a trap. But how could she forget everything that had passed between her and Cecil, try to save his life when he had only ever tried to destroy hers?

'Lady Frances — I beg you.'

She gazed at him a moment longer then slowly inclined her head.

The bitter stench of vomit pervaded the gloomy chamber. Frances drew a sprig of lavender from her pouch and pushed it into her bodice. The warmth of her skin soon released its fragrance. She breathed in deeply, then walked slowly to the bed.

Cecil turned to face her. His skin was the colour of beeswax, with a thin sheen of sweat. His dark eyes stared up at her and he smiled, though his jaw was clenched against the pain.

'William.'

His son was at his side in an instant. 'Do not be angry, Father. I did not know what else to do. You cannot suffer like this any longer.'

Frances busied herself with mixing a fresh tincture, plucking the tiny green leaves from the sprig of woad and grinding them with a little dried ginger and willow bark.

'I'll wager neither of us thought to meet like this, Lady Frances,' Cecil rasped.

She glanced at him and saw that he was watching her carefully, though his smile did not falter. 'Show me where the pain is,' she said, ignoring his remark.

He moved his hand to the right side of his stomach. She reached out but he grabbed her wrist so suddenly and with such force that it surprised her. 'You must let me examine you or I can do nothing to help,' she said firmly.

After a few moments, he relaxed his grip and she carefully lifted his nightshirt. The lump was visible beneath the skin. She placed her fingers gently on it and heard Cecil's breath hiss between his teeth. It felt hard to the touch. She knew that her herbs would work no effect upon it. She had seen the Reverend Samuels tend a woman in Britford with just such a growth in her abdomen. He had told her there was no remedy but to cut it out. The woman had refused. She had died within the month.

Frances had only ever used her knife to remove shards of wood and glass from wounds that had sealed over. To do anything more carried great risk, she knew. Many patients had bled out at the hands of inexpert surgeons.

Cecil's eyes never left her as she kept her own fixed upon the swelling, rapidly weighing the choices that lay before her. She could give him something to relieve the pain, but it would only be temporary. His torment would grow much greater as the tumour steadily consumed more of his stomach.

Better that he should die in torment than live to torment you.

She pushed away the thought. God had given her the skills to bring comfort and healing to the sick. She must not deny them. 'The tumour must be cut out,' she said, as she raised her eyes to Cecil's.

Behind her, she heard his son's sharp intake of breath. The older man's mouth twitched, but there was fear in his eyes.

'You can summon one of the court physicians to perform the task, if you wish,' she continued, holding his gaze. 'But it must be done soon. There is no other remedy.'

Cecil eyed her steadily. Though his body was racked with pain, his mind would be as sharp as ever as it ran through the possibilities. 'No. You shall do it, Lady Frances.'

The pulse throbbed at her temples but she took care to show no emotion. He had placed his life in her hands, just as hers had been in his these past six years.

She began to prepare a fresh tincture of elder bark and turmeric, to reduce the inflammation. 'I will need your help,' she said, to William.

He was at her side in a moment. She tore

off a clean strip of linen and soaked it in the mixture, then handed it to him.

'You must dab the wound with this, while I remove the swelling,' she instructed. 'Make sure to keep replacing it with fresh. It will soon become soaked.'

William nodded, but remained silent. Out of the corner of her eye, she saw him cross to the bed and kiss his father's forehead.

The knife glinted in the candlelight as she rubbed another piece of linen along it. 'Give your father some wine — as much as he can stomach.'

She saw his hands tremble as he poured a large glass and held it to his father's lips. Cecil took a long gulp, then spluttered. A few drops of the ruby liquid soaked into his white shift. His chest heaved as he gasped for breath, but he brought the glass to his lips again and took another sip. For a moment, Frances feared he would vomit, but his breathing gradually slowed and he sank back onto the pillows.

She reached into her pocket and clasped the rosary, uttering a silent prayer. Then she came to sit on the bed and gestured for William to stand close by. Cecil's eyes had closed, but not in sleep.

Frances took the linen from William and gently dabbed at the area around the swelling. Cecil flinched. She knew he was bracing himself for the pain. Slowly, she moved the knife into position. Its blade was now so close to Cecil's skin that if he moved even slightly it would pierce him. Her hand remained perfectly steady, though her breathing had become rapid. She pushed the blade onto his skin now. For a moment, it did not yield, then suddenly the knife sank deep into his flesh and a thick trail of blood ran down his abdomen. She heard Cecil suck in a breath.

Knowing she must work quickly, she drew the blade around the edge of the tumour. By the time the circle was complete, several pieces of blood-soaked linen lay discarded on the floor. Frances was glad that William's stomach was as strong as hers.

Carefully, she peeled back the skin to expose a fleshy white lump, about the size of a small apple. The blood was pooling around it so she could not see whether it extended any further. As soon as William had soaked through another linen, she eased her fingers around the tumour. Cecil gave a low moan. Glancing up at him, she saw that his face had a ghastly pallor and his breathing was shallow. *She must do it now.*

Taking the knife again, she began to cut around the growth. A foul odour rose up from it as she worked, her fingers slippery with Cecil's blood. At last she felt the tumour loosen. Another cut and it was free. She grabbed a large clot of linen and pressed it firmly against the wound, then pulled the skin back over it and gestured for William to hold the clot in place while she washed her hands. The ewer was soon filled with bright red liquid.

Once her hands were dried, Frances threaded her needle and moved quickly back to the bed. Cecil was unconscious now and she could not tell if he was breathing, but there was no time to check. Another few minutes and he would bleed out from the wound. She began stitching while William staunched the flow of blood, exposing a little of the cut at a time for her to work on. At length, it was done. Frances cleaned the wound as best she could, then applied a final clot of linen and bound it in place.

She gathered up the discarded material from the floor and threw it on the fire. It hissed and spat as the flames consumed the sodden rags.

'Will he live?' William's voice was barely a whisper.

Frances did not answer, but moved to the top of the bed and placed her fingers gently on Cecil's throat. After a few moments, she felt a pulse — faint but steady. 'If he survives the night, his chance will be greater,' she said, watching Cecil's face.

His mouth was still twisted into a grimace and there was a thin trail of blood from where he had bitten hard on his lip. The wound would pain him for many weeks yet, and it would be a long time before he was able to raise himself from his bed. *Long enough for the Arbella controversy to die down.* Even as she thought it, Frances knew that Cecil's memory was more tenacious than most.

'I am indebted to you, Lady Frances,' his son said quietly.

She wondered whether Cecil would be too.

CHAPTER 27
12 SEPTEMBER

'You have been cleaning the wound, as I showed you?'

William nodded. 'Every day. The swelling is slowly reducing, I think.'

Frances looked closely at the skin, which was puckered around her neat stitches but no longer inflamed. She pressed her fingers lightly around it and heard Cecil suck in a sharp breath.

'I will bring some more of the fleawort,' she said, as she continued to examine the wound. 'If you mix it with a little vinegar and rose water, it will take down the swelling even more.'

'I may be frail in body, Lady Frances, but my mind is undiminished. You may issue your instructions to me too.'

Cecil was watching her with his usual expression of mild amusement. It was the first time she had felt glad to see it, she realised. Her satisfaction at having brought him back to health was evidently greater than her instinctive fear of him.

'You may leave us now, Will,' he said, smiling at his son.

The young man bowed and left the room. Frances moved to stand by the bed and waited. Cecil listened until his son's footsteps had faded into silence before addressing her. 'I owe you a great debt, Lady Frances,' he began, his expression now serious. 'I know that without your skills I would not have drawn breath for long.'

She inclined her head. 'God gave me those skills for a purpose, my lord. I cannot gainsay Him, even if it means helping those who would do me harm.'

Cecil held her gaze for a long moment. 'You took a risk in attending me,' he said slowly. 'I almost had you condemned as a witch with far less proof than you have now provided.'

Frances stared at him. Surely even he would not use this against her, not after she had saved his life. 'Not as great as the risk you took, my lord.' Her voice was as hard as flint. 'I am sure your royal master would be shocked to know that the man he appointed to root out witches from his realm had secretly been attended by one.'

He flinched, but recovered himself. 'Then

337

it seems we have placed each other in danger, Lady Frances,' he observed. 'But only if we choose to act upon it.' His dark eyes appraised her steadily.

Frances knew that a pact had been made. 'There are other dangers, though, are there not?' he continued, after a pause. 'This troubling matter of the Lady Arbella.'

Frances's pulse quickened but her eyes never left his.

'It seems that Parry has neglected his duties, allowing all and sundry to visit the lady.'

Another pause.

'Even her husband.'

His eyes blazed into Frances's. She knew that William would have told him where he had found her that evening, that Cecil would have sent someone to question Arbella. They would have discovered the reason for Frances's visit soon enough.

When it was clear that she was not going to respond, Cecil continued, 'I will have to inform the king, of course. Pity those who attend him when my message arrives,' he added, with a rueful smile.

Frances thought of her husband. Pray God Cecil would not mention her in the dispatch.

'His Majesty will no doubt wish to review the couple's . . . accommodation,' he went on. 'Parry is an old man and might be forgiven his negligence, but that Seymour was able to pass in and out of his lodgings at the Tower without notice is of greater concern.'

'It was not so when you had me placed there,' Frances spat, fury mingling with her fear.

'Indeed. But you did not have the friends that Seymour has.' He let the remark fade into silence.

Raleigh.

Did Cecil know she had visited him too? That they had whispered treason while sipping wine in his lodgings?

'What do you want with me?' she asked, weary of the unspoken threats, of the web of lies and danger that surrounded her.

Cecil raised his eyebrows as if surprised by her directness. 'Why should any of this concern you, Lady Frances?' he asked, with exaggerated innocence.

Frances did not answer but continued to regard him steadily.

Eventually, he sighed. 'I would have ordered your arrest by now,' he replied, 'but William persuaded me to reconsider. My son is a sentimental creature, with greater honour than sense. He told me that the debt I owe you must be repaid with silence.'

Frances's lips curled with distaste. Even the act of saving his life would not have prevented him from destroying hers. She found herself wishing that her knife had slipped, that he had died from the wound. *Thank God that his son had a greater conscience.*

'For William's sake, I will honour that debt, Lady Frances,' he continued. 'But I have set my spies to watch you. If you are foolish enough to conspire with that woman again, I will not be so merciful.'

Frances held his gaze, searching his eyes for sincerity. She had no choice but to take him at his word. But even if he broke it, she would not break hers. Arbella would be as dead to her now as the child that had bled away.

PART 3
1611

CHAPTER 28
4 JUNE

The light was already showing between the cracks of the shutters. In the distance, Frances could hear the tolling of a bell. Five o'clock. George was stirring. He had woken with the dawn this past month. Often she had felt the warm press of his hand against her cheek as she slept, and had opened her eyes to see him standing by the bed, impatient for her to join him. That precious hour, before anyone else was awake, had become her favourite part of the day.

Sometimes they lay on the settle, George's back against her chest as they read together, Frances's fingers slowly tracing the words as he spoke them. At others, they would play a game — fox and geese was the one George loved best — and he would exclaim in triumph if he won, forgetting his mother's urging to be quiet lest they wake the entire palace.

She fought the urge to scoop him into her

arms and carry him to her bed. He would be awake soon enough. Rolling over, she reached out towards the small table next to the bed and quietly pulled open the drawer. Her husband's letter was nestled within it. George stirred again at the crinkle of the stiff paper as she unfolded it, but settled back to sleep.

We arrived at Belvoir late last night. It is a beautiful castle and the Earl of Rutland has already shown us the lavish hospitality for which he is famed. The king is anxious to begin the hunt, which we will do tomorrow. He is greatly distressed by the loss of one of his hounds — Esmé — who bolted as soon as I opened the door to their wagon upon our arrival. I was obliged to spend half the night searching the woods for him, but as yet there is no sign.

I trust you and George are well. Pray tell him that there is a chestnut mare in the stables here that much resembles Duke. I wish he were here to ride it. I wish you were here also.

Your loving husband,
Thomas

She had read it several times since it had

been delivered to her the previous day. Thomas had always been a faithful correspondent during his absences on the hunt, which had become increasingly frequent and prolonged this past year. She missed him more each time. Ending her involvement in the Arbella plot had made her feel closer to him somehow. She had hated the deception.

She wished Lady Vaux had been as easy to shrug off. The woman had continued to plague her with messages, urging her to keep furthering the suit of the King of Spain's nephew. That at least had proved easier of late, Frances reflected. Although she had continued to speak favourably of Prince Victor whenever she had had the opportunity, nothing had persuaded the young woman as much as seeing her prospective suitor. Two weeks earlier the Spanish ambassador had presented Elizabeth with the prince's miniature upon his arrival for the marriage negotiations. Elizabeth had been captivated by his shining eyes and seductive smile and had spoken of little else ever since. Frances had prayed fervently that the ambassador would enjoy similar success with the king's ministers — if not with Prince Henry, who had made his disapproval all too obvious. God willing, by

345

the time Thomas returned the alliance would be concluded.

She looked back at the letter.

I wish you were here also.

Closing her eyes, she sank back on the pillows. She wished she could still her mind and sleep a little before George awoke. She was to attend the princess as usual today and hoped her mistress would not wish to stir from the palace.

'Mama.' His voice was still heavy with sleep.

She smiled down at him on his pallet and held out her arms. With the sudden energy that children seemed able to muster, he scrambled out from beneath his covers and leaped onto the bed next to her. They lay like that for a few moments, Frances stroking her child's silken hair as he nuzzled against her chest. She wished she had a lock of Tom's to compare it with, though she knew it would be identical.

'I miss Papa,' George said, his words muffled by her linen shift.

It was a moment before Frances could reply. 'I miss him too, my love,' she whispered.

Frances watched as the stout gentleman stooped to receive his honour.

'On behalf of His Most Sacred Majesty King James, I confer upon you the baronetcy of Willoughby, to be held by yourself and your heirs in assurance of your loyalty to the Crown.'

Cecil's voice echoed around the silent hall as the newly created baronet made his obeisance.

Robert Bertie was the latest in a succession of Catholics whose loyalty had been bought in this way. That their faith could be so easily exchanged for such an honour was galling. Frances had to admit, though, that it had been a stroke of genius on Cecil's part, boosting the king's precarious finances while negating the threat posed by those 'infested spirits', as he called them, who still cherished the old religion.

Beside her, she saw the princess stifle a yawn.

'I hereby pledge my allegiance to the king, his heirs and all those who serve them,' the gentleman declared, placing his hand on his breast.

There was an answering cheer from the crowd and he bowed before them, his face red with pride. Frances's composure never wavered, though she silently cursed the man's weakness. Little wonder that none of the plots against the heretic king had amounted to anything. Cecil caught her eye and smiled. She diverted her gaze to another man looking in her direction. *Robert Carr.* He bowed as she inclined her head, wondering idly why he had left the hunt to attend this ceremony. Surely there were greater gains to be had at his master's side.

The princess had stood to leave. 'Thank God that is over!' Elizabeth exclaimed, as soon as they had reached the gallery that led to her apartments. 'We have had to endure twenty such ceremonies this past month alone. It is a wonder there are any baronetcies left to give.'

'Or to sell,' Frances muttered, under her breath.

They walked on in silence, Blanche making a show of fussing over the princess's train.

'I wish the prince would hasten his journey,' Elizabeth said, as they reached the door of her apartment.

Frances had thought the same. It was more than three weeks since her mistress had received a message from her father's ambassador in Madrid that the King of Spain's nephew had embarked for England.

'I shall be driven mad with boredom,' the princess continued. 'The court is very dull since my father left, and there is little chance of my mother leaving her beloved Greenwich to keep me company.'

Frances could not help but smile at her mistress's youthful impatience. She had a good deal more to occupy her than most ladies of her age.

'I have other news that may offer some diversion, Your Grace,' Blanche observed slyly.

'Oh?' Elizabeth said, while she searched her sewing casket for thread to continue her embroidery.

'Apparently the Lady Arbella will finally set out for Durham tomorrow.'

Frances's heart raced. The king had ordered that she be transferred to the custody of the Bishop of Durham more than four months ago, but Arbella had pleaded illness and he had grudgingly agreed that she might tarry at Lambeth until she had recovered. Frances had braced herself for a secret summons to attend her and had been relieved when none came. Her indisposition must have resulted from a different cause. Raleigh had mentioned the tightening of security around Seymour's lodgings at the Tower when she had seen him last.

'Is that all?' Elizabeth retorted scornfully. 'What that woman does is hardly of concern to me.'

'It would be if her plans had succeeded,' Blanche muttered petulantly. 'They say she still hankers after your father's throne.'

Frances looked at her sharply. 'That is enough, Blanche. Our mistress has told you the matter holds no interest for her, and neither should it. Lady Stuart is no more a threat to the crown than you are.'

The young woman fell into a resentful silence.

All of a sudden, the princess leaped to her feet, eyes sparkling. 'I know who shall entertain me this afternoon!' she declared. 'Come, Frances, we're going to the Tower.'

Frances was dismayed, but Elizabeth was already pulling on her gloves.

'Sir Walter always restores my spirits. I cannot think why it did not occur to me before. It has been too long since I last visited him.'

Frances knew it would be pointless to object, so she helped her mistress with her cloak and went to fetch her own. Blanche watched them for a moment, then made ready herself.

The tide was in their favour, so the journey along the river was swift. Although she relished the feeling of the sun on her skin, Frances felt a creeping unease as they drew closer to the fortress. It was a long time since she had visited Raleigh. He had respected her wishes to have nothing more to do with the Arbella plot, and she had not wished to rouse Cecil's suspicions by being seen at the Tower too often.

As they mounted the steps to his lodgings, the scuffle of footsteps could be heard inside. The guard bowed low as he opened the door for the princess. Sir Walter was in his accustomed seat by the fireplace, but he appeared a little flushed and Frances saw panic in his eyes. He soon recovered, though, and bowed before stepping forward to kiss Elizabeth's hand.

'What an unexpected honour and pleasure, Your Highness,' he exclaimed.

Elizabeth smiled gracefully and took the seat he indicated. Blanche sat beside her so Frances was obliged to occupy the window seat.

'Forgive me, Sir Walter, there was no time to send word of my visit. It was something of an impulse. There is so little company to entertain us at present, with my father away on the hunt and my mother at Greenwich.'

'Their loss is my bounty, Your Grace,' Raleigh said, with an easy smile. 'What of the prince? Surely he would not wish to leave his sister so neglected.'

Elizabeth sighed. 'Henry has been charged

351

with planning another reception for the Spanish ambassador in our father's absence, though he seems not to relish the task as he did when Prince Gustavus was here.' Her face clouded. 'I fear the ambassador will think it a slight.'

Raleigh shot Frances a knowing look. 'I wonder the Spanish prince himself has not arrived long before now. If I were in his place, I would have commandeered the swiftest vessel so that I might be at your side in an instant.'

The princess blushed prettily. 'His Excellency assures me that Prince Victor is preparing to embark,' she said, eyes shining.

'Well, I would not wish to hasten his voyage,' Raleigh replied, with a rueful smile, 'for you will have little time for an old man like me once he is at your side. I have heard it said that many ladies' hearts have broken at the news that he is to be your husband. I could not have surrendered you to any man who was less alluring than he.'

His honeyed words had worked their effect and Frances was grateful for it. She had had to be more subtle in promoting the match, for fear of exciting the princess's curiosity as to why she was so in favour of it.

Frances listened to her mistress's animated chatter as she regaled Sir Walter with the descriptions she had heard of the King of Spain's nephew, the letters she had received from him, and how well she might like being Duchess of Savoy once they were married. She started when she saw a man crouched in the far corner, just out of view of the others. He was sitting on a low stool; his features were obscured by a large black hat, and at his side he carried a rapier.

Raleigh was watching her. He gave the slightest shake of his head before focusing back on the princess, who was still prattling, blissfully unaware. Frances was grateful to see that Blanche was fiddling idly with the lace of her sleeve and had not noticed either.

'It is growing late, Your Grace,' Frances said, standing abruptly.

Elizabeth was about to protest, but Raleigh had risen to his feet too.

'I fear Lady Frances is right, Your Grace. Sir William does not like his . . . *guests* to entertain visitors after dusk,' he said, with a rakish grin.

The princess's shoulders sagged in defeat and she turned so that Blanche could put on her cloak. As she made to follow them, Frances glanced at the figure in the shadows, who turned to her at the same moment.

Staring back at her from the gloom was Arbella.

The bells were already chiming eight when Frances hastened to the princess's apartments. She had not slept the night before. The image of Arbella's face had flitted before her every time she had closed her eyes. She had tried to convince herself that she had been mistaken, that the figure had been a manservant or some agent of Raleigh's. But she had recognised those small blue eyes as they peered out of the shadows, the smirk . . .

She wondered how the woman had managed to escape captivity unnoticed, let alone gain access to Raleigh's lodgings in the Tower. Had Raleigh been helping her to visit her husband, or had she been in his lodgings for another reason?

As she reached the door to her mistress's chamber, she heard sobbing. Her heart gave a lurch and she rushed inside.

Blanche was kneeling in front of the

princess, whose face was buried in her hands.

'What has happened?' Frances asked, fearing the answer.

'He is not coming!'

Frances was astonished. She had been certain that whatever had caused Elizabeth's grief related to Arbella. The princess threw a crumpled note to the floor and began to pace the room. 'Am I destined never to marry?' she demanded between sobs. 'To remain a barren virgin, like the old queen?'

'Please — calm yourself, Your Grace.' Frances grasped her hand and guided her to the window seat, away from the other ladies, who were gawping helplessly at their mistress. Even Blanche seemed at a loss as to how to comfort her.

'Who do you mean?' she asked, though she already knew the answer.

'Prince Victor!' Elizabeth cried, then fell into a fresh bout of sobbing. 'Cecil writes that my father has reached a private accord with the King of Spain and no longer needs the assurance of marriage to forge their alliance. No doubt a consignment of Spanish gold was enough.'

Frances had spent the past few days willing the Spanish prince to arrive. It would give heart to the Catholics, whose hopes were vested in the match, and would make them less inclined to support Seymour and Arbella, should they make their move — which seemed more likely now those hopes had been dashed. 'But we had received news that the prince had already embarked for England,' she reasoned.

'His uncle recalled the fleet just a few hours after it had left the port at Cádiz — so Cecil says,' the princess mumbled, her chest still heaving.

No doubt Cecil had worked hard to bring this private accord to pass, Frances thought, tempting his royal master with the lure of riches. He could have no wish to see the king's daughter espoused to a Catholic prince — not when there were Protestant suitors with whom an alliance might be forged. Prince Henry would be crowing when they saw him next. She wanted to weep: the plans for which she had laboured so hard now lay in tatters. Tom had died in vain. Catholics would never thrive again in this kingdom. They would do well to cast away their relics and rosaries and find what solace they could in heresy.

Her thoughts were interrupted when the princess stood abruptly and marched to the dresser. Pulling open the top drawer with such force that Frances feared it would fall to the floor, she took out the miniature of the prince. She looked down at it briefly, then strode back to the window by which Frances was still sitting. She wrenched it open and flung out the portrait. Frances heard the faint splash as it fell into the river below.

'You may leave me now,' the princess announced imperiously, drying her tears.

Frances stood uncertainly. The other ladies hesitated too.

'Go!' Elizabeth shouted, then stormed out of the room, slamming the door behind her.

The sudden cawing of a bird made Frances start. It sparked a medley of screeches and twitters, which became deafening as she approached the aviary. After a time the birds' excitement died away and only the occasional flutter of feathers could be heard amid the silence that now prevailed. The royal beasts must be sleeping too, she thought, as she looked across at the tall cages silhouetted against the night sky.

Continuing past the menagerie, she soon reached the lake that had been dug in the centre of St James's Park. It was a clear night and the moon's rays reflected off the still, dark water. Frances peered into the gloom and thought she saw a shadow moving between the trees. She held her breath and watched as the shape drew closer.

'Lady Frances,' Lady Vaux said, in a low voice, drawing back her hood. 'Your letter was most insistent.'

'Our plans are in ruins,' Frances said, without preamble. 'The King of Spain has recalled his nephew. There will be no betrothal.'

A slow smile crept across the older woman's face. 'I have received the news already. It seems it travelled more slowly to court.'

'If you knew of it, why did you not send word? All of my endeavours have been spent in encouraging the princess to look favourably on the match — and I had succeeded. I did not know it was all in vain.'

'I knew you would find out soon enough,' Lady Vaux replied nonchalantly. 'Besides, you made it plain the last time we met that I should not write to you again, lest your involvement be discovered.'

Frances pushed back her rising irritation. 'Well, you will have no further cause to send me letters now that our scheme has failed. There are no other Catholic princes abroad with whom the king will consider an alliance for his daughter.'

'You should have more faith, Lady Frances,' Lady Vaux replied. 'God has shown us that we were in error, that there is another suitor — one who will prove a far greater match for the princess than some foreign prince.'

An Englishman? It was impossible. The king would never agree to his daughter marrying a Catholic, unless it was to forge a lucrative foreign alliance.

'And you are well placed to further his interests, since he is your kin.'

'My *kin*?' Who on earth could she be referring to? Her brother Edward might be ambitious, but even he would not venture so far.

'The Earl of Northampton. Your uncle.'

Frances let out a bark of laughter. The idea was so ridiculous that it could not be true — but then she noticed Lady Vaux's expression.

'He is a true Catholic, at heart,' Lady Vaux continued, 'though he has outwardly conformed since this king's accession — as so many others have been obliged to. And he is of sufficient rank to be a suitor to the princess. I hardly need tell you that he was cousin to a queen of England.'

Frances had suffered her uncle's boasts about his kinship to Henry VIII's last wife, Katherine Parr, many times, but she had never had such cause to regret it as she did now. 'But he is more than forty years her senior!' Frances exclaimed, setting aside the many other reasons why her uncle was such a terrible choice.

'That is no bar to the match,' Lady Vaux said, with a dismissive wave of her hand. 'Many men have taken brides far younger than themselves. Besides, the earl is still vigorous and no doubt capable of siring many heirs yet.'

Frances shuddered. If she was repulsed by the idea of her ageing uncle bedding the princess, with how much greater horror would Elizabeth view it? 'The king will never allow it. He seeks a foreign alliance through his daughter's marriage and will not give that up for a home-grown suitor unless he is of impeccable credentials — which my uncle certainly is not.'

Lady Vaux's eyes showed triumph as she held her gaze. 'I might have been inclined to agree with you, were it not for the offer of assistance from a quite unexpected quarter,' she said. 'Robert Carr will turn his master's mind to the match. By the time he has applied his efforts on our behalf, the king will think that there can be no greater union for his daughter. I hear that the young man can be most . . . persuasive,' she added.

Frances stared. *Robert Carr?* Why on earth

would that sly young man apply himself on anyone's behalf except his own?

'The earl holds a prize that Carr is eager to win,' the woman continued. 'He is greatly enamoured of your uncle's young ward. Though she is already his mistress, he means to make her his wife.'

This fresh revelation was so unexpected that Frances struggled to make sense of it. Surely Carr's passions would not be stirred by a woman, even one as beguiling as the earl's ward, Frances Howard. She had seen the girl many times since arriving at court, but had never paid her much attention. The same could not be said of the handsome courtiers who swarmed about her.

'But Lady Howard is married already, is she not?'

Lady Vaux inclined her head. 'It is a marriage in name only. The Earl of Essex has proved incapable of consummating it, though he blames his young wife for that. He must be the only man in England who does not wish to bed her.'

'Then what can my uncle do to help Carr?' Frances demanded, with rising impatience. 'An impotent husband is still a husband.'

'Your uncle has powerful connections at court and can petition for an annulment on behalf of his ward,' Lady Vaux replied, lifting her chin defiantly. 'Without him, their cause is hopeless and Carr knows it. That is why he has agreed to further our schemes.'

Frances fell silent. The prospect of her uncle marrying the princess seemed just as preposterous as when Lady Vaux had first mentioned it. Even if Carr did succeed in persuading the king, she knew that she had neither the power nor the will to convince her young mistress that a conceited, objectionable old man would make a good husband. 'I wish you well in your endeavours, Lady Vaux,' she said at last. 'But I will have no part in them.'

'You speak as if you have the freedom of choice, Lady Frances.' Her voice was cold. 'But you know as well as I that it is not so. The king may have lost interest in finding those who were involved in the Powder Treason, but Cecil has not. If you refuse to play your part in this, I will make sure that he discovers you were once involved in something far more deadly.'

The threat of being exposed if she did not do Lady Vaux's bidding had always been implied, never spoken. This had enabled Frances to push it from her thoughts. But it had lurked on the edge of her consciousness. It was all too clear that she could hide from it no longer. Seymour had used it to embroil her in his schemes — for a while. Now Lady Vaux had resolved to do the same. Frances felt as trapped as the beasts that skulked in the cages behind her.

CHAPTER 30
7 JUNE

A hush descended and the crowds parted as Cecil walked slowly across the centre of the hall. Frances watched him from the dais, where she stood behind her mistress's chair. They had been summoned there only an hour before, the messenger interrupting the customary ceremony of dressing the princess for the evening's entertainments. The dais had already been decorated for the masque and there had been no time to take down the brightly coloured swags that were strung between the marble pillars. They formed a stark contrast to the sombre atmosphere that pervaded the hall.

Cecil's messenger had given no hint as to why the entire court had been ordered to assemble so suddenly. When Frances had accompanied her mistress there, she had heard several courtiers grumbling that their dinner would be cold by the time the gathering was over and the tables had been laid. She herself had little appetite. Whatever the cause of this peremptory summons, it must be serious to interrupt the usual routine of the palace.

Frances had spent the past two days in an agony of suspense. While the princess had veered from tearful outbursts to sullen silences, her own mind had been filled with thoughts of Arbella. She wished she had asked Lady Vaux about her, but she had been so shocked by the scheme involving her uncle that she had been unable to think of anything else for the rest of their meeting.

When no word of Arbella had been forthcoming from anyone, she had resorted to asking Blanche — as casually as she could — whether the lady had set out for Durham yet. Blanche had delighted in chastising her for thinking of such trivial matters when their mistress was stricken with grief over the prince. Frances had not yet raised the subject of her uncle. It would hardly ease the princess's anguish about her lost suitor to know that a gouty old man stood ready to take his place.

'I hope he is quick about it,' she heard Prince Henry mutter now. 'I am entertaining the French ambassador this evening.' He was sitting between his two siblings, clearly bored. He seldom visited Whitehall these days, preferring the livelier company over which he presided at St James's. Although she lamented the failure of the Spanish match, Frances could not help but feel relieved that Henry would have even less reason to spend time with his sister now — at least, not until he found another foreign suitor for her.

Cecil was mounting the steps to the dais. Frances thought him even more stooped than the last time she had seen him a few weeks before. She had not attended him since his recovery from the tumour the previous autumn, so the wound must now have healed. From the way he held himself as he bowed before the two princes and their sister, it seemed no longer to pain him. As he straightened, his eyes darted to Frances. She regarded him steadily as he walked to the front of the dais to address the crowds.

'Your Highnesses, my lords. I have summoned you here to convey news of the gravest sort,' he began. 'It is almost a year now since the king's officials discovered a foul treason at the heart of this court. The Lady Arbella had contracted a secret marriage with William Seymour, intending to use their combined royal blood to usurp the throne. God in His wisdom guided us, His Majesty's servants, to uncover this unlawful union so that the perpetrators might be apprehended.'

There was a low murmur around the hall as people recounted to each other their memories of the event. Cecil held up a hand to silence them before continuing. 'But the devil has found means to make mischief once more. By his hand, the Lady Stuart and her unlawful husband have escaped His Majesty's custody.'

Frances was only vaguely aware of the collective intake of breath among the crowd as she clutched the back of her mistress's chair. It was the news she had dreaded ever since her visit to the Tower three days before. Many times since then, she had wondered whether to tell Cecil what she had seen. But some impulse had always prevented it. Though she was not willing to support the lady in her reckless quest for the throne, neither could she bring herself to betray her — or Raleigh.

'God damn the man,' she heard Prince Henry say, under his breath. 'He should have come to me with this, before announcing it to the court.'

Her mistress's hands were trembling in her lap.

'The king has instructed me to make a thorough search of the city, as well as of the ports,' Cecil continued.

Frances directed her gaze towards him as he faced the princess.

'And of the palaces too, Your Graces.'

'They are hardly likely to be hiding here, my lord,' Henry exclaimed scornfully.

Cecil spread his hands. 'You are right, Your Grace,' he replied softly. 'But they were able to escape your father's custody, which suggests that they may have had accomplices here at court.'

Even though she was innocent of any involvement, Frances knew that Cecil would not hesitate to use her earlier assistance of the lady to implicate her, if it proved to his advantage. The king would be convinced that this was part of a wider conspiracy and would be impatient for news of arrests.

'His Majesty requires all of his subjects to be vigilant,' Cecil declared, 'so I ask that you send word to me of anything you have seen or heard that might occasion suspicion — even among your closest acquaintances. Not since the Powder Treason has there been cause for such alarm.'

He bowed towards the princes and their sister, then slowly left the dais. In the time it took him to reach the back of the hall, the hum of chatter had risen to a deafening roar.

When Frances retired to her husband's apartments that evening, her head was aching. Sleep would be the only cure, but she was certain it would evade her. Even if she allowed her racing thoughts to still, the fear that Cecil would send men to arrest her had set her nerves jangling. The best she could hope for was to lie quietly in her chamber, waiting for the night to pass.

She paused at the threshold, her eyes slowly adjusting to the gloom. She was glad that George was spending the night in Prince Charles's lodgings, ready to depart early to hunt the next day, but longed to wrap her arms around his warm little body, to nuzzle the softness of his hair. She closed her eyes and uttered a prayer that God might keep him safe tonight, even if He could not perform the same service for her.

With a sigh, she undressed to her linen shift, then padded over to the ewer and splashed water on her face and neck. The cold drops made her shiver as they ran down her back and chest, but offered some respite from the pain that seared her head.

When at last she climbed into bed, she slipped into sweet oblivion.

A loud hammering shocked her awake.

Her eyes flew open. Had she dreamed it? She had no idea if she had been asleep for minutes or hours.

Another volley rang out across the chamber. Frances threw back the covers and ran towards the outer door. A faint light glimmered from under it.

He had come for her.

She pulled on her cloak and wrapped it tightly around her, then reached for the bolt. She pulled it back and lifted the latch.

Instead of the king's guards, there stood a young man clad in a livery she did not recognise. Sweat dripped from his brow and his clothes were caked in dust. Hastily, he removed his cap and gave a short bow.

'Lady Tyringham?'

Frances nodded.

'The Earl of Rutland has sent me here with ill tidings. Your husband fell from his horse during the hunt and was trampled underfoot. He lies mortally hurt at Belvoir. Please!' he urged, as she struggled to comprehend his words — so different from those she had expected. 'You must make haste. A carriage is ready. Pray God it is not too late.'

371

CHAPTER 31
11 JUNE

The rain whipped against the carriage window as Frances peered out. In the gathering gloom, she could just make out a dark mass covering the hill ahead: the Earl of Rutland's famed woodland, which surrounded his castle, whose turrets she could now see rising above the trees.

Their progress had slowed since Grantham, thanks to the arrival of the rains that had threatened all day, turning the dusty track into a river of mud. She could hear the horses whinnying as their hoofs slipped on the now treacherous path that led steadily uphill. Frances cursed her failure to persuade the coachman to press on to the castle, rather than rest his horses at the town, which lay just seven miles before it. They could have been there by now, sheltered from the elements, the horses dry and warm in the stables. The man had spent a frustratingly long time at the inn, taking his meat with a rowdy group, while Frances, having eaten a hasty meal, paced up and down outside. She had been at the point of leaving him there and walking the rest of the way when he had emerged, ruddy-faced, oblivious to her scowls.

Now the carriage listed to one side, precariously close to the edge of the path, which fell steeply away into the valley below.

'Whoa!' The coachman's shout was followed by a string of curses that were carried away on the wind.

For an agonising few minutes, they remained still, the carriage swaying in the gusts that blew across the valley. A fresh wave of fear assailed Frances. It had been four days since the messenger had arrived at Whitehall. If her husband was as gravely hurt as he was reported to be, she might already be too late. It was all too horribly familiar, she acknowledged, as she thought back to the cold March night when she had hastened to her dying father at Richmond. Surely God would not be so cruel as to take her husband from her so soon afterwards. No: they would have been intercepted by a messenger if Thomas had already died, she reasoned.

Frances looked down at the large leather bag that lay at her feet. Within her clothes, she had hidden her collection of dried herbs and tinctures. There had been no time to select those that would be of most use to her husband, so she had brought them all. It was probably wise not to leave any in Greenwich anyway. How she would treat her husband with them when the king lodged under the same roof, she did not know. She could only hope that they would be afforded some privacy as man and wife — the same privacy she had spent most of their marriage trying to avoid.

The carriage moved forward, throwing Frances back against the cushions. She could hear the slap and squelch of the horses' hoofs as they plodded up the track. Darkness was falling quickly now and Frances could see the faint glimmer of lights in the castle. She wondered which room her husband lay in.

At last, they reached the drive that snaked through the parkland to the entrance. Frances heard the sharp crack of the whip followed by the rapid crunch of hoofs on gravel as the horses finally cantered towards the gatehouse. Lowering the window, she felt heat as they passed the torches that blazed on either side of it. A few moments later, they were inside the courtyard. Not waiting for the groom, who was scurrying towards her from the castle, Frances stepped down from the carriage and hastened towards the large doorway from which he had emerged.

A sombre-faced footman stepped forward as she approached. He bowed.

'Have you been invited for dinner, mistress?'

'Lady Frances Tyringham.'

She saw his eyes widen briefly in alarm.

'Then please allow me to escort you to the hall, my lady.'

Frances tried to suppress her rising impatience. 'Thank you, but I will go straight to my husband, if you could show me to his chamber?'

'Of course, my lady. I will fetch someone to accompany you.'

Before she could protest, he had turned on his heel and stepped smartly away. She could hear the rapid clip of his heels on the marble floor as he disappeared.

The entrance hall was vast. At the far end a huge stone fireplace was surmounted by the head of a bull, its glassy eyes staring straight ahead. Above, on the first floor, three large archways had been cut into the stonework, through which Frances could see a white marble staircase with ornate black iron balustrades. The walls to either side of her were covered with halberds, swords and other weapons, all artfully arranged into geometrical shapes.

'Lady Frances.'

She spun round. A small woman was standing in the doorway that led through to the stairs. She was wearing a pale gold dress slashed with scarlet and edged with lacework at the sleeves and neckline. A large square ruff covered her neck, and her dark blonde curls were surmounted by a headdress of the same white fabric. Her features were pinched and her large grey-brown eyes were watching Frances intently.

'Forgive me, Lady . . .'

'Manners,' she answered. 'Cecily, Countess of Rutland. You are most welcome to Belvoir Castle,' she added, in a tone that suggested Frances was anything but.

Frances curtsied.

'Peake tells me you will not join us for dinner,' she continued. 'I assure you, it is no inconvenience — we have only just begun.'

'Thank you, Lady Rutland, but I am anxious to see my husband,' Frances replied. 'How does he fare?'

The countess's eyes were flitting over her, and Frances was suddenly aware of the shabbiness of her attire. She had dressed hastily before departing her chambers at Greenwich and had changed only her linens since. Glancing down, she saw that her simple grey gown was heavily creased, its hem caked with mud. But if the lady of the house objected to her appearing in such a state, having travelled for four long days to see her husband, who might even now be breathing his last, she must be cold-hearted indeed.

'I have had my physicians attend him,' she said. 'Their reputation is unsurpassed in the county.'

'You are most kind,' Frances replied. 'Now please, forgive me, I must see him.'

'Of course,' Lady Rutland said. 'Follow me.'

She led the way up the staircase, which was flanked on either side by numerous family portraits. As they mounted the second flight, one of the pictures caught her eye. It was of a young man with dark brown hair and a fashionably pointed beard. He was pleasant-looking rather than handsome, but what struck Frances was the sadness in his eyes. Tearing her gaze away, she hastened after the countess, who stepped nimbly along a gallery at the top of the stairs.

Frances hardly noticed the sumptuously decorated series of rooms through which they passed, her heart keeping time with her quickening pace. At length, they reached a dimly lit corridor. The countess stopped outside a door about halfway along it. For a moment, Frances feared that the woman would insist on entering with her, but instead she gave a nod and started back along the corridor.

Frances watched until she was out of sight, then lifted the latch.

The first thing she noticed was the heat, which hit her in a suffocating wave as she stepped into the chamber. An enormous fire blazed in the grate, and both of the small windows were tightly shuttered. Frances breathed in the sickly stench of decay. A young attendant dozed by the fire but stood as she entered. He looked at her in alarm, as if waiting for admonishment. Frances was sure the Belvoir servants received plenty from their mistress. 'Thank you,' she said. 'You may leave my husband now.'

The boy's face showed relief and he left the room, closing the door softly behind him.

Crossing quickly to the windows, Frances flung them open. A gust of cool, damp air blew into the room, making the glass rattle in its casement. Frances closed her eyes and uttered a silent prayer, then turned to the bed.

Heavy damask curtains were drawn around each side of it. Slowly, she walked towards it, straining to listen, but there was no sound from within. She felt the cold grasp of fear as she pulled back one of the curtains. Her husband was lying on his side, facing away from her. She padded around the edge of the bed, drawing another curtain as she did so. Her eyes never left his body, which lay perfectly still. When at last she saw his face, a small cry escaped her lips.

A large black bruise covered one side, which was so swollen that it completely obscured his fine features. Above his right eye, there was a deep gash that was crusted with dark blood and seeped yellow pus. There was more blood on the pillow, and as Frances looked closely, she saw that it came from a wound on the side of his skull, which glistened through his matted hair. His lips were parted and cracked. There was a yellow-brown stain on the sheets and the tang of vomit hung on the air. His knees were drawn up, and his right arm was bent at an unnatural angle across his chest. Frances placed her fingers around his wrist. He did not move. She waited, trying to still her own pulse as she felt for his. At last she found it — faint but steady — and let out a long breath.

Swallowing tears, she forced herself to look at her husband with the eyes of a healer, not a wife. His arm was dislocated, she was sure of that. Some, if not all, of his ribs were probably cracked. There were no signs of inward bleeding, but she could only guess at the severity of the wound to his head.

Working quickly, she took out her phials and dried herbs and set them on the table next to the bed, pushing aside the potions that had been left by the countess's physicians. With a sudden thought, she walked quickly to the door and was relieved to see a key in the lock. She turned it and heard it click into place.

Back at the table, she plucked some dandelion leaves and ground them with brittle elder bark until the mixture became a powder, then added a few drops of juniper oil. Tearing off a piece of clean linen from the bolt she had brought with her, she dipped it slowly into the mortar, then dabbed the yellowy tincture onto the gash above Thomas's eye. It felt hot to the touch. He made no move as she continued to clean the wound. It would need stitching. Reaching into her bag, she drew out the finest needle she could find, with some silk yarn. Her fingers shook as she tried to thread it and she cursed her clumsiness. When at last she had succeeded, she leaned forward and pinched one end of the wound together, then slowly pierced the skin. Thomas flinched, but after a few moments, his face relaxed and she continued to stitch, pulling the thread as tight as she dared so that the flesh would knit together.

In the distance, she could hear the chiming of a clock. Dinner must almost be over. She prayed nobody would disturb them just yet. Crossing to the ewer, she soaked a fresh linen cloth in the water, which had long since turned cold, and began to clean the deep gash on the side of Thomas's head. Her fingers gently parted the hair around it, but in the soft glow of the candlelight it was impossible to see the extent of the wound. Feeling inside her pocket, she drew out the scissors she had put into it the last time she had worn the dress so that she might work on her embroidery with the princess. They were not very sharp but would suffice. Coiling his thick brown hair in her fingers, she had a sudden recollection of Tom, his head on her breast as she stroked the curls at the nape of his neck. She began to cut the hair. It was sticky around the wound and she was obliged to keep wiping the blades, which were soon blunted.

When she had trimmed as close to her husband's scalp as she dared, she held the candle closer. Her breath caught in her throat and she stared in horror. A deep wound ran from behind his right ear to the top of his scalp, the bone showing in places through the swollen red flesh. A thin trail of blood pulsed from the deepest part and Frances could see that it was tinged with yellow. The wound was far too wide for stitching yet. The best she could hope was to stem the bleeding and stop the infection spreading.

She fetched more fresh linen, soaked some in the tincture she had made and applied it carefully to the wound. Folding a larger piece of the fabric into a thick wad, she placed it over the length of the wound, securing it with a long strip of linen, which she tied around Thomas's head. Then she made up a fresh tincture with anemone and honey, adding a little water so that it would slip easily down his throat. She placed the small glass phial between her husband's lips and gently tilted it. There was a gurgle as the mixture reached the back of his throat. Frances waited, fearing he might vomit, but after a few moments she saw his neck pulse as he swallowed. She gave him another tiny dose to swallow, then another, until at last the phial was empty.

Suddenly weary, she looked at the table, which was littered with discarded pots and herbs. She would need to gather more tomorrow. Kneeling at her husband's bedside, Frances closed her eyes in prayer. She had done all she could for now. God must take her husband into His care.

CHAPTER 32
14 JUNE

Frances rubbed her aching neck as she walked slowly down the stairs. She had kept vigil by her husband's side all night, dozing, then waking suddenly, fearful that he had slipped away while she slept. Each time, she had looked across and seen him lying there, as if suspended between this life and the next. She had been loath to leave him, but she must preserve her own strength for the days — perhaps weeks — to come, and had resolved to eat as hasty a breakfast as politeness would allow.

The smell of freshly baked bread and roasted meat wafted up the stairs as she descended, making her stomach growl. She had eaten little since her arrival three nights before, taking her meals in Thomas's chamber so that she could keep watch on him. Now, as she followed the aroma towards the dining room, she wondered if she might take some food back to his chamber, rather than eat with the assembled company.

A groom was standing by the door as she approached and escorted her into the hall. The day had dawned clear and bright, and sunlight streamed in, sparking off the jewelled candelabra and the ornate chandelier that dominated the ceiling, its crystals delicate as raindrops.

Two servants were busy clearing away dishes and platters from the table, and Frances was relieved to see that the chairs were empty. The king must have left for the hunt. She followed the groom to a seat at the far end of the table and helped herself to some fine manchet loaf, still warm from the oven. She wrapped it in her napkin, with some ham and plump figs. Pouring herself a large goblet of water, she drank it, then stood to leave.

'Lady Frances?' A man was standing in the entrance to the hall, his slender frame silhouetted against the light that spilled through the doorway. 'Forgive me. I did not mean to startle you,' he continued, walking slowly forward to greet her. He was of about her own age, Frances judged, and had a pleasant, kindly aspect. There was something familiar about him.

'How is Sir Thomas?'

His eyes were filled with genuine concern

— and, she thought, some hidden sadness. She realised why she felt she had met him before. The portrait on the stairs.

'Lord Rutland.' She curtsied. 'My husband has not yet awoken. His wounds are very grave. I fear —' She stopped.

'I am very sorry for it,' the earl replied. 'He was — is — a fine man and serves the king most loyally. He is a skilled horseman too. I did not witness his fall but understand that something startled his horse. There was nothing he could do to control it. I feel responsible, since it happened on my estate. I will do whatever I can to ease his suffering, Lady Frances.'

At that moment, a young serving woman entered the hall bearing a large platter of smoked herring and more fresh bread. As she set it down next to where Frances had been sitting, her large brown eyes flicked up to the earl. A shadow crossed his face as he looked at the girl with . . . fear? Desire? Both, perhaps.

'Thank you, Philippa,' he murmured, almost to himself.

She did not acknowledge him, but slipped away, her elfin face obscured by a mass of dark curls. As she reached the doorway, she almost collided with Countess Cecily, who stepped briskly into the room. 'Have a care!'

the woman chided.

The girl skittered away, but before she disappeared Frances saw her fingers flick out in a gesture so strange that she wondered if she had imagined it. *A witch's curse.*

'Ah, Lady Frances,' Cecily said airily. 'It seems you are destined never to dine with us. The king rose early for the hunt, the rest of our household with him.'

'Did you not wish to join them, my lord?' Frances asked, hoping to divert Lady Rutland's attention away from herself.

'Not today, Lady Frances. My limbs still ache from yesterday's expedition,' he replied, with a crooked smile.

His wife made an impatient clicking noise with her tongue, then turned back to Frances. 'I trust Sir Thomas has everything he needs? It must have been quite a shock to see him in such a state. My husband's physicians say he is beyond hope.'

Lord Rutland shifted uncomfortably. 'There is always hope, my dear,' he said quietly.

'My husband seems stable enough for now, but I will need fresh linens and . . . other supplies.' Frances was careful not to mention her herbs or tinctures. 'I have already exhausted those that I brought with me.'

Cecily looked at her in dismay. 'Surely you do not mean to treat him yourself, Lady Frances. He requires the skill of a physician. Besides,' she added, casting a sideways glance at her husband, 'I am sure you would not wish people to think you a wise woman.'

Frances opened her mouth to reply, but Lord Rutland gave a small cough, as if in warning. 'I would be glad to accompany you to Bottesford, Lady Frances,' he said. 'We can visit my apothecary. I am sure he will be able to advise upon the best remedies for your husband.'

His wife gave a snort of derision. 'Why trouble to go yourselves when we can summon him here?'

'It is only a short ride and I fancy Lady Frances would welcome some fresh air. She looks a little pale.'

Before Cecily could raise any further objection, Frances excused herself so that she could fetch her cloak and riding boots.

When she returned a few minutes later the earl was waiting for her. He seemed distracted, and though he smiled, his eyes were grave.

'You do not mean still to go, husband?'

They turned at Cecily's voice. She was standing at the entrance to the hall, hands on hips.

'I see no reason to delay our excursion, my dear,' Lord Rutland said.

'But the king may require your counsel,' his wife persisted, 'and that of his other attendants.'

Frances looked from one to the other.

'He has not told you, then?' the countess demanded. 'A messenger arrived a few minutes ago with news from the court. The Lady Arbella has been seized.'

Frances tried to keep the shock from her face.

'My dear, Lady Frances has troubles enough of her own. She does not need to hear this now.'

'No, please, go on,' Frances urged.

'She was taken on board a ship bound for Calais,' Cecily continued. 'It is said that she had arranged to meet Seymour in the Channel, but he was delayed and the king's officers found her first. She will be in the Tower by now,' she added, with relish.

Frances did not know if she felt relieved or afraid. 'What of Seymour?' she asked.

The countess pursed her lips. 'He escaped, though pray God the seas will take him.'

Frances hoped he had fled to Flanders. Tom and his associates would have lived out their days there, if only they had chosen to flee England, rather than stay to rally support among the Catholic community. She thought of how she could have joined him to revel in the intimacy they had enjoyed only fleetingly in England. But then an image came to her of Thomas lying unconscious in the chamber upstairs and the usual longing for Tom was replaced by remorse.

'You should have told him yourself.' Cecily was chiding her husband again. 'The king honours those who bring him welcome tidings.'

The earl shrugged. 'We have already received a great many bounties at His Majesty's hands, my dear. Besides, the messenger will have ridden with greater speed than I could ever have mustered.'

Cecily's scowl deepened but she pressed her lips together and turned on her heel.

'Well, now, Lady Frances. That is quite enough talk of treason for one day,' the earl said, with a touch of humour. 'Shall we depart?'

CHAPTER 33
14 JUNE

A towering spire rose into view as they descended into the valley. To Frances, it seemed almost as high as that of Salisbury Cathedral, yet the church was a good deal smaller. For all her worries, it had been a pleasant ride. She had longed to gallop through the open fields that surrounded the estate, but even at a more sedate pace the fresh air had cleared her mind, helping her to absorb the news about Arbella and Seymour. This was surely the end to their plotting. Seymour could not hope to challenge the throne without Arbella at his side, and Frances knew that Cecil would take no more risks with her safe-keeping. Sir William Wade would be only too happy to provide the most secure lodgings at his disposal in the Tower.

'St Mary's houses the tombs of my ancestors,' the earl remarked, following her gaze. 'They were generous benefactors —

as you can see. The locals boast that it is the tallest church spire in England. They call it the Lady of the Vale.'

'They are right to be proud,' Frances replied. 'It is magnificent — as is your home, my lord.'

'That is a mixed blessing, I find. The richer the home, the more likely the king is to visit.'

Frances looked at him sharply, but he was smiling.

'I am honoured, of course, but such visits leave my coffers severely depleted,' he continued. 'King James favours Belvoir for the hunting grounds. They are fine enough, but the woodlands give me greatest pleasure. I spend many hours there, hunting down plants and herbs, rather than foxes.'

Frances was surprised. 'You have some knowledge of such things?'

'A little, yes — though I wish it were greater. I think you share my interest.'

Though she judged the earl a gentle, kindly man, she hardly knew him and dared not place her trust in one so favoured of the king. 'I, too, was fortunate to grow up among woodlands rich with such treasures,' she said lightly. 'It inspired me with a love of nature that I cherish. Sadly, I have little opportunity to indulge it now. His Majesty's palaces boast many splendours, but the natural world is almost entirely absent.'

They lapsed into silence but Frances could feel his eyes upon her as they rode into the village. It was much larger than Britford and there were perhaps fifty houses lining the wide streets, all built from the honey-coloured stone that was quarried nearby. A stream ran along the periphery and there was a handsome bridge across its widest point. Frances was aware of curious stares as they passed through the market square, with its large stone cross at the centre, though everyone they saw was careful to show their deference to the earl.

There was a cluster of shops at the far end of the square, and outside one Frances could see a wooden sign painted with a pestle and mortar. She slowed her horse, but the earl continued straight past. Her confusion turned to unease as they reached the edge of the village, the handsome houses giving way to smaller, shabbier dwellings. As they drew level with the last, which lay close to the woods, her companion pulled on the reins and brought his horse to a standstill. Dismounting, he tethered it to the ramshackle gate. The unthinking way with which he did so suggested he was a frequent visitor — though, looking again at the cottage, with its crumbling stonework and frayed thatch, Frances could hardly believe it was true. After a pause, she took the hand he offered and climbed down from her horse.

He was already striding along the path as she tied her horse's reins to the gate but he waited for her at the door, then knocked softly. There was no sound from within, but Frances had the creeping sensation of being watched. She looked towards the dark thicket at the edge of the forest and thought she caught a small movement, but her attention was diverted by the light tread of feet within the cottage.

A moment later, the door was opened a crack and Frances could see a pair of eyes peering out at them.

'Mistress Flower, forgive the intrusion,' the earl said smoothly. 'My friend here is in need of your assistance.'

The woman grunted, then turned on her heel and retreated into the house, leaving the door open for them to follow. As she stepped inside, Frances had to pause until her eyes became accustomed to the gloom. There was only one small window, which looked out onto the woods and afforded little light. The room in which they were standing seemed to serve as kitchen, bedroom and parlour. There was a large bed in the corner, and a meagre fireplace on the opposite side of the room. Frances breathed in the sharp tang of rosemary and lavender, along with a scent she did not recognise. Bunches of dried herbs were suspended from beams across the ceiling. Underneath the window there was a table, its surface gnarled with age, upon which was set an array of clay pots and dishes, with a large pestle and mortar.

'What ails you?'

The woman was thin and stooped, and her face bore the lines of age — or hardship, perhaps. Her hair was streaked with grey, but her eyes were striking and Frances thought she must have been a great beauty in her youth.

'The lady has come on behalf of her husband, Joan,' the earl replied, before Frances could do so. 'He fell from his horse and is badly hurt.'

'His ribs may be broken and there is a deep wound to his head, which bleeds still and is inflamed,' Frances added.

'Is he feverish?' the woman asked, padding over to the table and holding up one of the pots to the light, then decanting some of its contents into a small bottle.

'His skin is hot to the touch, but he shows

no sign of delirium,' Frances replied.

Joan deftly plucked a few sprigs of different herbs, then began to grind them. Frances was mesmerised by the calm, rhythmic movement of her hands as she continued to work, pausing now and again to pour in a few drops of oil. She inhaled the pungent aroma of rue and yarrow, which soon filled the chamber. She looked with envy at the woman's collection of herbs, tinctures and simples, longing to examine them more closely. Even the Reverend Samuels had not possessed such skill.

At length, the woman set down the pestle and carefully poured the mixture into another small bottle. 'You must apply this to the wound twice a day,' she said, handing it to Frances. 'And give him this to drink — as much as he can stomach.'

Frances took the second bottle and sniffed it. 'What is it?'

'Clary sage and self-heal. It will lessen the inflammation and bring down his fever.'

'Surely elder bark is more effective?' Frances was suddenly fearful that her husband's life was now in the hands of this stranger.

Joan's eyes fixed upon hers for a long moment. The earl shifted uncomfortably. 'Have you brought a wise woman to keep me

396

company, my lord?' she asked, not taking her eyes off Frances. 'If you wish to use your own remedies, then it is of no matter to me. Perhaps you set little store by your husband's life,' she added slyly.

'I care a great deal for him,' Frances snapped.

The woman smiled. 'Then you will use my simples — though if his hurts are as grievous as you say, even they may be of little use.'

'Thank you, Joan,' Lord Rutland interjected, pressing some coins into her hand. 'We will leave you now.'

Frances turned to follow him but stumbled over something at her feet. There was an angry yowl and a cat scampered to its mistress. Joan scooped it up and pressed her lips to its neck, nuzzling the long fur. 'Hush, Rutterkin,' she murmured. 'Tell me, my lord, how do your young sons fare?'

The earl turned back. 'They are in fine health, thank you,' he said cautiously. 'Now, if you will excuse us . . .'

His fingers had just closed over the latch when the door was flung open from the other side. The elfin servant girl stood stock still, her eyes darting from her master to his companion. Frances wondered that she had not noticed the resemblance before.

'Mother,' the girl muttered, as she brushed past them and sank down onto the bed, pulling off her shoes, the soles of which were coming loose. She did not acknowledge the earl, who looked ill at ease. Frances was as shocked by the girl's insolence as she was intrigued by his reaction.

Joan gave a low chuckle, then turned her back on her visitors and began grinding a fresh tincture.

'Good day,' the earl said, and walked out of the house, Frances following.

They rode back to the castle in silence. Frances longed to question her companion about Joan Flower and her daughter, but something in his manner prevented it. She wondered if Lady Cecily knew that he visited their cottage. That he had lied about the apothecary suggested she did not.

As they neared the entrance to the castle, the shouts of the king's servants rang out across the courtyard. Frances's heart sank. She had hoped he would be out hunting for hours yet. Fighting the instinct to turn her horse and gallop away across the fields, she followed the earl into the courtyard and dismounted.

James was sitting on the mounting block, his face flushed from the ride. A number of attendants were fussing around him, drawing off his leather gloves, unlacing his jerkin and handing him a cup of wine. Frances recognised Robert Carr among them, his white hands brushing James's neck as he pretended to dust off his shirt.

'Your Majesty.' The earl bowed low. 'I hope you found good hunting today.'

The king took a long swig of wine and gave a grunt. 'The horses were sluggish and my hounds fretful.' His gaze moved to Frances. 'When will your husband be fit to attend me again, Lady Frances?'

'I hope Sir Thomas will recover in time,' she said, 'though if God sees fit to spare him, it will be many weeks yet before he is able to join the hunt.'

'Ach!' James exclaimed impatiently, batting away one of his attendants. 'That's of little use to me. If he does not make haste, I will find someone to replace him, eh, Rabbie?'

The young man bowed but kept his eyes on Frances. He held out his hand and helped his master to his feet. Frances watched the king turn and walk slowly back towards the house, his hand still clutching that of his attendant.

CHAPTER 34
6 JULY

The sun streamed through the open window, making the heat in the chamber even more oppressive. It had not rained since Frances's arrival at Belvoir almost a month before, and the earth was dry and cracked, threatening to ruin the harvest. Soaking a linen cloth in the fresh water that the charwoman had brought up earlier, Frances rubbed it slowly over her neck and chest, shivering as rivulets trickled down her back and stomach.

Thomas's eyes were still closed, his lips curled into what looked almost like a smile. She studied his face, her fingers resting on her collarbone. How many times had she inwardly recoiled as he had leaned forward to kiss her cheek? Even this chaste contact had felt like a betrayal of Tom. Now, as she gazed at her husband, she found herself longing to feel the warmth of his lips on her own, his hands pressed into the small of her back as he drew her closer.

She shook away the thought and turned back to the ewer. Her hands trembled as she poured more water and she set down the jug so clumsily that it knocked against the rim of the bowl, almost upturning it. She cast an anxious glance at Thomas, as if afraid to have disturbed him, even though she had spent the past few weeks willing him to open his eyes. Although she had carefully applied Joan Flower's tinctures to his injuries and had given him the clary sage and self-heal to drink, with small amounts of broth and water, he had not stirred. She drew some comfort from the fact that the inflammation had receded and he was no longer feverish, but she prayed that God would soon open his eyes.

From the window, she saw Cecily striding purposefully towards the walled garden that lay to the west of the house. Margaret Flower was tending the chickens, her blonde curls catching the sun as she stooped to scatter another handful of seeds. Frances had been surprised to learn she was Philippa's sister. She looked so unlike her — and her mother Joan — with her rounded curves and fair hair.

Frances had moved away from the window when a faint cry drew her attention back to the garden. Margaret was crouching, head bowed, her hand on her cheek. Cecily was standing over her, gesturing sharply towards the house and back at the girl. Frances could not catch her words, but she was clearly chiding Margaret for some misdemeanour.

Soaking another cloth in the ewer, she carried it over to the bed and peeled back the sheet that covered her husband's body. As gently as she could, she lifted his linen shirt and began dabbing at his chest. The bruising had faded now, and she hoped that the cracks in his ribs had begun to knit together. She pulled back the sleeves and sponged his arms. The muscles had begun to waste and they had grown thin, like the rest of his body. Wringing out the cloth, she moved to his hands, which felt cool to the touch, despite the searing heat. As she held his fingers, she felt a twitch so slight that she feared she had imagined it. She waited, gazing intently at his hand. There it was again, stronger this time.

Frances looked at his face. Though his eyes were still closed, his lips were moving, as if he was trying to form words. Still clasping his hand, she leaned closer. After a few breaths, there was a low rasping sound from the back of his throat. Quickly, she poured a cup of water and held it to his mouth, tilting it slowly as she had done many times these past weeks. He swallowed, then lifted his head for more. Frances's hand shook as she held the cup to his lips again. When she was sure he had had enough, she set it back on the table.

Her husband's eyes twitched and, slowly, he opened them. Blinking away the long weeks of sleep, he stared up at the canopy above the bed, his brow creasing.

'Thomas,' Frances whispered.

Slowly, he turned to look at her. For a moment, his expression did not change, then his brow cleared and his lips lifted into a smile. Frances blinked away tears. She had imagined this moment so many times, forcing herself to picture every detail, as if by doing so she could conjure it into life. She hardly dared believe that it was real, and as she reached out to touch his cheek, she feared he might dissolve into a dream, as Tom had so many times.

His skin still felt cool as she held her palm to his face. After a few moments, he lifted his hand and closed it over hers, wincing. His chest rose and fell in quick movements as he recovered from even this small exertion.

'Frances.'

His voice was as cracked and dry as the scorched earth that surrounded the castle. She helped him to another few sips of water and waited while he recovered his breath again.

'What has happened?' he rasped.

Frances smoothed a lock of hair from his forehead. 'You were thrown from your horse during the hunt. It trampled you underfoot. Several of your ribs were broken and you have a grievous wound on your head.'

'Let us hope it has brought me to my senses at last,' he whispered.

Frances laughed, almost giddy with the relief and joy that were surging through her. Tears spilled down her cheeks as she gazed at her husband. It was a while before either of them spoke again.

'How long have I lain here, like this?' Thomas asked.

'About a month.' Frances saw his eyes widen in shock. 'I began to fear that you would never wake. I —' She broke off, unable to continue.

Her husband squeezed her hand. 'I am sorry to have given you such trouble. It must have grieved you to be apart from George for so long. How does he fare?'

Frances smiled. 'He has been a faithful correspondent,' she said fondly. 'I will read you some of his letters later.'

She recalled her surprise and joy upon opening the first, a few days after her arrival at Belvoir. It was only a few lines, but she had cherished it, tracing the round, childish script as she read that he had been working hard at his lessons, that the prince was kinder to him, and asking when she might return. That he had written at all was thanks to the princess — the address was in her elegant script. She had feared that her mistress's affection, so recently regained, would quickly fade, and she did not doubt that Blanche would make the most of her prolonged absence.

'And the king? Is he still here?' Thomas asked.

Frances's smile became forced. 'Lord Rutland is a generous host. His Majesty seems in no hurry to return to London.'

'You have met the countess?' he asked.

'I have seen her but seldom. Most of my hours have been spent in this chamber.'

'Then I pity you, for I must have been a very dull companion.'

Thomas fell silent again, and Frances watched as his eyelids grew heavy. After a few moments, they closed and his breathing slowed. She was about to stand when his grip on her hand suddenly tightened.

'Thank you, Frances,' he whispered, as he opened his eyes to look at her once more, then slowly slipped back into sleep.

During the days that followed, Thomas's strength gradually returned and he was soon able to stomach more than the watery broth that had sustained him while he had remained unconscious. Though his chest still pained him, the wound on his head was healing rapidly and the hair surrounding it had begun to grow back. Soon it would be concealed altogether, Frances told him.

After a week, he was able to stand with her assistance, and even walk a few, faltering paces, leaning heavily on her. Though she knew it gave him pain, she gradually extended the distance they covered, so that his wasted limbs would begin to regain their strength.

'Tell me some news of the court,' her husband asked one day, as they sat at the window seat in his chamber.

Frances looked at him sharply, but then relaxed: he could hardly have heard about Arbella and Seymour without her knowledge, given that she had been present on the few occasions that a member of the household — usually the earl — had paid him a visit.

'There is little to tell,' she lied, looking down at the embroidery on her lap. 'The princess is thriving and grows daily more loved by the people. Her brother has established a lively court at St James's and welcomes all manner of dignitaries, now that he is Prince of Wales. Their mother is still at Greenwich, I believe. I hope she enjoys better health.'

'She must be glad of the repose — though her husband hardly troubles her when he is in London,' Thomas said. 'I wonder that they can live such separate lives.'

Frances could feel his eyes upon her. 'I suppose that royal marriages are different from those of their subjects.'

Thomas took her hand in his. 'Are they, Frances?' he murmured. 'Has ours been so very different from that? Though we have lived as husband and wife for five years now, I often feel we are little more than strangers.'

Frances felt her heart quicken. 'It is as you willed it,' she said quietly.

'No, Frances,' he said, with sudden force, withdrawing his hand. 'As *you* willed it. I have long since wished it otherwise. Even before —' He was struggling to contain his emotions.

Frances looked at her lap, where the embroidery lay untouched.

'Even before Tom's death,' he continued, sounding so sad that tears filled her eyes as she listened. 'I remember seeing you for the first time, as you danced in the masque that evening. Though it was clear that you wished to be anywhere other than the stage, you excelled all the other dancers as much in grace as in beauty. I can see you there still, your eyes burning, the blue satin of your dress swaying around you as you followed the steps. I had never seen anything so exquisite, and I know I never will again.'

He fell silent. Frances was suddenly aware of the clock's ticking and tried to slow her breathing to keep time with it. She thought back to when she had first met her husband and was ashamed when she recalled her coldness towards him. She had been furious with her uncle for parading her at the dinner, like a rare jewel that he hoped would fetch a good price. Thomas had been a gracious and charming host, but she had hardly noticed him — particularly after Tom's arrival. Her treatment of him had been as thoughtless as her uncle's had been of her.

'Forgive me,' she whispered, unable to raise her eyes to his.

He reached across and placed his hand over hers. The warmth of his touch was like balm to her soul. 'You have never wronged me, Frances,' he said gently. 'I knew that you still loved Tom when I offered to marry you, and you did not promise anything that you have not honoured. The deceit is not yours.'

Frances might not have deceived him in the way he meant, but in conspiring with Anne Vaux and Jane Drummond she had committed a far worse betrayal.

'I still ask nothing of you,' he continued. 'I know you cannot love me as you loved Tom. I want only to be with you — George too, whom I love as my own son. To share in even part of your life is enough. God knows it is more than I deserve,' he added.

Frances saw the shadow in his eyes at these last words. She tried to muster some of the anger she had felt upon seeing him leave Jane Drummond's apartment at court, but pity and remorse flooded her.

'It is not enough,' she said.

He turned to her in dismay, but she touched his cheek, holding her hand there for several moments as she gazed at him. Then, leaning forward, she kissed him.

Frances gazed up at the mellow sunlight through the leaves on the tall branches above, casting dappled patterns across the forest floor. A soft breeze lifted a strand of her hair over her shoulders, causing a shiver to run through her, though the afternoon was still deliciously warm.

'We should return to the castle,' Thomas murmured, his lips brushing against her neck as he spoke. 'The countess does not look kindly upon latecomers.'

Frances sighed and stretched luxuriantly, the gnarled root of the oak tree pressing against her naked back. Raising herself on one elbow, she gazed down at her husband, whose eyes were still closed. The bruising on the smooth contours of his chest was barely visible now and he was able to move his arms without wincing. She stroked his hair, her fingers gently probing the wound. An angry red scar ran halfway across his skull, but it was concealed by the hair that had grown back over it.

'Must I be forever subject to your examinations?' The corners of his mouth twitched into a smile. 'I begin to think that your only interest in me is as a specimen upon whom you may practise your spells and incantations.'

Frances grinned. 'I assure you that if my interests lay in that direction only, I would find a much finer specimen to experiment upon.'

Thomas clutched his hand to his heart as if wounded by her words but she caught it in hers and pressed her lips to it, then gently laid her head on his chest. It felt warm against her cheek and she could hear the steady beat of his heart. She traced her fingers down his stomach, brushing against the hairs that thickened below his navel. Desire flickered inside her again. She brought her lips close to his, savouring the warmth of his breath on her mouth, then kissed him, slowly at first but with increasing urgency as she moved to sit astride him. He was gazing intently at her now, his hips rising and falling with hers and his hands gripping her thighs. His chest glistened with sweat and his whole body seemed to tense before he gave a deep shudder of release.

Frances smiled down at him as her breathing began to slow. After a few moments, she lay next to him, nuzzling against his shoulder as his arms circled her. The sun had sunk lower now so that the clearing where they lay was in shadow. Frances felt a slight chill as the leaves rustled in the breeze, and pressed herself to her husband. 'I wish we could stay here and sleep under the stars.'

Thomas kissed her hair, breathing in her scent. 'So do I,' he murmured. 'But the beasts of the forest would be as nothing to the wrath of Lady Cecily if we failed to show ourselves at dinner.'

With a sigh, he withdrew his arms and tugged at the shirt that lay crumpled underneath them, then gathered up the other discarded clothes. Frances watched him, reluctant to move, despite the cold that was now seeping into her limbs.

'Will you not stir yourself, Lady Tyringham?' He grinned as his eyes roamed across her naked body. Slowly, deliberately, she uncurled herself, her arms stretching above her head, her back arching like a cat's. His eyes glinted with desire as he gazed down at her. He seemed to hesitate and glanced over his shoulder at the distant castle, which was now silhouetted against the darkening sky. Then his shoulders dropped and he groaned, lowering himself onto her.

'Will you not have more of the beef, Lady Frances?' the countess asked, with a tight smile, gesturing towards the dish that lay between them. 'It is not quite cold.'

Frances smiled pleasantly. 'Thank you, my lady, but I have had more than enough. Your hospitality has been as generous as ever.'

She stole a glance at Thomas, who winked.

'Indeed, Lady Rutland,' he agreed, setting down his glass. 'My wife and I will miss the delights of your table when we return to Whitehall. I fear we have imposed upon your kindness for too long.'

Cecily sniffed. 'Not at all, Sir Thomas. It has been an honour to have you and Lady Frances as our guests,' she said, without a trace of sincerity.

'You are sure that you are strong enough for the journey?' the earl asked.

'Quite sure, I thank your lordship. I am fortunate to have had such an attentive nurse,' Thomas replied, smiling across at Frances.

'It is a wonder that your wife was able to restore you to health, when even His Majesty's own physicians had despaired of you.'

Lady Cecily's voice rang out across the

dining hall. Frances's shoulders tensed. Though their hostess had pretended to share the relief expressed by the rest of the household at Thomas's recovery, her enquiries into his continuing health had been more insistent than those of the rest. Many times these past weeks Frances had caught the countess staring at her with something like suspicion. Had she found out that Joan Flower had supplied her with herbs and salves to aid her husband's recovery? The earl had gone to great lengths to ensure that they were delivered into his hands, but many eyes and ears at Belvoir might have betrayed him. Frances suspected, too, that Cecily knew she had once been imprisoned for witchcraft. The scandal had long since been forgotten at court, but it might linger here, where life moved more slowly.

'I am thankful that God saw fit to spare me, Lady Rutland,' Thomas observed. 'It is proof, as if we needed it, that He alone has mastery over our lives.'

The countess opened her mouth to reply, but a look from her husband silenced her. Frances exhaled deeply, then took a long sip of wine. Though she would always cherish this place for the happiness it had brought her, she was glad they would leave tomorrow.

The meal was swiftly concluded, the earl declaring that Frances and her husband must be in need of rest before their journey. She rose to curtsy to their hosts, and was turning towards the door when Cecily addressed her again. 'You must give my congratulations to your brother, when you see him next.'

'I have four brothers, my lady,' she replied. 'To which of them do you refer?'

'Baron Longford, of course,' Cecily said, with a sly smile. 'Surely you have heard of his ennoblement. The earl received news of it from court. It is a great honour for your family.'

Frances stared at her. *'Edward?'*

'Why, yes, of course. He is the eldest, is he not? And heir to your father's estate?'

Frances had heard nothing from Edward since their father's funeral and had assumed that he was living a quiet — if profligate — life at Longford. He could not have secured such a title unless . . . Edward must be at court. There could be no other explanation. She imagined him jostling for favour alongside all of the other ambitious place-seekers. How long had he been there? She had been absent for months now and the king had returned to London weeks ago — long enough, certainly, for a young man of

Edward's guile and looks to come to his notice. Was her brother there still? She prayed that he was not.

'Edward is the eldest, yes.' She tried hard to keep her voice light. 'But he is not my father's heir. Longford will pass to my son, when he comes of age.'

Even as she spoke, she feared it was no longer true, that Edward had somehow secured Longford for himself, as well as his new title. But the terms of her father's will were indissoluble — unless she or her son committed an act of treason and their property became forfeit to the Crown. An image of Arbella flitted before her and she swallowed her rising panic. If her part in that had been discovered, the king's officials would have been at Belvoir long before now, she reasoned. She darted a look at her husband, who was watching her with concern.

'How odd,' Cecily persisted. 'A man has four sons to inherit his estate, yet leaves it to his grandson.'

'My late father-in-law was very fond of our son, Lady Rutland,' Thomas cut in. 'Though his bequest was unlooked for, we will make sure that it is honoured.'

'Well, my dear,' the earl said, 'we must not keep our guests from their beds any longer.

Goodnight, Sir Thomas, Lady Frances.'

Thomas bowed and, taking Frances's hand, led her from the room before the countess could voice any objection.

CHAPTER 36
23 SEPTEMBER

Frances rubbed the sleep from her eyes as she peered out of the carriage window. She had slept only fitfully after hearing that Edward had been at court, that he was now a baron. What else had he been occupied with during his time at court? *Idle hands are the devil's instrument.* The words from scripture had tormented her, robbing her of sleep until long after the third chime of the clock in the hallway had faded.

'We will soon be there, my love,' her husband said, as he closed his hand over hers.

She had been glad to break their journey at Tyringham Hall, wishing they might remain there, that she had never taken George from its relative safety to the snakepit of court. Now Edward was among the vipers that awaited her there.

As the coach passed under the Holbein Gate and into the courtyard, Frances's fear was subsumed in excitement at seeing George. It seemed a lifetime since she had been with him and her arms ached to hold him. His letters had become less frequent, but she supposed that, with the unseasonably warm weather, he was spending more time out of doors with Jack.

Thomas helped her down from the carriage and they walked towards his apartments. The courtyard was strangely quiet and the last of the sun's rays cast long shadows over the cobbles. The evenings had grown chill this past week and soon would shorten, too. She quickened her pace as they reached the final corridor, though her fall months before had made her cautious and she kept hold of her husband's arm.

'Do not fret, Frances,' he said. 'I sent word to Mistress Knyvett that we would be arriving this evening so she will have kept him up to see us — not that she could have done otherwise, I'm sure,' he added.

When at last they reached the door of their apartment, Frances flung it open, her face alight with anticipation. Startled, Mrs Knyvett jumped up from her chair by the fireplace, dismay on her face. Brushing past her, Frances went into the bedroom, expecting to see her son fast asleep. But the pallet was empty. 'Where is he?' she demanded, striding back into the parlour.

'Forgive me, my lady,' the woman said, wringing her hands. 'Sir Thomas's message only arrived this morning and Master George had already left for St James's. I sent word for him to return but have heard nothing since.'

'St James's? But the king is in residence here.'

'His son is not, though,' Thomas reminded her. 'Prince Henry spends all of his time at the palace now and is seldom seen at Whitehall, even — or perhaps especially — when his father is here.'

Frances fell silent for a moment. Why was George at Prince Henry's court when he was a member of Charles's household? The younger prince still resided at Whitehall, and George's letters had been written from there.

'The invitation arrived early this morning, my lady, and your son was most eager to go.'

'You should not have allowed it without our permission,' Frances snapped.

The older woman looked stricken. 'I would not have agreed, were it not for the fact that the boy's uncle delivered the invitation and offered to accompany George himself.'

Edward.

Frances saw her alarm reflected in Thomas's eyes. 'We must go there at once.' She was already making for the door.

'But, my love, it is late.' Thomas grabbed her arm as she passed. 'George will already have retired by the time we get there. You are tired from the journey and should rest here tonight. We can fetch him at first light.'

Frances wrested her arm free. 'I will go alone if you do not wish to accompany me.'

She was halfway down the corridor when she heard his footsteps behind her. 'Frances, wait,' he said, as he caught up with her. 'You know I will not let you go there unaccompanied.'

The warmth of his hand on hers eased her agitation, and they hurried together towards the outer courtyard.

The sound of drums striking a lively tune was almost drowned in the shouts of revellers as the carriage came to a halt outside the great hall. Frances glanced up at the brightly lit windows, as if expecting to see George's face peering down, but she could make out only the silhouettes of ladies as they flitted past in the dance.

As she and Thomas mounted the sweeping staircase, lined on either side with vast paintings of biblical scenes, the noise from within the hall grew louder. One of the doors was flung open and a man staggered out. He took a few swaying paces before collapsing against a wall and sliding down it, his head lolling forward, like a marionette whose strings had been cut.

Frances steeled herself as she and her husband walked through the open doorway. The hall within was crowded with brightly dressed young courtiers, some dancing a galliard, others watching while they sipped wine and stuffed sweetmeats into their mouths. Frances's gaze swept the room. She was in search of an official who could tell her where George was sleeping, but everywhere was a riot of russet silks and chinking glasses. Clasping Thomas's hand, she pushed through the crowds, looking this way and that as they made their slow progress.

A tall man dressed in an elaborate masque costume came hurtling towards them, almost knocking Frances off her feet. Only the crush of bodies prevented her from crashing to the ground. But as she thrust out her arms to steady herself, she let go of Thomas's hand. A fresh wave of revellers closed around her, concealing her husband from view.

She was almost at the far side of the hall now and could see a small recess behind a pillar that was mercifully empty. With fresh resolve, she was soon inside it, her back pressed against the cool marble of the pillar.

'Will you not join the dance, sister?'

She froze.

'I wonder that you did not take part in the masque,' Edward continued. 'I hear that you were quite the performer in your youth. But, then, you are a respectable wife now. Tell me, how is Sir Thomas? He has been so long absent that the king has quite forgotten him.'

Frances ignored the barb. 'He is fully recovered and will resume his duties now that we are back at court.' She glanced over her shoulder hoping to see her husband, but her eyes alighted only upon the red faces and dishevelled hair of strangers.

'It was reported here that his life was despaired of. Yet you nursed him back to health.'

'I thank God that He saw fit to spare him,' she replied.

'You should not be so modest, sister. Everyone here knows how skilled you are in such matters.'

You will have made sure of that. 'Where is my son? You had no right to bring him here without my sanction.'

'Or that of his father?' He smiled, teeth flashing like a wolf's. 'But that would have been impossible, would it not, sister?'

She swallowed her rage. 'Where is he?' she repeated.

Edward gestured to the raised dais at the end of the hall, and Frances saw George standing next to Prince Henry, who was seated on an elaborate throne beneath a vast canopy of state. As she watched, the prince leaned forward and whispered something in his ear, then laughed uproariously. George laughed too, but as if he did not understand the joke. He was holding a bottle, which he raised to his lips. He took a swig, some of the wine spilling down his shirt, which was already marked with red blotches. Horrified, Frances surged forward, her brother following in her wake.

'George!' she called, as she came within a few feet of the dais.

Her son did not turn at her voice but continued to stare adoringly at the prince, who was regaling him and his other companions with some story. As she climbed the steps, the prince's eyes flicked to her, showing irritation at being interrupted, then triumph when he realised who she was.

'Lady Frances. What an unexpected

pleasure.' His words were as smooth as silk.

George whipped around and gazed up at his mother with a mixture of joy and alarm. He took a step towards her, then stopped, his cheeks reddening.

'I have come to take my son home,' Frances said, without preamble.

Henry stared at her as if waiting for her obeisance. When it became clear that she had no intention of making one, his expression hardened. 'George is my guest, Lady Frances.' A pause. 'Unlike you.'

'He is too young for such entertainment,' she hissed, looking down at her son, whose face was now pale. She reached out and put an arm around his shoulders, but he shook it off.

'Nonsense!' the prince declared, smiling at the boy's gesture of defiance. 'I was only five when I attended my first masque. You cannot keep him hidden from society for ever, Lady Frances. He will grow to lack refinement, as well as learning. He expressed some curious ideas about the scriptures when he first arrived at St James's. I have made him see reason, of course. Young minds drink in knowledge as a dried river-bed absorbs a sudden rainstorm. Don't you agree, Lord Longford?'

Frances's fingers itched to deliver a slap

to his smiling face. She could not bear to look at her brother, who now stood by her side.

'That is the very reason I brought my nephew here, Your Grace,' Edward replied, with a deep bow. 'I rejoice to see how he has flourished under your care.'

George was now swaying and clutching his stomach. She was about to step forward and take him from the dais before the prince could make any further remarks when she felt the warmth of a hand on her back. Thomas. He bowed before the prince.

'My wife and I are indebted to you for your kindness to our son, Your Highness,' he said, laying a hand firmly on the boy's shoulder. 'But it is late and we must return to Whitehall. His Majesty requires my attendance tomorrow.'

The prince opened his mouth to speak, but Thomas was already guiding George from the platform. Without troubling to bid farewell, either to the prince or her brother, she followed.

The courtyard was deserted when they emerged from the palace. Frances breathed in a lungful of the cool night air, willing it to cleanse her of the foetid stench of sweat and wine that had pervaded the hall. Her son was between her and Thomas, holding a hand of each. His eyelids had kept drooping as they had descended the stairs, but the shock of the cold jolted him awake. He made a small groan, bent over and vomited onto the cobbles.

CHAPTER 37
24 SEPTEMBER

Frances sighed and pushed her plate away, untouched. Her temples pulsed with a dull ache, which she knew would be as nothing to the pain in her son's head when he woke. They had walked back from St James's last night, her husband judging that the fresh air and exercise would help purge George's body of the wine more quickly than if they travelled by carriage. Though at first they had been obliged to stop every few paces so that George might retch, by the time they had reached Whitehall the colour had returned to his cheeks and he no longer shivered as violently. Ignoring his protests, Frances had administered a few sips of water before he collapsed into a deep slumber, illuminated by the moonlight that streamed through the window.

This morning she felt fury against the prince and her brother. She had fallen asleep with their smirking faces before her.

She had woken later, gasping for air, and Thomas had drawn her into a tight embrace, smoothing the damp hair from her forehead, his lips touching her ear as he whispered soothing words.

She looked at him now and love for him overwhelmed her. The dark shadows under his eyes told of a restless night for him, too, but he smiled with his accustomed warmth. 'You should eat something, Frances. You have had nothing since we arrived,' he said.

She sank down on the window seat and gazed out across the river, which despite the hour was already filled with barges carrying passengers, victuals and myriad other cargo. After a few moments, he came to sit with her.

'Will you attend the king today?' Frances asked.

Her husband shrugged. 'I must await my instructions from the Lord Privy Seal. I wonder he has not already issued them — we have been back for almost twelve hours.' He grinned.

Frances's smile soon faded as she thought of Cecil. When she had been summoned to attend him the previous year, he had looked so frail that she had not expected him to survive. That he had rallied was as much thanks to his doggedness as to her ministrations — of that she had no doubt. He could not abide the thought of his rivals taking advantage of his absence so he had returned to court sooner than she had advised. *A wounded beast knows its strength better than those who think themselves safe from its claws,* Raleigh had remarked when she had told him of the service she had performed for her old adversary. 'It seems this kingdom is truly cursed,' she mused now, 'for our heretic king will be succeeded by a prince who will drag us even deeper into wickedness and depravity.'

Thomas remained silent for so long that she began to think he would not respond. 'That may be true,' he said at last. 'But if our kingdom is damned, then the souls within it can still be saved. Inside the heads of wheat that are buffeted and doused by tempests there is a kernel of goodness protected by a hard shell. Nothing can penetrate this treasure. It remains, safe and uncorrupted, until the time is ripe for it to be revealed to the world.' He clasped her hands. 'It is the same with our faith, Frances,' he continued, his voice filled with ardour, though it was barely more than a whisper. 'We must continue to nurture and cherish it in our hearts, even as our mouths form words to deny it. Those words will be

430

heeded by the king and his son, and all those who seek to further the cause of heresy. But never by God. He sees what is in our hearts, Frances, and will bring us the joy of His salvation.'

Frances battled a series of conflicting emotions as she held his gaze. Though she wanted to believe as he did, she felt it a betrayal of everything she held dear. Surely God wanted His people to fight for the true faith, even if it cost them their freedom, their lives. His Son had done nothing less, and it had proved mankind's salvation. Then she thought of her own son growing up steeped in heresy, repeating the blasphemous words that his new patron spouted, and felt again the familiar anger.

It is better to hazard your mortal self than your immortal soul.

Her father's words came to her, as if he had whispered them in her ear, and she understood that she must continue along the path she had chosen, that she must do whatever she could to keep Longford in Catholic hands. She felt more at peace as she looked back at Thomas, but as his features slowly relaxed, she realised he had mistaken her reaction for compliance. In carrying out her father's wishes, she would be betraying those of her husband. Their marriage had been forged on the promise that she would keep her faith hidden and that Thomas would ask nothing else from her. He had stayed true to that pledge, but she had broken it. Her betrayal was made worse by the fact that, in all other respects, she was now his entirely, heart and body. But she could no longer deny her soul.

The guards nodded her through and she began to mount the steps that led up to the prisoner's lodgings. Although it was many months since she had visited, they had seen her enough times in the past to recognise her at once.

'Ah, Lady Frances!'

Raleigh opened his arms in greeting. Smiling, Frances crossed to where he was standing by the window. The bristles of his beard tickled her cheek as he kissed her.

'Come, come,' he said, guiding her towards the chairs next to the fireplace. Though it was a mellow autumn day outside, the thick stone walls of the Tower were impervious to the warmth of the sun's rays and a fire crackled in the grate.

'So you have returned to me at last?' he said, with a dolorous expression, clutching his hand to his heart.

Frances grinned. 'I am sure you have had

visitors enough to keep you entertained. The prince must know these lodgings better than your own wife does.'

Raleigh rolled his eyes. 'I would rather be driven mad with loneliness than have him for company. Though his visits have their uses, I admit,' he added. 'He brought that sour-faced girl with him last time — the one who fawns over him, with her pursed lips and mournful eyes.'

'Lady Blanche?'

Frances was not looking forward to being back in the young woman's company that evening, when she was to attend her mistress at the masque.

Raleigh nodded as he sucked on his pipe, then blew out a long trail of smoke. At first the smell had caught in Frances's throat, but she had grown accustomed to it.

'He is using her, of course — even a fool could see that. But she would willingly step off a precipice if it pleased him.' Another long drag on the pipe. 'I wonder if he has dipped his wick in her.'

Frances let out a bark of laughter. 'From what I have seen of Prince Henry's court, there is little room for morality,' she observed.

Raleigh must have heard the bitterness in her voice. He did not speak, but waited for

433

her to continue.

'Thomas and I went to St James's last night,' she said after a pause. 'We were in search of my son, who had been taken there by my brother.'

'Edward?' Raleigh sat up straight now. 'I thought he was at Longford, licking his wounds and frittering away your father's fortune.'

Frances's mouth twisted into a grimace. 'Just before we left Belvoir, I heard that he was at court, that he had been made a baron. I assumed he had won favour with the king, but perhaps it was the prince who bestowed the honour upon him.'

Raleigh gave a sardonic smile. 'I imagine your brother prefers his new title, even though it ranks below that of viscount.'

Frances gave a nod.

'I agree that this is the prince's doing,' Raleigh continued, his expression now serious. 'Certainly he is swelling his court with a coterie of flatterers and fawners. The more people flock to St James's, the greater his triumph over his father.' He paused. 'But what of Edward? Did ambition drive him to court or is he there for other reasons?'

'I wish I knew.' Frances was working at a thread that had come loose from her sleeve. 'Though I fear it is to serve me ill.'

'And your son — he is of an age with my Carew, is he not? A little young to be sampling the delights of the prince's court.'

Frances sighed. 'But not so young as to be able to resist the heresy that pervades that vipers' nest.'

'Ah.' Raleigh moved his chair closer to hers so that their knees were almost touching. 'I sensed your agitation as soon as you arrived. Your smile did not quite reach those beautiful eyes.'

'My husband urges me to keep my faith hidden, to deny it to all but God.' Her voice was rising now and she lowered it, mindful that the servants were within earshot. 'But I cannot — I *will* not — stand by and watch my son be damned. Longford too.' Tears of frustration pooled in her eyes.

Raleigh reached forward and patted her knee. He said nothing and she sensed he was waiting for more.

'The plots in which I have become embroiled have achieved nothing so far,' Frances said, her voice low. 'Arbella and Seymour were married, yet the King of Spain did not stir himself. Instead, Cecil discovered their schemes and the lady resides here, with you and God knows how many other failed Catholics. Forgive me,' she said hastily, seeing his wounded expression. He waved away her apology.

'And now the only means to stop the princess marrying a heretic is to persuade her to take my uncle as a husband.' She rubbed her hand across her forehead. 'Even if Elizabeth does marry a Catholic, what will that achieve? I have seen little evidence of the multitudes who are said to be ready to take up arms and seize the throne for her.'

Raleigh remained silent for a long time but his eyes never left her. 'What you say of the late plots is true,' he said at last, his words slow and measured. 'They have not delivered what was promised. It may be that Lady Vaux and her like play a longer game than we are aware of — that Arbella and your uncle are just two pieces on a board that is covered with hundreds more. But Copernicus has taught us to believe only that which our eyes can see.'

Frances recognised the truth of that. Though she was still engaged in Lady Vaux's schemes, she no longer believed that they would come to fruition, any more than those of Lady Drummond. She must find a way to escape her clutches and strike out on her own.

'I see the light of our faith burning even more brightly in your eyes,' Raleigh continued, bringing her back to the present. 'That same faith will light the path ahead, leading to everything you desire.'

■ ■ ■ ■

PART 4
1612

■ ■ ■ ■

CHAPTER 38
25 MAY

'Dead?'

Frances stared at her husband. Thomas nodded.

'Yesterday, at Marlborough. He had been to Bath, but the waters offered no cure this time.'

She sank onto a chair, her legs trembling. The idea that Cecil was gone seemed impossible. He had been a constant, menacing presence ever since her first arrival at court eight years before. Even the years she had spent at Tyringham had been blighted by the knowledge that he had set someone to watch her. He had superintended her torture as a suspected witch and had hounded Tom to his death. She had every reason to rejoice. Yet she felt only a creeping numbness.

Thomas came to kneel at her feet and took her icy hands in his. 'I know it is an even greater shock to you than it was to me,

441

given what you suffered at his hands.' His expression darkened briefly. 'Though it was obvious how ill he was, I thought he would outlive us all.'

'Do you know the cause?' she asked.

'They say it was a tumour.'

Frances knew that such growths could return, even if they were cut out. Yet she could not quite push away the feeling of failure. 'Then he must have died in torment,' she said, remembering the hiss of his breath as she had examined that first growth with the gentlest of fingers.

Then she thought of Tom, his frail, blood-ied body jerking over the cobbles as he was pulled on a hurdle to his execution. *It is mine to revenge. I will repay.* Frances felt shame that she had not placed greater faith in God's words. She had read them often enough since Tom's death, desperate to derive some comfort from them. But they had seemed like the empty promises with which a father pacifies a troublesome child. Now that she knew the truth of them, she should feel triumphant, at peace. But she experienced neither. Just a gnawing pity.

'They say he died in as much pain of mind as of body,' Thomas said, stroking her knuckles with his thumb.

Frances had supposed Cecil to be incapable of remorse. Certainly he had never shown any throughout the years she had known him. She had seen him dispatch opponents with unblinking efficiency. 'Surely he was not troubled by his conscience at last.'

Her husband shrugged. 'A man might set aside all of his former opinions when death is close at hand. Few can meet it with the same sanguinity that —' He stopped.

'Thomas?'

Frances could no longer see her husband's face but something in the way he was holding himself worried her. When he remained silent, she placed her hand on his shoulder. He started at her touch. 'What is it?' she asked quietly, keeping her hand quite still.

Thomas's shoulders sagged. When he turned to her, his eyes were filled with such pain that her heart contracted. He bent to kiss her fingers. 'I have seen many men die, Frances, most on the field of battle, their life ripped from them by arquebus or sword. Though such a death is quick, the terror still showed in their eyes. How much greater the terror must be if a man knows the hour of his death many days or even weeks before. And if . . .' he faltered '. . . and if it is brought upon him slowly, to draw out the terror, the agony.'

443

Frances's hands fell slack in his. She knew with a sickening certainty of whom he had spoken.

'I was there, Frances,' he said suddenly. 'I saw Tom die.'

Her breath caught in her throat as she stared down at him. She opened her mouth to speak but could form no words. For almost seven years she had closed her mind to what Tom must have suffered. Many times an image had shocked her — a rope being pulled tight, a knife slicing through flesh — but she had always pushed it away, busying herself with some task, fingers trembling. Only in her dreams had the full horror come rushing in and she had awoken screaming.

'You were at Westminster?' The words rasped in her throat.

Thomas inclined his head. 'I promised that I would not forsake him, that he would turn his face to me, keep his eyes upon mine so that all those filled with hatred or anger or vengeance might fade away and he would see only the truth and comfort of our faith reflected back at him.'

His words were coming as rapidly as his breath now. Frances wanted to shut her ears but could not.

'I would willingly have given my life for

444

his, Frances,' he continued, with sincerity. 'I knew what you were to him — and he to you. All night as I waited by the scaffold, I prayed to God that He might put me in his place.'

Frances thought of how she, too, had spent that night in prayer as she paced the floorboards of that attic room, her words disappearing into the darkness.

'Though He did not answer my prayers, He did at least give me courage to do as I had promised. But it was as nothing to the courage that Tom showed, Frances. He seemed impervious to the tortures they visited upon him. His gaze never faltered and his eyes were filled with such acceptance, such peace that it silenced the crowds who had bayed for blood just moments before.'

He stopped, as if the words were choking him, his chest heaving with silent grief.

'Why did you not tell me before now?' she murmured.

He raised his eyes to hers again. 'I wanted to — many times. But whenever I mentioned him, it was as if I had scalded you. I feared that if I spoke to you of his death it would be more than you could bear.' He bent to kiss her fingers. They were wet with his tears when he raised his head again. 'I feared, too, that you would never forgive me for failing him.'

'How did you fail him?'

Thomas could not meet her eyes. 'I stood by the scaffold, so close that I could almost have reached out and touched him. Yet I did nothing to stop the horrors that were visited upon him.' He was unable to continue.

Frances felt strangely peaceful as she looked down at him, as if something inside her had been set free at last. She touched his cheek, keeping her hand there as she spoke. 'You did not fail him, Thomas,' she said softly. 'You honoured your promise to be with him at the end, though God knows it cost you dearly. Thanks to you, he did not die friendless and alone. You gave him the courage he lacked,' she whispered, then knelt to hold him close.

The hall was crowded with courtiers and officials when Frances and her husband arrived. The king sat under the canopy of state, Robert Carr at his side. They were in whispered conversation, their heads close together, and every now and then James let out a bark of laughter. She should have known better than to expect a sombre atmosphere, Frances reflected, even though

446

the court had been summoned to be told the news that was already on everyone's lips: the king's chief minister was dead.

'His blood ran black when the surgeons tried to cut out the tumour,' Frances heard one woman mutter as they passed.

'What do you expect from such a black-hearted villain?' her companion retorted scornfully.

Their laughter still echoed in her ears as Frances moved through the throng, gripping Thomas's hand ever more tightly. Ahead, she saw the unmistakable figure of her uncle. He was whispering something to a young woman, his mouth close to her ear. She giggled as his hand trailed over the plump flesh above her bodice. Frances swallowed her distaste. Clearly the earl saw no reason to desist from his usual habits, now that he was courting the princess. She changed direction but at that moment he turned and saw her.

'Good day, niece,' he called, as she curtsied. 'Sir Thomas.'

'I trust you are well, my lord?'

Frances detected frost in her husband's tone, though she knew her uncle would not.

'Exceedingly so, now that churl is dead at last,' he replied, making no attempt to lower his voice. 'The pickings will be all the richer for the rest of us.'

'His Majesty has chosen a successor, then?' Frances asked. She had grown used to the speed with which the spoils from one official were divided among the others, like carrion among crows.

Her uncle gave a scornful grunt. 'There will be more than one, niece! The man was as rich as Croesus and had amassed enough titles and offices to sustain an entire court. I look forward to hearing which of them His Majesty has chosen to bestow upon me. After all,' he added, a slow smile creeping across his face, 'he will wish to enhance the status of his future son-in-law.'

Frances stifled a grimace. Even though she had done her best to further the match between her uncle and the princess for months now, she was no more reconciled to the idea than Elizabeth was. It felt like a betrayal of the affection and trust that had grown between them. She saw how the young woman recoiled every time another gift arrived from the earl, how she discarded each as soon as it had been opened.

'Silence for the king!' The lord chamberlain's voice rang out across the hall, bringing the excited chatter to an abrupt end. James got to his feet and surveyed the expectant faces before him. 'My lords,' he began, his voice echoing around the vaulted hall, 'it seems I have been nurturing a serpent in my breast these nine years.'

A frisson of excitement ran through the gathering. This was unexpected. Frances's pulse quickened as she waited for James to continue.

'You will have heard the tidings that the Earl of Salisbury is dead,' he continued, clearly enjoying the suspense that he had created. 'Ever since I inherited the Crown of this kingdom I have raised him up above all others. It has pleased me to shower him with titles, lands and offices. Never has so much power been vested in one man.'

Frances heard her uncle's grunt of assent, but kept her eyes fixed on the dais.

'And how did he repay me?' he continued, leaving the question to echo into silence. 'With lies and betrayal and heresy!'

The company descended into a din of animated chatter as everyone began to speculate what Cecil could have done to deserve such censure.

'During the earl's late absence from court, I received intelligence that he had fallen into the same heresy that he pretended to persecute on my behalf,' James continued, the colour rising to his cheeks as he spoke. 'I therefore ordered a search of his houses, wherein my officials found ample proof to confirm my suspicions. His private chapel at Hatfield was stuffed with relics, statuary and other tokens of popery.'

There was an audible gasp. Frances felt as if she had been dealt a blow to her stomach. Instinctively, she reached into her pocket and began working the beads of her rosary between her fingers. But it failed to calm her racing thoughts. Cecil a *Catholic*? It could not be. For as long as she had known him, he had pursued all those of her faith relentlessly, never flinching from meting out the severest penalties. That he had secretly shared the same faith was unthinkable. And yet . . .

Frances looked at her husband, whose eyes were still fixed upon the king. Had he not told her that Cecil had died tormented in mind as well as body? She had assumed that remorse had set in as the hour of death approached. How much greater his anguish must have been if it was caused by having betrayed his conscience all these years.

'And so I have appointed my trusted servant Lord Carr as secretary of state . . .'

Frances had hardly been aware that the king had begun to speak again. She forced her attention back to the dais.

'. . . with full powers to hunt down all

those associated with his predecessor in this post and bring them to face the king's justice.'

'*Carr?*' her uncle muttered under his breath.

'Furthermore, I have instructed my Lord Chief Justice to introduce stricter penalties for any subject who fails to swear the oath of allegiance, or who is otherwise found to adhere to the Catholic faith. From henceforth, no mercy will be shown to those obstinate papists who, through their wicked and wilful disregard for God's true word, seek the destruction of the king's person and of his entire realm. All of their property and goods will be seized by the Crown, to be dispensed with at the king's pleasure — along with their lives.'

Silence descended upon the hall. The only noise that Frances could hear was the pulse that throbbed in her ears.

'George!' Frances remonstrated. 'You must practise your letters, as I have shown you.'

The boy stared sullenly at the paper but made no move to pick up the quill that lay discarded next to it, a trail of black ink spilling from the nib. She quelled her rising exasperation.

'I do not like the text you have chosen,' he muttered, pushing the paper away and folding his arms in defiance.

Frances had selected a passage from the Book of Tobit, which told of the young boy Tobias's journey to collect a debt owed to his father. She had thought the story might appeal to George, who was close in age to the hero. That it was drawn from a text favoured by the old religion was no coincidence.

'But it used to be your favourite. You would always beg me to read it to you again, even though you had heard it the previous night — and the one before that,' she coaxed, trying hard to keep the tension from her voice.

George's scowl deepened and he pressed his lips together. 'I am no longer a child, Mama.'

Frances could not help but laugh. 'You are not yet seven, George. There will be many more summers before you are a man.'

'That's not true!' he shouted, leaping from his chair and pushing it back with such force that it clattered to the ground. 'Prince Henry says that I hold a sword better than many of his father's soldiers. He says it will not be long before I can join the crusade against heretics.'

Frances stared at her furious son and felt as if she was looking at a stranger. 'What do you know of heretics, George? Do you even understand what the word means?'

'Of course I do!' the boy shouted, stamping his foot. 'They are the enemies of God and the slaves of the devil. They are wicked and — and —' His face was puce as he tried to remember the other words the prince had used. No doubt they had been repeated to him often enough during her absence last year, Frances realised, with mounting horror. *What else had Henry said to him?*

'They would burn us all in our beds and

dance upon our graves,' George continued, eyes alight with triumph as the words came back to him, 'just like those wicked men who tried to blow up the king.'

Frances's mouth dried. She gripped the back of the chair, her fingernails digging into its smooth carvings. 'What did you say?'

George started at her voice, which was now dangerously low. The colour drained from his face. 'The men who . . .' he faltered, then cast his gaze to the floor.

'Go on, George. The men who did what?' Frances hissed, through gritted teeth.

Her son's hands, clasped tightly in front of him, began to shake. He bit his lip as if to stop the tears that threatened. All at once, her fury abated. He was but a child, for all his defiant words — words that had been put into his mouth by that devil the prince. She was at his side in a couple of strides. He recoiled, as if fearing she would strike him. Frances knelt in front of him and gently took his hands.

'You must forgive me, George, but you do not know of what you speak,' she soothed. 'It angers me to think that you have been so deceived.'

His eyes darted up to hers and she saw a flicker of their former defiance.

'Those men died for their faith. They held

it as dear to their hearts as you are to mine. Theirs —' She had almost said, *Theirs was the true faith,* but though she wished with all her heart that her son might come to share the same beliefs, she must have a care. 'We must always be true to our hearts, George,' she finished.

His brow furrowed, as it did when he was trying to sound out a word he did not recognise. He fiddled with the ties of his doublet, lacing and unlacing them until Frances gently stilled his fingers.

'But the prince never lies, Mama,' he said at last. 'And he says that there is only one true faith. All those who believe otherwise will burn in Hell.'

Frances knew she must not say too much, yet neither could she let George be corrupted by Henry's wicked lies. 'We must serve God before all others, George — even the king,' she said, clasping his hands again. 'Only He can guide us to the true path.'

She drew him to her and held him tightly. He stood stiffly at first, but then he put his arms around her and she felt his small hands press into her back.

'Well,' she said, planting a kiss on the top of his head, 'I think we have done enough work for today. How about a ride in the park? I am determined to reach the oak tree before you this time!'

George's face lit up and he raced off to change into his riding clothes.

The sun had sunk low in the sky by the time Frances and her son had returned from their ride, exhilarated but exhausted. For once, George had needed little persuasion to retire to his bed and she had heard his steady breathing before she had even reached the door of his chamber after bidding him goodnight. But while her body ached for rest, her mind would not allow it.

'Can you not sleep either?' her husband whispered, surprising her. He must have been feigning sleep all this time. Relief flooded her as she nestled against his warm chest. Though he had been lying next to her, she had felt so alone when she thought that she was the only one awake, tormented by the fears that ran incessantly through her mind.

'Is it Cecil?' he asked, when she made no move to speak.

Frances exhaled deeply. 'In part, yes. I keep thinking of the king's announcement. Can he really have been a Catholic, when he persecuted them so relentlessly?'

For a while Thomas did not answer. She sensed that he was choosing his words carefully. 'We know only that his private chapel contained remnants of the old religion,' he said slowly. 'But that is true of many noble houses in this realm — even of some churches. The late queen had just such a chapel for her private worship, though she espoused the reformed faith. It is possible to cherish remnants of the old, even when embracing the new.'

Frances considered this. 'You are right, of course. But *Cecil*? He, of all people, should have practised every part of the faith he imposed upon others. He should have known the dangers, too, of allowing any room for doubt. Many have perished for less proof than he left behind.'

Thomas traced a pattern on her shoulder, his fingers trailing idly over her cool flesh. 'It is perplexing,' he conceded. 'Cecil never betrayed any hint that he did not conform privately to what he pursued so forcefully in public. But how well can we know any man or woman, even those to whom we are close?'

It had been many months since her husband had looked upon her with suspicion. What had happened between them at Belvoir had changed everything. Now Frances saw nothing but love in his eyes. She hoped he saw the same in hers, even though there was much that she still concealed.

'You do trust me, don't you, Frances?' he murmured, when she gave no reply.

'Of course,' she said quickly. 'I would trust you with my life — George's too.'

'Good,' he replied, squeezing her shoulder. 'You must know that you can confide anything to me.'

Frances's heart was hammering now. She twisted her head to look up at him. Though he wore the same gentle smile, his eyes were clouded with concern. Her skin prickled as she thought of how she had betrayed him — and did so still. For all that she might try to convince herself that she was concealing her schemes to protect him from danger, she knew that the truth would destroy him just as surely. As she held his gaze, she felt an overriding urge to confide in him now, share the burden she had carried for so long. Her lips parted.

'Thomas . . .'

He looked down at her, waiting.

But then she imagined the hurt and fury her words would bring to him, how the love she saw in his eyes would disappear, replaced by loathing. He could not but hate her for what she had done — what she still sought to do. The love that had grown between them these past months was like one of the tender blooms she had nurtured in the woods at Longford, shielding it from the chill winds of winter so that it might flourish in the warmth of spring. She could not destroy it before it had even taken root. She pressed her lips to his chest. 'I love you.'

He gave a deep sigh and kissed her.

'And I you,' he said, his lips still brushing against hers. 'I always have.'

CHAPTER 40
8 JUNE

'I will be gone for just a few days,' Thomas assured her. 'Parliament will convene on Monday, so the king will need to return to Whitehall at least a day before.'

Frances felt suddenly desolate. He tilted her chin so that her eyes met his.

'You are quite sure that all is well, Frances?' he asked, lowering his voice so that George might not hear. He was sitting across the room, studying one of his books. 'You hardly touched your breakfast and you are so pale.'

'Nothing ails me, I promise,' she lied.

The truth was that she had been feeling wretched for days. She had barely slept, her mind turning ceaselessly over the revelation about Cecil, her worries about George and Longford, and the constant, gnawing guilt that she was betraying her husband. Her bones ached with fatigue and she had no appetite. She had laced her stays more tightly this morning, yet still her gown hung off her wasted frame.

Thomas looked at her for a long moment. Then, adopting a cheerful expression, he went to George and lifted him high into the air. For all that he liked to pretend that he was a man, George exclaimed gleefully, his feet kicking the air. 'Now then, young sir, can I trust you to look after your mama while I am gone?'

'Of course, Papa,' George replied earnestly.

'Good. Because if your attention should slip —'

At this, Thomas released his grip so that the boy started to fall, but caught him before he struck the floor. Even though his papa had performed the same trick numerous times, George whooped with delight.

'And you must work hard at your lessons,' Thomas continued. 'You are to be master of Longford one day, and your tenants will not take kindly to a dullard.'

He winked at Frances, who smiled indulgently.

'I promise I will, Papa. By the time you return, I shall have mastered all of my letters and will read to you from the king's new Bible.'

Thomas's smile became fixed. 'I shall look

461

forward to it, George,' he said quickly, before Frances could object, and ruffled the boy's hair. Turning to his wife, he took her hands in his. 'Take good care, Frances,' he said, then bent to kiss her.

She gave him what she hoped was a reassuring smile, then gazed after him as he walked from the apartment, the warmth of his lips slowly fading from hers as the door closed behind him.

Frances watched as the princess smoothed the skirts of her new gown. She was standing on a footrest while the seamstress adjusted the hem, her fingers deftly pinning the silk in place. The colour reminded Frances of the soft purple irises that had just started to bloom in the palace gardens.

'I don't see the need for such trouble.' Elizabeth sighed. 'There will hardly be much company, with my father away on the hunt and my mother still at Greenwich.'

'All the more reason for Your Grace to shine, as you will be holding court on their behalf,' Frances suggested. 'I am sure many will want to pay you homage. There has been little enough to lift the spirits lately.'

The princess twisted around to look at her. The back of her gown had not yet been sewn together and it hung open, exposing

462

the soft folds of her petticoat. 'You mean since Cecil's death?'

Frances nodded and returned to her needlework. Ever since the news had been announced, it was as if the entire court had held its breath. People spoke in whispers and eyed each other with suspicion. If the king's chief minister had been a papist, how many others might be skulking in the shadows?

'People are shocked by his betrayal, certainly,' the princess agreed, 'though it is a source of delight for his rivals. Your uncle expects to profit from the spoils, I think.'

Her mistress's expression was suddenly grave. Frances tried to keep her own neutral, but she knew that even the mention of his name was enough to open a chasm between them. She had done her best to adhere to Lady Vaux's instructions and make her uncle as appealing as possible to the princess, but the stories she had invented of his bravery, charm or ready wit had been exposed as the lies they were whenever he had come into Elizabeth's presence. She would do as well to pretend that a crow was a bird of paradise.

'He is a man of ambition, and always seeks to improve his prospects,' Frances agreed.

How she loathed this artifice. She knew

that the princess was no more fooled by it than she was, and resented the distrust that it had created. It was a constant check to Elizabeth's growing affection. How much closer might they have been if Frances had not been obliged to fall in with Lady Vaux's schemes? *Not for much longer,* she reminded herself again. She would find a way out of this labyrinth of lies and deceit.

Both women turned at the sound of footsteps. Frances rushed to the door so that she might intercept the visitor before they saw her mistress in a state of undress, but froze when she saw the prince.

He regarded her coldly but did not acknowledge her as she curtsied. As he strode into the apartment, another figure rounded the corner just behind him.

Edward.

Frances tried to keep the shock from her face as she stepped briskly forward, pulling the door closed behind her. 'You may not see my mistress at present,' she said firmly, ignoring the faint amusement on his face.

'I am sorry, sister, but your authority is exceeded by that of my master. Now, please,' he said, already reaching for the latch.

Frances was there before him. 'The princess is being fitted for a new gown. I am sure you would not wish to dishonour her by intruding upon her privacy.'

Edward was momentarily abashed. Through the door behind her, Frances could hear the clipped tones of the prince as he addressed his sister.

'I shall wait a few moments, then,' Edward said tightly.

Frances glared at him. 'Why are you here, Edward?'

'The prince invited me to accompany him while he paid a visit to his sister. Was I to refuse him, to spare you the sight of me? It is clear that you can hardly bear to breathe the same air as your beloved brother.'

'I mean here at court. Surely you have matters enough to occupy you at Longford. Or have you already ruined our father's estate?'

'Longford is thriving, I assure you,' he replied. 'I will make sure that it remains so for the day that I hand it over to the care of my nephew — if that day ever comes. Tell me,' he continued, before she could interject, 'how does George fare? Such a promising boy and so fast to learn. You must be immensely proud of how he is maturing.'

Frances would not rise to his bait. She would not give him the satisfaction of seeing her fury. 'My son is well, thank you. Now —'

'*Such* a pity that you have not allowed him to attend any more of our gatherings.' Edward gave an exaggerated sigh. 'He had a merry time of it on the last occasion.'

Frances pressed her lips together, not trusting herself to speak. *Why was he here?* He had been absent from Whitehall for so many months that she had begun to hope he had returned to Longford.

'Of course he will return to St James's soon enough,' Edward continued cheerily. 'Prince Henry has taken quite a shine to him. He does so enjoy the chance to mould young minds to his own opinions and beliefs, to bring them to the truth before they can be corrupted by lies and sedition.'

'George will be raised to know his own mind, free from the influence of those who seek to manipulate him for their own gain,' Frances retorted, her jaw tightening.

A ripple of laughter sounded through the door as they glared at each other.

'You should have a care, sister,' Edward drawled. 'Loose words might be twisted into treason, especially if they come from the lips of one who is already under suspicion.'

He stepped closer, gripping her arm. 'Your son will never inherit Longford,' he snarled, his lips almost touching her ear. 'I would rather see it razed to the ground.'

Frances pulled away from him, as if scalded, shock mingling with hatred. 'You can do nothing to prevent it,' she spat back, her voice rising. 'Our father willed it. His bequest cannot be disputed.'

Edward's lips curled into a slow smile. 'That is true, my dear sister,' he agreed. 'And I am a dutiful son — I would not dream of going against his wishes.' He assumed a sorrowful expression. 'But the will of an ordinary man is as nothing compared to that of a king.'

'What do you mean?' Frances demanded.

Edward continued to smile but said nothing. Then he took another step forward so that his face was close to hers and his cloak brushed against her skirts. She forced herself to hold his gaze, though her skin burned and her vision was blurring. He pushed past her, slamming his shoulder against hers so that she was knocked back against the heavy oak frame of the door.

'Ah, Your Grace,' she heard him say, as he walked into the princess's chamber. 'How well you look today.'

Frances made no move to follow him. The back of her skull throbbed from where it had hit the frame. She tried to steady her breathing, but the thought of Edward's parting words made her pulse quicken again. Though she had asked their meaning, she had understood it well enough. Her son's inheritance would be seized by the king if he detected any hint of treason on her part. What her brother could not know was that she was already up to her neck in it.

CHAPTER 41
22 JUNE

Frances turned her face to the sun as she trailed her hand over the side of the barge. The branches of the dogwood trees that lined the river on either side of them weighed heavy with blossoms, soft pink and white, the delicate fragrance carried on the warm breeze.

On days such as this, she could almost forget the troubles that weighed like a stone upon her heart and surrender herself to the pleasures that nature offered. Edward's sniping seemed far distant, Lady Vaux's threats as insubstantial as a dream.

She smiled as she thought of how she had lain in Thomas's arms last night, his fingertips toying with her breast as he kissed her. She had been overjoyed at his return, which was even earlier than he had predicted, thanks to a turn in the weather. It must have vexed the king sorely to see the sun shining as soon as he returned to London. Thomas had been as hungry for her as she was for him. Their lovemaking had been frenzied at first and they had tugged impatiently at each other's clothes, desperate for release. Only afterwards had they fully undressed and lain on the bed, their breath gradually slowing as the soft breeze drifted through the open window, cooling their skin.

The bark of her uncle's laughter intruded upon her reverie. She closed her eyes again as she tried to summon the delicious memory of last night, but it had already faded. With a sigh, she raised herself and looked to where the princess was sitting.

'I was quite the sailor, in my youth,' he declared, loud enough for Elizabeth's ladies to hear. 'The old queen would have put me in command of her fleet, if that fool Raleigh hadn't so beguiled her. It is a mercy that Your Grace's father has greater sense, eh?'

Elizabeth recoiled as he leered at her. He seemed blissfully unaware that she had not spoken two words together since they had left the landing stage at Whitehall. No doubt he thought she was in thrall to him, Frances mused disdainfully. She knew she ought to intervene, as she had during their other encounters, distracting the princess from his boorishness with a well-timed observation or deftly changing the subject of con-

versation during one of his dreary mono-
logues. If she had failed to make him more
appealing as a suitor, then she had at least
saved her mistress from the worst aspects of
his company.

After a few minutes, her uncle's voice
trailed off. Even he was incapable of sustain-
ing a conversation indefinitely, when the
other party failed to offer any response. In
the silence that followed, Frances was drift-
ing towards sleep, the soft lapping of the
waters against the side of the barge soothing her mind.

'The princess must keep late hours if her
attendants are so exhausted.'

Frances's eyes snapped open. Robert Carr
was sitting on the bench next to her, a
simpering smile on his face. She had not
heard him approach.

'The warmth of the sun lulls me to sleep,'
she replied, sitting up. Her temples pulsed
with the movement and she felt suddenly
nauseous. The barge was nearing London
Bridge now and the rapid waters were making it sway and lurch.

Carr glanced at the princess, the sun
catching his reddish hair as he turned. 'Your
uncle seems to be making some progress
there.'

It was more a question than a statement.

His piercing eyes studied her closely as he waited for her to answer. Frances knew that his hopes of marrying Lady Howard rested on her uncle's ability to secure her an annulment from her current husband. She had heard little of the matter since Lady Vaux first mentioned it, and the lady in question had been seen only seldom at court. But then, as the king's closest favourite, Carr was obliged to keep his liaison discreet.

'My mistress is pleasant towards all of her guests, my lord,' Frances replied evenly. 'Tell me, how do your own affairs prosper?'

She caught the flash of irritation in his eyes before he recovered himself.

'The king has been most generous since the Earl of Salisbury's death.' He smiled. 'He means to govern more closely from now on, rather than trusting his affairs to another chief minister, and has appointed me to undertake many of the earl's former duties.'

Frances hoped the scorn did not show in her face. Carr might be the chief favourite, but he had neither the ability nor the dedication to fulfil the duties of the late chief minister. Besides, she doubted that James's resolve to take control would last for very long. His obsessions burned brightly but were soon extinguished — excepting his obsession with witches, she acknowledged. 'Then I congratulate you, my lord,' she said pleasantly. She paused. 'I trust that your personal affairs also prosper?'

A slight flush crept up the white skin of his neck.

'We both know of what you speak, Lady Frances,' he said, in a low voice. 'But I can discern no progress in that quarter. Your uncle assured me that he would secure his ward's annulment by Shrovetide, but that has long since passed. If he does not soon arrange matters to my satisfaction, I will have little choice but to abandon his. God knows it is a thankless task, trying to persuade the king that your uncle would make an excellent son-in-law. He is more than twenty years His Majesty's senior, let alone his daughter. The only reason my master has not rejected the idea out of hand is that he knows it vexes the prince.'

Frances raised an eyebrow. 'So the king does not intend to support any of the suitors his son favours?'

'The prince might secure the most powerful man in Christendom for his sister and their father would still find fault with his choice. He would even agree to a Catholic son-in-law if he thought it would frustrate his son.'

'But the princess is greatly in thrall to her

473

brother and would do anything to please him,' Frances pointed out, glancing at her mistress to assure herself they were not overheard.

Carr's gaze intensified. 'Prince Henry might think that he holds all before him, but his power does not reach beyond the confines of St James's. Even now, in the absence of a chief minister, the king has no intention of bestowing any authority upon his heir. He despises him so much that I would not wonder if he found a way to disinherit him.'

Although she was well aware of the antipathy that had long existed between James and his son, Frances had not known how deep it ran.

'He could not do so, of course,' Carr continued. 'The laws of this kingdom are such that the rightful order of succession cannot be overthrown. Besides, even James knows that his second-born son is little more than a simpleton, much though he dotes upon him, and could never wear a crown.'

What of his daughter? Frances wanted to say, but knew she must keep her counsel. 'So the king contents himself with frustrating Prince Henry's ambitions?' she asked instead.

Carr gave a dismissive wave. 'And all those who pay court to him. Though they share in his bounty now, if their young master were to fall, they would collapse around him like a house of cards.'

An image of Edward's smirking face flitted before Frances and she was elated at the thought of his being ejected from court, disgraced, along with the prince's other minions. If only Henry might test the military prowess that he so often boasted of and go to fight in some foreign land. She pictured him lying on a battlefield, bloodied and defeated, his lifeless eyes fixed upon the sky.

The shouts of a small crowd that had gathered to watch the princess's barge as it passed the Tower jolted her from her thoughts. She was suddenly aware that Carr was watching her closely.

'He is hardly like to fall, though, is he?' Frances said carefully.

A slow smile crept across Carr's face. 'Perhaps not,' he murmured, leaning forward. 'But, then, life is sometimes short, is it not, Lady Frances?'

Upon their return to the palace that afternoon, Frances was unable to settle to her duties. She had given up on her embroidery, having pricked her finger more times than the silk that was stretched over the frame on her lap. Neither had she been able to muster even a feigned interest in the jewels her mistress should wear for the masque that evening.

'What ails you, Fran?' the princess asked gently.

Frances smiled. Even though Elizabeth had called her by the diminutive since the earliest days of her service, she still felt a swell of gratitude for the affection that had grown between them. Her smile faltered as she glanced at Blanche, who was sitting in the window seat, pretending not to listen.

'I have not been sleeping well these past weeks,' Frances answered truthfully. 'Perhaps it is the change of seasons — the daylight lingers far more now.'

The princess did not reply but continued to look at her. 'You have grown thin, too, and so pale,' she persisted, her brow creasing with concern. 'You are not ill? I could ask one of my father's physicians to attend you.'

Frances gave what she hoped was a reassuring smile and reached forward to kiss the young woman's hand. 'I am touched by your care, ma'am, but promise that I am quite well. I am sure that my appetite will return as soon as I am more rested.' Then Frances diverted the conversation to other matters. She had to force herself to concentrate as her mistress chattered on about the latest court gossip — how Lady Dorset had slighted the Earl of Oxford for speaking ill of her husband, the scandal that had been caused by the Countess of Pembroke's gown being trimmed with ermine, the lord chamberlain's disapproval of the masque that had been chosen . . .

'Of course, the topic that excites most gossip is who will be Your Grace's next suitor.' Blanche's silken voice floated across the chamber when the princess paused for breath.

Frances saw her mistress's animated face cloud. 'I am sure the princess does not wish to join the speculation, Lady Blanche,' she cut in sharply.

Elizabeth sighed. 'It's all right, Fran,' she said, with resignation. 'Blanche is right. The matter of my marriage has dragged on for so long now that everyone must wonder when a suitable husband will be found for me.' She stood abruptly and crossed to the small casket she kept locked on the dresser. Fumbling for the key that hung from a cord at her waist, she opened it, drew out a letter and unfolded it. 'My brother writes that another suitor has been found, that he exceeds all others as the sun outshines the moon.'

Frances hid a sneer. It was just the sort of overblown language that the prince would use. His speech was as gaudy as his attire.

'He is Frederick the Fifth, Count Palatine of the Rhine. A Protestant, of course, and very close in age to me — in fact, I am but a week older.'

'Better than forty or more years your senior,' Blanche muttered, her eyes flashing with triumph as she looked across at Frances.

'My brother has already sent an emissary to treat with him on my behalf.'

Frances was surprised. 'Without your father's sanction? Surely he holds sway in such matters.'

Elizabeth shrugged. 'Henry can be impetuous sometimes, but he is so anxious to secure my happiness.'

Frances bit back a retort.

'The count is a fine young man, by all accounts,' her mistress continued, 'very learned and devout.'

'When will he come to meet Your Grace?' Blanche asked archly. She seemed a good deal less surprised by the news than she herself had been, Frances noticed.

'Henry does not say,' Elizabeth replied, sinking back into her chair. 'Perhaps it is too soon to judge.'

Frances studied her closely. Though the princess had been careful to appear grateful for her brother's efforts, her flat tone had betrayed her fear that this prince, too, would soon prove a disappointment.

There was a long pause, during which Frances tried to convey her sympathy and reassurance with a smile.

'Well, this is wonderful news!' Blanche broke the silence. Both women turned to her. 'The count sounds like an excellent young man, and deserving of your hand. I offer you my hearty congratulations, ma'am.'

'You are too hasty, Blanche!' the princess almost shouted, pushing back her chair.

Frances saw the woman's eyes widen briefly before she composed herself again.

'Frederick and I have not even exchanged letters yet. We are very far from being betrothed.' With that she strode towards the door. Reaching for the handle, she swung around. 'Come, Frances,' she said briskly. 'There is light enough yet for a ride.'

Frances could not help but feel a rush of satisfaction at her rival's disgrace. How often she had suffered the young woman's jibes, always delivered with a smile so that the princess was not alerted. Now she allowed herself a brief, triumphant glance at Blanche, before following her mistress out towards the stables.

It was already dusk when Frances returned to her apartment. The princess had excused herself from that evening's entertainments on account of a headache, but had asked Frances to keep her company in her privy chamber. She had said little at first and Frances had maintained a tactful silence, knowing her mistress's temperament well enough to judge that it was better to wait for her to unburden herself unprompted.

At length, Elizabeth had confided that she had received a miniature of Count Frederick. It had not pleased her. Frances had understood why when she had shown it to her. With his large round eyes and plump cheeks, he looked much younger than his fifteen years — little more than a child, really, Frances reflected, as she studied the likeness. His lace collar was so high around his neck that it appeared to be choking him, and his narrow shoulders hinted at fragility.

But Frances knew she could not be complacent. For as long as Prince Henry championed the match, his sister would offer no objection. Indeed, she would make herself as pleasing as possible to her new suitor to show her gratitude to her beloved brother. Even so, Frederick's physical shortcomings, with Lord Carr's remarks about the king's stance, gave Frances cause to hope that she might yet steer her mistress towards a Catholic suitor.

Lord Carr's other remarks had played on her mind, too. *Life is sometimes short, Lady Frances.* Those words had come back to her time and again, sparking a torrent of dark thoughts. It was treason even to speak of the king's death, let alone do anything to hasten it. *The same was not true of his son and heir.* She tried to dispel the notion. Even if Henry's murder would rid the kingdom of a wicked heretic, it was sinful in the eyes of God, she reminded herself. He had commanded: *Thou shalt not kill.* Anyone who disobeyed would suffer the fires of Hell. Yet still the idea had gnawed at her, invading her dreams when she finally surrendered to sleep.

The sconces had not yet been lit and in the gloom of the corridor she was obliged to fumble for the latch. She startled when it

482

was suddenly lifted but relaxed when Thomas opened the door. Her smile faded when she saw his expression. *Did he know?*

'Forgive my tardiness,' she said, as she closed the door behind her. 'The princess was a little fretful this evening and it took me a long time to calm her.' She drew off her cloak and draped it over a chair. Seeing that a jug of wine had been set on the table, she made towards it but Thomas stepped in front of her. His eyes were clouded with something she could not quite fathom. Then she realised it was fear.

Without warning, he clasped her to him so tightly that he almost squeezed the breath from her. She could feel the rapid pulse of his heart against her cheek.

'Tell me what has happened.'

He did not answer at first, but held her even closer, as if he feared she might suddenly fade away.

'Come — sit with me by the fire,' he said, releasing her at last. 'There is a chill to the air tonight, is there not?' He was speaking quickly now, his movements awkward as he pulled out a chair for her.

'You are making me fearful, Thomas,' she said, a little too brightly, as she waited for him to speak.

He was immediately chastened. 'Forgive

me,' he replied, running his hand through his hair. 'That was not my intention.' He gulped some wine.

Frances noticed his hand tremble as he set down the glass.

'I accompanied the king on a hunt today, as you know,' he began. 'He did not plan to return until sunset, but our party was interrupted by the arrival of a messenger carrying grave tidings.'

Frances tried to stop her mind racing on, but she knew from her husband's behaviour that whatever those tidings were they must concern her.

'A conspiracy has been uncovered in Lancashire,' he went on.

Frances relaxed slightly. She had no connection in that part of the country. Neither, to her knowledge, did Lady Vaux's or Lady Drummond's networks stretch that far north.

'Catholics?' she asked.

Thomas shook his head.

'No, Frances.' A pause. 'Witches.'

The word seemed to hang in the air as she stared back at him. There had been no talk of witches at court for many months, the subject of the princess's marriage and her brother's ongoing feud with the king overshadowing all else. Frances had even heard one courtier say that James was more interested in hunting foxes than witches these days — though she had hardly dared give it credence.

She tried to swallow, but her mouth was as parched as the cracked earth in the old herb garden.

'Twelve people have been arrested and await trial at the York assizes,' Thomas continued. 'They are accused of bewitching one man to death and causing several others to fall grievously ill.'

'So it was not a conspiracy against His Majesty?' Frances asked.

'No, but he has taken a great interest in the matter. When the messenger told of how several of the women have already confessed to making a pact with the devil and letting him suck their blood, the king became greatly agitated. He questioned the man closely for an hour, devouring every word as if it came from God Himself. By the end, he was alight with such a passion that I have not seen the like in him before — even for his favourites. He —' Her husband shook his head slightly.

'What is it, Thomas?' she asked quietly, holding his gaze until she saw his shoulders sag, as if defeated.

'It is nothing. He was in a frenzy, that is

485

all, and seemed no longer master of his actions. After the conference was over, he crossed to the stag he had slain and ripped open its belly with his knife, then stamped the beast's entrails into the soil.'

A wave of nausea swept over Frances and she leaned forward, her head in her hands. She was only vaguely aware of her husband placing his arm around her shoulders, whether to comfort or steady her she could not tell. He continued to hold her as he began to speak again.

'It is as if the news has ignited something deep inside him, given him a purpose that he has lacked for several years. Already he has issued orders for the suspects to be searched for the Devil's Mark and has dispatched his own witch-pricker there for the purpose.'

Frances shivered, despite the warmth from the fire. She raised her eyes to her husband's to rid herself of the image of the blade as it jabbed at her flesh, probing ever deeper until she cried out in fear and pain. 'He will not stop there,' she said at last. 'I have seen the same light in his eyes, have suffered at the hands of his interrogators. Now that he has been reminded of the pleasure it gives him, he will hunt down other witches to sate his appetite. And it will not be long before his gaze alights upon me.'

Thomas looked stricken but said nothing. She knew she had spoken his own fear and that he could not lie to her by denying it.

'I will not let any harm befall you, Frances,' he vowed, clasping her hands as he knelt before her. 'I cannot lose you, not now that we are — that you have come to feel for me what I have long felt for you.'

Her heart swelled as she looked down at him, his head bowed. 'Thomas . . .' She trailed off, suddenly uncertain. He raised his eyes to her. 'It is not only your wife whom you need to protect.'

'Of course,' he said quickly. 'George too — I know that. If anything were to happen to you —'

'Not just George,' she interrupted, taking his hand and guiding it to her stomach.

Thomas's hand froze, like that of a statue. Then his eyes flew up to hers. 'You are with child?' he said, in wonder.

Tears spilled down her cheeks as she nodded. 'I think so. I have been so tired lately and find the thought of food abhorrent at times, though at others it is as if my hunger will never be satisfied. It was so with George.'

'How long . . .' His eyes, too, were glistening.

'I cannot be sure, but I have missed two courses now so perhaps two months — three at most.'

Thomas sat back on his heels, as if winded. Frances watched a succession of emotions cross his face but did not know which held sway. 'Are you glad?' she ventured, trying hard to keep the fear from her voice.

His features lifted and he gave a bark of laughter. 'Glad? Frances, you have made me happier than I have ever been in my life!' he exclaimed, then clasped her to him tightly.

She stroked his hair as he pressed his face against her belly. But then he pulled back suddenly, as if fearing he had been too rough.

'It's all right, Thomas.' She smiled. 'I am not made of glass — and neither is our child.'

He placed his hand on her stomach again, more gently this time. 'That may be so,' he said, returning her smile. 'But you are both far more precious.' He cupped her face with his hands and gazed at her, his eyes alight with joy. 'I will not let anything happen to you — to either of you.' His smile faded as he spoke, and fear assailed her as she thought of their earlier conversation. How precarious life was in this court, she reflected bitterly, where happiness was as fleeting as sunshine in a cloud-laden sky.

But then Thomas leaned forward and kissed her, and her fear began to dissipate as she savoured the warmth of his mouth on hers.

CHAPTER 43
15 AUGUST

'For the Lord knoweth the way of the righteous: but the way of the ungodly shall perish.'

The chaplain's voice rose and fell, like the swallows that swooped and soared over the palace gardens. The seasons passed so quickly now, Frances thought. When she was a child, each summer had seemed to stretch into eternity, the winters even more so. Only as she grew to adulthood and the cares of the world began to overtake her did time take flight, the months skittering by, like clouds on a stormy day.

She glanced down at her stomach. There was no sign yet of the child that grew within, but she had lain awake for hours last night, her senses trained on her womb so that she might catch the faint, fluttering movements that had first awoken her. Following her gaze, Thomas squeezed her hand. The secret joy they shared had brought them even closer and Frances felt a kind of wonder at the strength of her love for him. But it made her fearful, too. She knew what it was to have such a love snatched away and that her heart would not bear it a second time.

Seeking distraction from her sombre thoughts, her gaze travelled up to the exquisite ceiling, the tiny gold stars scattered across the azure blue, like a celestial miracle. At each corner, a fleshy cherub blew on a horn, as if to awaken any members of the congregation who dozed beneath.

In the pews that stretched in front of them, the courtiers' faces were turned towards the pulpit, where the chaplain, a stern-faced man in middle age, was still reading from the king's new Bible, his voice growing louder as he warmed to the themes within.

James was not visible, though Frances knew that he was watching from the gallery above, with the queen and their children. Even Henry had been summoned to Hampton Court for the occasion, his father determined he should witness this celebration of his theological achievement. For a year now, the King James Bible had directed worship in churches across the kingdom, but James was eager that his subjects should

491

not forget who had commissioned it. He had therefore invited all of his high-ranking nobles, churchmen and courtiers to the palace where it had been spawned to mark the anniversary.

This was the first of several days of ceremonies, feasting and entertainments. Frances's heart sank as she thought of the long, dreary hours that were still to come. Even the princess seemed to take little delight in the prospect. Perhaps Count Frederick's impending visit occupied her thoughts.

Frances was at least grateful that the Hampton Court celebrations had temporarily eclipsed the scandal of the Pendle witch trials. Reports from the York assizes had reached the court daily, sending the gossips into a frenzy of excitement as they pulled apart every detail. Frances had avoided the public dinners as much as possible, eating the food Thomas brought to her in their apartment. But she could not escape the court altogether, much as she wished to, and was astute enough to judge that her absence might excite more unwanted attention.

She was already the subject of gossip: a gaggle of chattering ladies would fall silent as she approached. So long as it remained idle chatter she could bear it, but the terror she repressed during the day crept into her dreams at night. Many times she had cried out and woken, her hands clawing at the rope around her neck. Thomas had always been there to soothe her back to sleep, suppressing his own fear as he whispered words of comfort and love. She stole a glance at him now, seeking the strength that the sight of him always instilled in her.

At last, the sermon drew to a close and the chaplain gave his blessing, then climbed down from the pulpit and walked along the aisle, pausing to bow to the king. There was a rustle of silk and the low murmur of voices as the congregation rose to their feet and began to file out after him. Frances waited until most had gone, much to George's annoyance. He had begun to fidget during the last half-hour of the service and was now desperate to free his limbs.

'You look tired, Frances,' Thomas said, as she rose to her feet. 'Why don't I take George for a run in the gardens before the feast begins? You can rest in the shade.'

Frances hesitated. She did not wish to be apart from them, but her back ached and the thought of finding a secluded bench to rest on was too alluring a prospect to resist. 'Thank you,' she said, with a smile, and bent to kiss her son's head. 'But pray do not be long. We will have little enough time to-gether while we're here.'

Thomas drew her towards him and kissed her firmly on the lips. 'We will meet you in the rose garden. Come now, young sir, who shall prove the fastest to the river?'

George raced off down the corridor that led from the chapel, Thomas following in close pursuit. Before he rounded the corner, he turned back to Frances. His smile fal-tered as he waved.

Frances walked in the opposite direction, breathing in the aroma of roasted meat as she neared the kitchens. She could feel the heat from the fires as she passed, her stom-ach growling. God willing, the feast would be served as soon as they were seated. She knew, though, that it was more likely they would be obliged to sit through a series of interminable ceremonies, watching the king dip his hands in the ewer and his page wipe them dry while the rich sauces congealed around the venison, trout and other dishes. She longed to be back at Tyringham Hall, free from the pageantry and entertainments, the sniping and intrigue. When the three of them had last lived there, she had feared the private hours with her husband. Now she yearned for them.

Emerging into the courtyard, she blinked

in the bright sunlight. Relieved to see that it was deserted, save a few liveried servants who hurried about their business, she made her way slowly across it and out towards the gardens. As she passed under the great gate-house, her eyes were drawn by a movement to her left. Shielding her eyes, she saw her son scampering along the river path, Thomas following. She watched them for a few moments, then continued to the enclosed gardens to the west side of the palace.

Though the roses had long since bloomed and had left only a few sagging petals on the bushes, their fragrance lingered. Frances breathed deeply and closed her eyes. She had a memory of her first meeting with the princess, many years ago now, when they had gathered rose petals in her private garden, bunching up their skirts to contain them. The young girl's shyness had soon been forgotten in her excitement at meeting her new attendant. She had been so open-hearted then, so trusting. It pained Frances to think of how that trust had been destroyed. But, then, if Tom and the other plotters had not deceived the girl for their own ends, she would have been spoiled by some other experience soon enough. Innocence was as fleeting a virtue at court as the roses in this garden.

Weariness overcame her. Spying a bench on the far side of the garden, she walked to it and sank down gratefully. There was not a breath of wind and the heat of the sun was entrapped in the walls of the garden. Frances's eyelids grew heavy as she gazed back towards the palace, its elaborately twisting chimneys rising towards the sun as if they would touch its rays. The low hum of bees sounded in her ears, gently lulling her to sleep.

'Are you always so neglectful of your duties, sister?'

Frances's eyes sprang open. Edward was standing before her. His features were in shadow but she caught his smile. She wondered that she had not heard him approaching. He must have padded across the grass that lay between the flowerbeds, rather than along the gravel path. 'Edward.'

She made no move either to stand or to gesture for her brother to join her on the bench. After a few moments, he swiped at a few leaves that had fallen onto it, then sat next to her. Frances had to stop herself recoiling as his arm brushed against hers.

'What are you doing here?' she asked, her gaze fixed straight ahead.

'Well, that is a fine greeting for your brother,' he retorted scornfully. 'You have so few friends at court that I wonder you do not welcome me with joy.'

Frances ignored the barb and waited for him to answer her question.

'You surely cannot be surprised to see me. The prince is here, after all,' he added haughtily.

'I did not see you in the chapel.'

She sensed him bristle. Perhaps he was not as highly favoured as he liked to boast.

'I had other matters to attend to,' he replied. 'Matters that concern you.'

He was goading her, she told herself, taking care to keep her expression neutral, though her skin prickled with apprehension. 'Oh?'

She saw Edward's mouth twitch at the corners, as it had when he was a child and concealing some carefully prepared jest. He had once offered their younger sister Bridget a comfit, knowing her weakness for them. Frances remembered the tentative delight on her sister's face as she had reached towards the box that Edward held, then how she had screamed as her fingers closed over a writhing mass of worms. Edward's cruel laughter had echoed around the hall long after Bridget had run sobbing from it.

'The trial of the Lancashire witches must soon reach its conclusion,' he said, after a deliberate pause. 'I am sure you have been awaiting news of it with the same interest as the rest of the court. More, perhaps?' He let the question hang in the air. 'It has served as a timely reminder to us all — His Majesty in particular — that we must be forever vigilant in order to root out this scourge upon our kingdom, before it takes so deep a hold that it destroys us all.'

Frances had to remind herself to breathe.

'The prince, too, is most anxious to hunt down the contagion so that it might be vanquished. He says that the devil and his minions shall perish when the light of the Lord is shone upon them. In this, at least, he is in accord with his father the king.'

Frances was terror-struck. It spelled danger enough for her that King James's fervour for witch hunting had been reignited. How much greater might the danger be now that his son had taken up the cause? The prince had already tried to poison her son's mind against Catholics and would surely delight in stirring up his fear of witches. How long before he planted the idea in George's mind that his own mother might be such?

'What has this to do with me?' Frances asked steadily.

Edward smiled as he would at a child who

had asked a naïve question. 'Come, sister,' he murmured, taking her ice-cold hand and pressing it to his lips before she could snatch it away. 'Even Master Shakespeare's players could not have maintained a pretence for so long. Yet here you are, seven years after first being discovered as a witch, and still disguising yourself as a loyal subject. Really, Frances, you are to be congratulated.'

She gripped the edge of the bench. 'You forget, Edward, that my innocence was proven and I was restored to the princess's service at their majesties' command.'

Edward waved his hand dismissively. '*Pardoned,* sister, not acquitted. The stain of witchcraft hangs over you still. Why do you think nobody at court wishes to be seen conversing with you?'

Despite her fury, Frances recognised the truth of his words. The princess aside, there were few others whom she could look upon as friends, rather than mere acquaintances.

'Your spell in the Tower taught you discretion, at least,' her brother continued, 'though you soon resumed your wicked practices, even sending your faithful old nurse to her death.'

Frances wrenched her hand free. 'How dare you?' she cried, rounding on him. 'Ellen was as dear to me as our own mother. I would have gladly risked my own life to save hers.'

Edward sighed heavily. 'Ah, but you didn't, did you? You were too preoccupied with birthing that bastard of yours to spare a thought for a frail old woman. God knows how many other lives you have blighted,' he went on, warming to his theme. 'I wonder that you used your potions to cure your husband. Perhaps you intend to ensnare him in your schemes.'

'Thomas has nothing to do with this.'

The words had come out before she could stop them. Edward raised an eyebrow. 'With what?' he murmured.

She glared back at him defiantly and pressed her lips together, inwardly cursing her indiscretion.

He leaned in closer so that she could feel his breath on her face. 'You are steeped in treason, sister. What they whisper about you here is true. I have always known you to be a witch, but it seems your wickedness runs much deeper. Tell me, whom do you con-spire against? Is it the king? The prince? Or perhaps you hope to finish what the Powder plotters started and murder them all.'

Frances bit her cheek so hard that she tasted the coppery tang of blood. Still, she held his gaze, unflinching. She did not trust herself to speak again.

Edward slouched back against the wall. He put his hands behind his head and stretched out his legs in front of him. Frances knew it was an act, but his nonchalance sparked fresh fury and she could no longer bear to look at him. She focused her gaze upon a single rose, counting the thorns that jutted out along its smooth green stem.

'It is of little consequence,' he said, with an exaggerated yawn. 'If your treacherous schemes are not uncovered, you will be hanged as a witch anyway. I have more than enough proof to send you to the gallows. You will not escape them a second time, Frances.'

The thorns seemed to grow sharper as she stared at them, so that they appeared as tiny, deadly blades. She imagined them piercing her skin, as the witch-pricker's knife had done.

'It is amusing to think that I will be master of Longford after all, is it not?'

Frances swung around to him.

'Our poor father's efforts to disrupt the lawful inheritance will come to nothing. But, then, he could not have foreseen that his precious daughter would turn traitor and ruin everything.'

'Longford will never be yours, Edward,' Frances hissed. 'If I am declared a traitor, the estate will be forfeit to the Crown.'

Her brother's smile widened and he closed his eyes as he turned his face up to the sun. 'That is true, my dear sister,' he purred. 'But the prince has promised that as soon as he succeeds to the throne, he will restore Longford to me.'

Frances gave a scornful laugh. 'And you believe him? It is obvious that you have not spent enough time at court, brother, or you would know not to take anyone at their word. Even — or perhaps especially — the prince.'

But Edward's smile did not fade. Opening his eyes, he leaned forward and reached inside the pocket of his doublet. 'How right you are, Frances,' he said brightly, unfolding the paper. 'Which is why I took the precaution of securing the prince's written pledge.'

She snatched the paper from his hands.

Indenture, made this third day of August in the tenth year of the reign of His Majesty King James the First . . .

The words seemed to dance in front of her eyes as she read on, fingers trembling. 'Longford' was repeated several times, as were the names 'Edward, Baron Longford' and 'Henry, Prince of Wales'. She recognised her brother's signature at the foot of the page, next to that of the prince. The large wax seal was imprinted with three elegant plumes. *The Prince of Wales feathers.*

Frances let the paper slip from her fingers. With a deft move, Edward reached forward to pick it up and made a show of folding it with elaborate care before putting it back in his pocket.

'Really, Frances, you should be more careful.' He clicked his tongue. 'Well, I cannot stay here all day exchanging pleasantries, no matter how diverting your company is.'

She kept her gaze fixed upon the ground as he stood up.

'Ah, Sir Thomas,' Edward exclaimed, 'and my dear nephew.'

Frances almost wept to see them approach. Seeing her expression, Thomas brushed past his brother-in-law and sat down next to her. 'What is it, my love?' he asked.

She gave a slight shake of her head and glanced at Edward, who had scooped George into his arms and was swinging him around. The boy's whoops of delight echoed around the walls of the garden. Sensing her discomfiture, Thomas stood and gripped

Edward's arm so that he was obliged to set down the boy. George swayed and staggered, then shot a resentful look at his papa.

'It is growing late, Edward,' Thomas said firmly. 'We must go in for dinner before the king is seated.'

Edward winked at his nephew, whose face brightened at once, then turned on his heel and strode back towards the palace.

CHAPTER 44
19 AUGUST

Frances stared down at her shift. The blood glistened red on the linen. She clutched her stomach as it contracted in a fresh wave of pain. As it slowly receded, she took a deep breath, trying to steady her heart. She thought of Arbella's haunting screams as her own child bled away. *Was this God's punishment?*

'Frances!'

She had not heard the princess return. The young woman stared from Frances to the stained linen. Then she ran forward and put her arm around her attendant's shoulder, guiding her to a nearby chair. Frances sat down gingerly, as if fearing that the movement might trigger another onslaught.

'Is it — is it your courses?' Elizabeth whispered. 'You are so pale, though. I will summon my father's physician.'

'No!' Frances cried, making the princess start. 'Forgive me . . . I will be well.'

505

Feeling suddenly faint, she lowered her head into her hands, centring her thoughts upon the slow intake and release of her breath. She had slept badly again, her exchange with Edward playing in her mind until she had had to bite down on the sheets for fear of screaming out her terror and rage. Though she tried to calm herself with the thought that no accusations had yet been made, and that life had resumed its usual pattern since their return to Whitehall, it was as if Longford was lost to her already.

A few minutes passed. The princess continued to sit quietly by her side, stroking her back. Frances felt her breathing begin to slow as the faintness receded. She placed her fingers lightly upon her stomach, but there was no more pain.

'I will fetch you a new shift,' Elizabeth said, stepping quickly out of the room before Frances could protest. She could hear the low hum of voices from the other side of the door. A moment later the princess returned, the neatly pressed linen draped over her arm. She helped Frances to stand, then began unlacing the back of her gown so that she could change into the fresh garment. Frances could not help smiling at the reversal of their roles. Though they were hardly practised at it, Elizabeth's fingers moved with surprising deftness and Frances soon felt her stays spring open as the final thread was released.

She breathed in deeply, relishing the feeling of lightness around her waist. Perhaps she should have loosened her stays before now, she reflected. A small swelling had begun to show a few days earlier. Thomas had seen it when she had undressed for bed, the light from the candle casting a shadow over the budding curve. He had fallen asleep that night with his hand still resting upon it.

'There!' the princess said as she smoothed the hem of the new shift, which skimmed Frances's ankles. 'I will have to gain a little in height before you and I can share our clothes, but it will suffice for now.'

Frances thanked her and stooped to pick up her discarded gown, but Elizabeth snatched it away. 'You have no more need of this today, Frances,' she said firmly. 'You must rest.'

Frances opened her mouth to protest but at that moment the doors of the outer chamber burst open and Thomas strode into the room. Seeing the bloodied shift that the princess had draped over one of the chairs, his face grew ashen. 'What has happened?' He drew Frances into an embrace as he sat next to her.

She hesitated and glanced at the princess, who discreetly left the room, closing the doors softly behind her.

'Is it . . .' he began, but the words died on his lips.

Frances could not bear to see him so stricken, but neither could she offer any reassurance. Though she could no longer feel the blood seeping between her legs, she did not know whether the tiny life still pulsed inside her.

'I don't know,' she said quietly. 'The pains started about an hour ago. They have stopped now but . . .' She gestured at the bloodied shift.

Thomas stroked back a strand of hair from her face, then leaned forward and kissed her forehead. 'Come now,' he said, as he scooped her gently into his arms. 'It is time to rest.'

By the time they reached their apartment, the rise and fall of Thomas's footsteps had almost lulled her to sleep. Setting her down, he unlocked the door and guided her inside. Frances was grateful to see that the parlour was deserted. Mistress Knyvett was a kindly woman but liked to gossip, and Frances was in no mood to indulge her. She followed her husband to the bedchamber.

'You are quite sure everything is well, Frances?' He pulled the covers over her.

She gave what she hoped was a reassuring smile, but she knew that he was talking about more than the bleeding.

'You've been so distant since our return from Hampton Court,' he continued, sitting beside her and taking her hand in his. 'You do know that you may tell me anything, without fear of judgement?'

'Of course,' she replied, too quickly. Her heart began to flutter, like the wings of a tiny bird trapped in a cage.

'Did Edward say something to trouble you?' His expression darkened. 'I do not trust him, after what he did to George.'

Frances could not form the words of a lie but neither could she confide in him, as she longed to do. To reveal even part of her conversation with Edward would lead to more questions — which she could not answer truthfully without destroying everything that had grown between them. She hated to keep another secret from her husband when the burden of the other already weighed heavily upon her, but she had little choice.

After a pause, she gave a slow shake of her head, then put her hand in front of her mouth, as if stifling a yawn.

'Forgive me, my love, I have tired you,' Thomas said, immediately contrite. He planted a warm kiss on her cheek, then left the room.

When would the deception end?

The next morning Frances heard muffled voices as she approached the princess's chamber. One was the prince's, she realised, recognising the high-pitched trill of laughter. She nodded to the guard, who opened the door.

'Frances!' Elizabeth exclaimed, clasping her hands. 'You should be resting. What were you thinking to return so soon? You are still so pale,' she gabbled.

Frances kissed the princess's hand. 'I am much better, thank you, Your Grace, and eager to return to your service.'

'Such dedication is commendable.'

Both women turned to see the prince staring at them. Frances bobbed a quick curtsy, her eyes travelling to his companion. It was a long time since she had seen William Cecil. He had not been at any of the court gatherings that the prince had attended lately, and Frances had begun to think that Henry was as fickle in his friendships as he was in his other pursuits.

'Your Highness, Viscount Cranborne.'

William gave a stiff bow, but the prince remained seated. His cold gaze was directed at Frances, who came to sit by her mistress. Blanche was standing by the fireplace, her fingers interlaced demurely. Frances suspected she had chosen to stand so that she might display her figure to best effect in front of the prince.

'My sister has been telling me just how far your dedication stretches, Lady Frances,' the prince continued.

Frances felt the princess flinch. She was staring intently at her brother, as if willing him not to say any more. Frances formed her own mouth into a pleasant smile as she waited for him to go on.

'As well as helping her dress, stitching her linens and whatever else you ladies do, it seems you have also taken it upon yourself to direct her choice of husband.'

Frances glanced at her mistress. A slow flush was creeping up Elizabeth's neck and she was looking down at her hands.

'Henry, please,' she said quietly, keeping her eyes lowered.

'Tell me, what was it about Prince Gustavus that you found so disagreeable?' His words were as sharp as flint. 'I should have thought you would rejoice to see your mistress betrothed to a prince from your mother's land. Perhaps his hair was too light, his expression too grave.'

Frances's gaze did not falter. How did he know of the part that she had played in dissuading her mistress from marrying the Swedish prince? She had always taken care to be discreet, only raising the subject when she and Elizabeth were alone. The princess had made her swear never to let another soul know of her own growing doubts about her suitor, which had given Frances assurance that her role in fostering them would not be discovered.

Out of the corner of her eye, she could see that Elizabeth's face was now a deep red. *It was she who had told him.*

'Or perhaps . . .' The prince paused for dramatic effect.

Even his sister now raised her eyes to look at him.

'. . . perhaps it was his faith that offended you, Lady Frances.' His eyes glinted with the same thrill she had seen in huntsmen as they closed on their prey.

'Of course not, Your Grace,' she replied calmly. 'Prince Gustavus shared the faith of this kingdom.'

'Ah, but did he share *your* faith, Lady Frances?' the prince asked.

She darted a look at William Cecil, who

was regarding her steadily. Blanche gave a small cough, but Frances could not bear to see the triumph on her slender face so she focused upon the prince again. 'I worship as the king directs,' she replied. 'As do all faithful subjects.'

Henry continued to stare at her for a long moment. There was a soft creak from a floorboard as the wood swelled in the rising warmth of the room, which the sun's rays had now penetrated.

'I hope for your sake that is true,' he said. A muscle in his jaw pulsed. 'But I am minded to take no chances with my sister's new suitor. Count Frederick will soon embark for England. We must ensure that he meets a compliant bride when he arrives.'

Frances glanced at the princess. A solitary tear was weaving its way down her cheek. She felt a surge of fury that Henry should treat her as little more than a brood mare to be traded at market.

'A great deal rests upon this alliance and I will not have it disrupted by meddlesome women,' he continued. 'I have therefore instructed my sister to speak of the count to no one but myself. I will know if she defies me. I have appointed Lady Blanche to be always in her presence.'

Though Blanche still affected a modest

demeanour, a sly smile played about her lips. Frances swallowed her revulsion and turned to the prince once more. 'I am sure Her Grace is grateful for your solicitude,' she said, taking care to keep her voice light.

'Do you presume to know my sister's thoughts, Lady Frances?'

The princess stood up suddenly, as if unable to bear the tension any longer. 'Forgive me, Henry. I am tired.' Her voice was broken.

After a long pause, her brother rose to his feet. Motioning to his companion, he held out his hand for his sister to kiss then walked slowly from the room. As soon as their footsteps began to fade, Elizabeth made a noise that was halfway between a sigh and a sob and ran into her bedroom, slamming the door behind her.

Chapter 45
22 August

'They say that the old woman took the longest to die.'

Frances tried not to listen as she tore off another piece of bread, but the rest of the chatter died down and all eyes were turned to her uncle, who was clearly relishing the attention.

'You would have thought her scraggy neck would snap as soon as the rope tightened around it, but it took a full five minutes for her to choke out her last breath.'

Frances repressed a shudder. An image of the woman she had seen hanged at Tyburn came to her. The glazed, bulging eyes had haunted her for many nights since. Thomas reached out to touch her knee. The reassuring warmth of his hand calmed her. Though she had expected news of the Lancashire witch trials to reach the court this week, she had dreaded it, too. Every mealtime passed in the idle chatter of court gossip had been a relief.

'Were all twelve hanged?'

The question came from the far end of the table.

The earl shook his head as he drank some wine. 'One was acquitted.' He wiped his mouth. 'Another died in gaol — fortunate for her, though she will not escape the fires of Hell so easily.'

'Why was she acquitted?' the woman next to Frances asked, sitting forward on the bench.

'Probably pleaded her belly,' another said, before the earl could reply. Instinctively Frances's hand shot to hers. 'They often use that trick. Did you hear about Old Mother Williams? When the verdict at her trial was pronounced, she claimed she had a child in her womb, even though she was nearly four score.'

There was a loud roar of laughter around the table. Frances wanted to shut her ears. Thomas's hand twitched on her lap.

'I doubt that was the reason in this trial,' her uncle continued, when the hilarity had died down, 'or she would have been thrown back in gaol to wait out the months while the guards watched for any swelling beneath her stays. Making such a plea buys only time, not life.'

Frances's vision blurred and she closed her eyes briefly. When she opened them, she saw that Thomas was watching her, his brow knitted with concern. 'Let us talk of other things,' he murmured.

Frances smiled. She kept her hand on her belly, as if to protect it from the horror that was being spoken of by their fellow diners. Still she did not know if she was protecting an empty womb, as a blackbird might sit on her nest after her eggs have been stolen by a crow. 'What time do you leave tomorrow?' she asked, saddened by the prospect of his absence.

'Before daylight, I fear,' Thomas replied. 'His Majesty has a mind to ride up to The More, some thirty miles north-west of here. He has heard that there is excellent hunting ground thereabouts, though the house itself has fallen into ruins since King's Henry's day.' He paused. 'I do not like to leave you at such a time.'

'You worry too much, Thomas,' she chided gently. 'I have plenty to occupy me here and will fare a good deal better without a troublesome husband to distract me.'

She was glad to see his eyes crinkle at the corners, and they resumed their meal in companionable silence. Frances felt hungrier than she had in weeks, so took full

517

advantage of the food that was laid out before them. As she reached to spear a piece of beef, she stopped, her fork suspended above the dish. There it was again — a movement so slight that it might be mistaken for the tickle of fabric against her skin. Discreetly, she laid down her fork and placed her hand tentatively on her belly. There was no mistaking it this time. The fluttering was rapid and strong, like the wings of a butterfly trapped against a pane of glass.

Frances felt a surge of joy, as pure and exhilarating as a crisp winter's day. She turned to her husband, beaming. His confusion cleared as she moved his hand to her stomach. A slow smile crept across his mouth and his eyes sparkled as he gazed at her.

'So perish all witches!'

Her uncle's voice dispelled the wonder of the moment, like a pebble hurled into a still pond. Frances swallowed. The elation she felt at knowing their child still lived was tinged with fear. She was hazarding another life now, too. *All the more reason to prevail.* She must find a way to rid herself of those who circled her, like wolves. As she imagined them now, eyes trained upon her, they dissolved and formed anew into a solitary dark figure.

Prince Henry.

Frances had not tarried in bed after Thomas set out. Leaving her son sleeping peacefully and Mistress Knyvett snoozing by the fireplace, she had left the apartment and padded along the deserted corridors until she reached the riverside gate. There were several boatmen clustered around it, heads bowed as they sucked on their pipes and waited for the court to awaken. Seeing her approach, one broke away and led her to his boat. The tide was in their favour and it took only half an hour to reach the Tower.

As she climbed onto the landing stage, Frances prayed Raleigh would be awake. The sky was lightening but on checking her pocket watch she saw that it was not half past five.

The guards at the outer gateway nodded her through and she made her way along the curtain wall before turning left under the archway that led up to the green. Climbing the steps, she peered across at Raleigh's lodging and was relieved to see a candle burning at the window.

He opened the door before she had knocked. 'You keep unsociable hours, Lady Frances,' he said, as he bent to kiss her

519

hand. 'It is usually only the cawing of the ravens that stirs me from my bed.'

She struggled to return his smile and took the seat he indicated.

'News of the Lancashire witches reached court yesterday,' she began. 'They were hanged a few days ago.'

Raleigh nodded, grave-faced. 'So I understand. The walls of the Tower are not so solid that they can keep out the news from Whitehall.' He sipped from the goblet next to him. 'They say it has reminded the king of his passion for witch hunting.'

Frances looked at him bleakly. 'That is true — and the prince now pretends to share his passion. It is one of the few matters upon which they agree,' she added bitterly.

'And what of Lady Vaux?'

Frances shrugged. 'I have heard little from her of late. Though I doubt she has been idle.'

'So she is not the one about whom you wish to confer?'

Frances admired his ability to get to the heart of the matter straight away, without ever making her feel hurried. She shook her head.

'Perhaps it is that troublesome brother of yours — ah, I see my aim is true.' He leaned forward, lowering his voice as he spoke again. 'Has he been corrupting young George?'

'Not since that night at St James's. He has found other ways to torment me.' She took the cup that Raleigh offered. Holding it beneath her nose, she breathed in the aroma of basil and something sweeter. Honey. As the liquid slipped down her throat, it seemed to warm her entire body. She began to relax.

'Edward's favour with the prince increases daily,' she continued. 'It seems they are kindred spirits, both intent upon destroying the lives of others to boost their own. He has persuaded Henry to sign an indenture, restoring Longford to him if ever it should be forfeit to the Crown.'

She could see the thoughts playing through Raleigh's mind as he watched her with steady, knowing eyes. 'Prince Henry is impatient for his own inheritance,' he said, 'if he makes such pledges while his father is still in good health. I wonder what other plans he is quietly putting in place.'

'I am sure he means to dictate the lives of all those unfortunate enough to fall within his orbit.' The scorn dripped from her voice. 'He has certainly resolved to dictate his sister's choice of husband and ordered me not to speak to her of it, lest I dissuade her from this latest candidate.'

'Count Frederick? A chit of a lad, by all accounts. I doubt he will be to the princess's taste.' He paused. 'So he knows that you sought to undermine the previous match?'

'I care little for that. I suspect the princess let it slip, though I know she would not have done so intentionally. In a way, I am grateful to the prince. He was quite clear that I should desist from any future discussion of the princess's marriage. I am therefore released from my obligation to further the suit of my uncle.'

'That at least is a blessing,' Raleigh agreed. 'I cannot imagine that your efforts in that quarter were thriving. Will you tell Lady Vaux?'

'It is Longford that concerns me most,' she replied, with a touch of impatience, eager to draw his attention back to the matter in hand. 'Edward has threatened to provide proof of my witchcraft. He knows that I treated my husband at Belvoir and has other evidence besides.'

Raleigh raised an eyebrow, but Frances remained tight-lipped. She had no wish to talk of Ellen. The guilt she felt over her death was still too raw, even after all these years.

'And he has the king's ear, as well as

Henry's?'

'I don't think so. But that hardly matters. If the king hears that the supposed witch who slipped through his fingers years ago can at last be brought to justice, he will not care who stands witness.'

Raleigh fell silent for a few moments. 'You may be right,' he said, resting his chin on his interlaced fingers. 'Though it is the prince with whom we should be most concerned. He has reason to punish you for disrupting his schemes. Edward will be quick to take advantage, we can be sure of that. Both men now share a common aim, Frances. To destroy you.'

He had voiced the thought that had been running through her mind since that encounter with the prince. Hearing it spoken aloud made her shake with fear.

'Of the two men, your brother can most easily be dealt with,' Raleigh continued. 'His ambition has blinded him to the danger that the indenture has placed him in. By making plans for Longford when Henry is king, he has countenanced the death of our present king — which, as I am sure you are aware, is treason.'

'Then the prince would also be implicated,' Frances said, 'if the indenture should come to light.'

Raleigh gave a shrug. 'Certainly, but it is doubtful that he would face the same consequences. Much as he despises him, even the king would flinch at putting to death his own son and heir.'

'Whereas Edward . . .'

'. . . has as good as signed his own death warrant,' Raleigh finished for her.

Frances sank back in her chair. She felt almost giddy with relief, but it was soon supplanted by shame. No matter what Edward had done, he was still her brother, yet she was talking of his death as if it were cause for celebration.

'Of course we have no proof,' Raleigh continued. 'Although Edward was foolish enough to boast of the indenture to you, he will have it safely locked away, until such time as it is needed.'

'And nobody else will know of it,' Frances added. 'I saw only his signature and the prince's. It is no surprise that they did not risk having it witnessed.'

She thought back to the document. That she had had it in her grasp was galling. Where could Edward have hidden it? She did not even know where his lodgings were at St James's — not that he would be fool enough, surely, to keep it there. 'I must find it,' Frances murmured, almost to herself.

Raleigh patted her hand. 'It is natural that you should wish to, but you must not allow it to distract you from the real matter in hand,' he said softly.

She looked up at him. 'You could spend weeks, months, searching in vain,' he went on. 'Meanwhile, Edward and the prince will be building a case against you, choosing their moment to strike.'

'What would you have me do?' Frances asked, rubbing her temples.

'Without the prince, your brother is powerless. Yes,' he held up a hand to stop her protest, 'it is possible that Edward will run to the king with his tales, but for as long as the prince draws breath he has no reason to do so.' He paused. 'Whereas if Henry's life were suddenly to be snuffed out . . .' He clicked his fingers, the sound echoing in the silence that followed.

Frances eyed him doubtfully, not wanting to believe that she had understood his meaning. 'There is no reason to suppose that such a thing might happen, though, is there, Sir Walter? The prince is in robust health, after all.'

Raleigh smiled. 'Of course, of course.' He took another sip from his goblet. 'But what if he were to choke upon his own poison?'

Frances pressed her mouth into a thin line.

'It would be a delicious irony if the woman whom he tries to incriminate for witchcraft escapes the rope by employing the same skills of which she stands accused. Would it not, Frances?'

She stared at him in horror. 'You mean that I should poison the prince?'

'God has given you great skill in such matters, Frances,' Raleigh continued, undaunted. 'You could stop his breath without leaving any trace of foul play.'

She made to stand up, but Raleigh grasped her wrist, forcing her back onto the chair.

'The prince stands between you and all you hold dear, Frances,' he urged, his voice low. 'He will take Longford from your son, bully his sister into marrying a heretic, and see you hanged as a witch. You stand to lose everything at his hands.'

'That may be true.' Frances wrenched herself free. 'But I have only ever used my skills for good. I will not stoop to murder. Even if I escape vengeance in this world, I will not do so in the next.'

She stood, her chair scraping loudly on the flagstones. Raleigh's smile did not waver as he watched her stride from the room. By the time she reached the bottom of the stairs, she had broken into a run, ignoring the curious stares of the guards as she passed. Only when she had left the confines of the Tower did she stop, hands on her knees, gasping in air as if it might cleanse her of the horror that had been spoken in that gloomy chamber.

CHAPTER 46
25 SEPTEMBER

Elizabeth gave a shiver and drew her cloak around her shoulders. 'Autumn comes early this year, I think,' she said, looking at the trees that rose above the wall of the orchard.

Frances followed her gaze. 'It seems to have arrived with the endless rain this past week,' she agreed.

It pained her that their conversation was now limited to such matters. They had not enjoyed even an hour alone together for more than a month now. Blanche had proved all too assiduous in keeping watch on them, as the prince had instructed. Frances was grateful that she was absent now, at least. Even Blanche would not relinquish the day of leisure that each of the princess's attendants was awarded every few weeks. But she had made sure to arrange for another to take her place.

They lapsed into silence as they continued their circuitous route around the privy

528

garden. When Elizabeth peeped over her shoulder, her attendant was still there, walking a few paces behind. 'Lady Anne,' she called, 'pray, fetch me my sable. This cloak is not warm enough and I do not wish to return indoors just yet.'

The young woman hesitated, then hastened away towards the palace. As soon as she was out of sight, the princess clasped Frances's hand. 'Forgive me, Frances,' she said, her eyes imploring. 'I have been wretched since that day when my brother spoke to you. I cannot bear to think that I have brought his wrath upon you, that this horrid distance between us is my fault.'

'Your Grace, please —'

'No, Frances, you must hear me. I cannot rest until I have told you what happened.'

She glanced towards the palace before she continued.

'I was in an ill humour when Henry came to speak to me about Count Frederick. I had slept badly and did not show as much obedience as he is accustomed to during our conferences.'

Frances felt a flash of annoyance at the arrogant young man, who had always used his sister's adoration to cajole and manipulate her.

'He kept repeating that I must not ruin

this latest match as I had the Swedish one, that Count Frederick might not be as pleasing as Gustavus but I must show myself a willing bride.' She slowed her pace. 'It was then that I lost my temper and started ranting about all of Gustavus's shortcomings. I don't know what possessed me — Henry is such a good brother to me and I have always sought to please him.'

Frances waited for her to continue.

'He brushed aside my protests, insisted that I alone had failed to appreciate the prince's many virtues.' She chewed her lip. 'It was then that I said you shared my view — indeed, that you had helped me to see myriad other reasons why I should not marry him.'

She stopped walking and turned to Frances, reaching for her hands. 'The words were out before I could stop them, and the look on my brother's face told me how great an error I had committed,' she said miserably. 'Can you ever forgive me?'

Frances bent to kiss her fingers. 'There is nothing to forgive.' She smiled, her heart swelling with affection for the young woman who had come to seem as a younger sister to her. 'You must not blame yourself for becoming vexed with the prince. He should not seek to direct your thoughts and opinions. You have intelligence and judgement at least equal to his — greater, even.'

She saw her mistress's eyes cloud with doubt and told herself that she must resist the urge to say anything more against Henry.

'Besides,' she continued, 'I should not have been so outspoken in my own opinions. If there is any forgiveness to be pleaded, then it is on my part only. I promise that I will never speak to you of such matters again,' she added, thinking not of Count Frederick but of her uncle. How glad she was to be relieved of that burden.

Elizabeth's shoulders sagged and her eyes filled with tears. 'Oh, Fran,' she sighed, 'though I know it must be like this, I will miss our confidences more than I can say. You are the only one to whom I can open my heart.'

She inhaled sharply, as if to suppress a sob. Frances ached to see her so utterly wretched. 'All will be well, Your Grace,' she said. 'You do not need my counsel, but must listen only to your heart.'

The princess nodded, then resumed her walk, Frances half a pace behind. *God give the girl strength to follow her heart,* she prayed silently.

Frances had waited until she was sure the princess was sleeping before stealing out of her bedchamber. Having unburdened herself, the young woman had been overcome with exhaustion and had retired to her bed for the afternoon, insisting that her attendant do the same, given her recent indisposition. Though Frances had acceded, she knew she must not let this opportunity slip through her fingers.

A few discreet enquiries had told her that Edward did not have an apartment at St James's but was staying at Whitefriars. It had been many years since she had visited their parents' lodgings in the old Carmelite monastery that lay between Fleet Street and the Thames. The sprawling priory was ranged around two large courtyards, and Frances remembered that the Gorges' apartment lay on the northernmost quadrant. She could just see the chimneys now, above the ramshackle houses that lined Fleet Street.

Though she knew it might be a fool's errand, she had to begin her search for the indenture somewhere. The document now seemed her only hope of saving Longford

— and herself. She thanked God that the memory had come to her the previous night as she had lain awake, turning over the possibilities of where Edward might be hiding it. An image of the painting came before her again, causing her steps to quicken.

The question of what she would do with the document if she was right about Edward's hiding place ran through her mind again as she raced along the crowded streets. The surest means of achieving her aim would be to take it straight to the king. Her brother would be arrested and the prince would be in disgrace, leaving their plans to have her accused of witchcraft in tatters. But she had not been able to silence her conscience, which had reminded her constantly that this would almost certainly lead to Edward's death. Although it held greater risk for herself, she had therefore resolved upon another plan.

Her pace slowed as she turned down the narrow passageway that led to the priory. The bustle of Fleet Street faded as she advanced, her steps echoing off the ancient walls that had once formed part of an outer cloister. She had not allowed herself to think of what Raleigh had proposed. It was too monstrous. She had been wrong to confide in him and must sever all contact with him now, she told herself.

The gloom of the cloister was lifting and soon the passageway opened out into a vast quadrant, lined on every side with apartments, four storeys high. Frances looked along the rows of large windows, hoping she might see something to prompt a recollection of where her parents' lodgings were situated.

At that moment, the sun appeared from behind a cloud, casting a shadow over the side of the building that she was facing. It was then she noticed the small crest above one of the window frames, a simple design that bore the three stars of the Carmelite order. *Of course.* She wondered that she had not thought of it earlier. Her father had always joked that he had had the crest installed above their apartment so that he would not go blundering into a neighbour's by mistake. Young as she was, Frances had believed him. It had been years later that she had learned the real meaning of the design.

She hastened towards the archway at the centre of the façade. As she mounted the stairs to the top floor, she felt again for the key, mouthing a silent prayer of thanks to her father for giving it to her when she had first come to court all those years ago. She had doubted that she would ever need it and had all but forgotten about it after putting it safely in her casket. When she had found it last night, she had slept with it under her pillow, afraid lest it be snatched away.

She had taken care to count the windows before coming inside. There were three to each apartment, so the lodging must be four doors along the corridor. As she passed the third, she paused. She knew that the prince was on a hunting expedition today and prayed that Edward had accompanied him. Glancing behind her, she edged forward, wincing as a floorboard creaked under her foot.

She was outside the door now and drew a breath as she pressed her ear to it. All was silence within. She waited a few more seconds, then slowly eased the key into the lock. It was stiff and would not turn at first so she applied more pressure, pausing between each attempt to listen. At last, with a loud grating sound, the lock gave way.

Slowly, Frances lifted the latch and pushed open the door. The first room was deserted. The furniture was much as she had remembered it, though it was shabbier now — clearly Edward did not use the apartment for entertaining, or he would have wasted more of Longford's fortune on expensive furnishings. As she inhaled, she caught the familiar scent of her father's tobacco and a wave of grief washed over her, as raw as it had been more than two years earlier. But the pulse of fear soon returned, drawing her into the other rooms of the apartment. When she reached the last, Edward's bed-chamber, and found that it, too, was deserted, she almost cried out with relief.

Suddenly she saw it. There, on the panelling between the pillars of her brother's bed, was the painting she remembered so well from their childhood. She took a step closer. The colours had faded, but the figure of Eve was still clearly visible, the apple concealed in her hand and the serpent coiled around the branch above. It had hung in their mother's chamber at Longford and she had often referred to it when telling the children that nothing must remain hidden from God. How like Edward to use it as a place to conceal the birds' eggs he had stolen from the hedgerows surrounding the estate. Frances had always retrieved them, carrying them carefully back to the closest nests she could find in the faint hope that the birds that lived there would adopt them as their own.

Glancing quickly behind her, she gently

lifted the painting from the wall. She could feel the small niche that ran along the inside of the thick frame. With trembling fingers, she turned it over slowly. Her heart sank as she saw that the back of the frame was empty. She had been so sure that the indenture would be there.

A bell sounded in the distance. She must not tarry: Edward could arrive at any moment. Pushing down her disappointment, she took a quick look out onto the courtyard below, then began to search the rest of the apartment. As she quietly pulled open drawers and lifted the lid of chests and caskets, she felt gratitude that her brother had not stuffed them with treasures. If he had, she would have been there for hours. Before long, she was back in the parlour. Aware that this was the final place to search, she took even greater care than she had in the other rooms, looking for hidden compartments under chairs, balancing on a chest so that she could search behind the picture frames, peering inside the fireplace and running her fingers along its inner ledge.

Nothing.

Frances sighed as she brushed the soot from her fingers. She was about to embark upon a second search when she heard voices in the courtyard below. Running to the window, she concealed herself behind one of the shutters and peered down. She glimpsed Edward's coat as he ducked under the archway beneath her.

Heart thudding, she tore out of the apartment, closing the door as quietly as she could. The voices grew louder as she fumbled with the key in the lock. *Please, please,* she mouthed silently, the iron digging painfully into her palm as she used all her strength to turn it. At last it grated into place and she raced along the corridor, away from the advancing footsteps.

She had just rounded the corner when Edward and his companion reached the top of the stairs at the other end. Clamping her hand over her mouth to silence her panting, she waited, crouching against the wall.

'And you are sure you were not followed?'

Edward's voice. Whoever he was addressing must have answered with a nod.

'Good. I would not want the prince to know that I am stealing his whore.'

He gave a bark of laughter and there was an answering giggle from his companion, followed by a rustle of skirts and a small moan. Frances's lips curled in distaste. Clearly her brother shared more with his patron than the desire to destroy herself.

She heard the key turn in the lock. Curiosity got the better of her and she poked her head around the corner. Her brother's back was to her, and she could see only the pink silk of the lady's skirts, which he had lifted up to her thighs. Her head was lowered against his chest as her fingers worked to unlace his breeches.

'I must have you now,' Edward groaned, pushing open the door to the apartment.

Just before he pulled the woman in after him, Frances caught a glimpse of her face, flushed with desire. She leaped backwards and waited until she heard the door close behind them.

Lady Blanche.

Frances watched as her son lifted the racquet, gripping it with both hands as he swiped it this way and that, following Charles's lead. Now and then, the prince leaned over him, drawing his shoulders back or repositioning his fingers on the handle. He would soon reach his twelfth birthday, Frances calculated, as she watched his slender frame. Though he still walked with a slight stagger, he seemed to have grown into his body in recent months and his face, if not quite handsome, was certainly pleasing. With his piercing eyes and brown hair, he resembled his father much more closely than his elder brother did. Perhaps that was why he was the king's favourite.

'Play on!' he called now, striding over to take his position on the opposite side of the court.

George did not turn to look at her, but she could see that he was apprehensive from the way he held himself, like an arrow pulled taut against the bow. As soon as the prince made his serve, he scampered after the ball, swiping at it vainly as it sped past him. He ran to retrieve it, face flushed more with embarrassment than exertion, Frances judged.

They played on, Charles winning virtually every shot and George becoming increasingly flustered as he tried to prove a more worthy opponent. Frances smiled. She relished these rare occasions when she could watch her son practising tennis, archery or one of the other sports beloved of his royal master. It pained her that she was not able to spend more time with him, particularly as he had become withdrawn again lately, even refusing the stories that he had always loved to hear at bedtime. Trying to coax the reason out of him had earned her nothing but more sulking. She had resolved to be patient and wait for him to unburden himself when the moment was right.

As the game wore on, she tried to focus on it with the same rapt attention that she usually felt. But her mind was still reeling from the events of the previous day — the coquettish smile on Blanche's lips as she followed Edward into the apartment. She had thought over the occasions when her brother had visited the princess with his patron, trying to remember if there had been any frisson between Edward and Blanche. But Blanche had only ever had eyes for the prince. Frances wondered that she could have blushed so prettily whenever he spoke to her, when all the while she was bedding his protégé.

The knowledge of their affair deepened her unease about Edward. Now that he had an ally in the princess's household — one so hostile to herself — he could wreak even more damage. Had he already drawn Blanche into his schemes? The young woman would prove all too willing an accomplice if she heard of his plan to have her rival condemned for witchcraft.

'Really, Charles! You should choose an opponent who at least stands a chance of hitting it back.'

Frances turned sharply and saw the prince walking down the steps of the viewing gallery, closely followed by her brother. She froze as Edward's eyes fixed upon her. As she rose to curtsy, she formed her features into an expression of what she hoped was polite indifference. Henry swept past her as if she were invisible. Leaping over the barrier with graceful ease, he sauntered over to his younger brother, who was eyeing him

542

resentfully.

'Master Tyringham, may I?' Henry said, with exaggerated decorum.

Frances watched as her son handed over his racquet with a stiff bow, then scurried from the court.

'Come, brother, as you were,' Henry called to Charles, who was standing mute with rage.

He stared at his elder brother a moment longer, then slowly walked to the back of the court, his eyes fixed upon the ground.

'This should be diverting,' Edward muttered, as he sat down next to Frances.

She remained silent, her eyes fixed straight ahead. Henry was bouncing the ball on his racquet while his brother waited for him to serve. At length, he unleashed a blistering shot, aiming it straight at Charles, who yelped and sprang out of the way. Henry's laughter echoed around the court.

'Bravo, Your Grace!' Edward bellowed, then guffawed loudly.

Henry gave him a wolfish grin, then prepared to launch another volley.

'You look so *serious,* Frances.' Her brother jabbed her arm with his elbow. 'Do you not delight in watching the prince excel in this, as he does all other things? Or perhaps your loyalties are divided?'

She knew that he was baiting her but did not rise, craning her neck as if to get a better view. As they watched Henry win point after point, Frances willed the charade to be over. Surely even the prince would tire of taunting his younger brother before too long.

'Have you reflected on what I told you?' Edward's voice was lower now.

She faced him. 'You mean the indenture?' she asked nonchalantly.

'That and other matters besides,' he replied, his expression darkening. 'I hope you did not think I was in jest.'

Frances's mouth lifted into a slow smile. 'On the contrary, brother. I knew you were quite in earnest, which is what made it all the more surprising.'

Edward raised his eyebrows, waiting for her to continue. Frances paused for several moments, enjoying his evident impatience. 'You must know that it is tantamount to treason, compassing the king's death?' she said, inwardly triumphant as she saw her words had hit their mark. 'If you succeed in having me condemned for witchcraft, then it will not be long before you follow me to the scaffold. You have signed your own death warrant, Edward,' she whispered, repeating Raleigh's words.

She could see a tiny vessel pulsing at his temple. As she held his gaze, his features began to relax and the familiar smirk returned to his lips. 'But there is only your word to sustain such a conviction, is there not, Frances? You have no proof that the indenture exists — indeed, I recall you being quite careless with it when I showed it to you. Ah, I see you remember that, too,' he said. 'Well, you shall never have it in your hands again. I have made sure of that. So we are back to the same conundrum, I'm afraid, dear sister,' he continued, with a heavy sigh. 'Your word against mine. Or, if you like, the word of a notorious witch against that of a favoured subject.'

Frances turned back to the court. She would not let him goad her. She had seen the fear in his eyes when she had spoken of treason. He knew the risk he had taken. She must not rest until she had found that document.

'Stop, Henry, stop!'

Charles's shrill cry echoed across the court and tears streamed down his cheeks. This prompted a fresh burst of hilarity from the prince, who began prancing about the court, aping his brother's awkward gait as he swished his racquet from side to side.

'Well played, Your Grace, well played!'

Edward shouted, as Henry made an elaborate bow.

Unable to bear the ridicule, Charles ran from the court.

The sun was glinting off the gilded weather vanes of the palace as Frances shielded her eyes to gaze along the wide expanse that stretched out beyond the Holbein Gate. Thomas had sent word that he would be returning with the rest of the king's hunting party in time for that evening's entertainments. She knew that he usually rode ahead of his master and the wagons that carried the hounds with their kill.

Though she had more than ever to conceal from him, she ached to feel his arms encircle her, to breathe in his familiar scent. He had been away for a month, but so much had happened since he left that it seemed a lifetime.

Her ears pricked at the distant blare of a trumpet. Jumping down from the wall that ran alongside the gate, she strained her eyes towards the horizon again and her heart leaped as she saw a group of riders silhouetted against the sinking sun. It took all of her resolve to stop herself running towards them. As they drew closer, she recognised her husband.

'Frances!' Thomas called in surprise, with a smile that warmed her more than the dying rays of the sun.

He dismounted and handed the reins to one of the grooms waiting by the palace gates, then swept her into his arms.

'I have missed you, Thomas,' she said, as she kissed his lips.

'And I you, my love,' he replied. 'But I did not expect such a greeting as this.'

Frances grinned. 'Is it wrong for a wife to anticipate her husband's return so eagerly, when he has deserted her for so long?'

He returned her smile, then reached out and placed his hand on her belly. 'And how does our young knave fare?'

'He — or *she* — is as restless as those hounds,' she said, with mock exasperation. 'I am woken several times a night. It does not bode well.'

Thomas stroked his hand across the small swelling that was still invisible beneath the folds of her gown. At the sound of the king's carriage approaching, they turned and made their obeisance, then walked slowly in its wake, Frances's arm on her husband's.

'Edward has not troubled you further?' Thomas asked, breaking the silence into which they had fallen.

'All is well,' she said. 'I saw George playing tennis earlier. I fear he is no closer to mastering it. Perhaps you could give him another lesson.'

Thomas opened his mouth to reply — but his eyes alighted upon something at the far end of the courtyard. Following his gaze, Frances saw the tall figure of the Earl of Rutland standing by a carriage. She watched as he held out his hand to guide someone from it and her blood ran cold as she recognised Countess Cecily.

'What is she doing here?' she breathed, looking up at Thomas, whose expression was inscrutable.

'The king has invited all of the great nobles to attend the reception of Count Frederick,' he replied evenly. 'I admit I am surprised that the countess has come with her husband. I cannot remember ever seeing her at court.'

At that moment, Cecily turned towards them. Frances could see her saying something to her husband.

'Sir Thomas!' the earl cried, striding towards them. 'And your beautiful wife. How good it is to see you again, Lady Frances.'

He bowed, despite his superior rank. Frances saw his wife's nostrils flare briefly.

She stared icily at Frances, waiting for her curtsy.

'We are all most anxious to meet the count,' the earl said, breaking the awkward silence that followed. 'He is a fine young man, I wager. I have heard it said —'

'I am no less eager to meet your brother, Lady Frances,' Cecily interrupted. 'He has won great favour with Prince Henry, I hear. Your family must be immensely proud.'

Frances inclined her head and held the older woman's steady gaze. Edward had already threatened to use her treatment of Thomas at Belvoir to strengthen his accusation of witchcraft. Now he had someone who was ill-intentioned enough to act as his witness.

'Well, you must excuse us, my lord, Countess,' Thomas said, with a quick bow. 'I am newly returned from the hunt and eager to see our son before the evening's entertainments.'

He took Frances's hand firmly in his and they walked briskly away. Frances could feel Cecily's eyes upon her as they passed under the archway and out of sight.

CHAPTER 48
17 OCTOBER

'Come, Lizzie! Do not stand there looking like a startled fawn.'

James leaned forward on his throne and held out his arms. Elizabeth darted an anxious look at Frances before stepping slowly forward, then stood stiffly as her father drew her into a rough embrace. His face was already flushed with wine. Beside him, Anne sat quietly, her mouth fixed in a demure smile. Frances was glad she had made the rare journey from Greenwich for the occasion. She had heard it whispered that the queen thought little more of the latest suitor than she had of the Swedish prince.

'But ye're so pale,' the king cried, pinching his daughter's cheeks so that a small, angry blush appeared briefly in each. 'I hope you're not coming to resemble that milksop brother of yours.'

Frances stole a glance at Prince Henry,

who was standing behind his father, jaw clenched. His skin was even whiter than usual, she thought, and there were dark shadows under his eyes. It was hardly surprising. She had heard it said that he spent every night doused in wine.

'I am a little tired, Father, that is all,' the princess replied.

James snorted. 'Ye'll be more tired still once ye're wed. The count will not let such a pretty wife sleep long.'

Frances noticed Elizabeth cringe away from her father's grasp and thought for a moment that she might run from the hall.

'Our daughter is right to be cautious, husband,' Anne cut in smoothly. 'Her previous suitors have proved lacking in one respect or another. We must reserve our judgement until we have met Count Frederick and can be sure of his character.'

'Ha!' James exclaimed scornfully. 'What does character have to do with it, when royal marriages are made? Even if I had known more of yours before we were wed, I would have had no choice but to go through with it. Danish gold was worth more to Scotland than a pleasing wife.'

Frances could hardly bear to look at Anne, but she withstood her husband's insult with typical sanguinity.

'Count Frederick will bring us a powerful alliance,' Prince Henry remarked haughtily. 'The Palatinate is one of the richest territories in Christendom and a strong advocate of the true faith. The papists have been utterly vanquished there.'

The king swung around to glare at his elder son. 'Cease your prattling!' he spat. 'This has nothing to do with you. The Swedish match was your idea and look how that turned out. I will have the governing of this one. Ye' are not king yet — God willing you never will be,' he muttered under his breath.

Frances watched Henry's pale cheeks redden. He was staring at the back of his father's head, mute with rage. Then her gaze rested upon Elizabeth, who looked utterly wretched.

'Sweet Liz, do not take on so.' The king tried to soothe her. 'It is a daughter's duty to lessen her father's disappointment in her sex by bringing him a profitable marriage.'

The princess looked down at her hands. Frances could not tell whether it was to conceal the anger that she herself felt, or her apprehension at meeting this new suitor. She was glad that their first meeting would be rather more private than the lavish reception that had been staged for Prince Gustavus. Only a few favoured courtiers and attendants were gathered in the king's presence chamber.

Everyone turned at the sound of advancing footsteps. A moment later, a liveried servant appeared. 'Count Frederick has arrived, Your Majesty,' the young man announced.

James gave a grunt and took a long gulp of wine, then swiped the remnants from his lips. 'Then ye'd best show him in,' he said brusquely.

The princess's eyes flew towards the door and she stood awkwardly, her fingers worrying at the lace on her sleeve.

'Come and stand by me, Elizabeth,' Anne said gently.

Her daughter obeyed, moving so close to her mother that her skirts brushed against the queen's arm. Anne clasped her hand. She did not release her grip as a fanfare of trumpets rang out across the corridor beyond, closely followed by the clipping of heels on the polished oak floorboards.

All the company below the dais made obeisance, heads bowed, as the count walked slowly into the room. Frances caught the scent of orange blossom and saw the flash of gold and green silk as he stepped lightly past.

'Count Frederick, ye're welcome.' James's voice, slightly slurred, echoed around the chamber.

'Thank you, Your Majesty.'

For a moment, Frances thought the princess had spoken. The voice was as delicate as the perfume she had inhaled as he entered the room. There was a rustle of skirts as the company rose from their obeisance. All eyes were trained upon the small figure kneeling at the king's feet. Frances stared. From this angle, the count looked barely older than George. His frame was as slender as a colt's and his skin appeared all the whiter against the dark brown hair that curled at his collar.

Frances turned to watch the princess, who was staring down at her suitor with near-amusement. As her father gestured for him to stand, he stepped lightly over to kiss Elizabeth's hand. She was a good deal taller than him, Frances noticed, even though the heels of his satin shoes were higher than was the fashion.

'Your Highness.' Prince Henry saluted him with an elaborate bow.

As Frederick turned to make his own obeisance, Frances studied his face. His deep brown eyes were so large that they gave him a look of surprise. He had dark, bushy eyebrows, a long nose and soft pink lips. His starched lace collar was so high that it touched his chin, just as it did in the miniature her mistress had been sent, and around his neck he wore a medal suspended from a green silk ribbon. He reminded Frances of the portraits she had seen of the old queen's younger brother Edward, the boy king, whose slender limbs had been disguised by thickly padded doublets to emulate his father's imposing silhouette.

At that moment, Frederick gestured to one of his attendants, who stepped forward carrying a box covered with red velvet. He handed it to his master, who addressed the princess. 'I would like to give you this as a token of my esteem,' he trilled, in perfect English, with only a hint of a Germanic accent.

Elizabeth accepted the box with a polite smile. But as she made to draw back the cover, a yelp came from within and she almost dropped it. Gingerly, she lifted a corner of the fabric and peered underneath, then exclaimed with delight. 'A puppy!'

The velvet dropped to the floor as she held the box close to her face and gazed at the tiny quivering creature, her eyes alight with joy. Frederick smiled at her excitement. Frances could not help but feel glad. This latest suitor might not be any more to her mistress's taste than the last, but at least he had already shown greater judgement.

Elizabeth set the box on the floor and crouched to open it. Reaching in, she scooped up the puppy and cradled it in her arms, stroking its head until it calmed. It really was the most exquisite creature — more like a baby badger than a dog, Frances thought, with black patches over its eyes and creamy white fur covering the rest of its body. Elizabeth's smile faltered when she looked at the prince, whose smug satisfaction was evident. He should not be so quick to triumph, Frances mused. It would take more than a well-judged gift to convince his sister — and their father — that the young count was an ideal suitor.

The king stood, signalling that the meeting was at a close. Count Frederick bowed as he stepped down from the dais, then waited until the rest of the royal party had departed before following in their wake.

Although the entertainments staged for Count Frederick had continued long into the night, Frances was awake early the next day. Thomas had already left, the king having decided to take his prospective son-in-law on a hunting expedition. She could not imagine the delicate young man relishing the prospect of joining that bloody spectacle, but the marriage negotiations were at too early a stage to risk causing offence.

Crossing to the ewer, Frances splashed water on her face, hoping to cleanse away the creeping unease she had felt since last night's reception. Although she had successfully avoided Countess Cecily, who had been seated with her husband at the opposite side of the hall, she had been aghast to see her in conference with Edward during a pause between the two masques. Their conversation had lasted for several minutes, and she had tried to judge from Cecily's expression whether its subject was more serious than the usual pleasantries of a first introduction. That they had not turned in her direction gave her cause to hope that it was not. But she did not doubt that her brother would soon devise another meeting with his new acquaintance.

'Are you really a witch?'

Frances swung around. Her son was watching her from his bed, the covers pulled up to his chin. She tried to soften her gaze as she saw his eyes widen in fear. Feeling as if the breath was being squeezed from her body, she said, 'Who would tell you such a thing, George?'

'Are you?'

Frances took a step towards him but was dismayed to see him cringe.

'Darling, you must have been dreaming,' she said as she went to him, disguising her anguish at the terror in his eyes. She reached out to stroke his hair, but he jerked away from her. 'George,' she said, more firmly this time. 'You must tell me who has been filling your head with such wickedness.'

'They put you in the Tower but you cast a spell on the king so that he would set you free.'

Frances felt the blood drain from her face as she looked down at her son. This explained his sullenness of late, the way she would catch him staring at her with something between curiosity and revulsion. She experienced a wave of guilt as she thought of how she had assumed he had been attending his lessons as usual. She had been too preoccupied with her own worries to enquire more closely into his activities in Prince Charles's household. Edward must have spent a few moments alone with his nephew.

'George, you must listen to me,' she said, as gently as she could. 'I am not a witch. I was wrongfully accused, many years ago.

When he realised that, the king ordered my release.'

Her son gazed up at her doubtfully.

'I speak the truth, George,' she continued. 'Whoever told you this did so out of mischief and malice. I am the same mother whom you loved and who has loved you since the day you drew breath.'

Her voice faltered as her throat grew tighter and she inhaled deeply to stop the tears.

'Besides, witches exist only in fables,' she continued, her tone lighter.

'That is not true!' George exclaimed, with such force that she was taken aback. 'The prince says that witches are everywhere and that we must hunt them down and burn them before they cast their evil spells.'

Frances had to remind herself to breathe. 'The *prince*? He has spoken to you of this — of *me*?'

Her son clamped his mouth shut again and stared at her, defiant.

'Tell me, George!' she cried, grasping his shoulders.

She felt him stiffen and saw his lips quiver. 'Or I will go and ask the prince myself.'

'No!' the boy cried, ashen-faced. 'You must not. He told me it was a secret, that I must not tell —' He covered his face with his hands and his shoulders heaved as he began to sob. A mixture of rage and pity made her fingers tremble as she stroked her son's arms, then pulled away his hands so that she could wipe his tears. Slowly, she lay down next to him, drawing his small frame to her so that his back was cradled against her stomach. After a while, his breathing grew calmer, the sobs less frequent. She had just begun to wonder if he had fallen asleep when he whispered, 'I am sorry, Mama.'

'Hush now, my love.' She kissed the back of his neck. 'All is well, all is well.'

They lay like that for a long time, until Frances heard his breath become shallower, his chest rising and falling in slow, rhythmic movements. She longed for the same sweet oblivion of sleep, but her whole body seemed to pulse with fury as she thought of how the prince had tried to poison her son's mind against her.

What if he were to choke upon his own poison?

Raleigh's words came to her suddenly. Though she tried to push them away, it was as if he was there now, murmuring them into her ear over and over again. She allowed her mind to wander. Root of mandrake would stop his breath, choking him within but leaving no trace outside his body.

A few drops would suffice. She imagined herself leaning over his sleeping form, the phial poised over his lips.

No.

She would not stoop to such wickedness. If she did, God would be her judge: she would live out her days sure in the knowledge that when her own breath stopped she would descend to the eternal fires of Hell. She must find another way to avenge herself.

Again, she thought of the indenture. Had she come close to finding it the other day? If she had had more time, had been more thorough . . . But there were many other places where Edward might have hidden the document. It was like searching the ocean for a single pearl. She must not give up, though. It was the only way to stop him carrying out his threat. She did not allow herself to dwell upon the possibility that, even if she succeeded, the prince might carry out her brother's work for him.

'There, my sweeting,' the princess said, as she gave the dog another comfit. Its tongue lapped at her outstretched palm long after it had swallowed the treat.

'You should not indulge him so,' Frances chided, with a smile, 'or he will grow too stout for those tiny legs.'

Elizabeth nuzzled the pup's nose, causing its little tail to wag furiously. 'Do not listen to her, Falstaff,' she said, casting a rueful smile at her attendant. She giggled delightedly as the dog licked her face, then set it on her lap. Within a few minutes, it was dozing contentedly. Elizabeth gave a heavy sigh.

'How do you like the count, Your Grace?' Frances asked lightly.

Blanche shot her a look of reproof. 'I wonder that you have forgotten Prince Henry's orders so soon, Lady Frances,' she remarked, with scorn.

'Forgive me, Your Grace,' Frances said,

ignoring Blanche. 'I did not mean to pry.'

She was gratified to see her mistress give the other woman a withering look.

'Frederick is a dear boy. So kind and attentive. But . . .' her smile wavered '. . . I cannot think he is only a week younger than me. It seems a year at least — more, even.'

'He will gain in height yet, ma'am,' Blanche opined. 'By the time you are married he will far exceed you in that respect.'

'*If* we are married, Blanche,' Elizabeth retorted petulantly. 'Nothing is decided yet.'

Frances smothered a smile. She must be careful to show no interest in the matter. God knew she had troubles enough to contend with. Out of the corner of her eye, she could see her rival watching her, but she directed her own gaze towards the window.

A knock on the door interrupted her thoughts. The little dog jumped up at once and began yapping frantically.

'Hush, little one,' Elizabeth said. 'It is only a visitor and you must get used to those.'

A moment later, the door was opened by one of the yeomen.

'Her Grace the Countess of Rutland, Your Highness,' he announced.

Frances rose to curtsy as Cecily walked in, straight-backed, her head held high.

'What a pleasure it is to meet you again, Lady Cecily,' the princess said, when they were all seated. 'I hope you enjoyed the entertainments the other evening.'

'Very much, Your Grace.' The countess simpered. 'My husband has often told me of the splendours of your father's court, and I can see now that he was in earnest.'

Falstaff gave a loud yawn as he traced a circle on his mistress's lap. Cecily's nose wrinkled in distaste.

'Pets are such a blessing, are they not, Lady Cecily?' the princess remarked, gazing down at the dog, who obliged her by licking her finger.

'Indeed,' the older woman replied curtly.

They lapsed into silence. Elizabeth seemed oblivious to the absence of conversation as she petted the little creature.

'I was very glad to meet your brother at last, Lady Frances,' the countess said at length.

Frances saw interest in Blanche's eyes. She smiled politely.

'He was every bit as charming as I had been led to believe,' Cecily continued, 'and clearly a doting brother. He wanted to know all about your stay at Belvoir. He must have found your prolonged absence hard to bear.'

'No harder than I did,' Frances replied,

her smile sweet as marchpane as she swallowed bile. She glanced at the princess, hoping she might change the conversation, but the girl was still too distracted by her dog.

'Baron Longford is indeed a fine young man,' Blanche observed smoothly. 'It is no wonder that the prince shows him such favour.'

The countess beamed at her. 'I said so to the earl, after our meeting,' she agreed. 'We have been invited to dine with them both tomorrow evening.'

At that moment, Falstaff leaped from his mistress's lap and scurried to the door, pawing at it frantically. The princess rose at once to follow him.

'Forgive me, Lady Rutland,' she said, 'but my dog needs to run about in the gardens for a while. Perhaps we might meet again another time.'

'Of course,' Cecily said tightly.

Frances allowed herself to enjoy a brief moment of glee that the countess had been superseded by a puppy. She knew it was a small victory, but it helped relieve some of the tension she felt.

She bobbed the briefest of curtsies as Cecily swept past her. Elizabeth stooped to gather the writhing animal into her arms, then hastened into the corridor.

'I will accompany you, Your Grace,' Blanche said quickly, glaring at Frances, then slammed the door behind her.

Frances was glad to be on her own at last. She was exhausted from the strain under which she had laboured these past few days. Thoughts of her conversation with George had churned in her mind, stoking her fury against the prince. She had said nothing of it to Thomas, afraid lest he chastise her son and destroy the fragile trust that the boy had come to place in her once more. But it had been a heavy burden to carry alone.

To stave off the feeling that she was powerless to do anything other than wait for Edward and the prince to destroy her, she had tried to focus upon the task of finding the indenture, considering all of the places where her brother might have lodged it, increasingly convinced that he had it in safe-keeping at St James's. That was where he spent most of his time, after all, and the prince would be only too happy to supply a discreet place for it. It might even be with one of his officials — someone he could trust not to read its contents.

Frances sank back into her chair and closed her eyes, pressing her fingers to her temples. She imagined herself in the woods at Longford, gazing up at the branches that swayed overhead as she breathed in the sharp tang of wild garlic and pine. Her breathing steadied, bringing a delicious calm, which lulled her to sleep.

She awoke with a start and rubbed her neck as she glanced quickly around the room. The princess and Blanche must still be in the gardens. She had no idea how long she had slept, but she must make haste and prepare her mistress's attire for the evening.

She stood abruptly, causing the blood to roar in her ears and her vision to cloud. As she moved towards the dressing room, her eye was arrested by one of the paintings on the wall opposite. It showed a hunting scene, which she had always thought at odds with her mistress's taste. Noticing that it was slightly askew, she reached to straighten it, but her sleeve snagged on the frame and it crashed to the floor. Cursing, she stooped to pick it up, and froze. Tucked into the back of the frame was a neatly folded document. Heart thrumming, she prised it free and turned it over. She gasped as she recognised the prince's seal. She cast an anxious glance towards the door. Her mistress would return at any moment, Blanche with her. With trembling fingers, she unfolded the document.

Indenture, made this third day of August . . .

Frances stared, as if fearing the words would disappear before her eyes. Quickly, she scanned the rest of the script, desperate to be sure.

Longford.

Her heart soared. She had found it. The signatures at the foot of the page confirmed that it was the same indenture that Edward had flourished before her at Hampton Court, the memory of which had plagued her ever since. *So he had given it to Blanche for safe-keeping.* How like him to make her hide it under his sister's nose. She thought of her mother's old painting, which she had been so convinced was where he had concealed the indenture. That had always hung in the room belonging to the most important person in the house. The same was true of this hunting scene, which was displayed in the heart of the princess's chamber. It was so simple, now she thought about it. Yet her brother would have outwitted her, just as he had when they were children, if it had not been for that blessed piece of lace, which now hung ragged from her sleeve.

Just then, Frances heard a distant yelp followed by footsteps along the corridor outside. Quickly, she folded the document and stuffed it inside the pocket of her gown. Her hands still trembling, she lifted the picture and positioned it over the nail in the panelling. The footsteps grew louder and she heard the princess call to her dog. Frantically, her fingers fumbled for the thin cord that was strung across the back of the painting. At last, she felt it snag over the nail. Releasing the frame, she shifted it over the panelling, careful to leave it slightly askew as before.

As the latch was lifted, Frances bolted to the dresser and pulled open the top drawer, riffling idly through its contents as if trying to find a particular accessory.

'Are you still here, Lady Frances?'

She turned to see Blanche watching her, eyes narrowed.

'You have had ample time to prepare our mistress's apparel. I hope you have not been sleeping. Your cheeks are very flushed.'

'Oh, leave her be, Blanche!' Elizabeth snapped, before Frances could answer. 'It is hours yet before the masque begins.'

Frances turned back to the chest, hiding her smile as she forced herself to concentrate on the gorgeous array of satin gloves and ribbons. 'The peacock blue this evening, I think, ma'am,' she said, still looking down into the drawer.

'I agree,' the princess called from inside her bedchamber.

Frances thought for a moment, then went to join her mistress. She could feel Blanche's eyes on her back but did not turn for fear of exciting her suspicion.

'Your Grace,' she said, as she stood at the threshold.

Elizabeth turned to her, brow creased with concern. 'What is it, Fran?' She pulled her into the room. 'Are you sure you are well? I have been so worried after what happened the other week . . .'

'I am quite well, I promise,' Frances said, with a smile.

The princess studied her face. 'You look better. The colour has returned to your cheeks at last.'

Frances's eyes sparkled with affection for her mistress. 'Will you forgive me if I miss this evening's entertainments?' she ventured.

The princess's smile faded. 'You *are* ill. Oh, Frances, I cannot bear to lose you again,' she cried, her eyes filling with tears.

Frances felt such a rush of love for her that, for a moment, she could not speak. She pressed her lips to Elizabeth's hands. 'I will never leave you again — not of my own free will,' she added quietly. 'And I assure you that I am in perfect health. But Blanche was right. I was sleeping earlier and I would rest some more this evening, if you will permit it.'

'Of course,' Elizabeth said, brushing away her tears. 'But what has made you so tired?'

Frances made a decision. 'It is the best of reasons.' She gestured at her stomach.

The princess gave a small gasp, then clapped a hand over her mouth. 'You are . . .'

Frances nodded.

'Oh, Fran! This is wonderful news. Thomas must be delighted. And I shall have a new playmate.' She hugged her tightly.

'Thank you, ma'am,' Frances murmured, when they parted. 'But I pray you, let it be our secret for now. Thomas knows, of course, but it is early yet and I would not have others thinking I am too fragile to fulfil my duties.'

She imagined Blanche with her ear pressed to the other side of the door. The princess nodded vigorously and pressed her fingers to her lips. Then she said, in a voice loud enough for Blanche to hear, 'Now go, Frances, and get some rest. It will look ill if my attendant sleeps her way through this evening's masque. But you must be here all the earlier tomorrow.'

Frances grinned and mouthed her thanks, then walked towards the door, trying hard

571

to appear downcast. Blanche was sitting close by, her needle suspended over a torn sash in her lap. Her eyes narrowed as Frances passed. It took a supreme effort of will not to glance at the painting as she left the room.

Chapter 50
27 October

Frances stole along the deserted streets. She had kept close to the river for most of the way, but as soon as she had seen the squat tower of Temple Church to her left, she had turned up the narrow lane that led towards it. Continuing north, she had soon reached the Rolls Chapel on Chancery Lane, its elaborate carved stonework casting shadows beneath her feet. *Almost there.*

Her breath misted in the chill air, but the blood was pumping so fast around her body that she felt as warm as if she had been sitting with Thomas by the fire. It pained her to think of how his eyes had clouded when she told him that she craved some fresh evening air. He had offered to fetch Mistress Knvyett to watch over George so that he might accompany her, but she had assured him that she would not be gone for long — that he must indulge the sudden whims of his pregnant wife. The lie was still on her lips as she kissed him goodbye. More and more, she hated the deceit. It lay like a cold stone between them. She prayed that he did not feel it too.

At last, Frances saw the bell tower of Gray's Inn silhouetted against the night sky. Her footsteps came to an abrupt halt, as if a great chasm had suddenly opened in the street ahead. She knew the risks involved, that doing what she had resolved upon might result in her brother's death. She reached into her pocket and ran her fingers along the smooth paper. *It is his death or yours.* The thought had run through her mind since she had discovered the document. Pushing it away now, she forged ahead towards the gatehouse, its marble archway ghostly white against the gloom of the buildings beyond.

She gave her name to the elderly porter, who showed no inclination to leave the warmth of the fire that she could see blazing within his small turret and simply gestured towards the chamber she sought. It lay at the north-eastern end of the first quadrant, and as Frances walked briskly towards it she uttered a silent prayer that the gentleman she had come to see would keep late hours. Glancing up at the windows, she saw that most were in darkness.

But as she drew closer, she could just make out a faint glimmer between the cracks of some shutters at a ground-floor window, close to where the porter had directed her. Her heart gave a lurch and she quickened her step as she made her way towards it.

She knocked lightly and listened, but could hear nothing. Perhaps he hadn't heard. She was about to knock again when the door opened. The young man regarded her closely for a few moments.

'Master Beecham?'

'Forgive me,' he replied, 'I am not used to receiving visitors at this hour, Mistress . . . ?'

'Lady Frances Tyringham,' she replied. 'But you may perhaps know me as Frances Gorges.'

She saw his eyes widen before he gave a tight bow and ushered her inside.

The chamber was smaller than she had imagined, and every wall was lined with books. On the large desk at which he had been working were numerous papers, some stacked precariously at the edge but all neatly ordered. Tom had always said that one could judge the skill of a lawyer by the volume of papers in his chambers.

His former colleague busied himself with clearing a space for her to sit. Jacob was younger than she had expected, though he had entered Gray's Inn at the same time as Tom. He was small in stature and his hair was even lighter than the princess's, which added to his youthful appearance. 'Please.' He gestured to the now empty chair on the opposite side of his desk.

He looked at her for a moment and seemed to hesitate, his clear blue eyes suddenly grave. 'Tom said that you might come here, though I expected you long before this. I still miss him, Lady Frances. He was a good friend and an excellent lawyer — a good deal more so than I, I fear.'

'Tom always spoke very highly of you,' she said. 'I know he trusted you, which gives me hope that I may do so too.'

'Of course,' Jacob replied earnestly. 'I would be glad to help in any way I can. Is it the deed? I notice that you have not yet drawn any interest from the land, though you might have done these six years past.'

Frances felt her throat constrict at the memory of what Tom had done for her. The land he had bequeathed her — in the queen's name, so that their association would not be discovered — had offered her the prospect of escaping court if his treachery was discovered. It had stood as a testament of the strength of his love for her. In time, she would transfer the land to their son.

Jacob gave a small cough, prompting a response.

'I am sorry, Master Beecham,' Frances said quickly. 'You are right — I must make arrangements for the deed. But that is not the matter I wish to discuss with you now.'

She took a breath, then drew the indenture out of her pocket and placed it on the table between them. Jacob's eyes lowered to it and she saw them linger upon the Prince of Wales's seal, but he remained silent and waited for her to continue.

'Tom may have told you that my family's estate is Longford Castle in Wiltshire.'

Jacob nodded. 'He said you were very fond of it.'

'It means a great deal to me, yes. When my father died two years ago, he bequeathed it not to my eldest brother, Edward, but to my son George. He doted on him,' she added, by way of explanation.

'And your brother accepted this?' Though his tone was light, his eyes were sharp, scrutinising.

'He had no choice — my father had made sure of the terms.' She hesitated. 'But he has determined to wrest back, by other means, what he sees as his rightful inheri-

577

tance. Please.' She gestured at the document.

Jacob opened it with the same reverence she had seen Tom employ when working on his deeds and conveyances. She watched his face carefully as he read, but his expression remained inscrutable. The only sound was the crackling of the fire in the grate and the soft rustle of paper as he made his way down the script. When he had finished, he folded the paper and kept his hands lightly resting upon it as he spoke. 'Your brother is determined indeed,' he observed quietly.

Frances nodded, her jaw clenched. She had no wish to give vent to the bitterness and fury that had lingered inside her since Edward had told her of the document. Lawyers responded only to facts.

'But in order for this indenture to come into force, you or your son would need to be convicted of some felony — or worse.' His eyes never left hers. 'Your son must still be a minor, so the onus rests upon you, Lady Frances.'

She tried to swallow but her mouth had dried.

'What is the likelihood that you will face such a conviction?' he persisted.

Frances let out a quiet breath before replying. 'My brother harbours no evidence

— to my knowledge — that I have been involved in any treachery,' she said, choosing her words carefully. 'But he means to have me convicted of witchcraft.'

Still he did not flinch, merely leaned forward and pressed his fingers together.

'That is a crime for which scant evidence is required, as I am sure you are aware,' he said slowly. 'In many cases, an accusation alone is enough to bring the alleged perpetrator before the assizes.'

'Yes,' Frances replied shortly. 'I know that, and I also know that my brother already has what passes for evidence against me. He also enjoys great favour with the prince — as you can see.' She waved her hand towards the indenture.

'You are fortunate indeed to have it in your possession, Lady Frances,' Jacob said. 'I will not ask how you came by it. Presumably your brother does not yet know.'

She shook her head. 'Neither will he, pray God, until I tell him.'

The young man fell silent again for several minutes. Then: 'A woman less shrewd would have burned this, as soon as she had it in her keeping. But you know what it purports, besides your own fate, and that of Longford?'

Frances's eyes blazed. She slowly inclined

her head. 'That is why I am here, Master Beecham. I would like you to make a copy of the indenture for me and retain the original here, in your safe-keeping, until such time as I instruct you to destroy it. You must say nothing of either to another living soul.' She saw his throat pulse.

'Your brother has committed treason by putting his signature to this indenture, and if I am found to have concealed it then I, too, would suffer the consequences. I would be condemned for misprision, Lady Frances — as will you, if the copy is found in your possession.'

She did not allow her gaze to waver. 'I know what I ask of you, Master Beecham,' she said steadily. 'And I do not ask it lightly, but for the love you bore Tom. By protecting Longford for my son, you will be honouring his memory.'

Though she had not spoken the words, she could see the light of understanding in Jacob's eyes as they searched hers. She was only vaguely aware of holding her breath as she waited.

At length, he gave the slightest of nods, then reached into the drawer of his desk and drew out a blank sheet of paper.

Thomas was already asleep by the time she

crept back into their apartment. She undressed quietly, taking care to fold her gown around the pocket. The paper gave a soft crackle as she placed the garment in the chest, as if reassuring her of its presence. Having stripped down to her shift, she padded over to George's bed and kissed his forehead. He did not stir, and she could hear his breath, steady and shallow. She climbed into her own bed.

'Where have you been?'

She jumped at her husband's voice. Either she had woken him or he had feigned sleep when she had peered into their chamber. She moved over to nuzzle against him but felt him stiffen.

'Forgive me, my love. It was such a beautiful, clear evening and I wandered further than I intended,' she whispered, drawing away from him so that he would not register the hammering of her heart.

'Where did you go?'

'Just along the river,' she replied calmly.

She heard him sigh softly.

'When will you trust me with the truth, Frances?'

His question hung in the air. Frances opened her mouth to make a denial, but could not speak it. She hated the deceit more with each day that passed, but she could not confide even little of the schemes in which she was embroiled. It would only spark more questions, more lies. She could no more bear to destroy their love than she could to entangle her husband in this web of treachery.

'I do trust you, Thomas,' she whispered at last.

That, at least, was true.

CHAPTER 51
28 OCTOBER

Frances waited for the groom to return. The sound of hammering carried to her from the range of buildings above her, to the right. She had heard it reported that Prince Henry had ordered a lavish new suite of apartments. Only a man of his pretensions could look at the cavernous palace of St James's and judge it too small, she thought, her lip curling.

'Sister!'

At Edward's voice she spun round. She had not expected him to come and greet her in person. Perhaps he did not wish to be seen with her in the palace, given what he planned.

Her smile was sickly sweet as she held out her hand for his kiss. 'Is there somewhere we may talk?' she asked lightly.

Edward glanced over his shoulder at the cluster of liveried servants who were standing idly by the entrance to the state apartments. One looked in their direction. 'Shall we walk in the park, dear sister?' he replied smoothly, maintaining the pretence that her arrival was a pleasant interruption.

Frances dipped her head and placed her hand on his arm as they went towards the gatehouse. She remained silent during the short walk across the promenade and through the large gilded gates at the southern end of the park. Her hand still rested on Edward's arm and she was gratified to feel him grow tense but, of course, he was too stubborn to ask the reason for her visit.

Only when they had reached the edge of the lake that lay at the centre of the park did she turn to address him. 'Tell me, Edward, how is Lady Blanche?'

He quickly turned his surprise into scorn. 'Why, sister, you are surely better placed than I to know.'

Frances gazed out over the calm waters and smiled. 'I see her often, certainly, but the hours that you spend with her are more . . . *intimate.*'

She let the word hang briefly, then continued. 'I should congratulate you, brother, on finding a lady whom you can trust so implicitly. Or perhaps she did not know what she agreed to conceal for you.'

She turned in time to see fleeting panic in

his eyes.

'You have always spoken in riddles, Frances. Riddles — and spells, of course.'

He ran his tongue over his lips and pretended to watch a swan as it glided silently towards the edge of the water.

'Then let me make it clear, Edward,' she said sharply.

She reached into her pocket and drew out the indenture. She saw her brother's jaw drop as he stared down at it. He made as if to grab it, but she was too quick for him. 'It is a copy, of course,' she said, with a smile. 'You accused me of being careless with the original once. I will not be so again — not when lives depend upon it.'

A thin sheen of sweat glistened on his brow, despite the autumn chill. 'What are you waiting for, sister?' he snarled. 'If you mean to have me beheaded as a traitor then why did you not take it straight to the king's officials?'

Frances tutted. 'Not beheaded, Edward,' she said, as if she spoke to a careless pupil. 'You surely know the punishment for treason. After all, you would have me face the same. Or perhaps you hoped to afford me the kinder death and see me hanged as a witch.'

He glared at her, mute with rage — and,

she sensed, fear.

'What a pity you will be denied both pleasures now.' She sighed.

'What would you have me do, Frances?' he hissed, teeth gritted.

'You will abandon your scheme to have me condemned for witchcraft,' she said slowly. 'Whatever evidence you believe you have gathered, you will destroy it. If you involved any accomplices, you must tell them you were mistaken, that your suspicions were sparked by malice, not truth. And you must persuade them to take no action. Your favour with the prince will be enough to ensure their compliance.'

She thought of Countess Cecily. How disappointed she would be to have her pleasure denied. 'Neither will you attempt to have me accused of treason,' she continued. 'You can have no proof of it, beyond your desire for it to be true. Yet the proof I have of your own treachery is written here.' She waved the document in front of his face. 'You must know that it is treason even to think of the king's death, let alone plan for it. Many men have been condemned for far less.'

Edward's breath was coming rapidly now. 'How do I know that you will honour your part, if I do as you ask?' he demanded, as he edged closer to her.

Frances's smile was like a splinter of ice. The knowledge of the power she now held over him was exhilarating. 'You will have to trust me, Edward,' she said, her eyes never leaving his. 'But you must act quickly. I know that the Countess of Rutland is due to dine with you and the prince this evening, presumably so that you can secure her as a witness.'

She saw the truth of it in his face.

'By the time she and her husband arrive, you must have convinced your royal master that your suspicions about me were groundless, that he will show himself a fool if he pursues them. He is vain enough to want to avoid that — as are you.'

Her brother turned away, as if unable to bear the sight of her any longer. Frances watched him carefully. *What if he failed?* The thought had plagued her since her meeting with Jacob Beecham. Would she still carry out her threat to have him exposed as a traitor? It would be her only chance of saving her life — and Longford. But she was repelled by the idea.

'Very well,' Edward muttered, almost to himself, and made as if to leave.

'That is not all, brother.'

He turned back to her, his face twisted in dismay.

'Although you must trust me in this, you can hardly expect me to take you at your word. I will want to see proof that you have done everything I asked, before I have the indenture destroyed.'

Edward threw back his head and gave a scornful bark of laughter. 'What proof can I give, for God's sake?'

Frances's mouth lifted into a slow smile. She reached into her pocket once more and drew out another document. Edward's eyes darted to it. 'This is another indenture, Edward,' she explained, as if to a child. 'It stipulates that Prince Henry shall transfer the barony of Longford from you to me, in recognition of my faithful service to the princess. You may read it if you wish,' she offered, pushing it towards him.

Her brother stumbled backwards, as if it were a snake. She gave a shrug and continued, 'You will tell the prince that you have had this drawn up as a penance for the false suspicions you harboured against me. In signing it, he will be declaring his own trust in me before the world. I am sure you appreciate my need to take such a precaution, given how fickle a man's word can be these days.'

Edward glowered at her, his face now puce with rage. 'You ask too much, sister,' he muttered. 'It is not just on my account that the prince despises you. He will hardly be disposed to show you such favour.'

'Then you must persuade him, brother, by whatever means you have at your disposal . . . Your life depends upon it.'

Edward snatched the document from her. 'After all this is done, you will be dead to me. I want never to see you again.'

'Then we are in perfect accord, brother.'

The fifth chime of the clock echoed into silence. Frances tried to concentrate on the princess's gown, but her hands fumbled with the tiny silk buttons and she gave an exasperated sigh.

'Is everything all right, Fran?' Elizabeth asked.

'Forgive me, ma'am,' she replied quietly. 'My fingers are not my own this afternoon. Perhaps I should light some more candles. The light fades so quickly now.'

While Frances searched for the candles, the princess occupied herself with trying on a sequence of necklaces, each piercing the shadows with tiny shards of brilliance.

Frances glanced again at the clock. Edward should have sent word long before now. The elation she had felt after leaving him in the park had quickly been replaced by a gnawing fear. She knew that the success of her plan rested upon his being able to persuade the prince to abandon his suspicions against her. But that prospect seemed to fade with every passing hour.

Frances started at the sound of brisk footsteps approaching. There was a sharp rap on the door and Elizabeth, still admiring her reflection, called distractedly for the visitor to enter.

A groom wearing the king's livery stepped into the room and swept a quick bow. 'Pardon the intrusion, Your Grace, but Baron Longford desires a brief conference with his sister. He is waiting in the privy garden.'

Frances glanced across at the princess, fearing she would catch her panic, but the young woman was absorbed in her task. 'Of course,' she said. 'But pray do not be long, Frances. My father will not be pleased if I am late to dinner again.'

Frances had almost reached the door when her mistress called: 'Could you take Falstaff with you? He missed his afternoon walk because of the rain.'

At the mention of his name, the little dog gave a bark and leaped down from the chair where he had been dozing.

'Of course, ma'am,' Frances said, with a smile, stooping to pick up the wriggling creature.

The sun was already casting long shadows over the garden as she passed under the archway that had been sculpted in the box hedge. She saw him at once, sitting on a stone bench towards the centre of the garden. As she approached, he seemed agitated, perpetually glancing over his shoulder. He leaped to his feet when he saw her.

'Well?' she asked quietly.

Edward did not meet her eye. 'I have done as you asked,' he mumbled.

She waited, her anxiety rising. 'So the prince will take no action against me?'

'Why don't you ask me yourself, rather than trusting the word of this miserable wretch?'

Frances swung around. Henry was standing behind her, a smirk playing about his lips. She looked back at her brother, who was staring at the ground.

'Did you really believe that your brother enjoyed such favour that I would agree to turn a blind eye to a treacherous *witch*?'

His spittle flew onto her cheek as he said the word. Frances was too shocked to reply.

The prince gave a derisive laugh. 'I mean, *look* at him! How could I take any pleasure in the company of such a man? I only ever showed him favour because I knew he would give me the prize I sought. He proved as biddable as that puppy.' He snorted.

Instinctively, Frances took a step away and set the dog on the ground. She was relieved when he scurried off to explore the garden.

'And what prize did you seek?' Frances spoke with an assurance she did not feel as she held his steely gaze.

His mouth twitched. 'Why, *you,* of course, Lady Frances.'

She drew in a quiet breath.

'Even before my sister let slip your confidence, I knew you had been dripping poison into her ear, persuading her against the suitors I had arranged so that she might marry a heretic.'

He took a step closer.

'I have many eyes and ears, even in my father's court,' he continued, 'but you were clever enough to leave no trace of your meddling, and I knew my sister clings to you, so I had to find some other means of wresting her away from your contaminating influence.'

Frances stared at him, unflinching.

'When I saw how the *baron* here thirsted for revenge against you for depriving him of his inheritance, it was all too easy to twist it to my advantage. A suggestion here, a hint there, and he soon believed it was his idea to begin gathering evidence of your witch-ery. Poor, simple fool.' He cuffed Edward's ear.

Frances bit the inside of her lip so hard that she tasted blood. 'You can have no evidence against me,' she said, measuring her words carefully. 'There is only malice and hearsay.'

Henry shook his head sadly. 'So it is with most witchcraft cases. But it does not stop the accused choking out their breath on the end of a rope.'

'What of the indenture, Your Grace?' she asked, her gaze intensifying. 'You must know it is treason to countenance the king's death.'

The prince's laughter echoed around the garden. It was so prolonged that he fell into a paroxysm of coughing. Frances watched as he banged his fist against his chest, try-ing to catch his breath, even as a fresh bout of mirth overcame him.

'Forgive me,' he wheezed, dabbing at his eyes. 'You shall be the death of me, Lady Frances, with jests such as that. The inden-ture will certainly spell the end of your brother, should it come to light, but it car-ries no such danger for me. Do you really think my father would put his own son and heir to death?' he sneered, echoing Raleigh's words to her in the Tower. 'Especially when the alternative is so risible. Poor Charlie.' He chuckled. 'No, my lady, the worst I will suffer will be chastisement and banishment from court — though that would be a positive reward.'

At that moment, Falstaff came scampering back and gave several excited yelps as he danced around the prince's feet.

'Damned beast,' he said, giving it a sharp kick.

The dog gave a high-pitched howl and ran to cower under a nearby bush, its little legs trembling.

'Will you treat your subjects thus when you are king?' Frances snapped, fury flaring in her breast. 'You need not answer — it is how you treat them now, and men's habits harden with time.'

Henry's eyes glinted dangerously as he stared back at her.

'Tell me, Your Grace, do you think to win their loyalty in this way?' she persisted, 'with childish tantrums and thoughtless cruelty? You may bully them into submission, certainly — for a time, at least. But they will soon grow to despise you.' She thought of Raleigh, his face twisted with derision whenever she mentioned the prince's name. 'Indeed, those who seem to revere you mock

595

you as soon as your back is turned. But you are too blinded by your vanity to notice.'

'Frances!' Edward murmured fearfully.

But she was too enraged to stop now. All of the fury and resentment that had been simmering inside her over the past few months now burst out, blistering as molten lava.

'Do you think the people of this kingdom want a preening, pale-faced boy for their king?' she went on. 'Why do you think the Powder Treason sought to place your sister on the throne? The plotters voiced what everyone else believes, that the princess would make a far more powerful monarch, one who would hold her subjects in thrall as the late queen did. I often wonder that you were born of the same mother.'

Without warning, the prince stepped forward and dealt Frances a stinging blow across the face. She stumbled back, sharp thorns digging into her palms as she grasped at the stems of the rose bush to try to stop herself falling. She landed awkwardly, and for several moments was too winded to speak. Her breath came in gasps and she cradled her belly, afraid for the child that grew within.

Edward was staring at her, clearly stricken. *You should have seen what he was,* she cursed inwardly, *instead of allowing envy and spite to blind you.* But she also railed against herself. She too had been blinded — by her love for Longford, for her son, for Thomas. She had been a fool to believe that the indenture would save her from the perils that swirled endlessly about her. Raleigh had been right. It was not enough.

Slowly, she got to her feet, wincing as pain lanced her stomach, and fearing a warm trickle of blood between her legs, but the pain soon subsided to a dull ache.

The prince was watching her with interest, as if she were a rare butterfly that he had trapped under a glass. 'I did not think you would be so easily silenced as that pathetic little dog,' he said, his voice as soft as silk.

He stepped closer again. She could feel the warmth of his breath on her face. Gently, he trailed his delicate fingers over her collarbone, his eyes following their idling movement. Then his hand snaked around her neck, stroking, caressing. She cringed and made to step back, but his hand suddenly closed around her throat, tightening. Desperately, her fingers clawed at his wrists, but he harboured a strength that shocked her. Her vision began to blur. Behind the prince, Edward was mute with horror. He made no move to help. As she began to faint, the garden disappeared and she was standing on the gallows, the rope chafing hungrily against her neck, its bristles rubbing her skin raw as it sucked the last breath from her lungs.

He released her and she stumbled forward, retching. A vision of the gallows still swam before her eyes and a fresh wave of nausea swept over her. She pushed it down, forcing her breathing to slow. Eventually she stood upright, her head pounding. Her eyes were dark pools of loathing as she stared at the prince.

'At least you are prepared now,' he murmured, in a sing-song tone. 'I have seen many women — men, too — piss themselves in terror as the rope tightens about their neck. But it will hold no such fear for you. You should thank me.'

He leaned forward, his mouth close to her ear. Idly, he traced his finger along the angry red welt around her neck. Her breath hissed through her teeth as she tried to stop herself recoiling. Slowly, he moved his lips to where his finger had been and pressed them against her burning skin.

'I have always known you were the devil's slave, Lady Frances.' His hand coiled around her waist and pulled her to him.

'Tell me, has he ever taken you as his whore?'

She could feel his arousal as he pressed his hips against hers. He held her there and moved his mouth so close to hers that she caught the stale odour of wine.

He stepped back suddenly, his mouth curling into a sardonic smile. His skin appeared so pale in the fading light that it was almost translucent. 'It has been a pleasure, Lady Frances, but the hour grows late so I must leave you now.' He stalked out of the garden, his cloak billowing behind him.

A strange peace crept over her as she watched his retreating form. With a sudden clarity, she saw now what she must do.

CHAPTER 53
31 OCTOBER

Frances peered into the looking glass, running her fingers along her neck. It was still tender, but the redness had faded. She had made a paste with egg white and alum to conceal the mark and was grateful that the turn in the weather had given her the excuse to wear a high-necked gown. She was grateful, too, that Thomas had not been there to see it. He had left for Hertfordshire on the day of her visit to St James's. Count Frederick had not joined the hunting party this time. Evidently he had not shown sufficient prowess, and the king had been heard to grumble that he did not wish to be hampered by him again. Frances wondered idly whether it would hinder Frederick's prospects as a suitor. It hardly seemed to matter now.

Her husband would return this evening. Though she longed to see him, the prospect made her uneasy, too. He had been quiet on the morning of his departure, his eyes searching hers as he bade her goodbye. The lies would soon stop, she told herself. When she had fulfilled this final act and freed herself from the plotting and contagion of court, they could live in peaceful harmony, cherishing each other and their children.

Nothing is hidden that will not be made manifest.

Frances stared at her reflection. She was a fool to think that what she concealed would fade with time. It would remain as a canker, slowly spreading until it choked the love between her and Thomas.

With an impatient sigh, she leaned forward and blew out the candle. She must not lose her resolve now.

The sky had lifted to a leaden grey by the time Frances reached the Tower. She had half an hour at most before she must board a boat back to Whitehall. At sight of the dark outline of the imposing keep, Frances felt a chill run through her. Would she soon return here a prisoner — a traitor? She knew all too well the horrors that Tom and his fellow plotters had suffered. But her crime would be poisoning as well as treason, and the punishment for that was to be boiled alive.

The possibility of discovery had played endlessly on her mind, these past few days, so that now it seemed as real and insurmountable as the solid stone walls of the fortress before her. She had considered her means of escape, should the hue and cry be raised. She could go at once to Whitehall, flee with her husband and son under cover of darkness. They could be far from London by the time their absence was noticed. But where would they go? There were no safe havens in this kingdom, and she could not bear the thought of exile in some foreign country, far from everything they knew and held dear.

Far from Longford.

She could never forsake her beloved home, her son's inheritance. What she planned carried great risk, but the rewards would be worth it. Longford would be restored to Catholic hands and this kingdom would be saved from another heretic king, even worse than the one who now sat on the throne. She sucked in the cold morning air, then walked briskly towards the outer bastion.

The guards eyed her curiously. She had only been there two days before. Her visits were not usually so frequent. She smiled, exhaling with relief as they nodded her through.

This time Raleigh was expecting her. He stood to greet her with his usual warmth when the guard let her in. 'Lady Frances, it is a pleasure to see you, as always.'

He seemed unconcerned, though he knew the purpose of her visit all too well.

She did not take the seat he proffered.

'You have it?' she asked, without preamble.

Raleigh spread his hands. 'My dear, you will wear out the flagstones if you continue thus. Pray, sit.'

Frances stopped pacing and sat on the edge of the chair opposite him. 'I have little time.'

'I know, I know.' He patted her knee. 'I do not wish to detain you but the guard will grow suspicious if you leave after only a few moments. Besides, there are details to discuss.' He reached into his doublet and drew out a small piece of folded linen. It was tied with a cord at one end. He glanced at the door, then handed it to her. 'The Arabs call it Satan's Apple,' he said, with a slow smile.

Frances felt its weight in her hand. Slowly, she lifted it to her nose. Even through the layers of fabric, she could smell the earthy, slightly citric scent of the mandrake root within. It hinted at something wholesome, healing. If taken in small doses, it could cure all manner of ailments. But a few drops more and it was deadly. She put it carefully in the pocket of her gown, next to her rosary. They would make excellent bedfellows. 'You are fortunate to have such a wide circle of friends, Sir Walter,' she said.

'A sailor makes many acquaintances on his travels. Each one has something to give: a fine wine, an old fable, an exotic spice . . . The old queen used to delight in the treasures I brought her. But none was as valuable as the one I have just given you, Lady Frances,' he added, suddenly grave.

'I will use it well,' she vowed.

'The prince still plans to dine with his sister this evening?'

Frances nodded. 'Yes — in Her Grace's apartments. Count Frederick will be there too.'

'And you are sure that Henry will not act against you before then?'

'Quite sure. The king will not return from the hunt until this evening so will take supper in private. His son will desire as great an audience as possible when he levels his accusations against me. Tomorrow is All Hallows when the court will gather for the feast. It is the perfect opportunity.'

'His Grace was ever one for theatrical

gestures,' Raleigh agreed. 'They play to his natural vanity. How sad that he will be denied this particular spectacle.' He smiled. 'And how apt that he will breathe his last on the eve when we remember the dead.'

Frances's mouth twisted in distaste. Though she was certain of what she had to do, she could not rejoice in it as Raleigh did. She stood and crossed to the window. The light was gathering quickly now and the sky was tinged pale yellow. Her gaze wandered to a solid, squat tower on the far side of the green, close to the one in which she had been tortured. A light flickered in a narrow window on the upper floor. As Frances watched, she saw a shadow move across it, then grow still. She strained her eyes to see. It appeared to be the outline of a woman, but perhaps the light was playing tricks with her.

'Lady Arbella is abroad early this morning.'

Raleigh's voice made her start. She turned to see him gazing at the same spot, over her shoulder.

Frances had not known the lady's quarters lay so close. 'How does she fare?' she asked, her eyes on the shadow.

Raleigh gave a heavy sigh. 'She has been driven near mad by her captivity, I am told,' he said, 'and means to starve herself to death.'

Frances's heart lurched with pity. Though she had disliked the haughty woman and had never wished to see her crowned, it pained her to think of her wasted body and wretched mind as she waited out the endless hours until death would claim her. 'Is there any news of Seymour?'

'Still in Flanders, as far as anyone knows. There is talk of him amassing a huge army with the King of Spain and sailing across the Channel to seize the throne. But it is only idle chatter. Seymour is not the stuff of which kings are made.'

As she watched the shadowy figure, Frances thought she saw a hand lift in greeting — or blessing, perhaps. She raised her own and pressed it to the glass. She might have saluted Arbella as queen, if Fate had twisted otherwise. Increasingly, it seemed that the distance between success and failure, righteousness and sin, was as insubstantial as a thread of gossamer silk.

'God speed your endeavours, Lady Frances,' Raleigh whispered behind her.

Frances lit the last of the sconces in the princess's chamber. The soft light reflected off the gilded frames and the intricate tracery around the windows, making the room appear so breathtakingly beautiful that she almost forgot what must take place there. She went to the large oak table, laden with wine and sweet delicacies, picked up one of the glasses and held it to the light. It would be easy enough to slip the tincture into the prince's wine. She would take care to do so towards the end of the evening, in case the mandrake should take effect sooner than she predicted. If it seeped into his blood while he slept, it would slow his heart gradually, luring him towards death as gently as a mother might coax her child to sleep with a lullaby.

She allowed her mind to drift ahead, imagining the consternation that news of the prince's death would cause. Elizabeth would be distraught. She loved her brother deeply, even though his control of her had become ever more suffocating. Frances hoped that, in time, her mistress would draw comfort from her new-found freedom. Her father had never shown the same obsessive interest in her marriage as his son. Neither was he so opposed to the idea of his daughter marrying a Catholic, if the rewards were great enough. Henry's death would at least hold out the prospect that Elizabeth might take a husband of the true faith. But Frances no longer felt any compulsion to influence her mistress's choice. Lady Vaux must find another pawn for her game. Tonight would be her final act — and it would be hers alone.

'I hope you have not tasted our mistress's wine?'

Frances set down the glass slowly. 'Good evening, Blanche.'

The young woman's eyes glittered in the candlelight. She was dressed in a new gown of pale blue satin, very fine. Her fair hair was swept up in an elegant coiffure and a necklace of sapphires sparkled at her throat. All for the prince's benefit, no doubt. She was beautiful, Frances had to admit. It must have been no chore for her brother to bed her. Had he told her about the indenture? If he had, Blanche was an arch dissembler, for her behaviour towards Frances had not altered. She was as coolly disdainful as ever.

'The marriage treaty is agreed, they say,' Blanche remarked. 'It awaits only the king's signature. There will be even more cause for celebration at tomorrow's feast, I am sure.'

She watched Frances closely. *Even more?* So she was right. The prince planned to accuse her there. 'What else shall we be celebrating, Blanche?' she asked lightly.

'Why, All Hallows Day, of course,' Blanche

replied, with a sly smile.

At that moment, the princess emerged from her bedchamber. 'I hope you have not been arguing, ladies,' she said, with a frown. 'You remind me of two cats with their backs arched, ready to pounce.'

'Of course not, Your Grace,' Blanche said, with a trill of laughter.

Frances merely bobbed a curtsy and smiled.

'My brother and Frederick will be here at any moment. Is everything made ready?'

'Yes, ma'am,' Frances replied. 'There is food enough for half the court, and a plentiful supply of wine. I ordered the Rhenish.'

Elizabeth nodded her approval. Frances noticed her hand shake slightly as she smoothed her skirts. She must be dreading the evening. Although she had got on well enough with Frederick during their private encounters, her brother would be pressuring for more than the polite, stilted exchanges they had shared. He wanted evidence that his sister would comply with his wishes.

All three women started at the sharp rap on the door. Blanche was first to it. Frances saw her curtsy. *The prince.* She waited for sight of the man whose breath she would stop before the night was over.

But it was Count Frederick who walked in first, head bowed and eyes darting nervously about the room. His childlike awkwardness was thrown into even sharper relief by the princess's easy grace. 'Good evening, Count Frederick,' she said. 'You are most welcome. May I offer you some wine?'

'No, thank you,' he said quickly, a blush creeping over his cheeks.

'Well!' Elizabeth declared, after a prolonged silence. 'I cannot think what is keeping Henry. He is not usually so behind his time. Perhaps we should be seated.'

Frederick nodded and went to the table. The princess chose a seat at the opposite end. If etiquette had not prevented it, Frances would have come to her mistress's rescue by making conversation. As it was, Elizabeth attempted a few remarks, but they elicited only a smile or a nod from her companion. Frances sensed her rising exasperation.

Two chimes rang out from the clock above the fireplace. Frances glanced at it. The prince was now half an hour late. What if he had decided to act sooner than she had predicted and was even now waiting in the king's privy chamber? No, she reasoned, his father might not return for another two hours yet and Henry would not keep the count waiting for that long.

Several more minutes passed. Then, at last, the sound of rapid footsteps could be heard. Instinctively, Frances's hand closed over the tiny glass phial in her pocket. *It was almost time.* She listened to the low murmur of voices on the other side of the door. Then it was flung open and Henry's chamberlain strode in.

He gave a swift bow before addressing the princess. 'Your Grace, I regret to inform you that your brother the prince can no longer attend. He is gravely ill.'

Frances's mind raced. *Was this a trick? Was he even now making the final preparations for her destruction?*

'Henry!' the princess exclaimed, her face ashen. 'I saw him only yesterday and he seemed well. A little tired, perhaps. What has happened?'

The man's face darkened. 'It was very quick, Your Grace. His Highness was fencing with one of his attendants this afternoon when he suddenly threw down his sword and collapsed, clutching his stomach. By the time he had been carried to his chamber, he was in a high fever.'

Elizabeth's hand flew to her mouth.

Frances forced herself to focus. 'Were

611

there any other symptoms?' she asked.

The chamberlain looked at her with re-proof, then turned back to address the princess, as if she had asked the question. 'There was a slight rash on his stomach.'

'My poor brother,' Elizabeth murmured, almost to herself. 'I should go to him.'

'No, ma'am,' Frances said. 'Until we know what ails him, you must not put yourself at risk of contagion. I am sure his physicians are taking good care of him.'

She imagined them now, with their leeches and potions. They were more likely to be inflicting harm than good.

'Well, give him this token of my love and esteem,' the princess said, taking off her ring and handing it to the attendant. 'And God speed his recovery.'

The man gave a curt bow and strode out. Seizing his opportunity to escape, the count stood abruptly, made obeisance and fol-lowed in his wake.

Frances glanced at Blanche, whose face was marked more with disappointment than concern. She would have to flaunt her finery on another occasion. Clearly having no patience to comfort their mistress, she too left the room.

As soon as the door had closed, Frances rushed to the princess's side.

612

'Oh, Frances! This is my fault!' Elizabeth cried. 'I have been dreading this evening so much that I prayed to God He might spare me. But not like this!' Her face sank into her hands.

Frances put an arm around her shoulders. The princess's anxiety and grief contrasted sharply with her own feelings. Although she was frustrated to have been denied the chance to put her plan into action, she could hope now that God might do her work for her.

CHAPTER 54
1 NOVEMBER

'Is there any more news of the prince?'

Frances took another sip of wine and pretended not to listen to the conversation on the opposite side of the table. She had spent the day trying to comfort the princess, assure her that all was well, while she had prayed that it was not. Eventually, Elizabeth had retired to bed, exhausted with worry, and had sent her apologies to her father for this evening's feast.

'None that I know of. They say he was delirious last night and ranted about sorcery and bewitchments.'

Frances's blood ran cold.

'Was this witches' work, do you think?' another asked.

'Who's to say? But when he recovers, I'm sure he will come looking for whoever cast the spell.'

Thomas looked anxiously at his wife. 'Ignore their idle prattle, my love. They have little enough news to feast upon so seek to invent their own.'

She gave him a weak smile and toyed with the stew, which was rapidly congealing on her plate.

'I have made my own enquiries, on behalf of the king,' he added quietly.

She swung around to look at him. 'Oh?'

'His Majesty did not wish it to be known that he was enquiring after his son's health, so asked me to find out for him. I have it on good authority that Henry is much recovered. His fever has broken and he is already calling for ale.'

Frances tried to hide her disappointment. 'The princess will be relieved to hear it. I must call on her before we retire.'

She said little for the remainder of the meal. Her mind was too preoccupied with the prince. She knew with a sickening certainty that the gossips were right. Henry would use his illness as proof that he had been bewitched. And there was only one possible perpetrator. Together with the stories that Edward had supplied, the prince's sudden sickness would eradicate any doubts as to her guilt.

Her thoughts ran on. If the prince recovered, she could not wait for another opportunity like the private dinner to administer the poison. By the time that such an event took place — if it ever did — Henry would have had her accused and imprisoned.

'Frances?'

Her husband was waiting for an answer.

'Forgive me, my love. My mind was elsewhere,' she said, giving his hand a pat. 'What did you say?'

'It was no matter.' His smile did not reach his eyes.

All of a sudden, there was a loud clatter at the end of the hall. All eyes turned towards the dais, where the king had staggered to his feet, his gilded chair lying on its side behind him. 'To the prince!' he cried, swaying precariously.

He thrust his glass to the ceiling, causing most of its contents to spill onto the floor. There was a brief silence before others repeated the toast. Frances stole a glance at her husband as he took a sip of wine. She raised her own glass to her lips but the wine that had warmed her belly earlier now tasted bitter. She swallowed it, fearing it might choke her.

Frances had attended the princess early the following morning, as much out of hope that she might glean some information about the prince as for concern about her mistress. The young woman had emerged from her chamber looking as if she had not slept at all. The same dark shadows marked her own eyes. The night had passed agonisingly slowly.

None of the diversions that Frances had suggested had won favour with Elizabeth, and they now sat in silence. The long hours of waiting reminded Frances of that other time, several years before, when she had been desperate for news of Tom, seizing upon reports that the gunpowder had been lit, the king and his parliament destroyed. It had all proved false. She shook away the memory of what had happened next. It was still too painful, and always would be.

Even Falstaff seemed to have picked up on the atmosphere and had sat on the footstool all day, his head resting on his paws and a mournful expression in his eyes. Little wonder that Blanche had found an excuse to absent herself, Frances thought. Not that she was sorry for it. Her impatient sighs and petulant remarks had grated on Frances's nerves.

The light was already fading by the time the messenger arrived from St James's. The princess leaped to her feet and waited, ashen-faced, for him to speak.

'Well?' she demanded, reaching out to clasp Frances's hand.

'His Highness's condition is a little improved, Your Grace,' the man announced. 'The physicians say that his fever has broken but he is still very weak so they have bled him.'

Frances felt the princess's hand relax.

'That is good news!' Elizabeth exclaimed, the colour rushing to her cheeks. 'Pray give him my dearest love and tell him I will visit him tomorrow.'

'Is that wise, Your Grace?' Frances asked. 'We do not yet know if the contagion has passed.'

'I cannot spend another day here, eking out the hours with worry and waiting.'

Frances could not deny that she felt the same.

'If my brother is not well enough to receive me tomorrow, we shall stay at St James's until the following day. I would like to be close at hand. You will come with me, Frances? I am sure that Henry will not mind if I am with you alone, just this once. We are hardly likely to discuss my marriage at such a time.'

Frances knew it was not a question. The thought of accompanying the princess to St James's was akin to entering a lion's den.

But she smiled and agreed.

'Then it is decided,' Elizabeth declared. She turned back to the messenger. 'Pray ensure that chambers are made up for Lady Tyringham and myself. We will ride over to the palace as soon as it is light.'

'St James's?'

Thomas was aghast. She gave a small nod.

'But what if the contagion has spread? I cannot let you risk your life — and that of our child — by going there.'

Frances took his hand in hers and kissed it. She smiled up at him. 'We will be quite safe, I assure you,' she said. 'There is no report of any member of the prince's household falling sick, and they would surely have done so by now if it was the sweat or smallpox. The likelihood is that he has had a cold in his head or some other trifling complaint.'

Thomas did not return her smile. 'I do not want you to go.'

Frances knew he suspected she was concealing something from him. Several times since his return from Hertfordshire, she had caught him staring at her. He had been quieter than usual, too, and she had filled the silences with idle chatter, fearful lest he ask the questions that she sensed were swirling in his mind. *He could not know,* she kept reminding herself. She was seeing meaning where none existed.

She wrapped her arms around him now, pressing her face into his chest so that he could not see the fear in her eyes. 'I will be gone for a day — two at most,' she assured him.

He did not reply but she could feel the rapid beat of his heart next to her cheek.

'Promise me you will do nothing to hazard your life,' he murmured into her hair.

She thought of the glass phial that still lay hidden inside her pocket. 'I promise,' she whispered.

Frances studied the prince's face. His skin was so pallid that it gave him an almost ethereal appearance. His dark eyes never left her.

She remembered the portrait being painted soon after she had first come to court. He had been ten years old then, but already insufferable in his pride and arrogance. How much worse would he become if he survived beyond his eighteen years?

There was no sound from the chamber beyond, though Frances strained to listen. Henry had insisted that the princess go in alone. No doubt he intended to use the opportunity to press her on the matter of her marriage, find out how well she liked the count. Or perhaps he was already slandering his sister's favourite attendant.

Frances turned at a soft sound behind her. William Cecil entered the room. She made to rise but he gestured for her to remain seated and bowed.

'Lord Cranborne.'

How like his father the young man had grown, she thought, though he was tall and straight-limbed. His lips were slightly parted, as if weighing his words before speaking them.

'His Grace will take comfort from seeing his sister, I am sure,' he said at last. 'It was good of you to accompany her, considering the risks.'

Frances eyed him closely. *What risks did he refer to?* 'Though we have received many reports from St James's, the princess was anxious to see Prince Henry for herself and be reassured that he is out of danger.'

William gave a small smile. 'Your mistress is very wise. My father always said that one should judge a courtier by his actions, for his words are meaningless.'

He was still dressed in mourning, Frances noticed. She wondered how deeply he had grieved his father's passing. They had served different masters and had seldom been seen together at court, but that signified little. She had rarely seen her own father since she had come to Whitehall, but the bond between them had never weakened. Neither had her pain at his loss. 'That is perhaps how we should judge all men, Lord Cranborne,' she replied.

William seemed to hesitate, then came to sit close to her. 'I will always be grateful to you, Lady Frances,' he said, in a low voice.

She looked up at him in surprise.

'You eased my father's suffering greatly and gave him more life than he would have enjoyed if you had not attended him. There are few enough people at court who would have done the same. He was not well liked.' He paused. 'And you, Lady Frances, had less cause than any to help him.'

She held his steady gaze.

'I know how he persecuted you,' he continued, when she did not reply. 'He told me of it, soon after I began my service here. The prince had made some remark about you, after we met for the lion-baiting at the Tower that day. He said he would not have a witch serving his sister.'

So Henry had been intent upon her destruction from the beginning. She glanced towards his chamber door.

'Henry would say nothing further, so I asked my father about it.' His voice was barely a whisper now. 'He told me you were innocent, that he had brought the accusation against you to win favour with the king.'

Frances had known it to be true, but to

hear the words spoken aloud smote her. She had been nothing more than a pawn in Cecil's game. And now the prince had taken up the pieces. 'I am no witch, Lord Cranborne,' she said at last. 'I have only ever used my skills for good, not evil.'

Until now.

The voice she heard was Thomas's. Her heart lurched.

'I know that, and I am deeply sorry for everything you suffered at my father's hands.' He looked down for a moment. 'He was sorry too, Lady Frances.'

She opened her mouth to protest but he held up his hand. 'Please — let me continue.' He took a breath. 'Our chaplain attended him at Marlborough. He said that my father was in great wretchedness of mind and took no solace from the rites that the old priest performed. He begged to make confession, though it is considered heresy now.'

Frances drew a breath.

'Seeing his distress, our chaplain eventually agreed,' William went on, his face ashen. 'My father told him of his crimes against you, that he would have seen you hanged, though he knew you to be innocent. Only when the priest had assured him of God's forgiveness did he quieten.'

There was a long silence. Frances tried to order her thoughts but she was still reeling from what she had heard. Even after his private chapel had been discovered at Hatfield, she had never quite believed the rumours that Cecil had been a closet Catholic. To act so contrary to his beliefs seemed impossible. But now she understood that he had spent his life sacrificing those same beliefs upon the altar of his ambition. Little wonder he had suffered such torment as death approached. He might have confessed many other crimes with his final breath. That it was his actions against her that had plagued him most shocked her to the core.

'My father raised me in the true faith, Lady Frances,' he whispered. 'Though he could never express it in life, I mean to honour his death by restoring this kingdom to the Catholic fold.'

The world seemed to shift around her.

'The prince is an even greater heretic than his father. England will surely be damned if he lives to take the throne. But his younger brother is sympathetic to the Catholic cause. He might become more so, in time.'

'Why are you telling me this?'

William's eyes burned with sincerity. 'Because I know how you have tried to advance our cause — how you might still.'

'What do you mean, Lord Cranborne?' she said slowly.

'You are wise not to trust the son of your enemy,' he said with the flicker of a smile. 'But you may depend upon my actions, even if you do not believe my words. We have a friend in common, Lady Frances. They told me to expect you.'

Raleigh?

'I will do everything I can to assist, of course,' he continued, as Frances tried to hide her confusion. She had been naïve enough to think she was acting alone.

At that moment, the door of the prince's chamber swung open and the princess stepped out. 'Oh, Frances, he is so much better!' she exclaimed, her face alight with joy. 'He is no longer feverish and his cheeks are rosier than I have ever seen them.'

'I am glad for your sake as much as his, ma'am,' she replied. 'I know how anxious you have been.'

'Does he require anything, Your Grace?' William asked.

Elizabeth shook her head. 'He still has no appetite — but that will return soon enough, I am sure,' she said quickly. 'But he asked to see you, Frances. He knows how distressed I have been and wants to make sure that you are caring for me.' She smiled. 'He is such a dear brother and thinks only of my happiness.'

Frances bowed her head to disguise the alarm in her eyes. 'I shall be glad to attend him,' she said, as she rose to her feet.

She glanced at William as she curtsied to her mistress. He was watching her closely.

Frances knocked quietly on the chamber door and it was opened a moment later by one of the yeomen guards.

'You may leave us now,' Henry called.

She waited as the two men filed out of the room, then walked slowly in, closing the door softly behind her.

The chamber was dimly lit, and the aroma of beeswax did not quite conceal the stale odour of sweat. Frances tried to calm her breathing as she made a slow curtsy.

'Do not stand there like some coy girl, Lady Frances,' the prince commanded. 'We both know you are very far from that.'

She gave a tight smile, jaw clenched. The stench grew stronger as she moved closer to the bed. Along with the sweat, she caught the sickly smell of decay. Henry was propped up against a large stack of pillows. His face was flushed, his hair matted at the temples. 'How is Your Grace?'

He smirked. 'I am sorry to disappoint you, Lady Frances, but as you can see I am much improved,' he sneered. 'You must have thought you would escape the rope a second time.'

Her gaze did not waver as she stared back at him. 'On the contrary,' she replied. 'It grieved me to see my mistress so distraught. I understand you wish to discuss my care of her?' she added, in mock innocence.

'Do not toy with me,' he murmured, leaning towards her. 'You know as well as I that my recovery spells death for you. That —'

He was seized by a violent fit of coughing. Frances watched as his chest heaved with exertion. His shirt lay open and the skin beneath had the soft sheen of wax. As she looked more closely, she noticed a slight red mark just beneath his collarbone. *Smallpox?* No, it was more like a freckle than the angry red sores that marked the disease.

Henry reached across to the jug on the table next to him, but stopped, his hand suspended above it, as another fit overcame him. Frances poured him some of the ale and held it to his lips. He gulped at it, then sank back against the pillows, gasping.

She waited.

'This sickness will soon pass,' he rasped, when his breathing had slowed. 'Already the fever has broken and I can feel the humour draining from my lungs. My physicians tell me that I will be well enough to receive my father within two days at the most.'

His eyes never left hers. She understood the threat that his words carried.

'I pray that God will speed your recovery,' she said.

The prince cocked his head, his lips twitching with amusement. Frances shifted slightly and felt the cool glass of the phial through the linen of her skirt.

'Indeed?' He raised an eyebrow. 'Then you are more of a fool than I thought.'

CHAPTER 56
4 NOVEMBER

Frances stopped pacing and stared out of the window. The great hall of St James's was in darkness now and the soft glow of candlelight spilled from only a few windows on either side. There had been no feasting again this evening, and though the prince had ordered the entertainments to continue during his confinement, in case his father should deign to visit, few had had the heart for them. Whenever a groom of his chamber appeared in the hall, all eyes would turn to him expectantly. But then the servant would walk past the dais, pausing only to bow to the princess and the empty throne next to her, and continue on his errand. The king had evidently chosen to wait another day.

Elizabeth had spent the afternoon with her brother, conversing and playing cards. Frances had been relieved not to be invited to join them. Instead, she had occupied her time in writing to Thomas and George, assuring them that she would return soon. Her husband would have been concerned for her since her departure. God willing, she would be with him tomorrow.

She glanced again at the clock. It was almost half past eleven, the time at which William had told her he would be taking up his post outside the prince's bedchamber. He had mentioned it as something of no greater significance than any other detail of his master's domestic arrangements. But she knew what it portended.

Was this a trap?

The thought had tormented her ever since William had told her that he knew of her plan, that he shared her faith. If he had said it to lure her into committing treason, she would face a terrifying fate.

Our faith will sustain us.

Her father's words. She had repeated them over and over to herself since that bleak night at Richmond almost three years before. They gave her strength now, as they always did. She must fulfil his wishes, protect her son's inheritance. There was no other way.

In the distance, she caught the solitary toll of a bell. Her heart skipped a beat. The hour had come. Mustering her resolve, she stole quietly out of her chamber.

■ ■ ■ ■

As she walked along the gallery that led to the private apartments, she heard the low murmur of voices ahead. Quickly, she moved into one of the window recesses, pressing herself against the pane as she gathered in her skirts. She held her breath as the voices grew louder. A few moments later, the guards passed by — so close she could almost have touched them. But they were too intent upon their conversation to notice her.

'It will be tomorrow,' one remarked. 'The chamberlain received a messenger earlier.'

'I'll wager he'll greet his son from a safe distance,' the other replied. 'Kings are always fearful of disease.'

'He need have no fear. Half the palace would have sickened by now if it was serious.'

Frances waited until their chatter had echoed into silence, then padded quietly along the rest of the gallery.

When she reached the room at the end, she paused and looked all around her. A single candle burned in each of the sconces on either side of the door, illuminating the faces of the characters in the rich tapestries that lined the walls so that they appeared eerily lifelike. The chairs upon which she and William had sat the previous day were empty. It was almost as if their exchange had never happened. Casting a glance over her shoulder, she saw that the gallery was still deserted, too, the paintings on either side stretching out into the gloom.

She turned at the soft click of a latch. The door of the prince's chamber slowly opened. There was a long pause. Frances held her breath as she waited. Then the familiar outline of William Cecil emerged from within. He drew the door closed behind him, taking care to make no sound.

Frances stepped out of the shadows. She saw him tense and place his hand on his sword, but his features relaxed as he recognised her. He waited until they had drawn close together before addressing her in an undertone. 'He is sleeping now. But you must make haste. The next guards will make their way here as soon as the others return to their quarters.'

William's face was in shadow but she caught the glint of anticipation in his eyes. He reached out suddenly and took her hands. 'God go with you, Lady Frances,' he said, then walked quickly back to the door and pushed it open just far enough for her to slip inside.

The narrow shaft of light disappeared as William shut it silently behind her. She blinked into the darkness. After a few moments, she could make out the silhouette of the bed, its canopy suspended above. She took a tentative step forward, reaching out as she did so, in case there was some unseen obstacle in her path. A few more steps and her fingers brushed against the soft damask of the bedcover. Using it as her guide, she moved silently around the bed until she felt the warmth of the prince's skin. He gave a moan. She froze and held her breath. But soon his breathing became slow and rhythmic again.

Frances edged closer, leaning forward so that her face was almost touching his. The same stale aroma emanated from his body, but there was no sign that the fever had returned. She started as his breath caught in his throat and he gave a loud, rattling cough. Glancing back towards the door she strained her ears to listen but there was no sound of the guards approaching yet. Henry's breathing steadied once more.

Frances could see that his lips were parted. She slipped her hand inside her pocket and pulled out the tincture. Feeling for the stopper, she gently prised it out. At once, the pungent, earthy aroma hit the back of her throat and her eyes watered as she swallowed a choking cough.

At that moment, she heard the creak of a floorboard outside the chamber.

She must do it now.

Leaning forward, she held the phial to the prince's lips. Her fingers trembled as she brought it closer and began to tilt it. One tiny move more and the liquid would begin to drip into his mouth, burning its way down his throat as it slowly sucked the breath from his body. She paused as, in the distance, she heard the faint chiming of a bell.

Midnight.

All of a sudden, it struck her. *It was the fifth of November.* The day when, seven years earlier, Tom and his fellow plotters would have blown up Parliament, if Fawkes had not been discovered with the gunpowder. Now was her chance to avenge their deaths.

He sees what is in our hearts, Frances.

Thomas's words sounded in her ears as clearly as if he had been standing next to her. She froze, the tincture suspended in her grasp. No matter how much the prince had wronged her — would do so still — this was murder. It was the devil's work. In saving her life, she would be destroying her immortal soul, condemning herself to eternal damnation.

Tears welled in her eyes as she tried to focus on the tincture. Slowly, she withdrew her hand and, with trembling fingers, pushed the tiny stopper back into the neck of the bottle. Just then, Henry gave another groan and turned his head away, as if he, too, knew that the moment had passed.

Beyond the door, Frances heard the low rumble of voices. The guards were almost there. She hastened to her feet and padded quickly out of the chamber, closed the door behind her. The outer chamber was deserted. William had gone.

There was no time to find him now, she thought, as she ran towards the doorway that led down towards the servants' halls. The guards' footsteps were so close now that she knew they would emerge into the antechamber within half a breath.

'Where's Cranborne?'

A man's voice rang out as she pressed her back against the wall, not daring to creep down the stairs until she was sure she was not in view.

'Young wastrel,' the other muttered. 'I'll wager he's already in his bed. We had best make sure all is well with the prince.'

Frances listened as they walked over to the chamber door. As soon as she heard the click of the latch, she ran down the stairs. The corridor below was in darkness but she hurried along it, reaching out for the cold stone walls to guide her. By the time she arrived in the courtyard, she was panting for breath and her skin was damp with sweat, but she did not stop running until she had passed under the gatehouse.

Ahead, she could see the dark mass of the park, the skeletal trees dimly outlined against the night sky, the moon obscured by heavy clouds. A fine drizzle cooled her burning cheeks. Crossing the deserted promenade, she passed through the gates. Her breath sounded in her ears as she weaved her way between the trees towards the path that led westwards through the park, breathing in the comforting scent of damp oak and grass.

Only when she had reached the westernmost edge, close to the lake, did she look back towards the palace. She could just make out the turrets of the gatehouse above the treetops. The rain was falling heavily now and she turned her face up to it, as if to cleanse herself of the sin she had almost committed.

'God forgive me,' she whispered.

CHAPTER 57
5 NOVEMBER

Frances shivered as a chill breeze whipped along the corridor. Her sodden gown weighed heavily upon her, and she longed for the comforting warmth of her bed, to feel Thomas's arms wrapped tightly around her. She wished that she might stay there for ever, safe from the horror that she knew must soon follow.

She knocked softly on the door, praying that Mistress Knyvett would not wake the others as she came to unlock it. As she heard the scraping of the bolt, she rehearsed the excuse she would give for the lateness of the hour, her dishevelled appearance. But as the door was drawn slowly open, it was her husband's eyes that met hers.

'Frances!' He drew her into the apartment at once, his face creased with anxiety as he regarded her soaking clothes, the hair clinging to her face. Quickly, he drew off her cloak and helped her out of her dress. It fell with a slap onto the stone floor as he pulled the last of the lacing free from its stays, his hands shaking. She stood close to the fire as he went to fetch a thick blanket and wrapped it tightly around her shoulders. He brought two chairs in front of the hearth and helped her onto one, as if she was as fragile as Venetian glass.

Frances felt so overwhelmed with love for him that she could not speak. She reached for his hand and held it tightly in hers. It felt cold, despite the warmth of the fire. She knew that he was waiting for her to speak and felt suddenly afraid. There could be no more lies, she knew, but she could not bear to see the love in his eyes turn to pain. Revulsion, even. She deserved nothing less.

Her throat constricted as she opened her mouth to speak, and her voice came out as barely a whisper.

'I have betrayed you, Thomas.'

She saw fear in his eyes, but he held her hand tightly as he waited for her to continue.

'You made me promise, when I married you, not to embroil myself in any more plots, but to keep my faith hidden, as you do.' She took a breath. 'I saw the wisdom in what you asked of me and thought I could stay true to it — indeed I did so, for three

639

years and more. But then I received a letter . . . from Dorothy Wintour — Tom's sister.'

She felt his hand go limp in hers and her eyes clouded with tears.

'I went to meet her in secret. She urged me to return to court so that I might prevent the princess from marrying a heretic. She said that many of our faith stood ready to take arms — the King of Spain, too, if a match was arranged between the princess and his nephew. I thought that if I helped to bring this to pass, Elizabeth might yet win the throne, as the Powder Treason had intended.'

She looked up at her husband. 'I was so blinded by my desire to honour Tom's memory that I could not see I would be dishonouring you.'

'Or perhaps you chose to ignore it,' Thomas remarked quietly, withdrawing his hand.

His voice sounded flat, lifeless, and he was staring at her as if she were a stranger. Frances's heart lurched as she saw the pain in his eyes. She longed to touch his cheek but could not bear to see him recoil from her.

'That is why you asked me to bring you here. Not for your son's advantage, but for your own,' he said.

It was pointless to object, to argue that she had acted only to further the Catholic cause, that it had been against her own wishes. Now that she had begun, she must tell him everything.

'Dorothy told me that Lady Vaux would arrange matters, that she would ensure the queen granted me my former position in the princess's household.'

'You put your faith in that woman?' Thomas asked, incredulous. 'Even Tom did not trust her. Though she pretends to be zealous for the cause, she has only ever acted for herself.'

Frances nodded miserably. 'I soon came to realise that, but it was too late. She threatened to expose my part in the Powder Treason, to reveal George's true father. I had little choice but to do her bidding — or, at least, appear to.'

Her husband's jaw twitched but he said nothing. 'But that was not the only scheme into which I was drawn, Thomas,' she went on quietly. 'I had not been at court for many weeks when I was told of a plot to further Arbella Stuart's claim to the throne by marrying her to William Seymour.'

Thomas was staring at her in open dismay now.

'I had little choice but to fall in with their schemes,' she continued, before he could speak. 'They threatened George — you, too — if I refused. So I stood as witness to their secret union. And I attended the lady when she miscarried his child.'

All the colour had drained from her husband's face. 'How could you?' he demanded. 'Even the Catholics would prefer to see this king on the throne than his treacherous cousin.'

'I share the same opinion, Thomas. But they had made sure of my compliance.' A pause. 'Lady Drummond had made sure of it.'

'Lady . . . What has she to do with this?'

The look on his face eradicated any doubt she might have harboured that he had been an unwitting part in all this.

'She is a Catholic, Thomas, and more dangerous than Lady Vaux or any of the other plotters in this court. She will not rest until she sees Arbella crowned queen.'

His face was now deathly pale. 'And what passed between her and me . . .'

'It was part of her scheme, Thomas,' Frances answered. 'Even though you knew nothing of it, your liaison with her would have been enough to see you condemned as a traitor.'

She saw understanding dawn in his eyes. He looked utterly stricken. 'And she used that to ensure you would fall in with her plans?' he muttered.

Frances nodded.

'What have I done?' he whispered, lowering his head into his hands.

'You were not to know, Thomas,' she urged, desperate to ease his remorse. 'Though it still pains me to think of what passed between you, I have long since forgiven you.'

He raised his eyes to her. 'But I shall never forgive myself.' His voice cracked.

Frances could not bear to see his wretchedness when her own guilt was far greater.

'As the months wore on and there was little sign that any of her schemes would bear fruit, I resolved to take matters into my own hands.' She was mustering her strength for what she must tell him now. 'Increasingly, I came to see that it was my mistress's brother, not her father, who presented the greatest threat to our faith — to me also.'

Thomas was gazing at her intently now.

'He plans to expose me as a witch,' she said.

Her husband's eyes widened with horror, but she went on before he could speak.

'Edward has provided him with more than enough fodder for his schemes — Countess Cecily, too. But still my brother wanted more. He threatened to have me accused of treason.'

Thomas's expression darkened.

'I do not know if he has proof,' Frances went on, 'but Henry encouraged Edward to find it by promising him Longford if I am convicted. I have the indenture they both signed. That is treasonous in itself, I know,' she added, before her husband could say it. 'I have the document in safe-keeping.'

Her husband's fury showed in his eyes but he made no move to speak. Frances tried to summon her courage for what she knew she must tell him now.

'I could not bear the thought of losing Longford,' she whispered, 'or you and George, and the child that grows within me.' A single tear rolled down her cheek and dropped onto her hand, which was resting lightly on her stomach. 'So I resolved to use the same skills that the prince would accuse me of to take his life.'

Thomas's eyes misted as he stared at her.

'I did not act entirely alone,' Frances continued. 'Raleigh has been my confidant since I came to court. He supplied the mandrake for my tincture.'

Her husband's expression seemed to harden slightly, but still he said nothing.

'I planned to slip it into the prince's wine, when he came to have dinner with the princess and Count Frederick, but a messenger arrived with the news that he had fallen sick. I hoped that God might do my work for me, but when we heard that the prince was out of danger I knew I must try again. So I took the poison with me to St James's.'

Her throat tightened, as if to stop the words before they reached her lips.

'The prince summoned me to his chamber soon after we arrived and repeated his threat to tell the king of my "crimes". He said he would do so when his father came to visit him. I knew I had to stop his breath before he made his accusations, so I entered his chamber last night, with the help of Lord Cranborne.'

'*Cecil*'s son?'

Thomas was wide-eyed with astonishment. She nodded quickly, not wishing to be distracted.

'The prince was sleeping so I went to his side. But then —' Her chest heaved with a great sob as she reached into her pocket and pulled out the phial. The liquid glistened gold in the firelight as she held it up

645

to her husband. 'I could not do it, Thomas. It was only as I held the poison to his lips that I fully understood the truth of your words. That we must cherish our faith in our hearts. To do otherwise can only bring suffering and turmoil. Though I must now face the judgement of an earthly king, I need no longer fear that of our Heavenly Father.'

The tears flowed freely as she lowered her head. Amid the wretchedness she felt for the pain she had caused him there was lightness that she had at last freed herself from the lies and deceit.

Thomas sat perfectly still while she surrendered herself to her grief. She longed to touch him, to feel the familiar warmth of his embrace but, with deep sadness, she realised it might be lost to her for ever.

After several long minutes, he reached for her hand. She felt a surge of hope, but it was extinguished when he merely wrested the tincture from her grasp. She watched as he took out the stopper, then stepped towards the fire and tipped the phial over it. The flames hissed and spat as the liquid fell onto them and an acrid smell filled the chamber, making Frances's eyes sting. But Thomas stood quite still, impervious to the searing heat as he held the phial over the flames until the last drop had fallen from it. He then wrapped it in his kerchief and put it carefully inside the pocket of his doublet.

'The river will carry this far from here,' he said, then sank back into his chair. He leaned forward and put his head into his hands. Frances could not tell if he was weeping. She longed to comfort him, but she clasped her hands tightly together.

When at last he raised himself to look at her, his eyes were filled with misery. 'Why didn't you trust me, Frances?' He sounded more tired than angry.

'I'm so sorry,' she murmured.

'Was I not a good husband to you? Did I give you cause to be afraid of me?' he persisted.

'Never!' she exclaimed. 'You have always been the best and gentlest of men, Thomas. More than I ever deserved.'

All too well, she understood the agony her betrayal had caused. The memory was still raw of that day in Westminster, when Tom had told her of the plot in which he had entangled her.

'I thought you loved me, as I loved you.'

'I did,' she protested. 'I do still. Although I have deceived you in so much else, my love for you is true.'

Loved, he had said. She could not have

expected anything else. What she had told him was enough to destroy tenderness.

'I could have helped you, Frances,' he said, 'made you see how reckless was the course you had chosen. But now . . . now everything lies in ruins.'

With every fibre of her being, she wished she had thrown Dorothy's letter into the fire and remained at Tyringham Hall, far from Lady Vaux, Lady Drummond and their twisted schemes. Far from the prince who was now poised to destroy her.

'Forgive me.' She mouthed the words silently.

They sat like that for a long time, each lost in their own thoughts. Frances was only vaguely aware of the frail grey light that had begun to lift the gloom of the parlour. Though her bones ached with weariness, she knew she would not sleep if she retired to her bed.

At length, Thomas stood up and walked over to the table. She heard him pour two glasses of wine. He held one out to her when he returned and she took it gratefully. He drank, then sat down.

'I will go to the king as soon as he has risen,' he said, with resolve. 'I will tell him that the prince has wronged you, that his accusations are groundless and that he seeks only to stir up trouble.'

This was more than she deserved, she thought, and her eyes welled with tears at his kindness. But she knew it was no good.

'Thank you, Thomas,' she said softly, placing her hand tentatively over his. 'But I would not have you hazard your reputation — your life, even — by speaking to the king on my behalf. Besides, it would be to no avail. He might despise his son, but he despises witches more. He will prove only too willing to give credence to Henry's tales.'

She made to withdraw her hand, but Thomas seized it, gripping it with such force that her fingers pulsed. 'I cannot let you die, Frances,' he said, his voice faltering.

They gazed at each other, unspeaking, for several moments. Slowly, he softened his grip and bent to kiss her hand before standing and striding from the room. Frances watched the door close behind him. Her fingers still tingled with the warmth of his lips.

CHAPTER 58
5 NOVEMBER

Frances stared up at the canopy above the bed. The damask had long since faded and the stitching around the edges was frayed in places. She had tried counting the leaves on the vine that twisted around the edges but it was no use. Sleep was as far from her as it had been when she had first lain down.

She turned to look at George's bed. It must be almost an hour now since he had left for his lessons. He had done so without protest this morning, knowing that most of the day would be spent in the tiltyard. She suspected that Prince Charles would be less enthusiastic. Though it was only two weeks until his twelfth birthday, he showed no signs of enjoying the boisterous sports so beloved of his elder brother.

The light was streaming through the gaps in the shutters now. Frances knew she should rise, send word to the princess that she had had to return to Whitehall, but her body felt as if it were weighed down with rocks. The slightest movement exhausted her.

Would this be her last day of freedom? She thought of Thomas pleading with his master to spare her, insisting that she was innocent of all the calumny of which the prince was about to accuse her. But she knew that James was too blinded by his obsession to show mercy. It hardly seemed to matter, somehow. The person whose forgiveness she sought was not the king, but her husband. She remembered the look in his eyes when she had told him of her betrayal. In trying to protect everything she cherished, she had destroyed it.

The click of the latch startled her from her thoughts. Frances threw back the covers and got out of bed so quickly that the blood rushed to her head. Gripping one of the pillars to steady herself, she brushed away her tears and walked slowly towards the door.

Her husband was sitting by the fire when she entered, his head in his hands.

'Thomas?' Her voice came out as little more than a whisper.

She saw his shoulders heave and, for a moment, he did not reply.

'I was too late.' He lifted his head from his hands as he spoke. His expression was

651

so anguished that Frances had to fight back the urge to run over and clasp him in her arms.

'The prince has made his accusations?'

Thomas ran his hand across his forehead and gave a heavy sigh. 'Perhaps — I don't know. I arrived at the privy chamber to find its entry barred. The yeomen told me that the king was not to be disturbed. So I waited, expecting him to emerge at any moment, but still there was no sound of his approach. The guards would only repeat the message they had given me before. I had no choice but to remain, watching as others came to seek entry and were also refused.'

Frances came to sit by his feet and waited for him to continue.

'At last, one of the grooms came out of the chamber and announced that the king had left for St James's at daybreak.'

Frances's heart began to pound. *The king was already there.* Henry would have wasted no time in telling him of her witchcraft, but had he been told of more besides? With every hour that had passed since she had fled the prince's chamber, she had become more and more convinced that William Cecil had betrayed her. Why else would he have left the anteroom before she had returned?

'Why was his absence concealed for so long?' she asked.

Thomas gave a shrug. 'I could find out nothing further — not even when he might return.'

Frances forced herself to focus upon the few details that they knew. It was almost eleven o'clock now, so the king must have left about four hours before. It was only a short journey by carriage to St James's. If Henry had made his accusations as soon as his father arrived, the king could have issued orders for her arrest long before now.

'I wish I could take you far from here,' her husband continued. 'I should never have agreed to your leaving Tyringham Hall.'

Frances laid a hand on his. 'You are not to blame for any of this, Thomas,' she said softly. 'It is my recklessness that has brought us here. I should have heeded your advice before we were married. I will never forgive myself for what I have brought you to — George as well.'

'You were acting according to your conscience, Frances,' he said. 'I cannot but admire you for that. You have shown great courage — far greater than I.'

Frances kissed his hand, then placed her head on his lap.

'What shall we do?' he murmured, as he

653

stroked her hair.

She closed her eyes as she breathed in his familiar scent. For this moment, nothing mattered but his forgiveness. 'We can only wait,' she whispered.

Frances watched as her son traced his finger down the windowpane, carefully following a droplet of rain. When it had disappeared behind the edge of the frame, he began again with another. She smiled at his concentration, wishing she could be so easily distracted.

It felt as if an entire lifetime had passed since Thomas had returned from the privy chamber the previous day. Her breathing had quickened every time she had heard footsteps along the corridor. Though he had pretended not to notice, she knew that Thomas had started at them too. Little wonder that neither of them had slept that night.

Frances had sent word to the princess at St James's that she had been summoned to Whitehall to attend her son, who had taken ill in the night. She had hated to fall back into deceit so quickly, but Thomas had urged the necessity and she had known he was right. As soon as George had returned from the tiltyard that afternoon, Thomas had ordered him not to venture out again. The boy had agreed all too readily, delighted to be spared the customary evening service in the chapel, and Frances was glad of the excuse to keep to her chambers with them. These precious hours might be the last they ever spent together.

She pushed away the thought and tried to focus on her stitching. With luck, she would finish George's new cap before the light faded. She glanced across at the clock.

Half past two.

Why was it taking so long? No doubt the king wished to draw out her agony. Or perhaps Henry had insisted on accompanying his father back to Whitehall. He would relish the spectacle of her arrest.

Just then, she caught the echo of rapid footsteps along the corridor outside. Thomas had risen immediately to his feet and was already halfway to the door by the time the volley of thuds sounded from the other side. George turned from the window, eager for diversion.

Her husband glanced back at her briefly before sliding back the bolt and opening it.

'You are to go to the hall immediately — all of you,' the man said abruptly.

Over Thomas's shoulder, Frances could see that he was wearing the king's livery.

Before her husband could speak, the man had turned on his heel. A moment later she heard him hammering on the door of the adjoining apartment.

Thomas pushed the door closed and turned to her, his face ashen. She forced a smile as George sprang down from the window seat and grasped her hand. 'Come, Mama!' he urged, pulling her to her feet. 'The man said we must go at once.'

Frances allowed herself to be dragged towards the door.

'Have courage, my love,' Thomas whispered, as she reached him.

His lips felt dry as he pressed them to hers.

CHAPTER 59
6 NOVEMBER

The hall was already crowded by the time they reached it and there was a loud thrum of excited chatter. Frances held her son's hand tightly as they pushed their way through the throng of courtiers. At length, they reached a small clearing at the far side of the dais, close to the large windows that looked out over the street below.

Nausea rose in Frances as she gazed across the room, searching the faces for any hint of what lay ahead. But it was clear from the snatches of conversation she heard that everyone was speculating about the reason for this unexpected summons.

She gave a start as her gaze alighted upon a familiar figure standing close to the dais. *Edward.*

Their eyes locked. Her brother's face was wan and there were dark circles under his eyes. In place of his usual swagger there was a new uncertainty. He was the first to look away.

All of a sudden, the doors next to the dais were flung open and six yeomen strode onto it. A hush descended as all eyes turned to the large doorway. Frances gripped George's hand so tightly that he frowned up at her. She glanced at her husband, who gave her a reassuring smile.

Several seconds passed. The guards had formed two lines on either side of the door. Frances saw them raise their halberds and a moment later the sound of footsteps echoed through the hall. She felt Thomas's hand on her waist as the king walked slowly onto the dais, followed by his wife, their daughter and younger son. They each sat on the thrones that had been set out for them.

Frances looked from one to the other. Anne's face was deathly pale and her lips were clamped tightly together. To her left, the princess sat staring at her hands. Her brother was seated next to her and was gazing out across the crowds, almost stupefied. Their father's expression was unreadable. His mouth was set in a grim line but his eyes seemed to spark with something like excitement.

It was all too similar to that other occasion in this very hall eight years earlier. Then it had been Cecil who had announced her 'crimes' to the assembled throng. Now, it seemed, the king was to have that pleasure.

She watched, almost as if in a trance, as James got to his feet and prepared to address his court. Her eyes flicked to the guards, who were now stationed behind the thrones, halberds glinting in the sunlight. Suddenly, one was staring at her. She took a step backwards and heard someone behind her grumble an admonishment. Thomas's hand held her waist as she tried to steady herself.

'Loyal subjects.'

The king's voice rang out across the hall. Frances stood perfectly still now and waited.

'I have summoned you here to convey the most grievous tidings.'

He paused again, as if enjoying the suspense he had created.

'I have just arrived from St James's where, as you know, my son Henry has lain ill these several days.'

Frances held her breath. This was the moment. She heard Elizabeth give a muffled sob and saw the queen clasp her daughter's hand.

'I must inform you that God has seen fit to claim him. The prince is dead.'

Time seemed to still as Frances stared at

the king, his gaze roaming steadily over the shocked courtiers crowded into the great hall. She barely heard their collective gasps and wails, and was only vaguely aware that George had let go of her hand and was now sobbing into his hands.

Had she imagined James's words, somehow willed them into being? The look on the princess's face told her she had not.

How could this be? Henry had recovered from his fever and seemed out of danger when she had seen him less than two days before. Certainly, his mind had been clear enough to focus upon her destruction. Her thoughts returned to that night in his chamber. Had a few drops of the tincture slipped into his mouth unseen in the darkness? No, she knew that was impossible. The phial had been full to the brim when she had replaced the stopper. With searing clarity, she knew that this was God's doing. That He had meted out His vengeance for Henry's wickedness. And that He had rewarded her for placing her fate in His hands, not those of the devil.

Frances turned to Thomas and saw that his eyes, too, brimmed with tears. The weeping courtiers on either side of them would have seen nothing amiss if they had glanced their way. Only she knew that her husband was experiencing the same joy and relief that was flooding through her.

'He succumbed to the sickness in the small hours of this morning,' James continued.

Frances looked towards the dais again as he spoke and felt ashamed as she saw her mistress weeping openly. The queen's mouth was working as she tried to hold back her grief.

'We must take comfort in knowing that, while my son has been denied an earthly crown, he has won a heavenly one.'

The king's voice was strong and steady as he continued to address his courtiers. Turning, he motioned for his younger son to join him at the front of the dais. Charles rose uncertainly to his feet and made an awkward bow. As he drew level with his father, James placed a hand on his shoulder. Frances saw the boy wince.

'But God in his great and bountiful mercy saw fit to grant me another son, just as able as the first — more so, even. I rejoice in the knowledge that when He has summoned me to join Him in Heaven, I shall leave my kingdom to be governed by so wise and capable a prince.'

Frances saw her son crane his neck to catch a glimpse of his master, who seemed to shrink beneath his father's grasp.

'God save Prince Charles!'

The king's cry was echoed around the hall. Frances whispered the words, savouring the sound of his name upon her lips.

As the royal party slowly left the dais, courtiers followed them, all clamouring to pay their respects to the new king-in-waiting. Just before she turned to go, Frances caught sight of her brother among them. She watched as he bowed low before the prince, who peered down at him, his expression icy. Edward was still kneeling, head bowed, as Charles swept past him.

'I am not yet free of danger,' Frances reminded her husband as they strolled through the palace gardens that evening.

Thomas clasped her to him again, kissing her fervently. 'But you very soon will be,' he insisted. 'Already the king has disbanded the prince's household and ordered preparations to be made for Charles's arrival. He and his attendants will be installed in St James's before the week is out.'

Frances shook her head. 'It is almost as if he had planned for this moment,' she remarked. 'I thought he might pretend to feel some regret, at least, but it seems he is content to leave that to his wife and daughter.'

She felt sad as she thought of her visit to the princess. Elizabeth had taken to her bed as soon as the assembly had ended that afternoon. Frances had heard her sobs before she had even reached the presence chamber. The poor girl had been utterly inconsolable. It had pained Frances to see her beautiful face racked with sorrow as she had lain on the bed, her knees drawn up to her chest as if to protect herself from the grief that threatened to overwhelm her. Frances had glimpsed her brother's miniature clutched to her breast.

'Forgive me,' Elizabeth had been saying, over and over, pressing her lips to his portrait.

Frances knew that she was riven with guilt for having defied her brother on the matter of her marriage, for rejecting one suitor and making her distaste for the other all too clear. There had been nothing she could say to ease her anguish. It was too soon, the grief was still raw — Frances knew well how she felt. For now, the only comfort she could give was by her quiet, steady presence.

'I wonder where Edward will go now,' Frances mused. 'Longford can hold no appeal for him, unless he is still intent upon bankrupting it before George can inherit. But I hold sufficient means to persuade him against such a course,' she added, thinking of the indenture that was still in safe-keeping at Gray's Inn.

'I am sure he will try to find favour with the new resident of St James's,' Thomas replied, his voice laced with scorn. 'He will hardly be alone in doing so.'

Frances tried to smile. 'And what of us, Thomas?' she asked. 'Where shall we go?'

Her husband stopped walking and turned to her. 'You do not wish to stay here?'

She fell silent. *Where was home, now?* Though she loved her mistress dearly, the thought of remaining here, among the relentless grasping and backbiting, the plots and intrigues, was insupportable. Even Longford had lost some of its lustre, as if it were still tainted by everything that had passed between her and Edward.

'I would like our child to be born at Tyringham Hall,' she said, reaching for Thomas's hand. Her heart swelled at the joy in his eyes and for a moment neither could speak.

'I will not desert the princess while she grieves so sorely,' she continued, 'but when her mind has grown quieter and she has begun to take pleasure in her life again, I will seek her blessing to leave — for a time. She will be expecting me to do so soon anyway,' she added, stroking her belly. 'I know that you cannot relinquish your duties for ever, but I hope you will come with me — George, too, of course.'

Thomas opened his mouth to reply, but she saw his expression change as he looked at something over her shoulder. She turned. A man wearing the king's livery was striding purposefully towards them. Thomas stepped quickly forward so that he stood between the servant and his wife. But the man showed no interest in Frances. Instead he gave a short bow and addressed her husband. 'Sir Thomas, the king has a fancy to hunt in Richmond tomorrow and has ordered that you ready his hounds so that he may ride out at first light.'

For once, Frances was glad of the king's heartlessness. It seemed that he regretted his son's death little more than she did. She saw her husband's shoulders drop as she exhaled quietly with relief.

He turned to her as the servant walked briskly back towards the palace. 'I suppose we should take comfort from how quickly the natural order of things is restored,' he said, with a grin, 'though I am sorry to leave you so suddenly. Shall I escort you back to the palace?'

Frances smiled. 'No, it is a beautiful evening and I would like to walk here a while,' she said, stepping forward to kiss him. 'Now that our plans are resolved.'

He hesitated, then kissed her firmly and strode away towards the stables, calling over his shoulder that he would meet her back in their apartment.

Frances resumed her steady walk around the knot garden, pausing every now and then to breathe in the tang of myrtle or stoop to rub the velvet sage leaves between her fingertips.

'You have done well, Lady Frances.'

The voice behind her was so soft that she wondered if she had imagined it. Swinging round, she saw William Cecil standing before her.

Frances glanced around the garden to make sure that they were not being watched. 'What are you doing here?' she demanded in a low voice.

'I came to congratulate you — and to thank you for your efforts,' William replied. 'I must confess that I feared you had strayed too far from the cause to be of use to us any more, but you have proved me wrong. Now that the prince is out of the way, we are a step closer to realising our ambitions.'

Frances stared at him in horror. 'What do you mean?' she said, though she already knew, with a sickening certainty, the 'efforts' to which her companion had referred.

'You played your part to perfection,' he continued. 'And I knew that Raleigh could be relied upon to supply the means.'

Frances felt as if the breath had been knocked from her. *Had the two men been in league all this time?* During their many confidences, Raleigh had often hinted of wider plots, but she had come to believe that he meant only the Lady Arbella, that he was little more than an observer of the intrigues that swirled about the Crown. The knowledge that he had kept this from her struck her like a blow.

'I played no part, Lord Cranborne,' she said at last.

The young man's smile broadened. 'Your time here has served you well, Lady Frances. You dissemble as skilfully as the most seasoned courtier.'

Frances pushed down her rising frustration. She knew how it must look to him — how she, too, would believe as he did if their roles were reversed. 'You are mistaken. I did not murder the prince. God stayed my hand before I could administer the poison.'

She saw uncertainty in William's eyes, but

his smile did not falter.

'And yet he had recovered from his fever,' he said. 'Is it not strange, then, that he should expire so suddenly?'

'The fever was just one symptom,' Frances insisted. 'It may have disguised something more serious.'

William's smile faded as he took a step closer. 'The prince's death aside, you cannot deny the part you played in my other scheme. I knew you could be relied upon to stand witness to the lady's wedding, to attend her when she miscarried Seymour's child.'

Frances thought back to that night in Lambeth. William had known she was at Parry's house. He had been waiting for her when she had emerged. But she had been so distracted by her attendance on his father that she had not thought to question it any further.

You must tell him.

The words that Arbella had spoken as Frances had left her chamber came back to her now. *It was William Cecil whom she had meant, not Seymour.*

'We came so close to success, did we not?' he continued now. 'But the devil thwarted our schemes. It is of no matter. God shone His light on the true path. The prince's death has brought us closer to success than Arbella ever could. This heretic king will be succeeded by an uncontested heir — one who shares our faith.'

Frances stared at him in confusion. 'Only Prince Charles can succeed without impediment.'

William's eyes sparkled. 'Indeed. And I have made sure he is surrounded by the right influences — your own son included. It took little to persuade the queen, given how highly she esteems you. By the time Charles takes the throne, he will be as true a Catholic as we are, Lady Frances.'

Frances tried to control her racing thoughts. 'But I have always concealed my faith from George,' she countered.

'Ah, but you have not been so much of a hypocrite as to raise him a heretic, have you? Your father wanted a Catholic to inherit Longford, after all.'

'My *father*?' She had never spoken of him to anyone, had never revealed the pledge that she had made as he lay dying at Richmond. She thought back to his words then. *Longford must remain in Catholic hands.* He had hinted at plots to return the kingdom to the true faith, but there had been no time to ask him more. Had he, too, known of what William Cecil planned?

'He was a great supporter to our cause and would rejoice to know that we have prevailed, thanks to you.'

'I told you, Prince Henry did not die at my hands.' Frances endeavoured to hold onto this truth amid the shock of William's revelations.

'Persist in this false modesty if you will, but there can be no denying that the prince's death will give heart to all those of our faith. They will take it as a sign that God favours our cause.'

Frances eyed him steadily. 'That may be so, but my husband and I plan to return to his estates. I will have no further part in your schemes. God alone knows the secrets of my heart.'

William took a step closer. 'Ah, but I know them too, Lady Frances.' His eyes blazed into hers.

With the slightest nod, he turned and walked slowly away, towards the riverside gate. Frances watched as his silhouette merged with the darkening shadows.

ACKNOWLEDGEMENTS

The crafting of this novel, like the first, was greatly assisted by Julian Alexander and Nick Sayers, my wonderful agent and editor. I am deeply indebted to them both for their inspirational ideas and steady, patient guidance throughout. The Hodder team has been as brilliant as ever, and I would particularly like to thank Cicely Aspinall, Hannah Bond, Jeannelle Brew, Caitriona Horne and Rebecca Mundy. Will Speed has designed a beautiful cover, and I am extremely grateful to Hazel Orme for her meticulous and insightful copyediting. On the other side of the Atlantic, my editor George Gibson has been unfailingly supportive and encouraging. I am also grateful to Ben Clark and Isabelle Wilson of The Soho Agency for their help and efficiency.

Huge thanks are owed to my fellow historians Alison Weir, Sarah Gristwood, Nicola Tallis and Kate Williams for being so generous with their time and support. I would also like to thank my colleagues at Historic Royal Palaces who read the first novel and were kind enough to give me such positive feedback, in particular: Nicola Andrews, Binita Dave, Sharon Kerrigan, James Peacock, Aileen Peirce, Adrian Phillips, Jo Thwaites and Jo Wilson. I am indebted to Rhona MacCallum for organising such fantastic events, and to the numerous HRP Members who have attended, among the most faithful of whom are Miriam and Peter Barton, Maureen and Anthony Hall and John Harding.

My friends and family have, as ever, been unstinting in their support. Stephen Kuhrt has again assumed the role of Principal Cheerleader — one in which he will never be surpassed. I cannot thank him enough for being such an assiduous and enthusiastic reader of all the early drafts, and for providing such encouraging feedback. Knowing of my sweet tooth, Beverley Lawrence kept me supplied with a delicious array of cakes, while Jeroen Verschaeren sent me a consignment of Belgian chocolate to sustain me during the edit, for all of which I am eternally grateful.

Each book presents a challenge of logistics, and for solving many of those I would like to thank my parents, Joan and John Borman. Despite the frequency with which it has been given over the years, I will never take their support for granted. I was very touched by the lovely feedback that my sister Jayne Ellis gave me on the first novel and hope that she will enjoy this one just as much. I will always be grateful for the interest and encouragement that my late father-in-law John Ashworth showed in my work, and for the encouragement of my mother-in-law Joy.

Those who live with me have had to bear the brunt of my frustration when the words wouldn't flow, and of the long hours spent hidden away in my office. Heartfelt love and thanks to Tom and Eleanor, as always. Finally, to my furry companions, Wiggins and her nemesis Cromwell (Thomas, not Oliver), for providing much-needed light relief.

AUTHOR'S NOTE

As with *The King's Witch,* the first book in my trilogy about the Gunpowder Plot and its aftermath, I have stayed as close as possible to the known history when crafting the narrative and characters. Details relating to my heroine, Frances Gorges, are scarce, but we know that she did marry Thomas Tyringham, Master of the Buckhounds to James I. His original home, Tyringham Hall in Buckinghamshire, no longer exists and the beautiful Palladian-style house that now stands in its place was designed by Sir John Soane in 1792.

Frances's parents, Sir Thomas Gorges and Helena (née Snakenborg), Marchioness of Northampton, did not win favour with the first Stuart king. Possibly this was thanks to Sir Thomas having played a part in the arrest of James's mother Mary, Queen of Scots, after the Babington Conspiracy in 1586. James did not keep him in office as

Gentleman of the Privy Chamber, and, despite being one of the highest-ranking ladies in the kingdom, Helena was not appointed a member of Queen Anne's entourage. Instead, the couple were assigned the keepership of Richmond Palace and rarely attended court. Helena did, though, help to broker the proposed marriage between Princess Elizabeth and Prince Gustavus of Sweden.

Edward Gorges was the second-born of Frances's five brothers and became heir to their parents' estate upon the death of the eldest son, Francis, in 1599. He was created Baron Longford in November 1611 — one of numerous others to be thus ennobled around this time. The sale of baronetcies was a deliberate ploy by Robert Cecil to generate funds for the crown, as well as to buy the loyalty of well-affected Catholics. The first round of creations between May and November 1611 saw eighty-eight baronets purchasing this new hereditary rank, twenty-six of whom came from recusant backgrounds. At the centre of the cohort was an interlinked network of families that had been implicated in the Gunpowder Plot.

The turbulent years following the discovery of the Plot in 1605 provided a rich seam of inspiration for the novel. The king's persecution of Catholics intensified and the 1606 Oath of Allegiance (or Obedience) required all his subjects by law to affirm their loyalty to him. Although the English Catholics were driven even further underground, their networks remained strong, and rumours of plots to depose James and replace him with a sovereign of the 'true faith' remained rife. Anne Vaux was typical of those who refused to be cowed by the persecutions. She was arrested in March 1606 on suspicion of involvement with the Gunpowder Plot, but was released a few months later. Her experience did not deter her from practising the Catholic faith, however, and she was convicted of recusancy almost twenty years later.

Although there is little evidence to suggest that Arbella Stuart was a Catholic, she did become a figurehead for those who were opposed to James's rule. Her clandestine marriage to William Seymour, who was sixth in line to the throne, in June 1610 led to their arrest and imprisonment. What happened next reads like fiction: Arbella escaped dressed as a man and made for the Channel, where she hoped to intercept her husband, who had succeeded in breaking out of the Tower. She was overtaken by the king's men and brought back to London, but Seymour managed to reach safety at Ostend.

As well as threats to James's throne, the years following 1605 were dominated by the question of whom his daughter Elizabeth would marry. All of the suitors I mention in the narrative were considered, but there were others: Frederic Ulric, Duke of Brunswick-Wolftenbuttel, Prince Maurice of Nassau, Lord Howard of Walden and Otto, Prince of Hesse. Queen Anne did object to the idea of her daughter marrying Prince Gustavus on the grounds that Sweden was then at war with her native Denmark. Despite his unwavering commitment to the Protestant faith, King James did give serious consideration to the suit of Victor Amadeus, Prince of Piedmont and nephew of the King of Spain.

The king's obsession with witches showed little sign of abating during the period covered by this novel. The most notorious witchcraft trial — that of the Pendle Witches — took place in 1612 and resulted in the execution of eight women and two men. Meanwhile, another, less well-known case was unfolding at the Earl of Rutland's estate at Belvoir. I hinted at this in the narrative and will bring it to life in the third novel.

Queen Anne's relationship with her husband deteriorated sharply after the birth and death of their last child, Sophia, in 1606. Anne had almost died during the birth and her decision to have no more children widened the gulf between her and James. She spent most of her time apart from her husband, at Greenwich Palace and then Somerset House, which she renamed Denmark House.

James's relationship with his eldest son and heir, Prince Henry, was little better. Although they both strictly upheld the Protestant doctrine and shared a passion for hunting, the two men had a series of high-profile clashes. Henry disapproved of the way that his father conducted the court and harboured an intense aversion towards his close favourite, Robert Carr. By contrast, as I have illustrated in the narrative, Henry adored Sir Walter Raleigh and bitterly resented the king for refusing to release him. The prince is said to have disliked his younger brother Charles — who suffered fragile health and was slow to learn — and made fun of him in front of the court on at least one occasion. Henry's early death in November 1612 was probably due to typhoid fever, but there were rumours of poisoning.

The other notable demise covered by this novel is that of the king's chief minister,

Robert Cecil. Although he had brought the Gunpowder Plot to light, Cecil experienced mixed fortunes in the years that followed. James increasingly preferred the company of his favourites and poked fun at his 'little Beagle' in public. Nevertheless, he continued to entrust him with affairs of state, telling him: 'Though you are but a little man, I shall shortly load your shoulders with business.' Worn down by the burdens of office, Cecil suffered from increasing bouts of ill health and died (probably of cancer) in May 1612 at the age of forty-eight. His private chapel at Hatfield House was found to be adorned with lavish decorations more akin to Catholicism than the Reformed faith. There is no other suggestion that Cecil was a closet Catholic, but this presented too delicious a prospect to ignore.

ABOUT THE AUTHOR

Tracy Borman is England's joint Chief Curator of Historic Royal Palaces and Chief Executive of the Heritage Education Trust. She is the author of a number of highly acclaimed books including *Henry VIII and the Men Who Made Him; The Private Lives of the Tudors: Uncovering the Secrets of Britain's Greatest Dynasty; Thomas Cromwell: The Untold Story of Henry VIII's Most Faithful Servant; Queen of the Conqueror: The Life of Matilda, Wife of William I; Elizabeth's Women: Friends, Rivals, and Foes Who Shaped the Virgin Queen; Witches: A Tale of Sorcery, Scandal and Seduction;* as well as the novel *The King's Witch.* Borman is also a regular broadcaster and public speaker.
tracyborman.co.uk
@tracyborman

The employees of Thorndike Press hope
you have enjoyed this Large Print book. All
our Thorndike, Wheeler, and Kennebec
Large Print titles are designed for easy reading, and all our books are made to last.
Other Thorndike Press Large Print books
are available at your library, through selected bookstores, or directly from us.

For information about titles, please call:

(800) 223-1244

or visit our website at:

gale.com/thorndike

To share your comments, please write:

Publisher
Thorndike Press
10 Water St., Suite 310
Waterville, ME 04901